NOBODY KNOWS

WHAT WE SWEEP UNDER THE CARPET

NOBODY KNOWS

WHAT WE SWEEP UNDER THE CARPET

LARRY SCHNEIDERMAN

— Beaver's Pond Press —
Minneapolis, MN

Edited by Angela Wiechmann

ISBN: 978-1-59298-792-4
Library of Congress Catalog Number: 2017913288
Printed in the United States of America
First Printing: 2018
22 21 20 19 18   5 4 3 2 1

Book design by Athena Currier

Beaver's Pond Press, Inc.
7108 Ohms Lane
Edina, MN 55439–2129

(952) 829-8818
www.BeaversPondPress.com

To order, visit www.LarrySchneiderman.com.
Reseller discounts available.

To Gary Mortenson
Fighting his battle with Parkinson's for almost twenty years,
Gary doesn't let the awful symptoms keep him from loving his
family and friends. He goes toe-to-toe with Parkinson's disease
every hour of every day.
Gary, you inspire!

PSALM 121

I will lift up my eyes to the hills—
From whence comes my help?
My help comes from the LORD,
WHO MADE HEAVEN AND EARTH.
HE WILL NOT ALLOW YOUR FOOT TO BE MOVED;
HE WHO KEEPS YOU WILL NOT SLUMBER.
BEHOLD, HE WHO KEEPS ISRAEL
SHALL NEITHER SLUMBER NOR SLEEP.
THE LORD IS YOUR KEEPER;
THE LORD IS YOUR SHADE AT YOUR RIGHT HAND.
THE SUN SHALL NOT STRIKE YOU BY DAY,
NOR THE MOON BY NIGHT.
THE LORD SHALL PRESERVE YOU FROM ALL EVIL;
HE SHALL PRESERVE YOUR SOUL.
THE LORD SHALL PRESERVE YOUR GOING OUT AND YOUR COMING IN
From this time forth, and even forevermore.

—New King James Version

INTRODUCTION

T HE OFT QUOTED SAYING, "YOU CAN FOOL all the people some of the time and some of the people all of the time, but you cannot fool all of the people all of the time" is sometimes wrongly attributed to P. T. Barnum, the great showman and salesman. In fact, Abraham Lincoln seems to have first spoken these words of wisdom.

Barnum and Lincoln were smart men but had far different reasons to be interested in the science of fooling people. There's a fine line between manipulating people and leading them.

Sometimes to fool others, you must first fool yourself.

Here I am—Jake Horton, age seventy-five, former business owner, retired pastor, widower, father of two, grandfather of four—feeling my productive years were an elaborate sham.

What the hell happened?

As I reflect on my whirlwind of a life, I am quite confident I managed to fool all the people all the time. It takes creativity to keep secrets, but I willingly expended the time and energy to do just that. I don't remember questioning my own motives much then. But now I wonder what flaw in my DNA led me to risk being exposed as a thief, a cheat, and a fake.

I knew the satisfaction of being successful in the eyes of the world: a beautiful wife; two great kids; the biggest and most expensive house in an affluent neighborhood; two luxury cars; a winter place in Nevada; and, most important, a reputation as a man of integrity.

I even became a pastor. How could a pastor—a man of God—go over the line as often as I did? And really, why did I become a minister, anyway? I owned a business. I liked it. I was good at it. I could have been successful doing many things. So why a pastor?

Christians believe one is "called" into the ministry. If God called me, I wonder if he held second thoughts. Then again, God doesn't make mistakes. He has his reasons, and I guess that should be enough.

To fool somebody is to trick or deceive them. A fool is a silly or stupid person who often lacks good judgment. I was not a fool, but in retrospect, I made fools of the people around me. And I am not proud of it.

Men were easier to fool. With rare exception, men avoid diving below the surface with other men.

Women, on the other hand, want to know what you're thinking and even why you're thinking what you're thinking. Fooling the women in your life takes dedication and practice. It's not for the faint of heart. And now I see it was not worth the high price I paid for doing it.

I was married twenty-six years to my wife—a beautiful, smart, and genuine person. Did she die fooled into believing I was the man I appeared to be? Or did she love me despite the truth she may have known? I'm not so sure. Who's the fool in this?

It's not like I didn't know the difference between right and wrong. My parents did their job. We worshipped at church every Sunday. We understood that the Ten Commandments were not just to be memorized but followed.

I grew up in a home where honest work and respect went hand in hand. My dad was proud to be an ironworker. He worked hard and provided well for his family. My mother managed the household and assumed nearly all the responsibilities for raising the four of us kids.

I wanted to be a better husband than my dad. I wanted to be a more involved father. But I am Roy Horton's son on this count: throughout my entire life, I found meaning and satisfaction in my work. I often worked long hours while my wife kept our family together. Our kids, JJ and Lindsey, knew we both loved them, but they accepted that I had other important priorities. It's clear now I should have given my dad more credit.

Sometimes when I crossed over the line, behaving in ways that would have embarrassed and angered my parents, I imagined what they would have said had they known what I swept under the carpet.

But they didn't know. Nobody knew.

PART ONE

1

BEFORE I EVEN BEGIN MY STORY, you must understand where I came from—my home, my family, my world.

I was born in 1946. Back when I was a kid, the population of Mesabi, Minnesota, was about eight thousand. It's about half that now, mainly older people. One thing hasn't changed: the community was dependent on the iron mining industry then and remains so even today.

Without iron mining, no reason exists for Mesabi, Virginia, or any of the towns on the Iron Range. While the mining companies provided thousands of well-paid jobs, the Rangers viewed the companies as tired puppets might view their puppetmaster. They knew all too well outside forces decided how much they moved and how high they would jump. The story of the companies bringing European immigrants to work in the mines and break the unions is well documented . . . and not forgotten.

In time, the pendulum swung the other way, and the iron miners' union became extremely powerful. If you belonged to the union and had worked for a few years, you were pretty much guaranteed your job. Stories were commonly heard about men who held unnecessary jobs in the mines and slept their whole shifts, night after night.

Most young people knew the future of the Range wasn't bright, so they planned accordingly after graduating from high school. Most commonly, that meant a move to the Cities, meaning Minneapolis–Saint Paul. When you left Mesabi, those remaining behind often perceived you had rejected them. You became an outsider—too "good" for them. You left. You were no longer part of the tribe.

The town suffered from a collective shortage of self-esteem, which led to a prevailing negativity noticed by visitors as well as by those of us who had left but still held ties to the community.

And this was unfortunate. Most of us raised in Mesabi, whether we stayed or not, still felt a sense of place that remained with us throughout our lives. We got a decent education there, and most of us did well when we left.

I know a lot of people complain about their upbringing, but I sure can't. For the most part, my memories of growing up in the Horton home are good.

There were four of us kids. Anna was older than me by three years. In a lot of ways, Anna embodied the role of the oldest child. She tended to be quiet and soft-spoken, but she was responsible and helped Mom remain sane. Sadly, she moved to Colorado almost immediately after her high school graduation.

My little sister, DeeDee, was three years younger than me. Thinking of her brings images of my dad tossing her up in the air and catching her. We all could see she was Dad's favorite. I was okay with that. After all, I was Mom's favorite. DeeDee, a people pleaser and a genuinely nice person, was fun to be around. She made friends easily.

And then came Mike, two years younger than DeeDee. Opposite in temperament from DeeDee, he was, as my mom once described, "a handful." Mike presented a challenge right from the start as a colicky baby. Mom tried valiantly to comfort him, but sometimes nothing could be done except to let him cry himself to sleep. By that time of night, Dad had often left the house to meet his buddies at some bar.

Little kids, little problems.

Nothing would be easy when it came to Mike. Mesabi could be tough on people who weren't mainstreamers.

As a family, though, we had far more good times than bad. We sometimes enjoyed the public beach at a nearby lake. We went to movies. For a special treat, we ate at one of the local restaurants. For the most part, we experienced growing up without undue supervision. As long as we didn't cause the family any embarrassment, we were free to make our own friends and choose our own activities.

I'm not one of those bitter souls who dwell on the alleged unfairness, incompetence, or whatever in regards to their parents. Instead, I will say what I know to be true: while they weren't perfect, who the hell is?

My dad was one of those people who are often referred to as "rocks." You know the expression "solid as a rock"? You could count on Roy Horton. He could outwork anybody. He could and he did. Just over six feet and 175 pounds, his daily uniform consisted of a white T-shirt and worn jeans held up by a western-looking leather belt.

As a teenager, I watched more than once as women eyed and even squeezed his muscular biceps. He had the looks to go along with his physique—thick black hair, dark-brown eyes, and olive skin that gave him a tanned look year-round. He gave little thought to impressing anybody, which only added to his appeal. People sometimes commented I could be Roy's clone. I did sort of possess the looks to be a watered-down version of the man.

His most often stated words of advice to his kids—"If your word is no good, you're no good"—always sounded more like an accusation than advice. I heard it more than the others.

Dad invented a "Bullshit Meter." When a neighbor, for instance, tried to impress us with a story but the tale did not add up for my dad, he would later tell us he had to plug in his equipment to check out the story. He'd act out inserting a plug in a wall outlet. Next, he'd summarize the story or at least a questionable sentence. Finally, he'd move his right index figure shakily in a circle left to right, indicating a high "bullshit rating." If Dad was in an especially good mood, he'd accompany his pantomime with sounds as well.

From time to time, as I'd tell a story, Dad would hold up an imaginary plug, showing everybody he was ready to plug in the machine. Once only, I mimicked plugging in my own machine while he told us something seemingly farfetched, at least it seemed so to me. Dad was not amused. As I recall, he made some reference to shoving the machine up my rear corridor. Dad rarely got physical, but we all felt danger could be imminent if he became upset.

Men in the 1960s often were defined by their jobs, and this was true in the case of Dad. He was an *ironworker*, heart and soul. From all accounts, he earned his working brothers' respect as a man who brought excellence to his craft and who stood up for his union and for his friends. He loved to work jobsites high up in the air, riveting gigantic beams and playing a role in building "giant Erector sets," as he would say.

Dad was a perfectionist. This trait, along with his pride in his ironworker brotherhood, could make him difficult and demanding. I heard him say on several occasions, "I want to work anywhere except on projects in the iron mines. What a bunch of lazy crybabies those guys are. I won't call them 'workers' because I would be lying."

As a boy, I remember Dad once worked on an office building in Michigan. I visited him with my mother. Mom brought binoculars. After a couple of minutes of searching, she pointed skyward and helped me focus them on my father many stories up.

I remember thinking, *Dad is working in the clouds.*

Dad arranged for the job supervisor to bring Mom and me up about thirty floors to see him. The supervisor gave us each a yellow plastic hat. Then, up and up the temporary elevator carried the three of us. I closed my eyes. When we got to where Dad was working, Mom climbed out, but I clung to the lift for my life. I never wanted to do that again.

"Are you ever afraid when you're working up so high?" I asked him.

He didn't hesitate. "No reason to be worried if you and those around you follow all the rules."

Roy Horton lived by his rules, and it could get him into some trouble at work. If he felt another worker was taking unnecessary chances—not following safety rules or simply "screwing around"—Dad would go to the supervisor. And if the guilty party wasn't removed, Dad would simply leave. These men, in his opinion, had not only broken the rules but he considered them to be "fakes." They were not ironworkers. "They will get somebody killed someday," he'd say. "It won't be me."

As a young boy, I knew I did not want to be a fake.

Like all men in Mesabi, my dad lived by the mantra "Work hard, play hard." Realistically, you could substitute "drink" for "play." To wear the title of Ranger, you really needed to be a drinker. It wasn't just men either. While the legal age to drink was twenty-one, many young people drank almost every weekend at sixteen.

Booze owned a key role at most social events, whether it be a major holiday, a high school graduation, a first date, or a get-together at a bar. Booze could provide the encouragement to act, and if the action took a bad turn, booze could provide the excuse.

Most of the men frequently claimed, "I could quit if I wanted, so I'm not an alcoholic." I honestly never thought of my dad as having a "drinking problem." Booze never affected his ability to make a good living or provide for his family.

Now, I'm not so sure.

I was perhaps twelve, and Dad and I were in his pickup coming back from somewhere late Christmas Eve afternoon. Church service would begin at 7:00 p.m., then we would go home and open presents. I could hardly wait. But rather than head home, Dad pulled up to the Galaxy Bar in downtown Mesabi.

"Jake, I'm going in for a quick one. Want to come in with me?"

I remember feeling proud as he introduced me to his friends. The woman behind the bar poured a "Christmas shot" in a tiny glass for my dad and opened a bottle of Dr. Pepper for me.

My eyes were drawn to the lighted wall of bottles behind the bar. There were more types of liquor than I could have imagined. I read the labels—and as it turned out, I had plenty of time to read them all.

The red and blue neon signs in the windows flickered. I especially liked the Hamm's sign with brightly lit stars and the well-known bear mascot. Under my breath, I repeated the words from their TV ad: "Hamm's, the beer refreshing. Hamm's, the beer refreshing."

The bar itself, made of solid oak with a brass counter, seemed to beckon, "Belly up and get comfortable." And that's what my dad and a handful of guys did. Behind the bar, a little artificial tree adorned with blinking lights and beer bottle caps reminded me we were AWOL from home.

The privilege of being at the bar changed to dread as my dad downed his third shot of Seagram's 7 whiskey. Three hours later, I grew nervous and impatient as I watched him drink two big mugs of beer. We had already missed Christmas Eve church service.

"Dad," I begged for the third time, "*please* can we go home?"

"Geez, Jake. You're worse than your mother. Okay, I'll finish this last beer. Do you want to try one?"

I caught the glare the bartender shot at him, but Dad didn't. I shook my head.

Before he finished the beer in front of him, one of his buddies bought a round for everyone, and my dad and two other guys started playing some sort of dice game.

Eventually, the bartender began shutting off the lights. "Merry Christmas," she said with some sincerity. A couple of the men gave her a kiss good-bye and left their crumpled dollar bills on the bar as a thank-you.

We finally left. It was dark and the streets were vacant. As we opened our back door, I could sense regret on my dad's part. He fumbled for the light switch and caught himself as he stumbled briefly over the door threshold.

"When did they put that there?" he slurred.

Under our tree, the unopened Christmas presents in their red, green, and silver wrapping provoked feelings of guilt. Mikey had been so excited about opening his presents tonight. Now, the boxes looked like empty promises. Instead of representing God's gift to mankind, they were evidence of Dad's thoughtlessness towards his family that night. Mom and my sisters and brother, tired of waiting for us, had gone to bed.

Christmas morning, I caught the tail end of an argument between my parents before they saw me. Mom had spoken the final word to Dad, "I wish you could have been here to see DeeDee and Mikey looking out the window crying while they waited for you to come home."

To Dad's credit, I guess, nothing like this happened again. It wasn't like him to disappoint his family like that. But Dad had his secrets too.

As a child, I thought Dad was courageous, loyal, smart, decisive, and confident. I remember thinking this was how a true man should be and that I'd never measure up to him. He had his weaknesses, though. For instance, he cared very little, if at all, about anybody's feelings. Yet this mattered little because, well, it just didn't matter to him.

Meanwhile, my mother reacted to my dad's downsides as though they were a small price to pay for the privilege of being Mrs. Roy Horton. At least, it seemed that way.

The embodiment of childhood sweetheart romance, they first met each other in church. Evangeline Carlson, known then and forever as Eva, age fifteen, volunteered to work at the Saint James Lutheran Hunter's Dinner. Roy, age seventeen, acknowledged he had been gazing at her for a while. Soon they were going steady, and five years later, they became husband and wife in the very same church.

I am told, and old pictures offer proof, that Mom was an attractive young woman. In contrast to Dad, she was fair-skinned and slightly built, with long, straight blond hair—understated, not showy in any way. Perhaps it's because people don't think of their parents as sexual beings, but I don't remember her wearing anything one would consider sexy. I'm reasonably sure, though, from the photographs I've seen, her appeal would have been enhanced by the clothing styles women wear today. Among the old photos, I found a couple of pictures Dad had taken at the beach. Mom, wearing a swimsuit, showed a lot of leg and a playful spirit.

My mother managed the household and assumed nearly all the responsibilities for raising the four of us. As Dad once said, "I'm responsible for the house and paying the bills. Mom is responsible for everything in the house, including you kids."

Though my grandmother enjoyed a reputation as an excellent cook, she didn't inspire her daughter, my mother, in the realm of culinary excellence. Mom made just basic meals. Occasionally, Mom would announce she had cooked a new dish for us. Inevitably, this provoked our anxiety because these new meals were almost always failed experiments.

But one time she made potato pancakes in a new blender she had gotten as a Christmas present from Dad. She fried the batter in a skillet and served those pancakes just right—I loved those crispy edges. A couple of months later, she asked what I'd like for dinner. I thought for only a moment.

"Potato pancakes!"

She shook her head. "They are too messy. Choose something else."

Mom taught Sunday school, participated in the women's group, helped at funerals, and saw to it we children attended church and behaved. When I attended grade school, she sang in the choir. When she sang solos, she took on a whole different presence. The church would become unusually quiet as her rich voice simply captivated the congregation.

One Sunday, she left our pew to sing a solo in front of the church, but Mike, age five, started screaming and wouldn't stop. That was the last time she sang in church—or for that matter, in public—again.

Not a real fussy housekeeper, Mom made sure our place was at least presentable. She often didn't get much help, though. And one weekend, this brought out Eva Horton's feisty side.

Mom had been after us all to stop leaving our clothes around the house. We had ignored her. So, right after the "amen" of our family prayer and before we tasted the stew steaming in the bowls in front of us, she asked softly, "Do you think I'm your maid?"

We all looked up as she scanned the table.

She repeated the question. This time her voice was louder and more confident. "Do you think I'm your maid?"

Even Dad had no clue what she was talking about or why she was so upset.

She set her spoon down loudly on the dinner table. She now had our full attention.

"I have been nagging all of you to just put your dirty clothes in the hamper so I can have the *privilege* of washing, drying, and pressing your stuff. I guess it's asking too much. Maybe it's my fault for spoiling you all."

She sat up straight and leaned toward us.

"As of now, I am on strike. If you want your clothes cleaned, you'll have to wash them yourselves."

To our surprise and regret, she meant it. For a full month, she did no laundry except her own. Dad had never used a washer or a dryer in his life. Now, he blamed us kids for his miserable plight. He tried to reason with Mom.

"I have my own job," he argued. "You shouldn't be including me in this."

She refused to discuss it.

A few days later, I heard him ask Mom in a challenging tone, "Don't you care if your husband looks like a bum?"

She responded as if she had been waiting for him to ask. "No, I really don't care. *I* know you're not a bum."

That month, we all learned to put our clothes away. Dad, Anna, and I also learned how to wash, dry, and iron.

Growing up, I thought Dad was witty and funny with his jokes making fun of Mom. People laughed, and she would laugh with them. Later, when I got married, though, Anna gave me only one piece of advice: "Don't talk about your wife like Dad talked about Mom."

This took me aback—Dad wasn't mean.

But then Anna repeated several comments Dad made about Mom being "a typical blonde," along with several other questionable jokes.

"Do you remember," Anna asked, "Dad's clever little joke, "What does a blonde consider 'long and hard'?"

I grinned. "Oh, yes. I do . . . the fourth grade."

As I thought about this, I could think of many "funny" comments he had made over the years about my mother's intelligence, common sense, parenting skills, cooking, even her activities at the church.

Years after the good man died, I was talking with Mom and asked her about Dad's humor.

She rocked my world a bit when she offhandedly mused, "I may have stopped loving Roy along the way."

Our eyes met. The two of us were now coconspirators of this truth that couldn't be spoken.

I changed the subject. I didn't want to visit this dark topic. I knew it would challenge everything I understood about my upbringing. And by that point in my life, I wasn't in a hurry to shed light on any dark topic, lest that light turn on me.

2

I F AT AGE SEVENTY-FIVE YOU CAN RECALL embarrassing situations from your school years, it's safe to bet those moments caused enough trauma to affect your entire life. As I tell some of these stories even now, I still blush in shame. You wouldn't think these school-age events would mean anything in the larger picture of life. Yet here I am, convinced otherwise.

It was my very first day of school. Each first grader was given a phonics book. The pages contained rows of various images. Miss Novak instructed the class to open our boxes of crayons and color the figures on the first two pages.

I missed her additional instructions: "But don't use purple. I hate purple."

So I plunged forward, boldly and unwittingly coloring cars, trees, moons, people, cows—everything—purple.

Miss Novak started walking down the aisles, commenting on each student's work. The girls generally got accolades, and they likely deserved them. The boys more often got suggestions.

Then she arrived at my desk. Something in Miss Novak just snapped. I wanted to disappear as she waved her index finger in my face.

"Why would you color a barn purple when I told you not to use purple at all?" she demanded with a whiny voice.

Without even thinking, I blurted, "For the purple cows."

With that, she grabbed my left arm and led me into the cloakroom. There among the coats and extra books and school supplies, Miss Novak administered her version of solitary confinement.

"You will stay in this room until you're smart enough to know which color is purple. Do you understand?"

I tried not to cry, but she pinched my ear as I replied, "Yes, Teacher." It did sound as if I were crying.

That night, I sat glumly watching TV after school. Mom came over and sat next to me.

"Jake, how was school today?"

Again, I tried to hold back the tears, but ultimately, Mom listened to the whole story between my sobs.

When we went to conferences a few weeks later, Miss Novak told the story with a smile on her ugly face. She left out the important details and made the whole incident sound like a source of great humor to her. What a fake!

Day had become night by the time Mom and I headed out of the school. It was moonless, and large drops of rain stung us as we hurried to the car.

"Mom, that isn't what happened—she's lying," I said.

Mom started the motor, turned on the wipers, then looked over at me. "I believe you, Jake. It's wrong she wasn't telling the truth tonight. But remember, none of this would have happened if you had just listened to her full instructions."

I knew then that if I had trouble in school, I would have to buck up because Mom would always side with the teachers.

Years later, other guys told similar stories about Miss Novak. She came off as a kind and committed teacher to the moms, but she could be diabolical when she didn't like you. And I knew she didn't like me.

I tried hard to do what Miss Novak wanted. I did the same for all my teachers for the first few years. For the most part, I avoided being called out, but I just knew these teachers didn't like me. I thought it was because I was stupid.

Then I reached fourth grade. The night before the first day of school, Anna told me, "You're going to like school this year. You have a really good teacher."

Mrs. Demming was an ordinary-looking woman in her forties. She was thin with brown-and-gray hair pulled back tightly into a bun. She possibly wore too much makeup. The vertical wrinkles above her nose unfairly made her look crabby because in truth, she owned a smile one would work for.

That old saying, "You may not remember what people say, but you'll remember how they made you feel" is so true. Mrs. Demming loved to teach . . . and it showed.

In the middle of the afternoon, when we kids got tired and mainly just stared at the clock, she would announce, "Story time!" She invited us to take turns standing in front of the room to share anything we wanted. Some of the kids would talk about a TV program they liked. Others would say something about a special event in their family. It didn't matter.

I always wanted to go up there and take a turn at it, but I remember being afraid of looking stupid.

One afternoon, it surprised me when Roger Anderson, one of the shyest in the class, raised his hand and walked to the front of the room.

"Why did the man put his car in the oven?" he asked.

It grew quiet.

He smiled slightly. "Because he wanted a hot rod."

I remember Mrs. Demming laughing out loud. The whole class laughed too and clapped. A couple of days later, Roger told the same riddle, and Mrs. Demming laughed even harder.

With more than a little fear, I decided to finally raise my hand. Mrs. Demming smiled broadly at me as I walked up. I had a riddle of my own.

"What's black and white and red all over?"

I shook my head at several wrong guesses, then said, "A newspaper."

Mrs. Demming started clapping, and the rest of the class joined her.

I became a frequent contributor. Like many of the others, eventually I told wild stories of fairies, dragons, and anything else imaginable. It didn't take long for my confidence to build.

As I enjoyed these small successes, I began to like school. My self-perception changed. I knew I was not stupid. Everything changed that year. By the seventh grade, I was considered one of the "smart kids."

In contrast, though, school wasn't as easy for Mike. As he advanced from class to class, he fell further and further behind. He simply couldn't read. When Mom forced him to practice reading at home during the summer, he sounded as though he were making progress. In reality, though, he was just memorizing words but retaining almost nothing.

Some teachers tried hard to get through to Mike, but they all gave up. On the other hand, other teachers exhibited little or no sympathy to what appeared to be a spoiled and demanding kid. His mantra became "School is stupid." This reflected poorly on my parents.

When he turned sixteen, he begged Mom, "Let me quit. I hate my teachers, and they hate me."

Mom was prepared for this possibility. She told Dad, "I don't want to fight Mike anymore. I don't think more school will do him any good—he hates it."

The only dropouts I had ever heard about were considered idiots destined to poverty and the misery coming with it. I could hardly believe Mom would go along with Mike quitting school. I thought she had just given up on him. In reality, his bottom-of-the-barrel view of himself caused her heart to ache almost every time they were together.

School was much more than academics on the Iron Range. Hockey was clearly the number one sport, football was a distant number two, and the rest followed far behind.

Much to my dad's obvious and frequently mentioned disappointment, I just didn't possess the interest nor the skating ability to compete in the Mesabi Raiders hockey program.

I did play basketball and knew to expect sparse, flat crowds. My dad attended a couple of games; Mom sometimes showed up with Mike and DeeDee. While most of my basketball career was forgettable, I did get named to the All-Conference team as a senior.

Football was where I stood out. The junior varsity coach put me down as starting halfback for our first game, and I never moved from the position all through high school. What I lacked in speed, I compensated by being unusually tough to tackle. It usually took two or more players to bring me down. I had perfected a spinning move that often frustrated would-be tacklers.

Unlike with basketball, my dad attended every game and got pumped by my running toughness. In my senior year, Coach Lyttinen found out I could set the all-time Mesabi record for carries per season if I carried the ball forty-two times in my final game. We were playing for second place. Our opponent, McKinley High School, was known to have a fast and athletic team. But our players were bigger and tougher.

Coach L decided on a basic running strategy. Our line against their line. Mano a mano. All week at practice, he exhorted me to punish the McKinley tacklers on every play. "Make them pay," he repeated over and over. This would be a test for toughness and durability.

Game day, we were an inspired team with a mission. Up and down the field we went, over and over and over. In the end, I had my 43 carries for 305 yards and three touchdowns in a 27–13 victory. We didn't throw a single pass. We simply wore them down.

A coach from the University of Minnesota happened to be at the game. Afterward, he invited me to sign up for football tryouts. I hadn't thought of competing at that level, but I promised him I would show up.

As my senior year came to an end, I was named valedictorian of the Mesabi High class of 1964. This was a big deal to my parents. In hindsight, I realize my commencement speech was filled with your garden-variety clichés, but it also included an important moment I'd never forgotten—and haven't since then.

I told my "Purple Cow" story with some humorous twists. I thanked the school board for not counting my first three years in elementary school toward my grade point average, then I thanked Mrs. Demming for guiding me on a better road. I knew she made a point of attending every high school graduation ceremony. We made eye contact, and she smiled brightly at me.

Near the end of my speech, I left the podium and walked past thirteen rows of chairs to Mrs. Demming. Hidden under my gown I carried a small box of chocolates I had bought at the drug store. I had already spoiled her makeup by thanking her during my speech; now tears rolled down her face. Mrs. Demming could not have fantasized she would be given a standing ovation on that memorable evening. I nearly choked. The other teachers on the stage came over and shook my hand. While I had been a little nervous about making the speech, I felt very good indeed about the outcome.

That night at home, I asked Mom if she remembered the "Purple Cow Affair." She surprised me with her answer.

"Yes, Jake, I do remember. Miss Novak wasn't one of my favorites either, but I think she taught you to listen better."

Incredible.

"Mom, she was a fake and an absolute bitch," I protested.

She weighed her words. "I'll admit—I didn't care for her personally, Jake. But you try teaching thirty first graders."

As for my dad, all he had was a single comment, "I hope you're finally ready to leave those first three old biddy teachers behind you."

As high school came to an end, so did my participation in the Young Christians organization at school. I was president in my junior and senior years, though I found the meetings tedious at best, a complete waste of time at worst. Fact is, I could hardly wait to get rid of this burden. I mentally counted down the meetings remaining.

I had almost dropped out of the club at the beginning of my junior year, but that's when Pastor Lund arrived. I liked him. It was funny—he seemed so much older, but he was only ten years my senior.

Roger was about six-two, trim and muscular, with blond hair and blue eyes. He downplayed his classic good looks by sporting a stubble of a beard, rarely combing his hair, and exhibiting no apparent taste when it came to buying clothes.

With Pastor Lund's good looks, it was no surprise that he had an equally good-looking "helpmate." His wife, Colleen, starred in many of my fantasies. She was "choice," as we said back then. She was five feet six inches tall with brown hair that lightened in the summer, green eyes, and a curvy but slim figure.

Despite her looks, it would be a mistake to take her lightly. If someone challenged her, she could easily dismantle the affront with her wit, her strong opinions, and her willingness to take a stand.

Much later, I would learn of a story that captured Colleen to a tee. One day, Colleen was sporting a mini skirt, tanktop, boots, and, for fun, a blond wig. Roger loved the way she looked, but he became self-conscious as others couldn't stop staring at her. He was a little surprised at her unawareness.

Finally, he whispered, "I'm not sure what you're wearing is totally appropriate for a minister's wife."

Colleen looked surprised, then whispered to him, "You may be right. Next time, I'll wear panties."

At first, I tried to keep her out of my thoughts, but finally I just gave up. Sometimes it seemed she could read my dirty little mind, which caused me to be even more nervous around her. Early on, I overheard my father comment to my mother, "I wonder how long that fashion-plate wife of his will be satisfied living up here?"

No doubt, it wasn't easy for a young couple to move to the Range and feel accepted. We had seen it happen before. In Pastor Lund's case, though, he didn't seem to care about being liked. He merely lived to serve. Some people saw this and liked him even more.

This was saying a lot, considering that Mesabi was worlds away from where the Lunds had envisioned themselves serving. Even before Roger had left the seminary, he and Colleen had high hopes he would be called to a church in the Cities. They both had grown up there, and Roger had graduated at the top of his class. A prime assignment in the Cities seemed within reach.

They were dismayed, then, when the synod sent them to Bismarck, North Dakota. Roger served as associate pastor to Senior Pastor Paul Lutz. Lutz had been diagnosed with pancreatic cancer. Rather than accept their beloved pastor's resignation, the congregation brought in Roger to support him.

Perhaps the Hand of God had orchestrated the Lutz-Lund partnership. For two more years, Pastor Lutz lived out his life in faith and grace, doing what he loved best—proclaiming the "Good News" of Jesus Christ. Sunday after Sunday, the congregation witnessed his conviction and courage. The experience influenced Roger in his future ministry style as well as his life.

About a week after Roger arrived in Bismarck, Pastor Lutz invited him to his office. With a flair for drama, he handed his new, young associate pastor a print-out. It even had a place for both of them to sign at the bottom.

"These are 'Paul Lutz's Eleven Commandments,'" he said. "But I want to be clear: these are commandments, not suggestions. Please read aloud Commandment Number One."

Roger responded, "Thou shalt not meet privately with a woman at any time."

They continued through the other commandments until Roger read Number Eleven: "Thou shall follow Commandment One in every circumstance."

Roger thought this "commandment" regarding women to be somewhat archaic. He wasn't sure how to reply. He had never considered himself particularly vulnerable to such temptation. Then again, others told stories about "jezebels" who took satisfaction in helping pastors slide into infidelity.

"I'm happy to follow these commandments," Roger said, picking up a pen to sign and make it official. "But just to reassure you, I'd never cheat on Colleen."

Lutz smiled indulgently. "When Adam said to Eve, 'You're the only one for me,' he was the last man who could honestly say that."

Pastor Lutz passed on many more pearls of wisdom before he died of his cancer. When it came time to find a replacement, it was understood the associate pastor could not accept the call. This is the way it worked, and the synod held firm.

Once again, Roger and Colleen applied for a church in the Cities. And once again, the synod had different plans. Because Roger had kept such an "open mind" during his assignment to Bismarck, the synod felt he could do the same in Mesabi.

"It's up on the Iron Range," the synod president told him. "Have you ever been there?"

In a lot of ways, the people in Mesabi shared similarities to the people in Bismarck. For the most part, they were both solid folk who were satisfied with the basics in life. What he detected in many of his new flock, though, was a sense of inferiority. But to his core, Roger believed in the message of the Bible that God loves us and never gives up on his people.

In particular, I felt sought out by the young pastor. I soon considered him a mentor.

One day during my senior year, Pastor Lund asked me, "Have you ever considered becoming a pastor?"

I was flattered but relieved Pastor Lund didn't know what went on in my mind. Yes, I believed in God. And yes, I knew my sins were forgiven. But I also knew my feelings were mixed about the church. I didn't relate to most of the kids in the Young Christians group.

Furthermore, I cozied up to sin probably more than others. My desires to get a little drunk on weekends and look for like-minded girls conflicted with the alleged morals of the other Young Christians. Then again, I was well aware a few senior girls in the group exuded sexuality, thus guaranteeing I would be too timid to ask them out. I would need a six-pack of courage to do that. At least.

As high school came to an end, I felt a nervous excitement. Yes, the Cities would be my destination. I had a vague sense of blame toward my hometown. I had achieved some success here, yet I didn't feel Mesabi had fully prepared me for life. Feeling little pride, I too would leave the Range behind.

3

T HE DAY I LEFT THE TOWN OF MESABI and headed for my new life in Minneapolis remains fixed in my mind for several reasons. My dad had gotten work outside of town and wasn't present for the good-byes. Maybe it was for the best.

Dad was not an emotional man. I always thought he held conflicted feelings toward me. One Father's Day, I took a risk and mumbled, "I love you." Dad looked at me and said, "Thank you." I would have liked to have taken those three words back. We butted heads on what was said and knew we would butt heads on what wasn't said. So we said very little at all.

I had packed my orange Pontiac GTO Judge the night before so I could avoid too long of a sendoff with my mother. Mom held back the tears right up until I hugged her. I assured her I would be coming home often, and this would turn out to be true.

DeeDee now became the eldest child at home, but she looked twelve to me, not fifteen. Still, a quick thought came to me as we hugged good-bye. *She's starting to look like Mom.*

Mike squeezed my hand, and I cried out in fake pain, which was our routine. I doubt Mike understood the implications of what I was doing.

As I headed south on Highway 53, I could see the three of them waving to me in my rearview mirror. Once they were out of sight, I pulled off the highway, parked the car, then ceremoniously kicked the iron ore dust off my tires. I couldn't remember where I had read of somebody doing something like this, but I liked the symbolism.

My best buddy, Gary Halstead, would be meeting me at the apartment we had committed to in Minneapolis. Gary and I had been friends since grade school. We had plenty of history to draw from when we ran out of things to say. He was not a stellar student and appreciated my help in getting him through some math classes. Neither was he any kind of an athlete, as he had quit competitive sports in eighth grade.

His father worked in the mines, and his mom stayed at home with the kids. Gary was the youngest of four. His dad often told people, "When Gary leaves, the old lady needs to get a job." He was also proud to state, "None of my kids get a handout. When they're done with high school, they are out on their own."

While I was expected to earn some income to pay for my room and board, my parents planned to help me with tuition and loans. We would figure it out together. The Halsteads—or at least Mr. Halstead—was a believer in independence and self-sufficiency. At least when it came to his kids.

He was also a believer in the benefits of hard and frequent drinking, even for a Ranger. On several occasions, Gary and I saw him in varying degrees of drunkenness.

Drunk or sober, he liked to lecture. I didn't like him much. I thought he was a blowhard. He carried himself as if his opinions were common sense and even smart, but I knew he was an idiot where it mattered. It's harmless to sit at the bar and bore people with your parenting theories and to rant about the younger generation. But to believe your childrearing skills are superior to others because you provide no financial help seems like nothing to brag about.

He regarded me as a "Big Christian," so he weighed his words some around me. Both Gary and I were amused by this because he often referred to Christians as "weaklings." I guess he had figured out it was more admirable to be dependent on a bottle rather than a god.

Despite this disagreeable man, all four of the kids, especially Gary, were popular in school and well-mannered. When school started at the U, Gary joined the Young Christian's Club, mainly so the two of us could do something together. He seemed to get more out of it than I did. Candidly, I could feel he was a better person inside than I was. I always had.

As we entered seventh grade, we had a black classmate for the first time in our lives. For the most part, the student body treated Allen decently. It didn't take a great heap of empathy to consider how it felt to be outwardly so different than everybody else. But behind Allen's back, some students made jokes and comments that were clearly racist.

Allen joined Young Christians with Gary and me, and his knowledge of the Bible amazed me. After one meeting, he needed a ride home, and I asked my mom if she would mind bringing him to his home. It was a fifteen-minute drive, and my mother and Allen never stopped talking.

The next day at school, one of my idiot football teammates commented to me, "I hear Allen is really your brother."

I knew what he was saying. But while I stood there, unable to come up with something suitable in response, Gary got in this student's face.

"I think Allen is a great guy. Smart too. What do you think?"

As the kid fumbled to recover, I couldn't help but be proud of Gary—and jealous at the same time. He had the guts to speak up. Later, I thanked Gary for standing up for Allen.

"Hey, Jake," he replied, "don't forget you've been a friend to Allen from day one."

That made me feel a little better, but I still couldn't help but note the difference between Gary and me. That feeling would always be there.

Joining us at our new place would be Trent Podominik. I hadn't spent a lot of time with Trent back in Mesabi, but Gary and he were long-time friends. We needed a third guy to share the rent and split the driving costs back to the Range as well.

While Trent had been only a decent student at Mesabi, he clearly was more focused in college. He wanted to own a business and, in his words, "make a shitpile of money." But along the way, Trent changed his major and became premed. I don't know why this surprised me, but it did.

When we all discussed our futures, Trent would say without hesitancy, "I'm going to be a surgeon." Gary would sometimes perform hilarious parodies of "Dr. Trent, Gynecologist." A good-looking young woman would elicit a comment from Gary such as, "Dr. Trent, GYN, please report to the exam room."

As I got to know Trent better, he invited me to his house and introduced me to his father. Afterward, I asked Trent, "Your dad looks very tired and weak. Is he okay?"

Trent seemed to consider his response. Finally, he replied, "No, he isn't okay. He has Parkinson's disease. There's no goddamned cure. He's depressed and says he wants to die. My mom has aged ten years in the last two. I never hear her laugh anymore."

Eventually, Trent's dad had to quit working because of his tremors and his tendency to fall.

One Sunday night on the way back to the U, we picked up Trent, and he took his usual spot in the back seat. I caught his face in my rearview mirror. He looked sad and troubled.

"Trent, I don't mean to pry, but you look upset about something."

He continued to stare out the window. "Dad needs to go live at the nursing home. Probably forever."

No immediate comforting thought came to mind.

———

As promised, I showed up for football tryouts at the U and did my best. From the moment I arrived, I felt like the walk-on I was. Compared to the recruits, I didn't get much of a chance to make the regular squad as a running back. I was a nobody here, and I wasn't used to that.

I did accept the offer to be included on the practice team. This worked out to some extent. We practiced less, so I had more time for other activities than the varsity guys. Still, I harbored some regretful thoughts and often fantasized starring as a Minnesota Gopher running back. I hoped someday I would be given a chance to prove myself.

I didn't waste any time looking for a job to earn money for my living expenses. I saw an ad in the local paper for part-time work at Sommer's Carpet and Tile. The last place I expected to land was at a carpet and tile store, but my interest was piqued by the line, "If you're a go-getter, we'll teach you to sell, and you can make a nice commission above the hourly wage." I had never sold anything in my life, but the hourly wage was decent, and any commissions would be gravy.

I called the store, and they connected me to Leo Sommer, the owner. When I expressed my interest in an interview, he asked, "Well, what are you doing now?"

"I go to the U," I responded.

"No," he said, "what are you doing *right now*?"

"Oh, I'm sorry. I guess I'm not doing anything."

"Aren't you talking to me right now?" he asked.

He had me confused.

"So, Jacob, if you took the job and you liked it, how long would you stay?"

I thought for a moment. "If I liked the job, I would stay until I graduate four years from now."

"So . . . what are you doing now?" Leo responded.

I thought for another moment, finally getting it. "I'm asking you for a job," I said.

He laughed. "You think on your feet. I like that. Why don't you come over here now, and we'll talk."

We liked each other immediately. Leo and his wife, Fern, had two daughters, neither interested in joining the business. He loved to mentor. He showed patience when I asked the same question more than once.

After a few weeks of doing odd jobs around the company, he told me, "You're ready to start selling."

I wasn't so sure. There was a lot to know about flooring—far more than I had imagined. I had also witnessed several situations where customers were unhappy with their purchases and they blamed their salesman. Such is the carpet and tile business. It was tough to solve these situations. As Leo would say, "It's not like they're returning a shirt."

Sensing my hesitation, Leo asked, "Do you think my other salesmen are Rhodes scholars?"

"I guess not."

"You have all the tools, except one, to become a great salesman," he assured me.

"Okay. I don't know if I can do it or not, but I'll give it a try."

"You didn't ask what tool you're missing," he noted.

I smiled. "I just need a customer with an open mind."

He glanced to the door, then smiled back at me. "And she's coming in right now."

Turns out, I sold that woman carpeting for three rooms. I went to her home, measured the rooms, and accepted her check for $1,000, along with six chocolate chip cookies. The commission was $50.

A few days later, her neighbor came in and insisted she work with "Jake." As I developed a following, I began to make a lot of money—really. I felt a lot of satisfaction as well. To my own surprise, this had become far more than just a job. I found myself daydreaming about the business.

Over dinner during one of my weekend visits back home, I thought I may have found a new commonality with my father.

"Dad, I'm beginning to see how you love your job."

He finished chewing the piece of roast he had just put in his mouth, then said, "There's quite a difference between building something and being a salesman."

I could have argued the point, but then I thought, *Why do I even care?*

4

I T WAS 1968, AND I WAS NOW ENTERING my fourth year of college. Despite all the beautiful young women in the Cities, and despite all the talk of "free love," I still hadn't hooked up with the girl of my dreams. Or really, any girl. And I did a lot of dreaming. It was frustrating.

Gary, on the other hand, seemed to find these women. More to the point, they found him. I didn't begrudge him. Gary was a good guy, and I was beginning to see how women were drawn to his sincerity and sense of humor.

Plus, Gary wasn't very fussy. For several months, he dated a girl from Des Moines, new to the Twin Cities and noticeably overweight. I remember Trent teasing him about this, but Gary made some comment about her being one of the nicest people he knew. And he added, "She is very giving." He loved women in general and wasn't hung up on their looks.

More times than I could count, I asked myself, *Jake, you're a decent-looking guy, an athlete, an honor student. You're a good conversationalist with a sense of humor, a nice car, a good future. Why can't you score?*

As good a friend as Gary was, I couldn't discuss my shortcomings with him. Still, maybe Gary could just sense it. "Jake, stop looking for a wife," he told me a couple of times. "Just have some fun."

Gary, Trent, and I went home every chance we got. I felt a new status of sorts on these return trips. When we showed up at the various parties, the young ladies were impressed. They knew we had escaped to the Cities and would soon have college degrees and, hopefully, good jobs.

By happenstance, a life-changing event fell into my lap on one these weekend retreats. We had cut our Friday afternoon classes so we could make it to the big Mesabi football game against the evil archrival, Virginia. We agreed to meet for the game at the Virginia football field and go to the dance at the armory from there.

I got to my parents' house about five o'clock and walked in through the back door. Mom and Dad were standing in the kitchen and looked surprised to see me.

Mom smiled. She came over, gave me a light hug, and asked somewhat flatly, "Jake, how was your week?"

Dad looked at the two of us, then directed his attention back at Mom. "Just remember what I've been telling you. Mike isn't a kid anymore. If you keep babying him like this, it'll only get worse with him." He looked at me. "Maybe our big-shot college kid has the answers. Maybe you'll listen to him. You don't seem to think I know anything." With that, he walked out the back door, slamming it as he left.

"What's going on with Mike now?" I asked.

"Well," Mom said, "you know he got caught with a small amount of marijuana a couple of weeks ago. He got expelled from school. And this morning, I got a call from some idiot who says he saw Mike with a gun outside a bar. I asked Mike about it, and he promised me it wasn't him."

Mom's expression was grim. I knew we both were thinking the same thing: this disturbing news about the gun was more likely true than not. Mom gave me a silent exasperated gesture as if to say, *What can I do?*

"What does Dad want to do?"

"He wants you to move your goddamned car."

Dad had come back inside rather quietly, considering. I had parked my car directly in front of the garage door, where his Ford pickup was now running.

"I'm sorry, Dad. I didn't know you were going somewhere." I got up to comply.

There were many things Roy Horton didn't like—one of them being Mom and I talking about him. Dad was agitated, so moving my car and getting him out of the house would be good.

He headed briskly for his pickup as I got into my car and backed it up slowly to the street. Of course, it was now "Mesabi rush hour." I had to wait while all three cars passed. I avoided looking through the windshield at Dad.

Then, at long last, the third car passed by slowly. I maneuvered into the street, allowing my father to escape. As he did, he gave me a quick wave—really, a pitiful wave, like *Okay. You're here. Big deal.*

I didn't want to be late for the game, but I also didn't want to leave Mom on such a note.

"I really can't believe Mike would have a gun," I said as I came back inside for a moment. "Geez, he's fourteen. But what does Dad want to do?"

Mom wiped her eyes. She seemed more tired than sad. "Well, your dad thinks we should send him to a reform school because we don't know what'll happen next with him. Last week, Mike looked like he'd been in a fight. Of course, he wouldn't talk about it. I don't know. Maybe he's right. Or maybe he just doesn't want Mike around here anymore." With that, she said, "Maybe we can talk about it tomorrow. You better get going. Be sure to look for your sister—she's cheering tonight. Say hi to Gary. And don't drink too much, Jake. They've been giving out a lot of tickets."

As I headed for my car, I wondered how a half hour at home could change my mood from happy to crappy. Mike, what the hell? A *gun*? I decided to at least talk with the little delinquent when I had a chance.

I felt bad for Mike. We all did. From the start, he did poorly in school, and his self-esteem took an awful hit. Mike did own one special talent, though. That would be boxing. His quick hands could decimate an unsuspecting opponent—whether in the ring or in some alley. I suddenly realized that even Mike's one talent might turn out to be both a blessing and curse.

Once I got to the Virginia football field, I was back in my element. Gary and Trent waved when they saw me, and we found our way to the Raider side of the field. The fall night was crisp but nice. Maybe sixty, and no wind.

The conversation turned to football. We agreed with the locals around us that it was too bad Mesabi had to play Virginia so early in the season. Virginia would likely win by three touchdowns, maybe more.

In between sports talk, the locals shared recent news and rumors.

"Gary, you hear the mines are laying people off again?"

A few moments later: "Say, Jake, is it true your dad was sent home from some job in Chicago?"

I could only say, "I have no idea." I looked over at Gary. He returned the look and shrugged.

The referee blew his whistle, and the Virginia Blue Devil kicker raised his hand to signal readiness to begin the game. I was ready to tone down the local chitchat.

Moments later, we were screaming at the top of our lungs. A Mesabi player received the kickoff, juggled it briefly, then zigzagged his way, breaking tackles, all the way to the end zone for a touchdown. Our voices became hoarse, then we yelled some more.

It felt like one of those moments when nothing else counted and you were lucky enough just to be where you were.

The Raiders simply dominated the Blue Devils on offense and on defense. At the end of the first quarter, it was Mesabi 13, Virginia 0. Our cheering section sounded as if we had just won the state hockey championship or something. In contrast, an eerie quiet came from the Virginia fans' side of the bleachers.

Mesabi kept the lead at the half 20–13 and still led 28–21 entering the fourth quarter. But then Virginia connected on a long pass for a touchdown to tie it up with a couple of minutes to go. As the momentum shifted, I could feel the collective fear of the Raider fans: we were going to lose.

I hadn't paid much attention to the cheerleaders during the game, but now I saw DeeDee's enthusiasm. For whatever reason, I wanted to give her a hug. I was suddenly overwhelmed with thoughts about our family.

First, Anna left immediately after graduation, as if she had all but given up on the family. Then I left for the Cities. Who knew what Mike would become. At least DeeDee was there for Mom. For now.

Virginia attempted an onside kick. Lame. The Raiders easily recovered it. Three running plays brought a first down.

"Hey, Jake, that kid remind you of anyone?"

I didn't recognize the older guy who asked, but it was meant as a compliment to my past running glories. I simply turned to him and raised both thumbs up.

Now with just a minute left in the game, Mesabi got penalized for too many players on the field. It wasn't surprising to see Virginia get a break from the refs on their home turf. Some of the Raider fans laced their screaming with expletives.

With the game still tied and time for only one or two plays, Mesabi snapped the ball. The quarterback rolled left and looked left—receivers on the left, but they were covered.

But what I didn't notice, nor did any player in the Virginia secondary, was one lone Mesabi player far to the right. He had been kneeling, pretending to be tying his shoelace, but he was on the line of scrimmage and eligible to receive a pass.

The quarterback turned quickly to the right, straightened up, and tossed the ball to the player. Nobody was near him. He caught the ball and held it tight against his chest. Incredibly, he ran casually into the end zone. It was one of the biggest upsets ever in Mesabi football history.

Never in my own football career had I experienced anything like what I saw next. Almost everybody in the Raider section, myself included, ran, walked, or stumbled onto the field to hug their heroes for the moment, the Mesabi Raiders. Later, one of the players joked the smell of booze from the fans' breaths almost made him drunk.

I sought out my sister. She was jumping and hugging with another pretty cheerleader, so I grabbed them both.

Next I looked for Coach L in hopes of congratulating him. Nobody could question his coaching abilities now. I spotted him near the players' bench. He was same as always—never up and never down. I felt a little sorry for him. I remember thinking, *Coach, you won the biggest game of your life. Enjoy it. At least pretend you're happy.*

———

That evening, we altered our usual pattern a bit. Rather than go to the armory dance, we decided to visit Buck's Bar in Virginia before we hit a party north of town. If there were no unattached women at the party, plan B would be to go to the armory. Of late, the armory dances made me increasingly uncomfortable, with their mix of older townies, who likely didn't care for us college boys, and high school girls a bit too young for us.

Multiple times, I watched guys my age leaving the armory with half-buzzed girls who looked about fourteen or fifteen. I drew the line at that. But to be honest, a year earlier, I had unwittingly gotten involved with a girl two years younger than my sister. She had lied to me, but I should have known better. Never again.

At Buck's, we had a good time toasting Coach L and the boys while getting a little toasted ourselves. Trent assured us he was good to drive, so I parked my car near the armory before we headed out to the party.

I listened as Trent and Gary bantered about the various women they were hoping to run into. With these guys, it wasn't idle talk. Back at our apartment, Gary slept in the bedroom next to me. He amazed me with the sex he was having one wall away from me. I didn't like to think about it, but no doubt it made me feel as if something were wrong with me.

It wasn't just a lack of making out and sex. Why wasn't I capable of enjoying women? While I enjoyed many guy friends, I honestly couldn't name one close female friend. When I talked with attractive girls, I simply froze up. Often they were interested in me, but I'd say something goofy or get too nervous to speak at all. And when it came to making out, I graded myself an F. The whole thing was enough to lead one of the idiots from nearby Hoyt Lakes to ask Gary, "Does Jakey swing the other way?"

By the time we arrived at the party, I had worked myself into wishing I had just stayed at Buck's. I was in no mood to scope for girls. Well, it turned out to be a moot point anyway. They did have a keg of beer, which we took quick advantage of, but there were only two girls there. Not only were they homely, but they were steadies with boyfriends who were out-of-it drunk but still awake.

We gulped a couple of more beers, then headed back south to the armory for plan B. Now inebriated, we expected little but weren't ready to give up hope.

We paid our five dollars each, endured having our hands stamped, and headed in to look over the women. As we neared the dance area, a couple of cute girls looked thrilled to see sophisticated college students. They began flirting shamelessly. Without even trying, it became obvious Gary was home free with one of the girls. Looking at the other girl, I didn't feel like getting into a competition I would likely lose to Trent.

"It's been a long day," I said. "I've had enough beer. You guys go ahead. I'm going to head home shortly."

I walked over to the vending area, thinking a Coke might make me feel a little better. It sounds corny, but the scene would have made a great ad for Coke. The noise and crowd faded to the background. I dropped my change in the machine. Out came a can of cold Coke. I opened it and watched the bubbles form on the top of the can. I tipped my head back, enjoying a deep drink. At that moment—and I swear it's true—I saw the most beautiful young woman I had ever seen.

The first thing I noticed was her curly black hair feathering its way down that beautiful face and resting on her shoulders. Then those eyes, deep brown.

And the cutest freckles I had ever seen. She was slender but with an attention-getting body.

She had my attention, for sure. I almost spilled my soda on my jacket. She noticed this and giggled. What a smile.

Now what?

I felt a hand on my shoulder. It was Gary. He had his arm around the girl we had met moments before.

"Hey, Jake, we're heading over to a party on the north side. Candy here has a girlfriend she wants you to meet."

Ignoring his invitation, I instead asked, "Do you know that girl in the white sweater?"

Candy answered for Gary. "That's Frankie Nazar's girl, Margie Kolar. I didn't see Frank around tonight, but they're tight. The two of them have been a thing forever. I guess. She's in my grade, but I don't really know her that well."

"Nazar is an asshole," Gary warned. "You don't want to get involved with that."

Apparently, it was common knowledge, at least among the guys, that Margie was out of reach because Frank would likely kill any guy moving in on his girl. And let's face it, she was just too damn beautiful—she likely didn't want anything to do with anyone else. At least, that's what my cowardly thoughts told me every time I considered trying to date an attractive girl.

But because I didn't know anything about Nazar, and because I was almost in a trance between the liquor and the sight of this young woman, I did the unfathomable. I sauntered slowly toward Margie, who was still smiling at me. I smiled back.

"I hear you're Margie. I'm Jake, and I can't decide."

Margie looked confused. "Can't decide what, Jake?"

"I can't decide whether it's your smile or your eyes that make you so beautiful."

Surprisingly, she blushed and looked down shyly.

Hell, Jake, just try asking, I thought.

So I added, "How about letting me take you home so I can figure it out?"

She looked at me with those dark eyes and lashes, blinked in surprise, then said, "Sure. Why not?"

I hesitated for a moment, but then she took my hand. She wanted to leave, and I didn't want to share her with these people. We headed for my car.

5

I ABSOLUTELY COULD NOT BELIEVE THIS WAS HAPPENING. I noticed Gary and a couple of other guys looking on in amazement as Margie squeezed my hand and I escorted her to my car.

I opened the passenger door and watched her climb in gracefully. When I opened my door, there she was sitting on the middle console, close to the driver's seat.

"Nice car, Jake," she complimented.

A little voice inside said, *She's just a young girl . . .* I rebutted back to that voice, *Yeah, but she sure looks like a woman.*

The evening progressed in a previously unimaginable way. I drove my GTO to a secluded spot, and we made out. After all my strikeouts with girls, I remember thinking to myself, *Don't let this be a dream.* I reclined my seat as far as I could, and Margie moved on top of me. I concluded in my mind, *This is a dream. A dream come true.*

I don't remember which of us brought up Frank, but I'm guessing it was goofy me.

To my infinite relief, she told me, "I'm tired of Frank. I want to go with a guy with a brain."

Hey! That's me.

We made out some more, then out of the clear blue, she asked, "Jake, do you believe in God?"

I ignored the question, hoping to keep the dream alive.

"Jake, do you believe in God?" she persisted. "I need to know."

There I was, confronted by personal conflict. I did then and I do now believe in God. But even in my diminished mental state at that moment, I knew my religious beliefs and my wild attraction for Margie were not necessarily compatible. Yet she made it plain she wanted an answer before further affections.

So I in turn asked her, "Margie, do you believe?"

She looked at me seriously with those beautiful eyes. "Yes, I do. But Frank says it's all a myth."

Seeing an opportunity, I looked back at her and said firmly, "Well, then, Frank having a brain is a myth. Of course there is a God. How does Frank think human beings come into being? How could something as beautiful as you not be from God?"

We got back to kissing. Eventually, things got a little heavy for a first date, so to speak.

"Whoa, it's almost one," Margie said, pulling away. "I need to get home."

It was a memorable half-hour drive. She continued to sit close to me and kiss me as I drove. I brought her to her door and enjoyed one deeper kiss.

"Are you around next weekend? Or how about tomorrow even?"

I couldn't believe my good fortune when she said, "Sure. I'll stop by your house tomorrow afternoon."

I woke up Saturday morning feeling very, very good. But doubts started to nibble into my mind, though. Would she really come over? Or would she stand me up? Some guys have a way with women. Much to my personal disappointment, I didn't seem to be one of them. Even with Margie seemingly interested in me, I still felt out of her league.

I decided to take her at her word rather than call her. I had homework to finish. Instead of working at the dining table, I sat in a chair near the front window, where I could watch for Margie.

Sure enough, around two o'clock, I could see her approaching the house. She hesitated for a moment, then moved slowly toward our door. She wore a short white ski jacket, a close-fitting black sweater, boots, and very tight jeans.

Be still my heart!

I let DeeDee open the front door. I heard, "Hi, I'm Margie Kolar. Is Jake around?"

DeeDee faltered for a moment, then turned and said, "Hey, Jake—Margie is here."

At that moment, I don't think I'd ever been much happier. I helped her with her jacket, then introduced her to Mom. The two of them hit it off right away. This was a relief. It helped me get my bearings.

Then Dad came up from the basement. Maybe I was imagining it, but he seemed to take a little too much interest in her too soon.

"What was your last name again, Margie?" he asked after a few minutes.

"Kolar," she responded.

"Are you Cy's daughter, then?"

"Yes, and my mother is Alice. Do you know them?"

Dad paused, then said, "Well, I've met him, and he's a good guy."

"Well, let's go and get some pizza or something," I said, moving things along.

Outside in the car, I turned to her. "Where would you like to go?"

She ignored the question. "I want you to know I broke up with Frank. Jake, you have given me something to think about."

No doubt, this was good news. I found myself proud I had kicked Frank Nazar's ass.

We skipped dinner and drove out into a rural area south of Mesabi. As I drove, Margie settled on an 8-track by Gary Puckett and the Union Gap and slid it in. I wondered if she were thinking the same thing as I was. We got to kissing.

Just when things got a little heavy, Margie once again said she needed to get home. Well, I needed to get back to the Cities too. As we headed back to Mesabi, we both grew silent. The lyrics, "Young girl, get out of my mind . . ." played. I hoped she wasn't paying attention.

I drove her home slowly, kissed her good-bye, and promised I would call her during the week.

Once I was back home, Mom hugged me, then held my hands as she smiled and looked up to my face. "What a beautiful, sweet girl, Jake. And so polite."

Dad added, "And she sure looks great in a black sweater. Doesn't she, Jake?"

Mom looked at him with daggers in her eyes. I didn't have to respond.

"I heard Cy's daughter goes with that dink, Frank Nazar," Dad went on.

I was surprised Dad knew this. It turned out the Nazars owned the local hardware store in Virginia. Nazar Senior had replaced the roof on the building and done the unforgivable—he used a nonunion contractor. Nazar and his hardware were on Dad's permanent shit list.

"Well, Dad, Margie isn't going with him anymore. He's past history. I couldn't care less about the guy."

Of course, this was a lie. I did want to know more about Frank Nazar. Margie was eighteen, and Frank twenty-two, like me. They had been going steady for two years. Doing the math, that meant she was sixteen and he was twenty when it started.

Frank was a cliché in some ways. He liked his motorcycle, he made good money as a welder, and he had a definite James Dean look—wavy dark-black hair, good-looking by all accounts. He was a chick magnet, hanging around with a younger crowd. The high school girls begged him for rides, which often turned into make-out sessions. He bolstered his bad-boy image by getting into fights periodically. I tried not to think about running into him, but I couldn't put it completely out of my mind.

When I picked up Gary for the journey back to Minneapolis, he wasted no time.

"*Are you out of your fucking mind?*"

I had anticipated this, so I responded, "Yes. Out of my mind in love."

He went on, gesturing almost frantically. "Jake, you don't know what you're into here. Not her. We're talking about 'Fast Frank.'"

Not wanting to seem concerned, I just grinned. "Frank is a wiener."

Gary looked at me. "You better watch your back, my friend. This guy's been in the can for assault. You're messing with somebody else's woman. You can joke if you want, but I've heard he's a hardcore badass. His whole family is messed up. You should hear the stories Clay Fortson tells."

Clay was a friend of Gary's. His family owned Fortson's Welding, where Frank worked. As Clay told it, Frank had the best skills of any of the workers, no question. But his interpersonal skills were lacking, to say the least.

One time, Clay had even told him, "Off the record, Frank, if you'd be willing to take anger management counseling, we would pay for it."

"Anger management," Frank seethed. "I'll show you fucking anger management."

Clay had heard all the rumors. Anger existed in large quantities in the Nazar household. Management of that anger was almost nonexistent. Frank Nazar Senior smacked his wife, Ina, around. He wasn't much easier on Frank or his older brother, Vince.

One rumor told of a time when Frank was ten and Vince nearly eighteen. Apparently, the old man had ordered the boys to restock the nail display at the hardware store. Vince was more of a supervisor than a brother to Frank, so once their father left, he put the ten-year-old to work while he snuck off to the football game. When Vince returned, however, he discovered Frank had made a mess of the display.

And when Frank Senior returned, he responded by locking them both in the store's pitch-black basement to "teach them a lesson."

When her sons still hadn't returned home hours later, a panicked Ina made a decision she had never made before—she called the police.

When the cops and social worker arrived at the store, they tried to piece together what had transpired: They had two boys who had been locked in a blackened basement for hours. They had a ten-year-old with a freshly bloodied nose, most likely broken. They had a teenager riddled with regret. And they had a mother who wanted to go to a shelter to protect herself and her sons.

Ultimately, though, the three Nazars went home. No charges were pressed against Frank Senior. Vince refused to answer when asked point-blank, "What is life like around your father?"

Frank was too young to understand, but Ina and Vince knew they couldn't take the chance. The idea of turning on Frank Senior made them fear for their lives more than if they just went home and let life return to its former dreary and abusive state.

Which it did, for a while. Then Vince skipped town once he turned eighteen. He wrote a short note to his mother that said simply, "Mom, only you can help yourself. Don't try to find me. Down the road, I will someday find you. It's not your fault. I love you. You can show this note to the old man so he knows you have no idea where I am."

Vince became persona non grata. Frank Senior made sure his youngest son understood Ina was just a stupid woman to blame for it all. On his end, young Frank knew his dad hurt his mother, though he never witnessed it. Over the years, he began to wonder why she stayed.

When Frank turned eighteen, he quit school, bought a beat-up rambler on the outskirts of Mesabi, and started at Fortson's Welding. Frank thought of himself as rebellious, mysterious, and at least superficially cool. His father bought him a newer motorcycle to complete the James Dean look.

Ina disappeared two days after Frank's birthday, most likely checking herself into a battered women's facility. Neither of the Franks had a clue as to where she lived. Neither of them cared.

"You don't know what trouble you're getting into with seeing Margie," Gary concluded.

We drove in silence for a few minutes. I played with the radio setting.

After a while, Gary added, "But no doubt—she is hot."

6

I CONFESS: I LOVED BEING SEEN WITH MARGIE. After all, I was usually on the other side, watching guys with good-looking girls and wondering what they had that I didn't.

As our relationship grew, she tended to be more and more affectionate in public. One day, I was at the Loon having a hamburger with Pastor Lund and a couple of the guys my age from church. Pastor Lund, only in his late twenties, dressed casually and didn't wear a clergy collar.

When Margie walked in and saw me unexpectedly, she gave me a smile and a hug. Before I could say anything, she was sitting on my lap—or rather straddling my left leg rather suggestively. I wasn't embarrassed. Well, maybe a little.

"Guys, this is my girlfriend, Margie Kolar," I announced a little more proudly than I should have.

Pastor Lund reached over and took her hand. "Hi, Margie. I'm Roger Lund, pastor at Saint James Lutheran. This is Bill Hicks and Luke Avery. So nice to meet you."

Margie shot up from my lap. "Oh, I'm sorry," she awkwardly uttered. "I didn't know you were a minister."

"Nothing to apologize for, Margie. Again, nice to meet you. A friend of Jake's is a friend of mine."

Later, after the three of them left, Margie looked at me. "I'm so sorry I embarrassed you like that in front of the pastor."

"No, no—it's fine," I reassured her.

I didn't know how to say it, but I sure as hell hoped she wouldn't stop showering me with affection like she did. I loved it.

"You're so smart, and I'm so stupid," she said, fighting back tears.

I felt bad for her. "Margie, you're plenty smart. Please don't say that, because it's not true."

Margie possessed at least average intelligence and likely beyond. But starting in grade school, teachers began to make fun of her because her mind seemed far away, somewhere far from the classroom.

Margie got through the day by being a consummate dreamer. Often, her very pretty face would sport a red spot on the right side of her forehead. No need to go to a dermatologist—this mark resulted from her tendency to lay her head down on her arms during class.

Some teachers attempted to discipline Margie by sending her out of class, but this didn't help anything. One wise teacher spent much of his lecture standing right in front of her desk. This worked fairly well. But most teachers tended to just shake their heads and let her sleep and dream.

Margie shared this fascination with dreams with her parents. It seemed the three of them talked more about dreams than their lives. And why not? Their dreams tended to be far more interesting and conversation worthy than their realities.

When Margie's mind drifted toward dreaming, she just hated to be awakened. Low grades held no concern for Margie because her parents set no standards. They knew they wouldn't be able to help her with college anyways, so why encourage her?

That night, we made out on the back seat of the GTO at a secluded spot on the Saint Louis River. She had some surprising news for me.

"Jake, I hope you'll like this—I'm moving to the Cities. I got accepted into secretarial school."

It took me a quick moment to gain my composure. She noticed.

"Jake, don't worry. I'm not moving to the Cities because of you. We'll go on just like we are."

I searched for the right words. I decided to say what I thought she wanted to hear.

"Margie," I said as I brought my arms around to hold her closer, "you make me happy. And seeing you more will make me happier yet."

As we lay there facing each other, she brought both hands to my face and kissed me. My mind raced. I thought of my dad's rather vulgar little advice he had shared with me more than once: "Don't let your little head do the thinking for the big head."

I could feel my heart pounding. I put my dad out of my mind. I knew this was a special moment. I wanted to be truthful, but I wanted *her* more than anything.

The words sounded as though they came from someone else as I whispered, "I love you, Margie."

I guess this is what she had been waiting to hear. She reached down and worked my zipper. We made love for the first time. I won't lie—I'm guessing Margie knew it was my first time ever.

I had a bizarre thought as we remained in each other's arms. Strangely, I felt a little lonely right at that very moment. Hollow. I couldn't understand it. Here was someone I had craved for since the first time I laid eyes on her.

It was late, very late, when I brought her home. Before she went in, we kissed some more and decided to get together at her house tomorrow.

What a night. I began to smile as I drove home. I can't think of any other way to put it, but I was proud of myself.

Then as I turned toward Fifth Street, just a few blocks from my home, my thoughts turned a little darker.

She's moving to Minneapolis.

I didn't use any protection.

I told her I loved her.

She didn't say she loved me.

Maybe that's good.

———

When I stopped by the next day, I wondered if Margie's mom could read my look of guilt. But I need not have worried—Alice had liked me from the start.

Alice was a traditional-mom type. As far as I could tell, she had never worked outside their home. She didn't enjoy drinking or going out. In fact, she detested bars. She spent most of her days reading everything from paperback passion novels to the Bible. While she seemed sad to me most of the time, when she smiled, I could see where Margie got her good looks.

I liked Cy, which was short for Cyril. One night at their house, we found ourselves talking about Margie. He looked around to be sure nobody could hear him, then he leaned over and whispered.

"Margie better marry somebody with lots of money. It's expensive to live in the clouds."

Cy was the franchise owner of Stories, the only bookstore in town. From time to time, I would drop by the shop. He would show me new book releases, and sometimes we would listen to a new album. The half-empty shelves should have clued me in—he had been on the verge of going broke for a long time. Ultimately, the bank would take the building from him.

Both Alice and Cy were religious people, Roman Catholics. Margie, Alice, and I would sometimes talk about various verses from the Bible. For a Catholic, Alice was well-versed in Bible study. When I stopped in that Sunday, they were just returning from Mass.

Alice smiled at me and asked, "Jake, do you have a favorite Bible verse?"

I liked the discussion. "Yes, it would have to be John 3:16: 'For God so loved the world, he gave his only son, that whosoever believes in him will not perish, but have eternal life.'"

She smiled again. "All of Christianity is summed up right there, don't you agree?"

I nodded.

She went on, "I don't know what I would do if I didn't think I would see my parents again."

We were going deeper, I could tell.

"Margie, have you told Jake about your grandparents?"

Margie got up. "Mom, that's depressing. I don't think we need to talk about that. Jake, we better go."

I wanted to hear more—I could tell Alice wanted to share something important. Without even knowing the story, I couldn't help but feel sad for her.

But Margie was almost out the door. I gave Alice an apologetic look and barely beat Margie to the car door so I could open it for her.

The ride was awkward. After a few minutes, Margie broke the silence.

"I will tell you the story, Jake, but only this once, and I don't want you to ever bring it up again. When my mother was fourteen, her parents were both killed in a car accident. I never even knew them, so they weren't really my grandparents."

Another awkward silence fell over us. I tried to imagine what it would be like to lose your parents so young. I thought about Alice's sadness. I thought again how Alice's features reminded me of Margie's. I thought about John 3:16.

I also thought, *I really don't know Margie at all.*

I broke the silence this time. "Okay, Margie—I won't bring it up again."

Yet I wanted to talk more about it. I wanted to know her better. Since I first met her, I thought having sex with her would be the total answer to all of life's problems for me. But already I knew we needed more. Maybe not now, though.

When I got back home, I asked my kid sister what she knew about Margie. DeeDee gave me a surprised look.

"She's beautiful, and I really like her. But she doesn't have friends. I think her old boyfriend was her whole social life. I don't think she played any sports or anything." She paused. "She's nice, Jake."

It was time to head back to Minneapolis, so I picked up Gary. Though I had become good friends with Trent too, I was glad it was just Gary and me this time. I hadn't told anybody about having sex with Margie, and it had been eighteen hours ago. But then I felt a little ashamed for wanting to tell him, so I held back.

An hour later, as we passed Moose Lake, I couldn't hold the news back any longer.

"Well, we did it last night."

"Did what?" Gary deadpanned.

I shot him a mock pissed-off look. "Screw you. You know what I'm talking about."

"Screw me? Sounds like you want to screw everybody now." He smirked as he reached over to turn down the radio. "Honestly, I thought you two had been doing the dirty deed all along."

"She's moving to the Cities to go to secretarial school," I added. It was strange, but I wanted his opinion.

I could tell he was thinking. "So, did you consider asking Margie to move in with us?"

"No, not at all," I said with complete honesty. The thought hadn't even crossed my mind.

Gary seemed satisfied with my answer, then he moved on to a related topic.

"Well, her moving to the Cities seems to mean Frank is really out of the picture. Every time we go up there, I think we're going to run into that asshole, Jake. Trent and I were going over to Buck's last night, but we changed our minds when we saw he and his buddies were there."

This surprised me. "Why would that stop you? What does he have against you?"

Gary sighed. "Jake, for a smart guy, you can be such a fuckin' idiot. Are you kidding me? I better have something to protect myself besides that sissy Trent if I'm going to be around Nazar. By the way, speaking of protection . . ."

Gary looked at me as if asking a question.

I changed the subject. "How are you doing in that statistics class."

He shook his head. "You really are an idiot, Jake."

———

I was glad for Monday morning, a return to my routine. The early-morning session for the Gopher practice team brought a pleasant surprise. Due to injuries with several varsity players, I was being upgraded to varsity, starting with practice tomorrow.

Even though I had gone nowhere with the program for almost four years, suiting up for varsity would be exciting. Of course, these injuries were unfortunate developments for the players involved and the team as a whole, so I needed to keep my excitement to myself. I felt vindicated, though, for hanging around the past three seasons. I decided I would do everything I could to impress the coaching staff. I wanted to contribute, and I believed I could.

I called Margie with my big news. At first, she seemed decidedly underwhelmed. As we talked longer, however, she asked if I could get her a ticket for the next game.

"Of course," I said. "The next home game is in two weeks against Michigan State. Do you want to go with Gary and Trent?"

She seemed pleased by the offer. "That would be fun," she said with some enthusiasm. "Oh, and Jake, I'm moving down there on Friday. I need to find a job. Any ideas?"

"What kind of a job are you looking for?" I asked.

She didn't respond at first. Finally, she said, "I don't really know. Maybe when I'm down there, you can give me some suggestions."

"Sure thing," I said. "I love you," I added a little meekly.

A moment passed, then she replied, "I love you too."

7

ONE OF THE BEST PARTS ABOUT WORKING AT Sommer's Carpet and Tile was spending time with Leo and his wife, Fern. I often had dinner with them at their home. Fern was a fabulous cook. She always asked questions about my life and was a good listener.

Fern liked to talk about her two daughters. Lydia lived in Washington, DC, married with no children yet. Cynthia was finishing college in Saint Louis with a major in political science. She planned to attend law school and become a patent lawyer. Fern proudly showed me Cynthia's picture every time I was there. Photos can be misleading, but this one showed Cynthia to be very pretty, indeed.

When I first started working there as a dateless freshman, Fern always made a point to compliment me on not getting involved with anyone until I was "on my feet." Then, she would add, "That's like my Cynthia."

"Fern, for the love of God," Leo would say in pretend disgust each time, "we're not running a dating service here."

This banter between the three of us went on for several years. But now I was dating Margie. While I paraded Margie all around Mesabi, I never brought her down to the Cities to visit the store. I never even mentioned her to Leo, Fern, or anyone at the business.

In retrospect, I should have asked myself, *Jake, why is it you never brought Margie to your store? Why have you never mentioned your relationship to Leo and Fern? Is it because you are ashamed of Margie for some reason? Is it because you suspect you'll be leaving her? Why? For someone "better"?*

The Monday after Margie and I each said "I love you," Leo pulled me aside at work and invited me to dinner later that week. Cynthia was home from Saint Louis, and they wanted me to meet her.

Before I could come up with an excuse, Leo added, "Fern will never talk to either of us again if you don't."

Really, I was flattered—and Cynthia looked darn good in that photo. So I told Leo, "I would love to meet her and enjoy another nice dinner with you and Fern."

Leo gave me a quick hug. "Be there at seven on Thursday, my good man."

As I got ready for dinner that Thursday night, I was a little nervous. I just hoped that photo was a good representation.

Then in the back of my mind, I thought about Margie. But I reminded myself we had made no pledges of exclusivity. I wondered if she would even care.

It got me thinking about her "You're so smart and I'm so dumb" comment, which she kept saying over and over. God, I hated that. Then I realized I would probably be the dumb one with Cynthia. A patent attorney to be. She may be too classy to like me.

Gary noticed my nervousness—and compounded it. "Just don't be yourself," he suggested as I headed out the door.

My anxiety compounded even more as I reached my car. Some genius had broken the driver's side window. The shattered glass was all over the front seat and the floor.

"Goddammit!" I yelled.

Inwardly, my wrath surprised me. I rarely used the Lord's name in vain.

The commotion brought Gary out to see what was going on.

"Holy shit! Did the bastard steal anything?"

"I don't know," I blurted. Nothing seemed to be missing, but I didn't have time to figure it out. I didn't want to be late for dinner.

Before I even thought to ask, Gary tossed me his car keys.

"You can't do anything about this tonight, but you'll want to call your insurance company tomorrow." As I rushed to his car, he added, "Don't leave any stains on the back seat."

I flipped him the bird, then thanked him and drove off.

I arrived right at 7:00 p.m. with a bouquet of flowers for Fern. As it turned out, the photo of Cynthia was a few years old and not totally accurate. Cynthia wasn't pretty. She was a knockout. A redhead like her mom with light-blue eyes, strikingly fair skin, a perfect little nose, and soft lips. She was about five-feet-five, and as the saying goes, "every brick was in the right place."

The old Jake would have withered like that flower bouquet after a week with no water. Now, with newfound confidence, I could sense we liked each other. I could sense the positive feelings coming from Fern and Leo as well.

I should have controlled my intake of wine a little better—a mistake Cynthia made as well. Leo's eyebrow arched a little when Cynthia asked him to open another bottle.

Cynthia sat across the table from me, and her feet touched mine. At first, I thought it was an accident. However, as the wine did its magic and the attraction grew, she was smiling at me as she continued to tease me with her bare foot.

It was about ten o'clock when she realized she had forgotten her purse at the store earlier in the day. She was flying back to Saint Louis in the morning, so she needed her purse tonight.

She looked at me. "Jake, I know you have early classes tomorrow, but could you please bring me to Dad's shop so I can get my purse?"

I couldn't say "Of course" fast enough.

At this point, Leo chimed in. "Jake, I hate to ask you to do this too, especially at this hour, but since you're going to the shop, would you check to make sure your customer brought those Wellington samples back? I need to show them to a good friend tomorrow first thing."

I made a note to do so, I thanked Fern for a wonderful evening, then I led Cynthia to Gary's car and opened the door for her.

Until that moment, I hadn't noticed how badly the car's interior needed a good cleaning. So I found myself telling her the story of why I was driving somebody else's car. Somebody else's dirty car. Somebody else's dirty car with a bag of aluminum beer cans on the back seat and a cardboard air freshener in the shape of two boobs hanging on the rearview mirror.

She just smiled.

It was no more than a ten-minute drive with little traffic. The whole time, I was torn between making a move and not. If I did and she refused and told her dad, that could only be bad. A voice rang in my head, *Don't let the little head think for the big head.*

Silence. I turned the radio up a bit.

Cynthia turned to me. "My parents adore you, Jake, and I can see why."

I didn't want to think about Leo and Fern right now, but the expected reply was my honest reply: "The feeling is mutual."

We drove in silence the last few minutes. I could see the mood had evaporated. I was angry with myself. Yet I could see the upside too. Maybe it was best if nothing happened between us.

I unlocked the back door and entered the code for the alarm. I let Cynthia in. Her eye was drawn to a new Alexander Smith display I had just set up. It read, "More Than Just a Rug, 'Romance' Makes Life Better." Leo had purchased a six-by-eight area rug for the "Romance" display in a deep-red thick plush. The spotlight above focused on the rug. With darkness surrounding it, the rug looked amazing.

And Cynthia wasn't bad either.

I turned, and there we were, facing each other and very close. I tentatively kissed her gently on her lips and placed one hand on her hip as if to ask her to dance. Moments later, we were on the rug together.

She stopped. "Jake, redheads don't look good wearing red, do they?" she asked while lying flat on her back and spread out on the rug.

I recalled a saying I had heard from a guy who was discussing the color of a woman's hair—something about the drapes and rug matching . . .

I held her. I at least had wised up in one way since my first time: I now carried protection in my wallet. In this case, so did my partner.

I could have gazed into those baby-blue eyes for a long time, but time was short.

"Jake," she said afterward, "'Romance' is a good choice. Is it stain-proof?"

With that, she slowly ran her hand through my hair and kissed my forehead softly, almost mother-like. She sighed.

"I suppose . . ."

She almost added something more but instead reached for her sweater nearby.

In the darkness and silence, we eventually found our clothes. I sat watching her silhouette as she slipped her skirt on, then she came over and kissed me gently.

"Jake, you better get me home."

Cynthia sat next to me with her left hand on my shoulder. I turned and kissed her. I liked her. I thought to myself, *What kind of excuse can I come up with to go to Saint Louis?*

As we headed back to Leo's, the air freshener bounced up and down, adding a comic asterisk to the evening.

"Be sure to call me next time you're home," I said.

To that, she said quietly, "Jake, home isn't here for me. Home is Saint Louis. It's where I live. With my fiancé. But my secret is safe, and so is yours."

I can't even express how cheap I felt at that moment. I wanted to pray and beg God to change me. But deep down, I didn't know if I truly wanted to change. God knew that too. I drove home feeling ashamed.

I sure got what I wanted, I thought. *All I wanted was her—someone who sleeps with a guy the night she meets him, when she actually lives with a guy she plans on marrying. Good luck, guy. Whoever you are.*

Then my thoughts turned to Margie, making my mood darker. I got to thinking, *Margie, good luck with Jake too.*

Part of me didn't even want to walk Cynthia to the door, but I reminded myself the evening really had been fun, with lots of laughs and great sex. I enjoyed her lingering kiss at the door, inwardly hoping it wouldn't be the last kiss but knowing in all likelihood it was.

She kissed me once more, and I could see her smile. "Jake, take good care of my parents. You're a special guy."

With that, she opened Leo's door and was gone.

I was thankful the guys were sound asleep. I knew they would be curious about how the night had gone with Cynthia. I felt like a rat on many levels. I went to bed hoping I'd have a better perspective in the morning.

I got up at about seven o'clock for my eight thirty elective class, anthropology. As I was ready to head out the door, I thought of last night's transgressions there on the rug display.

Then it hit me. *Oh my God.* The store opened at ten, but Dan, a full-time salesman and "office manager," would be there at eight thirty to do some cleaning. No, there were no stains or any other evidence on the rug. But a glance into my garbage can at my desk would reveal more than I wanted to reveal. I grabbed my keys and rushed out the door.

"Shit," I said out loud as I was reminded of my broken side window. The wind tunneled through the car as I raced to the carpet store.

My face flushed in anger and fear as I spotted Dan's Ford Triumph parked by the rear entrance. I slammed my palm on the steering wheel in frustration.

I slowly opened the back door. I could hear the vacuum from the far side of the showroom. Though I had been very quiet, Dan somehow knew I was there. Without turning around, he shut off the vacuum.

"Jake, I saw your note on the Wellington samples. Nice of you to do that so late at night for Leo, even after having dinner with his daughter. Wow." His tone turned ugly now. "And if you're wondering, I emptied your garbage already. I figured you wouldn't mind if I threw the thing out. You can only use it once."

"Dan—" I started.

"Don't say a thing, you horse's ass. I'm just thinking of the old man's comment about you being like a son to him. So I guess this means you fucked your sister. Nice going. And oh, nice hair," he added, referring to the result of my drive in with the broken window.

With that, he shook his head and made it plain he didn't want to talk to me.

8

Time passed. It blew over. For whatever reason, Dan didn't say a word to Leo or anyone about the incident. I was excited when Springer Carpets, a competitor, offered Dan a job. Then to my distress, Leo upped Dan's salary to keep him working at Sommer's. Eventually, I had bigger issues to worry about than Dan. Leo confided in me his plan to cut his hours and delegate some of his day-to-day tasks. In fact, he and Fern would soon be leaving on a ninety-day cruise.

"Good for you, Leo," I said sincerely.

"Well, I'm not getting any younger, and Fern has her health issues," he said.

A few days later, Leo called a rare store meeting to announce the ninety-day cruise. To that, he added, "And Jake will take on owner responsibilities in my absence."

I was as shocked as the other employees—maybe more so. Leo had put me in a bad position by announcing this to everyone without consulting me first. If I didn't accept the challenge, I would look as if I were ungrateful or not man enough for the job.

Thankfully, Leo motioned me to stay after the meeting had ended.

"Jake, I know you've been taking accounting at the U, but even if you weren't, I know you could handle running this place. You're the sharpest guy here—and that includes me. I trust you. So trust me. How about being in charge while Fern and I are gone? I mean it—you'll be in charge of it all. You can make any decision you want. And I'll pay you whatever you think is fair."

I paused. Something told me to accept Leo's offer. Maybe it was because I was flattered by the offer and his faith in me. Maybe it was my greed to make more money. And in some remote part of my brain, maybe I thought helping him out would counter my guilt for having sex with his daughter.

I didn't doubt Leo had good intentions about making me boss, but I wondered how the other employees would feel about it. With the exception of Dan, I liked the others, and I think they liked me.

"Leo, I'll do it as long as I'm truly in charge. And just remember—I'll be done with school in a few months and will be leaving then. This can't be a permanent position. If you're looking for someone to take over, it can't be me."

"I understand that," he replied. "But I'd rather have you now, even if it means training in someone else later."

"All right, Leo," I finally said. "Let's do this. When do you want to get started?"

"What are you doing now?" he asked back.

I grinned. After four years, I knew this game well. "Getting you to sit down and explain your system so you can take Fern on a nice cruise."

So we walked into his private office—more of a cubbyhole.

"Your first priority," he said, "will be to learn our bookkeeping system, which will take you about an hour."

We went over the ledger, which was basic bookkeeping. I was already a bit familiar with it. All of us at one time or another had been at Leo's desk with the ledger sitting there open.

Looking closer now, I noticed the bank balanced out at $46,812, but there was a 1 penciled up to the left of the column.

"Leo, what's this?"

"That's a reminder I actually have $146,812 in the business account," he said sheepishly. "You know, Jake, some of the guys would think I'm rolling in money if they saw the ledger balance of over a hundred grand."

I couldn't help but smile.

"Your next priority," he said, "will be to write yourself a check for whatever bonus you feel is fair for your new role these ninety days. I want to pay that in a lump sum now to save taxes."

I hesitated, then waved my hand. "Let's skip that for now. I can figure that out later."

It didn't make sense to pay myself before I even stepped into the role. I wanted to prove myself.

And prove myself I would. I already had ideas that I put into practice not long after Leo left for the cruise.

A well-known carpet brand, Persian Luxury, had recently offered Leo the opportunity to sell their products at Sommer's Carpet and Tile. But Leo had demurred. He felt this exclusive carpet brand was too expensive for our customers. But as a salesman, I had heard many customers ask if we carried Persian Luxury. I knew we could sell this product for less than other stores and still make good margins.

So I met with Ralph Snyder, the Persian Luxury rep, and asked about us carrying their line. At first, he was hesitant, hemming and hawing, but then he laid it on the line.

"Jake, I know you're in charge while Leo's gone, and I really would like to work with you. But what if Leo comes back and still doesn't want the line? Our setup charge to get all the samples is three thousand dollars."

I looked at him. "I can write a check for three thousand dollars today."

He thought for a moment. Apparently, there was more to lay on the line.

"My big downside," he said, "is that Springer Carpet wants the line too. If I give it to you, and Leo sends it back, I'm out in the cold with Springer. They'll think it was a bust with your customers."

I reflected on that. "Let me say, Mr. Snyder, I believe Springer would still want the brand even if Leo sends it back. Jerrod Springer knows Leo. He'd be wise to the whole situation. But you'd still have our three grand, so you could be a hero with Springer and give him the samples free if you want to.

Ralph stroked his chin a bit. "That's an interesting angle. You know what, Jake? I'm going to do it. Don't make me regret this. Please."

I didn't want him changing his mind, so I insisted on giving him the check right then and there, as I promised. I wanted to get this set up so we could start selling and so Leo could see it was a good move.

We received the samples two weeks later. Ralph came and put together a bang-up sales meeting. He explained that Persian Luxury offered salesmen an incentive of fifty cents per square yard.

The sales team looked at me, waiting for me to nix this plan. Leo never allowed incentives to go directly to the salesmen. He didn't for two reasons. First, he said it encouraged people to sell what was good for them rather than what was good for the customer. Second, and more to the point, he said, "Why should salesmen get extra money for doing their jobs? They have no risk—I do. That's why I keep the incentives."

With everyone waiting on my response, I asked Ralph, "How long will these incentives be available?"

He ruminated. "How long do you want?"

"Let's go sixty days."

The salesmen looked at me with shock. I turned to speak to them now.

"And when you guys sell any Persian Luxury carpet over fifteen dollars per yard, I'll kick in another fifty cents. Then you'll earn a dollar per yard plus your regular commission."

I thought Ralph would wet his pants.

One of the salesmen asked my permission to raise two Persian Luxury carpets we had at thirteen to fifteen dollars per yard so they could get the buck commission.

This likely was the first time in the history of carpet stores when a salesperson suggested *raising* prices as an incentive. Usually, salesmen whined our prices were too high, which was really just their go-to excuse to shift blame from themselves when they failed to sell a customer. But now, the sales team was so excited about the incentives on this brand of carpet, they were clamoring for higher prices.

That's what you call "buy-in."

Over the next sixty days, our only problem with Persian Luxury was that we had only one set of samples, which meant many of the top colors were often out on loan. The salesmen—including myself—were making money like never before, the store was making money like never before, and Persian Luxury was amazed with our success.

Except for fly-in-the-ointment Dan, everyone was excited. With all the money flying around, I brought Gary on as a salesman too. I knew he would fit in with the others, and more important, I knew customers would love him.

I took advantage of the positive environment and asked Ralph to get me $10,000 from Persian Luxury so I could boost our advertising. He blanched. When he reported back, he said his boss could only go to $3,000.

So I asked for his boss's phone number. I knew they were liars—they had money to help promote their brand and Sommer's. All the manufacturers included advertising in their budgets. The key to our getting these funds was to present a case showing how the funds would be leveraged to increase sales of their products.

Ralph's boss tried to take control of the conversation right away. "Mr. Horton, you guys are doing wonderful. But we don't typically have any advertising funds. My three thousand dollar offer is a big deal for us."

"I'll tell you what," I challenged, "you get me the ten thousand, and I'll put a deal in writing: if we don't do at least two hundred and fifty thousand dollars with you this year, we'll refund the ten grand."

We got the $10,000 and ran Persian Luxury commercials every week throughout the Twin Cities. Customers came in and asked to see Persian Luxury. Sometimes they would ask, "Do you personally like Persian Luxury?" I would be thinking, *Let me count the ways.*

Leo called me from time to time. He was thrilled about the Persian Luxury sales. He admitted he hadn't been willing to take the risk himself.

After the second month of selling the new carpet line, I proudly told him, "Leo, our sales are up by almost fifty percent!"

"You must be way behind on installations," he replied.

"No, we're in good shape. I hired two independent crews to help get us caught up."

There was a pause. "Jake, what have I always said about installers? We want our own, so they're loyal to us, remember?"

I thought for a moment. "Well, Leo, I think all four of these guys would work for us full-time if I offered. I just thought this was safer, in case business slowed down."

Leo thought for a moment too. He could be pragmatic, of course. Finally he said, "No. You're there, I'm here, and you're doing great. Just make sure we don't lose customers because of lousy installers. Did you pay yourself that bonus?" he added.

"Not yet, but I will by the end of the month."

Fact is, I wasn't sure what to do about the bonus.

When Leo first mentioned the bonus, I was thinking $2,000—good money for a part-time job. But now when I looked at all the profits I had made for Leo, I felt I deserved more. Much more.

I likely had the bonus on my mind when I received an invoice from Roxbury Carpet Mill and I noticed our check was to be sent to Wells Fargo, a large financial institution with many branches. I myself had a student loan there.

As I wrote and signed the check, I had two thoughts. One was, *I wonder if Roxbury might be in financial trouble, seeing as they're paying interest to Wells Fargo to finance our account.* The other random thought was, *When I graduate soon, I'll have to pay Wells Fargo a lot of money for my loan.*

The coincidence of Wells Fargo financing Roxbury as well as financing me intrigued me. In fact, I couldn't get it off my mind for some reason.

Three weeks passed. Leo and Fern were due home soon. Leo's accountant dropped off our latest financial statement. We had another record month. In the ninety days since Leo had left and I had taken charge, Sommer's had earned over $50,000 more than it did the same period the year before.

I liked to write all the business checks on Fridays because I didn't have morning classes. I could get to the office before the others and write the checks in private. As I drove in, my mind couldn't stop thinking about the money I had generated for Leo. He didn't even need the money.

I tried to push it out of my mind as I wrote checks for all the typical carpet store stuff. But then I sat there with the checkbook in front of me. My mind whirled:

I'm due this money, but Leo is too conservative.

I've been working a lot of hours.

Getting the Persian Luxury brand was almost an annuity for Leo in itself— and he wouldn't have gotten it without me.

I got up from my chair and looked out the window. I could feel my heartbeat throbbing on the right side of my temple. My mouth felt so dry my tongue stuck briefly to the roof of my mouth. My hand shook.

I was back at the desk. I shut the ledger with a bang.

Idiot Dan had arrived. He chose to start his daily vacuuming routine in my office.

"Good morning, Mr. Horton. Any garbage you want me to empty?"

I didn't know if it was a cloaked reference to Cynthia and me. And I didn't care. Leo wasn't around, and one day I would get Dan out of here. The only reason I had to deal with him was because Leo had paid him extra to stay. I grimaced.

I shook my head at Dan, and he moved on. I entered the checks into the ledger.

But I had two more to write.

I don't know what made me take the plunge. Perhaps it was my annoyance with that incompetent asshole Dan. At any rate, I closed my door, opened the checkbook, and wrote a check to Wells Fargo for $20,130.58.

For a ledger entry, this would note, "Carpet purchase, Roxbury Mills." But I mailed the check to the Wells Fargo student loans division. My loan would exist no more—it would be paid in full.

Then I wrote a bonus check for $2,000 to myself.

You might wonder why I did this. I know I wondered. Why would I risk my reputation? Why I would do this if my faith meant anything to me? Was I money hungry? Was it the thrill of the risk? Did I think Leo owed it to me, but I didn't want to ask? Was I a compulsive cheat and thief?

In the days that immediately followed, I couldn't believe I had sunk that low. In the grand scheme of things, that twenty grand would make little difference in my life. Yet I had embezzled it just the same. I hated to use the word, but that's what I had done. I could rationalize it, but I also knew I could go to jail if discovered.

But as the days went by and the business continued to do well, I put it far back into my mind. I decided to see it in a new light. *One day*, I thought, *I'll pay him back.*

That's what all the crooks say.

9

As I approached my college graduation, I knew my life, in many ways, mirrored the good life I had imagined for myself. But whenever I felt happy, an ugly figure popped up in my mind, holding a sign: "Jake, you are a filthy thief."

Shame is like walking around in a good-looking new sweater that has a huge spot on the front. So long as you hide the spot with your arms, people comment how beautiful the sweater looks. You want to put your arms down and relax, but you can't—then everyone would know you don't own a beautiful sweater at all.

I needed something to take my mind off the Wells Fargo deal, Leo, and how bad I felt. My opportunity to play varsity for the Gophers did just that, at least for the time being.

My football career at the U would come to an end in one week. I had played on the special teams the previous game and made a solo tackle. But my mind was soured toward the backfield coach, Harry Little.

I often thought back to my very first day of practice, when all the running backs were put in a line for forty-yard sprints. I never was fast—they knew that. Yet Coach Little commented loudly, "Horton, you run like molasses in January. You think you're a running back? More like a crawling back." I never got a chance to prove myself.

So, here we were with the last game of my career. It was Senior Day, with all the seniors' parents in attendance. While I wasn't proud of my football career, I was proud to have my parents introduced to the crowd and to have Margie, Gary, Trent, and some other friends sitting together to cheer me on.

The Michigan State Spartans had clinched a bowl invitation, while the Minnesota Golden Gophers had clinched an end to another lackluster season.

Our bad luck with injuries continued as the third-string running back came out of the game with a twisted ankle.

With moments left to go in the first half, I heard Murray Warmath, the head coach, say, "Horton? Who the hell is Horton?"

I grabbed my helmet and reported to him. "That would be me, sir."

He pointed at the team huddling up. "Better get in there, son, at blocking back."

Our quarterback, Blaze Hart, was a fellow Ranger, graduating from nearby Mountain Iron High School. Blaze and I got to know each other at a couple of "Ranger Parties." Being from smaller schools, both of us had played both offense and defense in high school. While Blaze starred as a quarterback in high school, he wasn't shabby at middle linebacker either.

At one party, he motioned for his buddies to come over, and he introduced me as the "slipperiest dick" he ever played against. He started calling me "Slippery Jake." I didn't like the name, and I was glad nobody jumped on the bandwagon. I liked Blaze overall, but I didn't like the one eye he had fixed on Margie while the other eye was on me. I knew that look.

In the huddle to start the second half, Blaze surprised everybody, including me, when he called a play where I would be carrying the ball.

"But Coach said I'm just supposed to block . . ."

"Coach doesn't know what you can do, but I do." Blaze pointed his finger at the right tackle, Rory Moore, and told him, "You better get off your ass, or Slippery Jake's going to run over you. Guys, we can win this game!"

I took my first handoff and cut back to Moore's left. The middle linebacker grabbed me by my shoulder pad, I spun, and he came loose. I cut back at another linebacker, lowered my head, and spun as he tried to put his arms around me. I dove forward for a twelve-yard gain.

Hart slapped me on the helmet. The next play was the same plan, the other way.

This time, there was a hole. I lowered my head, hit the hole, and veered back toward the center of the field, surprising the linebacker who held on for the ride. A gain of nine.

In what turned out to be beyond my wildest fantasies, the Gophers beat the Spartans 28–23. Here I was, a senior playing my first and my last game. In just one half, I carried 13 times for 106 yards, scored two touchdowns, and was awarded the game ball—no thanks to the coaching staff, but thanks to Blaze.

Coach Warmath put his arm around my shoulder in the locker room. "Where have you been?"

After the game, my dad ignored the rules and came into the dressing room. He gave me a bear hug. He grabbed my jersey below my neck and pulled me close to him. His words, spoken slowly with deep emotion, will be something I will never forget.

"I always knew this is what would happen if you got the chance," he said. "Jake, I am the proudest man on earth right now."

For the first time, Dad actually verbalized he was proud of me. It was wonderful—but deep down, I realized his pride came from a football game meaning almost nothing. We all celebrated into the night—then Margie added the exclamation point at the end of the unforgettable day.

As we laid there together, I thanked God for the opportunity I had been given that day. Then I thought again about Leo, and I knew I would have to endure another lousy night.

Margie surprised me by saying, "Jake, even people who don't know you were happy for you today. But you don't seem to be happy. What's wrong?"

"Oh, it's nothing. I'm just tired," I replied.

It floored me she had picked up on it. I could tell she didn't believe me either.

Perhaps my tortured thoughts should have served as a premonition. That Monday, Leo called and asked me to meet him for a private discussion at his house. This was business—no food, no Fern, certainly no Cynthia.

"Jacob," he started once we were both settled in the living room, "I wanted you to be the first to know: I'm selling the business. I already have a buyer. I need your help in getting this done. The buyer has hired an auditor, who will go through our accounts to make sure our statements are one hundred percent correct. I need you to cooperate in every way, Jacob. I want to get this done."

Leo could see my face had drained of color. He likely thought it was sadness or disappointment, but it was fear. Real fear.

Any auditor would match the numbers on the simple ledger. I would be found out. The only question was, would Leo be forgiving and let me pay it back, or would I go to jail? Here I was, almost finished with my four-year degree and already on the verge of personal disaster. I tried not to think of how I would be a pariah to my family, my friends, my girlfriend. I could never show my face in Mesabi again. My father would likely disown me. My theft was the opposite of everything he stood for.

I looked at Leo and felt myself perspire. "Leo, I'll cooperate in every way. But I don't know what to say right now. Can this wait until next week?"

Leo crossed his arms in front of himself and looked at me in a bewildered way. "I don't know why the delay, Jake, but please get the process started no later than Wednesday. And please keep all this confidential. I'll tell the others when the time is right."

With that, Leo, hugged me.

"Jacob, I am so proud of you."

Heat radiated from my face and neck, as if Leo had put my head in an oven. His words almost matched the exact words my dad had uttered after the game.

Leo yelled up the steps, "Fern, do you want to say good-bye to Jacob?"

My dad's praise was for nothing more than a good performance for thirty minutes on a football field. Leo, on the other hand, was proud that I was learning to be a respectable businessman, and he could feel he had done his part. Different men. Would either ever speak to me again if my theft were discovered?

I put my hand on Leo's shoulder. "Tell Fern I had to go, but tell her I said good-bye."

I needed to get out of his house. I needed some alone time. How could I turn this around so the accounts weren't audited?

The answer came to me early in the morning of a sleepless night. I called Leo and asked him if I could come by the house later that day.

"Sure, but why?" he asked.

"Leo, we need a face-to-face conversation."

Fern let me in with a smile. "Leo," she called, "Jake is here to see you." After we moved to the living room, she disappeared.

I had practiced my conversation and was anxious to get it out. "Leo, don't sell your business to an outsider. Sell it to me."

Leo was plainly surprised by the request. "Jacob, where would you come up with that kind of money?"

"Well," I countered, "I need the chance to get the financing, but if the selling price is within the realm of your balance sheet, I believe I can get it done. I think I have a pretty good track record here."

I could see he was frustrated because this foiled or at least delayed his plan. But I could also see he was pleased.

"Okay, Jacob. I'll give you two weeks to put a proposal together. But if you can't come up with the financing, I expect you to get the audit done with my buyer."

I gulped. I had two weeks. I was still alive. Or to put it another way, the bogus Wells Fargo check remained quietly in a grave for now. Resurrection could very well mean prison time.

10

THE ONLY WAY TO MAKE THIS HAPPEN was to get a business loan. I knew only one person who specialized in business loans in the banking profession, Carol Lupich. Carol was VP of commercial lending at First National Bank in Virginia. I knew her from interactions at our church in Mesabi.

She listened to my proposal, but the bottom line was she couldn't do anything until I had an appraisal of Leo's building included in the deal. She said any bank would require an appraisal, which would be costly and might take weeks.

She suggested I call the Small Business Administration as another financing option. I found out, though, the first step was to fill out a sixteen-page application they would mail to me within five to ten days. I scratched the SBA from consideration.

I was barely into this process, and already I had hit two brick walls. With bank financing now out of the question, my options were getting fewer and farther between. Then two possible resources came to mind: Leo himself and Jerrod Springer, the owner of Springer Carpets.

Leo would be my final desperation choice. Getting a "loan" from Leo would mean, essentially, having him just hand the business to me for free. Sure, we'd make a plan for me to pay him over time as contract for deed. But what Leo wanted was a check outright—and he had another buyer ready to give him that.

Even though it was my own skin I was worrying about, I knew in my heart of hearts, there could be no good reason why Leo would or should do this for me if I couldn't come up with the financing on my own. I would be asking him to give up his dreams to some extent to fulfill mine. Though I had not met Leo's son-in-law, I guessed he would advise Leo to tell me to take a hike. Or he might even tell me directly.

I needed to get in front of Mr. Springer. I had always wanted to meet the guy, anyway. I wondered if he had any clue how much business I had been taking from him.

So I called him on Wednesday, told him who I was, then said, "Mr. Springer, I would like to discuss a business proposal with you."

Springer paused. "I hope you want to buy me out of this miserable business. How soon can you get here?"

When I arrived at the store later that afternoon, my first impression was that Springer's felt more upscale than Sommer's as far as layout, lighting, and display.

I gave my name to the receptionist.

"Jerrod will be back any minute," she said. "He's running late. Please have a seat."

Twenty minutes past our appointment time of three o'clock, I had to fight the urge to give up on the meeting altogether. The receptionist must have read my mind or was just used to similar situations. She gave me a friendly smile.

"Jerrod runs late all the time. He's a nice guy. It's just that he has a lot of stuff going on. If I could ask, what are you wanting to see him for—the sales job?"

I would have liked to have said, "I'm here because I need about a million dollars from him so I don't have to hide in South America for the rest of my life." But rather, I responded, "I just want to run an idea past him."

She was about to ask more questions, but then she changed her tone and announced, "Here he comes now!"

Jerrod was younger than I pictured. As he approached, I guessed he was in his early forties—balding some, but he was fit and tanned, wearing khakis and an untucked orange shirt.

He offered his hand, "So, you're Leo's genius and a man very hard to bring down. Nice to meet a smart young man in the carpet business."

We were a half hour late from our appointment time, but I felt better when he asked his secretary to not disturb us. Then he added to her, "And if that builder calls again about his pissing contest with the installer, tell him there's nothing more I can do."

While I wouldn't describe his office as plush or even classy, it was neat and the furniture had a Scandinavian look to it with simple lines. The swivel chair behind the desk likely cost more than every piece of furniture at Sommer's added together.

Jerrod closed the door and caught me eyeing the chair. "Ever sit in a Stressless leather chair, Jake?" He sat down in his prized chair and moaned as if to imitate an orgasm.

"No, I don't believe I've ever sat in one, sir," I said.

He grinned. "Then don't ever sit in one. If you do, you'll have to own one. I paid over two thousand dollars for this at Schneiderman's Furniture. You married?"

"No, Mr. Springer, I'm not," I politely responded.

"Well, when you get married and want some decent furniture, go to Schneiderman's," he said almost too seriously.

I was getting impatient to discuss my proposal with him. But just as I began to speak, he asked, "So are you engaged to anyone?"

Now I was annoyed, but I looked at him and replied, "No, I'm not engaged either."

He studied me. "Well, I guess you're not here for counseling, then?" He leaned toward me. "So, Mr. Horton, what can I do for you today?"

The conversation thus far had left me somewhat unbalanced. I had prepared a whole pitch, but I decided to alter my approach on the spot. Springer liked me to do all the talking while he sat back and took pot shots at my points. I wanted to convey I wasn't desperate, but I could feel myself reaching to make the deal sound better or him.

"Mr. Springer, I have a very rough proposal I would like you to consider. First, though, I need you to guarantee that what I will share with you will be confidential."

He became serious. "Look, call me Jerrod, and I'll call you Jake. Now, Jake, I can give you my word I won't repeat whatever you tell me. But experience has taught me the cat is halfway out of the bag somewhere else."

I met his eyes. "Jerrod, this is the only bag, and so you and I can keep the cat in there."

He grinned again. "Okay, you have my word. Let's hear what you have to say and find out if anyone would be interested in the cat in the first place."

I hesitated for effect, then drew a breath and began. "Leo Sommer is retiring and—"

"Really?" he interrupted me. "I didn't know that. What's he going to do with himself without that store?"

I decided to just ignore the question. I needed to get this guy's attention. "Leo wants to sell the store . . . and I want to buy it."

Springer leaned forward. "So Leo wants to sell the business as a going concern, and he's selling the property along with it?"

I nodded.

He paused. "But Leo won't sell you contract for deed, and you don't have the money to get a loan, right?"

I weighed how I should respond to this. I said simply, "I haven't approached Leo with alternatives because at this point, he would like a cash deal."

Now, at last, I had Springer's full intention. He got up from his Stressless chair, stretched, sat down again, rocked backward, then asked, "So you have a going concern plus a piece of property and an old building to sell. What else?"

I thought for a moment. "Included in the price is about sixty-five thousand dollars worth of inventory at cost; twenty thousand dollar book value on equipment; and, of course, goodwill from the long history of the company. And some important relationships with key vendors."

He almost smirked at me, knowing I added that last piece as a reference to Persian Luxury.

"You did read their contract, yes? So I assume you know the part where Persian Luxury must agree to any transfer of ownership?"

Frankly, I hadn't, but I still responded, "They're very pleased with what's going on right now. We're selling that product on all cylinders."

Jerrod ignored this comment. He leaned back. "So what are you proposing?"

I had thought out this part of the pitch to some extent. "Well, you're right—I don't have the money or the credit to make this happen. Certainly not alone. What I propose is for you to cosign a loan with me and we become partners, with you getting seventy-five percent of the net profit and me twenty-five percent each year. You get me working full-time for you for fifty thousand dollars per year."

I paused, waiting for him to ask *the* question. I didn't wait long.

"Interesting. What did Leo net last year—and I'm warning you, no bullshit."

I let him wait a few seconds. "I will give you only last year's net, and it was almost two hundred thousand dollars."

Jerrod shook his head. "That's impossible. What's he selling over there, heroin?"

I met his eyes. "He has me . . . and I was just part-time."

No doubt, Jerrod Springer loved dealing. I could almost hear the gears turning in his brain.

"Jake, I won't say no, but I can't say yes either. I need to do some snooping. How about stopping by at five on Friday?"

I felt cocky and almost ribbed him about the likelihood of his actually being on time. Instead, I simply said, "Five on Friday. I look forward to it."

As I headed outside to my car, I felt as though Springer was watching me. I made a point to walk confidently with big strides. By the time I was in the car, I felt as though I were suffocating. I took off with the window open. I felt a little better as the wind blew through the car. I had just gotten the window fixed, yet here I had it all the way down anyway. Maybe I wasted my money.

My mind zeroed back to Springer. I had my whole life at stake here; Springer only had money at stake. Then again, whose fault was that? I knew the answer all too well. Unless this made money sense for Springer, he had no reason to consider it.

I also knew the danger of bringing this information about Leo's retirement to Springer—nothing could stop him from going directly to Leo to purchase the business outright. That remained a possibility, though it depended on whether he saw me as an important component of the deal. If he asked what I'd bring to the table to deserve my 25 percent cut of the net profit, I would explain that I not only brought in money as a salesman but that I also could run the business. As I saw it, $25,000 per year plus $50,000 in salary was darn cheap.

Of course, if I were a key component of the deal, Springer would no doubt want to nail me down with a contract to protect his investment. But those types of agreements can be sticky. If somebody wants to leave, it's better if they go.

Another thought came to mind: if Springer were interested, he would need to see the financials. How would Leo feel about that—especially if Springer decided to back out of the deal? Then Sommer's main competitor would have inside information. There was much out of my control.

The more I thought this through, the less sure I became. In just one meeting with him, I could sense he no longer enjoyed the business, if indeed he ever did. So why would he want two stores if he had a tough time with one?

According to the rumor mill, Springer had made some big money the past year by partnering with an old college buddy. Initially, the two of them developed and sold acreage in Argentina. In fact, the *Star Tribune* featured him in an article reporting how local entrepreneurs were investing in South American businesses to avoid the high Minnesota tax rate. Springer gained some notoriety with his carpet cronies from the story.

And not that long ago, he purchased two dilapidated brick buildings on Hennepin Avenue. Either he got lucky or he somehow knew the city would target that area for renovation. He sold the buildings for a handsome profit as they became part of the new and hip Hennepin Commons. Yet he was still working, which likely meant he wasn't financially independent, despite these deals.

I had a nagging feeling I was making a mistake negotiating on my own with this guy. But it was too late to figure out a different strategy.

———

Friday came around all too quickly. I drove up to Springer's Carpet and Tile just before five. It surprised me a little to see Springer's car in the lot. I headed inside.

Jerrod's secretary gave me a suspicious smile. "Mr. Springer is expecting you."

As I entered his office, Jerrod looked up, rocking in his prize chair behind the desk. I figured he would want me to talk first, so I jumped right in.

"So, Jerrod, what are you thinking?"

He shrugged. "I don't like deals where I'm not dealing with the decision-maker—and I have the feeling this is what I'm doing here. I'll be honest: I think we could have a great partnership, but will Leo want to make it happen?" He shrugged again. "So I had an attorney buddy of mine draw up a couple of documents. One is just a recap of what the offer will be. The other is a confidentiality statement I've signed so you can get the information I've requested here about Sommer's Carpet and Tile."

I did a quick read of the preliminary documents. They seemed reasonable.

"Any other questions, Jerrod?" I asked.

He rose out of his chair and stuck his hand out for me to shake. "Jake, get to Leo as soon as you can, then call me no matter what does or doesn't happen, understand?"

"No problem," I answered, feeling far less confident than I sounded. "I better get going," I added. "I have tickets to Herman's Hermits tonight. My girlfriend begged me to get them."

Jerrod half rolled his eyes. "Jake, get that agreement from Leo—the sooner the better. Let your girlfriend take one of her girlfriends to go see that gay band."

"It's a little late for that. I need to pick her up in forty-five minutes to make the concert on time. Can't disappoint my Margie."

Honestly, it wasn't the Hermits or even Margie making me want to get out of there. I didn't know whether Jerrod was seriously interested in the deal or not. One thing I did know, he made me feel way over my head. I knew every time I opened my mouth, I was in danger of saying something that made me seem like a ten-year-old.

I found myself almost gasping for air. I needed to get the hell out of his office and regroup.

11

I HEADED FOR FRIDLEY, WHERE MARGIE NOW LIVED with her aunt. If I made it by six, we could be at Metropolitan Stadium before seven.

Margie had just gotten off work as office assistant at Century Tile Distributors, a position I had helped her land. She appreciated that I had found her a decent job. But when I first brought her over to Century and introduced her to the owner, I almost changed my mind about her working there. The place was essentially a warehouse and a man's world. Margie's looks drew stares often. She was like eye-manna from heaven to guys who stared at concrete and cardboard all day long. I should have told them to pay her a buck more per hour just for that. Call it hazard pay.

As I drove, my mind wandered to Leo and Jerrod. I had left two messages for Leo without a return call. I shook my head and tried to set my problems aside, at least for tonight.

But that only left me wrestling with thoughts about Margie. I didn't know where our relationship would ultimately go.

Sometimes I thought of her in the longer term, maybe even as my wife. We attended worship together from time to time. We went on double dates, and while Margie felt nervous, my friends liked her.

In other ways, though, our relationship came to represent my shallowness. I said I "loved" her, and in a way, I think I did. But "infatuation" may have been closer to the truth. I realized much of my newfound confidence came from being with this sexy creature four years my junior. I loved the sex with her, though lately it seemed something was missing. We seemed to have less and less in common.

Margie was excited to go to the concert, and I wanted it to be a special evening for her. I hoped to score extra points for taking her to see a group she knew wasn't my favorite. I had also made dinner reservations at Fox340, near Met Stadium.

Traffic cooperated to and from Fridley. Just before starting time, we found our seats on the second level near the stage—great tickets. While I wanted Margie to just enjoy herself tonight, the vibes I was feeling told me otherwise. She looked happy but oddly preoccupied.

In between sets, we took a break from the uncomfortable seats to go get some refreshments from the food vendors. I planned on asking her if she felt okay and if she thought the Hermits were as good as she expected.

But before I could say a word, she unceremoniously said, "I need to pee," then headed for the ladies' room.

As we settled back into our seats, she took my hand and smiled. "Thanks, Jake, for being so nice and getting these tickets. I'm sorry I'm not the best company tonight."

I put my arm around her shoulders and hugged her. "Is it something I did?"

She looked at me and said, "No." Then she didn't say another word.

When the Hermits played their finale, "Mrs. Brown You've Got a Lovely Daughter," the crowd gave them a standing ovation. The band waved and disappeared for a minute, then came back to the wilder applause of the audience. The lead singer delivered his "You're the best audience ever" speech, then silence filled the stadium as the band set up for their encore.

"Jake, I'm pregnant," Margie said in a monotone voice and without even looking at me. It was like somebody saying, "I'm getting a loaf of bread" or "Gee, it's a little cold" or "I have to pee."

"What did you say?" Maybe I had misheard her.

She looked at me this time with tears in those beautiful brown eyes. "I said, I'm pregnant. I'm so stupid."

I didn't need to hear that last comment, which by now she knew I just despised.

My mind whirled: *Who is the stupid one here? Will she have the baby? What if she wants an abortion? What will her parents think? My pastor? Do I want to get married? Do I want to get married to her?*

I took her hand so we could leave. Maybe this was just a bad dream. We walked in silence to the car. I held the door open. She looked at me sadly.

I gathered all the goodness in me I didn't feel. "Margie, we'll get through this."

"It's not your kid, Jake," she responded in a flat tone, looking down. "It's Frank's."

Rage.

It was a feeling I hope to never feel again. A burning sensation spread from my abdomen to my chest. I breathed heavily.

Margie had fear in her eyes.

I just knew there was no way I could be in that car with her. I didn't trust myself. Some men would have yelled, "Find your own ride home, you goddamned whore!" Me, I handed her the car keys and just walked off. I would find my way back to the apartment. She could take my car and go to her aunt's or Frank's or wherever.

As I walked briskly between the cars in the mammoth lot, I couldn't decide which part of my brain to call into action. I just wanted to drink into oblivion. I didn't want to think about Margie or this whole pregnancy mess. I didn't want to think about the fraud I'd committed, how I'd shafted a man who had treated me so well, and how I had to rush to purchase his business to cover the fraud.

At long last, I was out of the lot. I flagged a cab, gave him a twenty, and told him, "Bring me to the closest bar." It turned out to be at the Metropole Hotel.

The bartender was a rather rough-looking dude, medium height and build with a pock-marked face. His name was Ryan. I asked him for a vodka martini. I drained it. I put some money on the bar and ordered a second. I slowed down to enjoy that warm feeling. I felt some relief just being alone. I ordered a third.

Ryan leaned over. "You're Jake Horton, right?"

This surprised me. "I don't think I know you, or do I?"

"You don't know me, but your third and final martini is on me. How you played against Michigan State was incredible. I don't want you to ruin your life by getting a ticket for drunk driving."

I could feel the vodka doing its work. I looked across the bar and met the gaze of a woman I can only describe as an updated Marilyn Monroe. She looked to be in her early thirties, and she had two guys twice her age putting their moves on her.

Ryan had noticed my glass was empty, so he filled it with sparkling water.

"Do you know who that gorgeous blond is?" I asked him.

"She hangs around here sometimes. I guess her name is Crystal—at least for tonight," Ryan responded with a knowing look.

I forced myself to look at Ryan instead of Marilyn. "I need to talk to her," I mumbled.

"Look, Jake, those two guys are bidding for her services. I think they're up to two hundred dollars for an hour."

"Give me a piece of paper," I said. "And a pen."

I caught her attention, sustaining a nasty look from the older of the two guys. I wrote "$300 NOW" and asked Ryan to deliver it.

She smiled at the note, put it inside her low-cut black cocktail dress, then dismissed the two guys.

I knew I was staring like a zombie as she sauntered over and sat down next to me.

"I'm Jake. You're Marilyn. Let's go somewhere."

She looked at me suspiciously. "Jake, you sure as hell better have three hundred dollars for me. I could have gotten at least that from those guys."

"I do and I don't," I slurred.

She wasn't liking this. "What do you mean? Either you have the god-damned three hundred dollars or you don't."

"I do have it, but it's at my apartment. We'll have to take a cab there, then I'll give it to you."

She thought for a moment, then looked over at Ryan. "Do you think I can trust this guy for three hundred dollars? He says he has it at his apartment."

Ryan leaned close to my face. He took my hand and began what looked like a normal hand shake, but then it felt as though my bones were turning into powder as he unleashed his bone-crushing grip. I nearly shrieked in pain.

"Jake, do you have three hundred dollars for the lady or don't you? If you don't, then tell me right now."

In a way, I was back in first grade. Others around the bar were trying hard to look the other way.

"Damn it, let go. Yes, I have the money."

"You damn well better. Now that I know you're taking a cab, why don't you and Crystal sit in that nice booth, and I'll buy you both a drink while we wait for my friend Luis and his cab."

We moved to the booth, her on one side and me on the other. After the drinks arrived, she took my hand.

"Jake, I sure hope your hand is okay, but I couldn't take the risk."

She looked spectacular in that short black dress. She started kissing my hand, one finger at a time.

"Can I sit next to you while we wait?"

I moved over so she could join me. My little head had taken the reins.

Luis came in and got us. It was about a half-hour drive, thirty-four dollars. I gave him forty dollars.

He ignored me and looked over at Crystal.

"Do you want me to stay and wait?"

"Thanks," she responded. "I'll call you when I'm ready to be picked up."

I alternated between dropping the keys and struggling to line the key up with the lock. I giggled.

"Can I help you with that?" Crystal offered.

"Hold that helpful thought," I answered.

I giggled again. I was thinking about the Freudian connection between inserting the key and inserting my manhood. Finally, I matched the key to the hole and opened the door.

Gary and Trent weren't home yet, thankfully. Once in the apartment, I started kissing her and started to pull down the zipper on the back of the dress. She gently separated us, though made no move to pull the zipper back up.

"Jake, I've always found it best to take care of business first, then we can relax and have fun."

I honestly didn't know what she meant, then it hit me. "Oh, the money. The money. Don't go anywhere."

Crystal sounded a little out of character when she responded, "You can count on that."

I left the room and found the book *The Fundamentals of Accounting*, where I kept my stash.

"Thank you, Persian Luxury," I said quietly.

I brought three hundred dollars out. She took it from me and put it in her purse.

"Okay, Jake, I'm here to please you. Let's take it a little slower so you get your money's worth."

I took her hand, brought her up to my room, and shut the door.

I now did what I wanted to do right from the first time I saw her, I unzipped the zipper slowly. As the pretty black dress dropped to the floor, I discovered to my delight that all she had on was her makeup.

She was loud and wild and gave herself fully.

"That was nice," Crystal said softly. "Now I need to call Luis, please."

"Now wait—that's not right," I replied. "You said it was three hundred dollars for an hour. It's only been forty minutes."

So she stuck to her end of the bargain, and I stuck to mine. When the hour was done, she slipped her dress back on, and we went down to the kitchen. I noticed an extra set of Gary's car keys on the table.

"Can I drive you back to the bar or wherever you need to go?" I asked, despite my drunken state.

She looked at me. "Jake, that's nice, but I want you to know this is business. Nothing more."

I liked her. But she went home via Luis.

———

The morning sun caused me to squint tightly. My head felt as if it had doubled in size without the skin around it changing. What a god-awful headache. I felt like crap.

My phone rang, and I fumbled picking it up.

"Hello? Is this Jake?" the voice finally asked. "This is Jerrod. What's going on?"

"A lot," I said truthfully.

"Don't be screwing with me, Jake. Have you gotten hold of Leo?"

My head was killing me. "What are you doing right now?" I asked.

"I'm getting ready to come over there and break your goddamned neck," he threatened with a raised voice.

Springer annoyed me. "Well, how could I call Leo then?" I asked.

Jerrod paused. "Stop fucking with me, Jake. I'm serious." He hung up.

I stood there in a daze for a moment, then noticed a note from Gary: "Leo called and says important. Call him Saturday at home."

As much as I wanted to call Leo immediately, I needed a shower and coffee first. I plugged in the pot and filled the filter.

The shower was good, and the coffee even better. Just as I started to feel human again, the phone rang. I took a deep breath. It had to be Leo.

Actually, it was Margie. "I just wanted to make sure you're okay," she said.

My mouth went dry. I could barely speak. "I can't talk to you now," I mumbled, then hung up.

I no longer felt like calling Leo. I thought about getting in my car and just driving up north to see my mom and dad, my brother and sister. Turn back the clock. Run away from these overwhelming problems I could thank myself for.

I'm so dumb, and you're so smart. Those words came to my consciousness seemingly out of nowhere yet everywhere.

"Yep, I'm really smart," I said out loud. "Jake, you're a joke."

I picked up the phone and called Leo.

Fern answered. "Sommer home—this is Fern."

"Hello, Fern. You sound particularly happy this sunny day."

"Oh, hi, Jake. I guess I am! Both of my daughters and my son-in-law are flying in today to spend some time with us."

I hated myself a little more. "Can I speak to Leo for a few moments?"

"Yes. He's been hoping you'd call before our family got here."

Leo came on the phone. After exchanging pleasantries, I asked, "Leo, could you meet me at that diner down the block from you? I have some important things to discuss."

Leo hesitated. "Is it about you buying the business, Jake?"

"Yes."

I could feel his discomfort, but I waited for him to speak. I had a feeling we wouldn't need to meet at the diner after all.

"My son-in-law is sharp about this stuff. He thinks I shouldn't sell the building but instead rent it out. For tax reasons. The girls agree."

It was simply second nature for Leo to use a tone of voice that felt warm and encouraging. I wasn't hearing it now.

I felt as if I were sinking. "Well, Leo, let me know what you decide to do."

Leo went on. "Wouldn't it be easier for you to buy the business without the building?"

I could see where he was going with this. Without the building as an asset, the selling price would be less, possibly making it easier for me to get the loan.

"Well, as you speculated, I don't think I can get a loan. But I did find a potential partner who is considering cosigning. But he wants the building."

Leo weighed his words. "Jake, let me see how this shakes out, and we'll discuss it. You know how I feel about you, but this is our retirement."

I sucked it up. "Leo, no argument from me. Please call me as soon as you know where we're at. Enjoy the weekend. Say hi to Cynthia."

What an insane thing to say.

"Oh, I meant to mention to you—she's engaged now. She just announced it, and we're so happy."

"That's great news." I choked on the words.

As we exchanged good-byes, my head felt ready to explode.

12

BARELY HAD TIME TO TAKE A SIP OF MY COFFEE before I was interrupted once again by the phone. I figured it was Jerrod calling back. My earlier view of him as a laid-back, fun guy had been exchanged with a more realistic picture of a single-minded, egotistical, and demanding jerk. I didn't want to think about what life would be as Jerrod's "junior partner."

I told myself not to pick up the phone, but I grabbed it anyway.

"Hello, this is Jake."

"Glad I caught you, Jacob. This is Dan, your favorite salesman at Sommer's. Say, I'm having a problem with a customer who's unhappy with our installers. They can see a seam in their living room."

I stiffened. "Dan, nobody guaranteed that they won't see a seam. Did you tell them that? A plush carpet often does show seams. We talked about that."

Dan persisted. "Well, Jacob, they won't take my word for it. You're the boss, so here's the phone number. It's seven four one—"

I didn't need this. I cut him off. "Wait a minute, Dan. Who installed this for us?"

Dan paused. "Team Two—Dick and that new guy."

"Okay," I said, "then get Dick to go back and inspect it. But be sure to tell your customer that even when the seam is tightly together, sometimes they show. Do you understand?"

Dan's mission in life seemed to be to piss me off. "A-OK, boss. I will do that. Does this mean you won't be inspecting it?"

"Yes, Dan. It means exactly that. I have to go."

I hung up. How could I get rid of that pain in the ass?

Then the damn phone rang again. I pledged to myself, *If this is Jerrod, I'm just hanging up.*

"Hello, this is Jake."

I was only slightly happier it was my mom.

"Hi, son. How are you doing this morning? I hope you're okay."

I knew she had already heard about the sudden breakup with Margie, likely from DeeDee. She launched into full mother mode.

"Jake, I really liked Margie. I'm sad for both of you. She's so young and probably confused."

I didn't know what to say.

She went on, "Do you still love her?"

The whole dialogue made me ill. I couldn't believe I had become this pathetic object of pity. It's one thing to change your mind about a relationship or even be the guy jilted when the girl changes her mind. But in my case, Margie had pretty much ripped my testicles from my crotch—without my even knowing it.

Those damned words, "You're so smart, and I'm so dumb," kept messing up my mind. How many times did she spoon out that crap, only to feed another sentence in her head when she was screwing Nazar behind my back: "But maybe you're not as smart as you think you are . . ."

Mom mistook my silence for grief. "Jake, do you still love her?" she repeated.

I felt bereft of any emotion except anger.

"Mom, you did hear she's pregnant, right? And you did hear this child will not be a Horton, right—that it will be a Nazar? Mom, what do you think I should do? Do you want me to marry somebody who lied to me every single day?" Anticipating her next question, I continued right on. "And what if it is my baby? Should I marry somebody who wants the baby to be a Nazar?"

Mom hesitated. "Jake, who said anything about marriage? I know it's a terrible situation. I'm horrified and shocked Margie would do this to you. I don't blame you for being angry, beyond angry. Yet don't you think you should ask her to tell you her version of the story?"

"No, Mom," I said, infuriated. "I know enough. Margie was screwing Frank while going with me. That's enough."

"Well," Mom said slowly, "maybe someday you'll want to know why."

"Maybe and maybe not," was the best I could respond.

Eva Horton had made the point she wanted to make. It annoyed me. She acted as though I should say, "Margie, honey, I understand why you can't get enough of that stud Nazar. I'll marry you, and he can live with us so you guys can screw anytime you feel like it."

I was ready to just end the conversation when her voice turned cheery and she abruptly announced, "We got an invitation from your sister to attend her wedding in Boulder."

It took me a few moments to take it all in. I hadn't talked to Anna in years. No one had. I couldn't believe Mom was even speaking of her, let alone saying she was getting married. This really came out of left field. As far as I knew, Anna hadn't talked with *anyone* in the family for years.

"Really? Did you even know she had a boyfriend? How long have they been together?"

For a moment, the phone was quiet. I could feel Mom taking a deep breath.

"Anna moving to Denver was a sad and an incredibly difficult thing—the fallout between her and your father . . . We just lost touch with each other." She took another deep breath. "But Jake, just so you know this, and before you hear it from somebody else, her spouse will be another woman."

I usually think before my emotions take over, but I couldn't this time. "What the hell! Did you know she was *gay*?"

My mother considered her response. "Does it matter if I knew or if I didn't? She is my daughter. She is your sister. The wedding will be on Memorial Day. I hope you'll be there."

This was unbelievable. "Mom, they can't get *married*. How could you even think that? Marriage takes a man and a woman. You know what the Bible says about homosexuality."

Her voice raised. "It also says, judge not. Doesn't it also tell us to love one another? Yes, we all know it isn't an official marriage, but Anna and Judy love each other, and they want their friends and families to know they plan on staying together. It's symbolic but still important."

Usually, I felt good after I talked with Mom. Not this time. The conversation had started with Jake the victim. Now, it had moved to Jake the bigot. I wasn't sure which of the two I despised more.

I said slowly, "Mom, I'm having a bad day. I'm just shocked by this whole conversation. I certainly hope it works out for Anna."

"We're going to the wedding," Mom added. "Actually, we're going out there soon for a visit. Please think about this and come with us."

———

"Is Dad going?" I asked, though I knew the answer.

"I'm sorry to say there are still issues between the two of them. Maybe there always will be. So, no, he is not going. He will not even think about it. I am so sad about that. But she's my daughter, and I love her. I won't continue to be a stranger to her, even if that's his choice." She sighed. "Jake, it would mean more than I can say if you came too on this trip. Not just for Anna, but for you. At the very least, you should call her today."

My head throbbed, and my mouth was parched. "Let me think about it, Mom. When are you thinking about going out there to meet Judy?"

She perked up. "DeeDee and I plan to leave on Tuesday. And Jake, I'm not just going to meet Judy. I'm really excited to get to know Anna again. She told me her love for me had never changed. I told her I felt the same way. I just want to make up for lost time."

But you can't, I thought to myself. As my grandmother often said, "You can't unscramble eggs." Indeed.

I didn't say that out loud, though. My people-pleasing side was telling me to support my mom, especially if Dad was clearly being a real jerk.

"Mom, she's lucky to have you for a mother. I am too," I added, softening.

"Just give your sister a call," she repeated. "She's expecting it today."

"I gotta go now. Love you."

As I hung up, I realized life had become very complicated. I tried to focus.

I needed to tell Jerrod the bad news about the building not being included in the deal. Would he still be interested?

Margie kept creeping into my mind.

Now this about Anna. For the moment, Margie and Jerrod were off my mind.

I had never asked what happened between Dad and Anna, and now I wondered if it had something to do with her homosexuality. In a convoluted way, I could see how Dad had unwittingly forced her to leave Mesabi. It was the right decision. In Mesabi, she would have forever been known as a lesbian first, no matter what she may have accomplished. And in that redneck culture often apparent on the Iron Range and elsewhere, people would have seen her as an embarrassment to our family.

But if the fallout was between Anna and Dad, why didn't Anna call Mom a long time ago? Did she think Dad wouldn't allow it? And why didn't Mom reach out to Anna? Dad may have been in charge, but when Mom wanted to do something, she did it. We all knew that, even and especially Dad.

None of it made sense to me. Part of me wanted to just let sleeping dogs lie, but part of me wanted to know more—when the time was right.

————

For some reason, I postponed calling Anna. I tried rehearsing the conversation in my mind, but too many skeletons were rattling in the closet.

But then Anna called me.

We talked about Mom. We talked about DeeDee and Mike and how much they've changed. It was awkward at first, but overall, I was surprised at how natural it felt after three years.

When the conversation paused, Anna said quietly, "Jake, I don't expect you to accept my relationship with Judy, but I think you'll like her. Everybody does. I hope you'll come out here and meet her."

I felt embarrassed for my first reaction about her and Judy. I hoped Mom hadn't told her what I'd said.

"Anna," I tentatively started, "it's not for me to judge. It really isn't. I'm just happy you've gotten back in touch with the family. Your family. Our family."

"Jake, do you remember that old photo of us in front of the house after it had just been painted?" Anna asked.

"Yeah. I do."

I remembered not just the photo but the day it was taken. Dad had hunted down a neighbor to take the picture so we all could be in it.

Mom's arm was around my shoulder, and we smiled at each other. Dad held DeeDee in one arm, biceps looking impressive, as DeeDee stared admiringly up at him. Mike is tugging at Dad's pants leg in his grasp. I kind of remember Dad yelling at Mike right after the picture was taken. Anna, off to the side, was the only one not smiling. The only one not touching anybody. Or being touched.

"I framed that photo and look at it every day," she said. "It's honest."

It was honest. No doubt whatsoever, the photo proved I was Mom's favorite and DeeDee was Dad's. That much was fact. And Mike was fighting for attention. That was fact.

I suddenly wondered why Anna hadn't picked up Mikey—Dad could have used the help. But the minute that thought came to mind, I realized it made me sound like Dad. And that wasn't a compliment.

As for Anna, I guess the photo proved she was different—even before the blowout with Dad. Was it because she was hiding a secret? Or was it for a hundred other reasons that would make any teenage girl feel out of sorts at a moment in time? Frankly, that's all the photo was—just one fucking moment in time. In one day, how many of these moments are there?

Anna spoke in nearly a whisper as if to say something she didn't want repeated. "Judy said our family is so photogenic. But let's face it—I don't have the looks the rest of you do."

Anna had inherited Dad's features, while DeeDee had inherited Mom's feminine looks. Mom's nose was perky and turned up a little; Anna's nose was wider. Mom's and DeeDee's hair was longer; Anna's was very short and didn't compliment her facial features. In that photo, especially, Anna's complexion was ruddy. But that could have been typical for a teenager.

Still, I would never say Anna was *unattractive*. She was attractive to Judy, I realized, and that's all that mattered.

Talking to Anna also made me realize that though we all felt the loss of not having her in our lives, the past six years had been good for her.

Right after moving to Denver, she roomed with a high school friend and found work as a waitress at an upscale restaurant. In the evenings, she attended junior college and developed an interest in modern art. She possessed some talent drawing illustrations and won some contests, including the grand prize for one year's tuition at the Greater Denver School of the Arts.

For a brief period, she thought she would try to make a living as a painter and wood sculptor. But ultimately, she realized her talents were just not that unique. When she was offered a job at a local museum, she knew she should take it.

A year later, her manager retired, and she took over the position. She organized presentations for artists from around the world. She earned the respect of the museum board with her enthusiasm, her attention to details, and her impressive work ethic. She may have been different, but she was still a Horton.

Anna explained that when she arrived in Denver, she was "shy." I understood that she meant she was shy about being attracted to other women. When she met Judy Morris, however, it was not sexuality but rather a mutual love of art that made them friends.

Judy, almost ten years older and well-connected in the Colorado art scene, became Anna's mentor. Several weeks passed before Anna realized Judy was as drawn to her as she was to Judy.

As Anna described, Judy had been raised in a wealthy, privileged home in Golden, Colorado, not far from Denver. She was a talented and refined person, but she had experienced serious issues with her family—and not for the reasons I had assumed.

Like her father, Thomas, Judy graduated from Stanford University with a PhD in computer science. The two had always been best friends. For Thomas, it was a dream come true when Judy also became his business partner. He specialized in complicated medical devices mostly used in new forms of heart surgery. Judy worked with her father as they traveled back and forth to Europe meeting with the top surgeons on the two continents. While they worked hard and smart to grow their business, they enjoyed exploring the world, especially the local art scenes.

Thomas was a brilliant man in many ways but also quite private. Thomas strove to advance science while at the same time advancing his own finances. Judy's mother, Connie, however, strove only to advance her status in the Denver social scene and her addiction to pain killers.

Connie became suspicious and jealous of the relationship between her husband and daughter. Connie and Thomas had not been intimate in years, and she knew her daughter was not interested in men. Unable to comprehend the depth of a father-daughter bond, she could only speculate they were sleeping together. Her paranoia grew until she believed they were planning to leave her, at the least, and kill her, at the extreme.

Not to be outdone, Connie began an affair with a prominent Denver doctor—a fact Judy discovered while reading a *Denver Enquirer* article about a recent cancer benefit. Judy almost gasped when she saw a photo of her mother smiling broadly in a sexy dress along with the doctor. She couldn't recall her mother looking as attractive nor as happy as she did in the photo. Perhaps for that reason, she hid her discovery from her father.

Or perhaps, seeing her mother's unhappiness for so long, she harbored a hope her mother may have found somebody she could love. Judy had more than a little blood spattered on her from the verbal wars her parents had been fighting. She wanted no part of their war, but of course both parents drew her in.

Eventually, though, she decided the truth had to come out. She arranged a family meeting over dinner. While Judy knew her mother was aware of her homosexuality, Judy planned to announce her and Anna's upcoming commitment ceremony. By opening up about herself, Judy hoped her parents could address their relationship and specifically the affair.

By the time Judy and Thomas arrived at the restaurant, Connie was on her third drink.

Connie was nearly expressionless when Judy told her about the commitment ceremony.

"What do you want me to say?" Connie loudly asked. "In a thousand ways, you and your father have made it plain: I am not part of your private, little family." At last, her face distorted to reveal her true emotions. "And now you come and ask me to support your pathetic lesbian love affair? I don't think so."

Connie stood up, stumbling slightly. She regained her balance if not her composure.

"Now, let me share *my* news," she nearly shrieked. "I am divorcing your goddamned father, and he can have his fairy daughter in the deal. Congratulations!"

With that, she spun around to leave but bumped into an unfortunate server who couldn't pull away his platter of drinks quickly enough to avoid losing them on the four shocked customers at the next table.

Connie drew close to one of the women at the table. "Is that an orange and a cherry in your hair, or is it the ugliest goddamned hairpin in history?"

The people in her path to the door gave Connie plenty of space as she strutted out.

"In Connie's eyes," Anna told me, "Judy's biggest sin was not her sexual preference but her close relationship with her father."

"I can't even imagine," I replied truthfully.

"Rather than focus on the negatives, though, I like to think Judy possesses the positive traits of both parents," Anna continued. "Perhaps she's not as outgoing as her mother, but she can be quite engaging with people. We have a lot of fun. And like her father, she's extremely successful in a very complicated business, but she's also sensitive, caring, and trustworthy.

"And now we're celebrating two years together and looking forward to publicly pledging our devotion to each other with our family and friends.

I'm actually the one who proposed the notion," she added. "I surprised even myself! But I guess I've just come to the point where I don't even want to think of life without Judy. I truly believe nobody else in the world could fill the void I'd felt for so long."

"I'm so happy for you, Anna," I said. "I look forward to being there for you two at your ceremony."

After we said our good-byes, I found myself smiling. I understood what drew Anna to Judy more than anything else: Anna had found somebody interesting and trustworthy, yes, but also somebody who loved her simply for who she was. Anna, for the first time, could be herself.

13

AFTER THE BARRAGE OF PHONE CALLS on Saturday morning, I opted for radio silence for the rest of the weekend. Whenever the phone rang, I shook my head and waved my hands wildly at Gary and Trent, giving the international symbol for "I'm not here." In a way, it was true. Between the business deal, Margie's pregnancy, and now my family drama, I was beyond lost.

Thankfully, only one call was for me. It was my kid brother, Mike. Gary said he sounded excited. I decided to call him back as soon as I could get the mess of unfinished business out of my way. I hated clutter.

Monday morning, I had to head to work and start facing the music. It was the first of November. I reviewed the sales activity and was pleased to see we had beat last October's sales by 24 percent. I knew these numbers would only intensify Leo's prick of a son-in-law's opinion of me. I didn't even know his name—didn't even care. The wannabe lawyer was here at the store as Leo's consultant "going over things," as he put it. The guy seemed to take some perverse joy in my squirming.

The son-in-law already thought Leo was offering me too good of a deal. Leo, though, would stick to his guns with the asking price. His word would be good, and it would be final.

My message light blinked at me, reminding me to check out who wanted me for what.

"Ten new messages," the recorder braced me.

I listened to all ten. I deleted two, which were solicitations; took notes for three from customers and two from carpet reps; and deleted one from idiot Dan. That left me with a message from Pastor Roger Lund and one from my mother.

I was intrigued Pastor had called me. He mentioned he and Colleen were staying in the Cities for a couple of days with his in-laws and wondered about getting together. He left his in-laws' number for me to call. I wasn't ready to talk to him, though.

Mom's message was, "Jake, I need you to call me right away. Nothing bad. Good news."

I knew it had to be about the family trip to Denver. She probably wanted to make one last run at me to join them. Before I could even think about leaving with the rest of the family, though, I had to take one last run at my dream of buying the store and burying my "misallocation." I had to call Jerrod.

But before I could do that, I had to get past the son-in-law. The first thing he did that morning was demand I go over the ledger with him so it would be ready for the audit before the presumed sale.

I already couldn't stand the guy, and I had nothing to lose, so I said, "Look, I'll have you know I plan on buying it myself. I'm happy to report that the loan is coming through, but it will take my investor a little more time to close on the deal."

This was one big lie. From the expression on the son-in-law's face, he knew it.

"Well," he said, "the family wants me to get the audit going now—in case you can't get the funds by next Tuesday." Now his expression showed he highly doubted my ability to pull the money together. "I'll go over the ledger myself, then. I'll come to you if I have questions."

Which he did. I was in our showroom with a couple hopefully on their way to a big job of Persian Luxury when he walked right up to me with the ledger in his hands.

"Jake, who is Nick Petrovick, and why was he paid four thousand dollars?"

The couple looked at each other in surprise. No question, it sounded as though the son-in-law was accusing me of something serious.

"Excuse me for a minute, folks," I said to the couple, though I was certain they would leave the moment I stepped away. Then I turned to the son-in-law. "Would you please come into my office?"

There, in private, I took a deep breath to try to calm my indignation.

"We owed Petrovick the money for installation on a HUD project not yet billed out because the building supervisor wasn't ready."

The self-important little prick pointed his pencil toward me to make his point. "My marching orders specified installers don't get paid until the order is billed and the customer is satisfied."

Incredible. I took a deep breath.

"Petrovick has worked for Leo for ten years. He has a family. He did his part. It's no fault of his this couldn't be billed. You want us to lose him as an installer? Talk to Leo."

I knew Leo never would have put up with this. I had reached the point of no return. Still indignant, I decided to lay it on the line. I leaned forward.

"If you ever imply I am dishonest again in a public setting, I will take that pencil and shove it up your ass." I looked at him hard. "Do *you* want to manage the store every day?"

When he said nothing, I said, "I thought not."

The son-in-law took his pencil and scribbled something on his notepad. "Jake, I'll leave you a note of what I need from you so you don't forget. Look especially at the last item when you get a chance."

He handed me the note. I waited for him to shut the door, then read his memo. There were three questions and a cynical reminder at the bottom: "$250,000 down. Good luck."

The phone rang. It was one of our new installers, Wayne Feldman.

"Jake, you told me you would talk to Dan. We have two things here I like to avoid: a pissed-off customer and a lying salesman."

"Wayne," I interjected, "if what you say is true, I'll take away his whole commission and donate it to charity."

Wayne had shown himself to be a bright guy in sizing up people. He once told Gary, "I wonder what that clueless asshole Dan has on Jake."

After hanging up with Wayne, I found Gary and filled him in.

"I think Wayne's on to something," Gary said. "What *does* Dan have on you?"

I tried to keep my reply casual. "Hey, he's been loyal to Leo, and I want to give him every chance."

I could see Gary was pondering my response. "Well, Jake, you're the boss. But as my friend and the man who brought me to this promised land, I want to give you a heads-up: the other salesmen are wondering the same thing Wayne is. Dell has been working with the dickhead for five years, and he told me if you don't get rid of him soon, he's gone. Just so you know, Dell supports you—or at least supports the way you've made him money. Still, you may want to think about it."

I feigned an overly proud expression. "Honest to God, Gary, you are becoming a rug man right before my eyes! I don't know why you're going for your master's when your final step of competence is right here!"

Gary rolled his eyes. "Just think about it Jake. That dumb shit Dan can cause you a lot more grief if Dell leaves."

I lowered my voice. "Thanks, Gary. I'm on it."

The afternoon was slipping away. Between the prick son-in-law and the Dan issues, I still hadn't had a chance to call Jerrod. I felt some relief when his secretary said he was in. I needed to get this burden off my back, one way or the other.

I heard him pick up. "What's the word?" There was little patience in his voice. I was ready.

"Jerrod, three things: One, the building will not be sold because his son-in-law plans on inheriting it. Two, it's a half-mil on the business with a two-hundred-fifty-thousand-dollar down payment. I need to know if you will commit to the down payment, one way or the other, by next week. Three, you're going to do a personal favor for me."

It was risky to make demands on someone like Jerrod Springer, especially when most of our conversations lately had ended with him threatening me. But for whatever reason, this little mystery completely disarmed him. I pictured him leaning back in his prize chair and stroking his chin, all the time sporting a smirk on his face, as though he held a secret.

"I'm listening—as long as the favor doesn't involve signing anything or giving you my money."

"It doesn't," I replied.

"What then?" he asked.

I felt almost euphoric when I said, "You're going to place a help wanted ad for a salesman with administrative skills, and you're going to offer a salary and commission at scale, with an extra two thousand dollars per month to help with administrative duties."

Springer laughed. "I don't need administrative help. What I need is psychiatric help for staying in this business."

A bit disappointed Springer didn't follow, I simply said, "Well, just let me know if anybody I know applies. I'd sure hate to lose one of my guys—especially

Dan. You offered him a job once, but Leo made him a counteroffer to stay. I just don't know if we could top your latest offer, though . . ."

Springer paused. "So, Jake, you manipulative bastard, how long does Dan need to work here before I can fire him? I don't want an unemployment claim."

"Since he quit at Sommers, we wouldn't have to pay anything. If he works less than thirty days for you, then you won't pay a dime. I'm not sure after that. No matter, you'll get rid of him, and I'll owe you one."

"As for the business deal," Jerrod said, his voice terse again, "I've got to think it over now that the building is out. I'll get back to you."

"When might I hear from you? I've only got about a week before Leo will sell to the other buyer and—"

"I said I'll get back to you," Jerrod snapped. Then the line went dead.

Oddly, I felt a little better already. I still didn't have an answer about buying the business, but at least the wheels were in motion to get one nagging problem—idiot Dan—off my back.

On to the next issue. I dialed Mom's number with a strong premonition of where this conversation would go and that I would pretty much need to say yes.

The phone rang only twice. DeeDee picked up with a cheerful, "Hello, this is the Horton residence."

DeeDee usually answered the phone and did so quickly, likely to avoid the third degree from Mom. I could picture her sitting in the recliner with her legs folded up under her and the phone braced between her neck and shoulder so she could talk and paint her fingernails to a new level of beauty at the same time.

"Hey, this is Jake. How are you doing?"

DeeDee nearly squealed into the phone. "Well, I'm doing great now that you called. Let me get Mom."

Oh, boy, I thought. *Now saying no to the trip would disappoint them both in one swoop. Damn.* Now I pictured DeeDee hovering right by Mom so she could listen in.

Mom picked up and after a little small talk, she got to the matter at hand.

"Jake, DeeDee and I leave tomorrow for Denver. We're flying. Your dad doesn't want to fly and is planning on driving with Michael. We sure hope you'll be with them."

I couldn't believe I had heard her right. "Did you say Dad is going? What changed his mind?"

Mom hesitated. "Your dad is a good man, Jake. He knows this is his one chance to get his daughter back. I didn't really push him at all."

Her words had barely registered before my mind moved to the logistics of this trip from hell.

"So, Dad and Mike are driving? How will that work? That's, what, about fifteen hours one way? They'll kill each other before they even cross the Minnesota border."

Mom expected this. "Jake, you'll be surprised how Michael has grown up. The two of them get along now. I know they'd enjoy your company too. Will you do this for me? I don't think I've ever asked a favor from you before."

I let out a sigh. I wasn't really getting anywhere with Jerrod and Leo, and I didn't know what to do next. Maybe going away for a couple of days would be a good thing.

"Okay, Mom. I'm nuts to say yes because things are pretty crazy at work right now. But I'll go."

Mom and DeeDee sounded like a couple of excited teenagers as they celebrated together. Apparently, Mom had expected that I couldn't or wouldn't come.

"Your father and Mike have the trip all planned out," Mom said. "Jake, you won't be sorry. They'll pick you up Thursday morning."

14

TRUE TO PLAN, AN AQUA STATION WAGON ARRIVED outside my apartment 9:00 a.m. on Thursday. When I came out the door with my brown leather suitcase, Mikey came over, hugged me, then took the bag.

Every time Mike saw me, he wanted to hug me. This always surprised me and made me feel guilty at the same time. I didn't spend much time with Mike.

He fit my suitcase carefully in the back of the station wagon, then sat in the back seat behind Dad.

I couldn't count the number of times Roy Horton had told people he could never live in the Cities. He said he'd feel like one of those hamsters on a wheel, running for dear life but not understanding why. Yet now he was behind the steering wheel—driving at Iron Range speeds and drawing horns, shaking fists, and middle fingers—all because he didn't trust anyone else driving.

We had been in the car only about fifteen minutes when Mikey asked me, "Did you hear about Frank Nazar?"

Just the sound of that name caused me to grimace. I looked in the rear-view mirror. "No, Mikey, I haven't heard anything. What's up?"

I could sense tension.

"It's no big deal," Dad interrupted. "He's just working for his old man part-time now, and he gave me the shaft on a circular saw. I couldn't believe it. I used the damned thing twice, and he wouldn't replace it because it was over a year old. Unbelievable."

It was clear Mike didn't have a circular saw in mind when he brought up Nazar. I glanced at him again in the mirror, and he reminded me of a child who'd had his hand slapped. Dad, meanwhile, set his jaw. I'd have to interrogate Mikey later without Dad present.

I just looked out the window. "Unbelievable, yes," I repeated softly but loud enough for Dad to hear. "That was unbelievable."

At this point, we had been together for twenty minutes of a fifteen-hour drive. Eventually, Dad pierced the quiet. "So, what's your buddy Gary doing now?"

I didn't want to leave the Nazar gossip, but I forced myself to play along.

"Gary's doing great. He's planning to attend graduate school, and he wants to be a teacher. In the meantime, I hired him to sell carpet. He also operates as my assistant manager. He's doing well, and he's been a lot of help."

I was well aware of Dad's antibusiness bias, so I wasn't surprised when he said with some disgust, "Four years of college, and he's selling carpet."

Silence again.

This time, it was Mike who finally broke it. "Jake, have you talked at all with Pastor Lund?"

He had my attention again. "Well, no. But just yesterday, he left a message for me at the store. I don't have a clue why he called, but it sounds like you do . . ."

Again, Dad jumped in. "Have you been to church lately, Jake?"

This was ridiculous. I knew it. He knew it.

I speculated out loud. "What do Frank Nazar and Pastor Lund have in common?"

"Eight miles to next rest stop," Dad announced. His tone indicated that all conversation would cease for those next eight miles.

Once we arrived at the rest stop, Dad all but grabbed Mike. "Let's go to the restroom."

Just to put a little pressure on Dad, I followed them into the building. It was laughable. I wasn't so sure I wanted to know what was up with this Nazar and Pastor Lund situation, but it was more than a little humorous being part of this masquerade. I guess I'd have to find my chances with Mike later.

There was silence again when we got back in the car.

After many miles, Mike tapped my shoulder. "Jake, did Mom or Dad tell you? I'm signed up to go into the army, like Dad did."

I regret my reaction. I whirled around to face him.

"Mikey, tell me you're joking!"

Mike was dismayed. "It'll be my special surprise to announce to the whole family in Denver."

"Mikey," I continued, "don't you know guys in the army are sent over to Vietnam now? Don't you know they're being killed? Do you even know, goddammit, where Vietnam is?"

It was Dad's turn. "Jake, just because you didn't serve doesn't mean you have the right to lecture someone who wants to. Do you think making money in a rug store is more important than serving the country?"

I didn't want to go there. "Mike, all I want to know right now is whether you're for sure signed up or whether you're still thinking about it."

Mike's reply showed some defiance. "I'm reporting to Fort Leonard Wood, Missouri, on December 15. Dad and Mom said we can have Christmas early."

I turned back around and stared out the windshield. It was irrevocable.

The mood in the car reminded me of a thick fog engulfing what was once fresh air. The fog had been forming since the beginning of the trip, but now my comments had made it hard to breathe.

I realized then just how important my opinion was to him. He looked up to me in a way I took for granted. All he wanted was to share his excitement and earn his older brother's respect. But instead, I insulted him. I was no better than those people back home who called him Loser, Retard, and Spaz behind his back—sometimes to his face.

As the hilled terrain moved by, Mike sat slumped in the back seat, staring at his refection in the window. I imagined he wanted to yell "Loser!" at himself about right now.

"Well, brother, you're certainly braver than I am. That's something," I offered. "What made you decide to do this?"

Mike sat up and smiled. He was back in it. "Dad said the army taught him a lot. And I want to serve my country."

I nodded and tried to smile with him, but I couldn't force it. His response sounded a bit canned. There was more to this story—I could feel it.

As we traveled through the beautiful but boring Black Hills of South Dakota, all I could think about was an argument between my parents a couple of years ago, when Dad wanted to send Mike to reform school. Had Dad found the ultimate reform school with the US Army? At that moment, I hated Dad, a feeling I had never felt before.

We traveled on, each in his own world. When we stopped for gas, Mike headed for the gas pump. He liked to operate the pump.

"Mike," Dad said, "don't overfill the tank. Jake and I are going inside." He motioned me over.

When we walked out of Mike's view, Dad's expression grew cold. I thought he might have hit me as he gripped my arm.

"Listen to me, Jake. I know what you're thinking. But goddammit, I did not talk Mike into this. He's almost twenty years old. He wants to serve his country. Let him feel proud. Be proud of him, Jake. You were a sports hero, top student, popular—all that shit. He's had nothing. Don't take this away from him."

Dad loosened his grip. I met his eyes.

"Tell me, Dad—can you picture Mike in a jungle with an M16, hunting down the Vietcong?"

At that, he pointed his finger at me. "Just remember what I said." He headed into the station.

Here I had my opportunity to question Mike about Frank and Pastor Lund, but I felt almost sick with anger toward Dad and with regret for Mike. I just couldn't pile more on top right now.

Here I was, in the middle of nowhere. I had agreed to this trip to escape my problems with Leo and Jerrod. Now I just wanted to escape my problems with my family. I felt as if I were wearing a necktie and somebody kept tightening it to see how much I could take. I wanted to scream at Dad, but I couldn't help but imagine he was also thinking, *Why the hell am I going to Denver?*

I found a pay phone and called Gary at the store. "Hey. How are you doing?"

"Hey, Jake," he said, "you called at a good time. I'm here by myself. Where are the Horton men right now?"

I thought for a moment. "In the fucking wilderness, Nebraska, pig country. I can smell every one of them."

"Say, I heard something odd. Don't get your hopes up, but I think Dan has been offered a job somewhere. I heard him saying something about it to a customer—imagine—but he stopped talking when I got within earshot. Man, if he leaves while you're gone, I'm going to have a big party to celebrate."

I didn't want to appear too happy yet. "Really? Huh. Yeah, that might be good for everybody," I offered with no honesty whatsoever. "What else is going on?"

Gary thought for a second. "Pastor Lund and his hot wife stopped by. They wondered how you were, and he wants you to call him when you get back."

A quick picture of Colleen came to mind. "Okay. I'll do that. Anything else?"

Gary was waiting for that. "Well, yes, I sold him some carpet and found an installer up in Virginia for him."

I smiled. "Gary, you amaze me. You need to stop talking foolishly about being a teacher. The carpet world needs you. Gotta go—bye."

I ambled out of the station. Dad gestured for me to take the driver's seat. He didn't like driving at night.

As I drove through the night, Mike slept. Dad kept his eyes fixed on the road, staring through the windshield. I could see his reflection, and I wondered if he could see mine.

I don't know why, but this saddened me. I realized we didn't truly know each other. It was like knowing someone's reflection instead of the real person.

I decided to break the silence. "Dad, it's about three thirty. Per the directions, we would get to Anna's at five. That's a little early for anyone to be up. What do you want to do?"

Dad thought for a moment. "Why don't we just grab breakfast somewhere near her place? Your mom will be up by seven, I'm sure." He turned toward me now. "And I don't want any more discussion about Mike and the army while we're here, understand?"

"Why not? Doesn't Mom know? I don't get it."

He grimaced. "Yes, of course she knows. I'm not going to argue with you. Just don't say nothing."

I ignored the double negative but not the message. I continued to drive.

Mike woke up just as we could see thousands of lights from Denver dotting the dawn sky. He sat up and gazed at the sight.

"One of those must be Anna's place," he said.

We found a diner and ate breakfast. A little after seven, we rolled up to Anna's apartment. A light was on. Dad knocked on the door softly. Mom came to the door, gave each of us a hug, then invited us in.

With modern décor, the apartment was cool. Mom woke DeeDee, and the five of us talked quietly while Anna still slept. Mom and DeeDee were excited telling us about Anna and Judy and how they'd been busy touring art galleries with them the past two days. Dad was fidgety.

At last, Anna came down the steps in her robe. She just stood there and looked at us, tears welling up.

Somebody had to make a move, so I did. I got up and hugged Anna.

"Thanks for inviting us," I said.

Mike fell in line. "Yeah, thanks," he said.

Dad approached Anna. He tentatively hugged her, as if afraid she wouldn't allow it. But when she wrapped her arms tightly around him, he returned her full embrace.

I don't think I'd ever seen my father cry. But he did so now, though he tried to hold it back.

"I am so ashamed," he uttered.

He tried to whisper, but he choked and we could hear him. "I don't deserve your forgiveness. I will take my guilt to my grave."

Anna sobbed and shook her head.

DeeDee put her arm around Mike, and the two of them looked on in amazement. This was not what they expected.

I caught Mike staring at me, waiting for me to say something, but I said nothing. All of this shocked me too. I wanted to know more, but this was clearly between Anna and Dad.

My mind swirled with everything that had happened in the twenty-four hours since the station wagon pulled up at my door. I looked down, not wanting eye contact with anyone. I thought, *What did Dad do?* I found myself feeling sorry for him, but then I thought of Mike going to Vietnam, and I felt my face flush. *What the hell did he do?*

15

WE SPENT THE DAY CHATTING AND getting to know each other again. By late afternoon, Dad went down for a nap, and Anna and Mom began preparing dinner. Judy would be coming over at six thirty.

At six thirty sharp, Judy entered the kitchen through the back door. The first thing she saw was the three Horton guys sitting on stools, each with a bottle of beer in front of him.

Judy wore a gray-striped sports coat, fitting her business persona. She wore her blond, layered hair in a shorter style than most. She exuded contentment in being who she was, yet she was warm and genuine.

Anna was obviously nervous, yet she beamed as she introduced each of us to Judy. I understood her nervousness. Sometime we're so afraid something will go down poorly and then, Mother of Jesus, it all goes beautifully. Our worry was totally unfounded.

My mind scrambled to remember when that had last happened to me. *Probably when I met Margie. Shit, no doubt.*

Nerves settled, now Anna said with obvious pride, "Judy, this is my brother Jake."

I hugged both of them at the same time. Anna's eyes filled with happy tears.

As Anna excused herself to regain composure and find a Kleenex, Judy and I shared a few moments of comfortable silence. We looked at each other with an expression that seemed to say, *She loves us best out of anyone. Let's both make her happy.*

When Anna came back, she tried to relinquish center stage to Judy, but her girlfriend knew just how to send the ball back to her court.

"Anna, did you tell your family about your promotion?"

I had never spent time with a gay couple. I felt relieved they weren't holding hands or showing outward physical affections—but then I realized what a double standard that was.

Margie and I are far from demure in public, I thought. *Or should I say, we weren't?* I quickly pushed thoughts of Margie out of my head.

Dinner was awkward at first, but again, Judy to the rescue.

"Mr. Horton, what do you like most about being an ironworker?" And "Mike, Anna tells me you're quite a boxer."

I kept waiting for Mom or Dad or even DeeDee to bring up Mike's joining the army, but no one did. Mike didn't show it, but he had to feel diminished.

After dinner, we headed to the living room to watch a movie on Anna's new television. I decided I could handle another beer, though I had consumed a six-pack already. I slipped into the kitchen to grab one, then noticed the phone hanging on the wall next to the dinette set.

It was Friday. Jerrod said he'd have his answer by today.

I sat down and dialed. The phone rang several times.

Just as I considered hanging up, I heard his usual greeting: "Jerrod."

That one word wasn't enough to give me a good read on whether he would agree to my deal or not. The burden was now on me to ask him directly. I didn't want to sound desperate, so I started with a few pleasantries. Then I simply came right out with it.

"What did you decide about our partnership deal?" I asked, then held my breath.

"The more I've thought of this," he said in a voice sounding both apologetic and wise, "the more I realize I don't want twice the headaches. Not without the building. Sorry, Jake, but I've decided against it."

My heart sunk. "Okay, Jerrod. I understand. See you around."

I hung up. The entire call had maybe lasted sixty seconds. It was over. At least I didn't have to pretend I liked the bastard anymore.

I pushed away my beer and put my head down on Anna's table. Maybe it was because this was yet another piece of terrible news piled on all the others. Or maybe I just couldn't take all this emotion.

Or most likely, it was reality setting in. I had no choice now but to have the audit done. I had to be honest with myself: all along, I had known this would happen. Buying the company had just been a pipe dream, a naïve attempt to avoid facing the music.

I just shook my head back and forth.

No, no, no.

"Are you all right, Jake?"

I jumped. I hadn't noticed Judy enter the kitchen. She put her hand on my shoulder.

I felt silly and weak, slumped over at the table like this. I straightened myself as best I could. I suddenly wished I hadn't had the beers, at least not as many. Judy had a civility about her. She was classy, easy to be around. I couldn't believe I had said ignorant things about her and Anna.

Judy poured herself a glass of wine, sat down across from me, and smiled.

"Your sister has followed your life the best she could. Your football and basketball success in high school. Your graduation speech. And then there was that amazing Spartan-Gopher football game. Your mom says you're managing a carpet store and may buy it?"

I thought briefly about shading over this disaster with some frosting, but I had heard enough lies the past couple of days. I shook my head. "I'm sorry—I shouldn't have brought all my personal problems here."

"Jake," she said softly, "everybody else is watching the movie. Tell me more. I'm intrigued. Give me the details about the rug business."

I found myself telling her the whole story—except for the embezzlement part. I told her how we were making record profits at our little company and how this had worked against me. Now that the company was turning big profits—thanks to me—Leo's "consultant" son-in-law knew how easy it would be to sell. There was no need to go out of their way to work out a deal with me.

I detailed how I had looked for ways to buy the place and how and why I still needed a quarter of a million dollars by Tuesday. And then I explained that just a few minutes before she came into the room, Jerrod had turned me down and ended my only chance.

After going on and on, I put my beer down. "I'm sorry, Judy, for the tale of woe. It's not like it's the end of the world. I'm still managing the store and making good money."

My words probably sounded as insincere to Judy as they did to me. I couldn't tell her it *was* the end of the world—Anna's favorite brother might go to jail. Fuck. Anna's favorite brother *deserved* to go to jail.

"How is Sommer's different from the other carpet stores?" she asked.

It was a good question, and the answer was easy. "We have the best service anywhere. We rarely advertise because word of mouth brings them in."

"Won't customers buy elsewhere once Leo isn't there, though?" she challenged.

"No, not at all. Our sales have grown since he's been away."

Judy nodded wisely. "Ah, so *you're* the key, then."

I shrugged and waved my hands. "I don't want this to be all about me. Judy, I heard you're in business too."

Judy shared how she had always wanted to work with her father and how they'd done well in a small niche in the medical-device field.

"Is it difficult to get into that business?" I asked. "It sounds much more fascinating than carpeting."

She smiled. "It's pretty tough for a woman. I've never run into any others. It's very specialized, very uncertain, but it's been good to my father and me."

We talked about Colorado, Mesabi, and the family. She was so easy to talk with. Judy laughed naturally and easily.

She was in the middle of one of those laughs when Anna and DeeDee came into the kitchen. The movie was over, and everyone was getting ready for bed.

"I guess I should say my good-byes before heading out," Judy said, standing. She paused and touched my arm. "Jake, you're delightful. Thanks for the conversation."

"I can't remember when I've enjoyed a conversation more—outside of those with my mother, of course," I responded with sincerity and a little humor.

It had been a long day of strong emotions—some verbalized, some silent under the surface. The result was exhaustion.

Nobody knows when these hidden thoughts may jump out of the darkness and demand their due, I thought to myself.

I lay on the couch with a sheet and wool blanket over me, but I didn't want to fall asleep right away.

With all the highs and lows, I found it difficult to attach an adjective to how I felt. Yes, I hated that Jerrod. He had the money to make my problem go away, and it had been a decent deal for him.

I grimaced. *I will put that son of a bitch out of business.* Then I thought, *Oh, sure, "Tough Guy Jake"—you who tells his employees competition is good.* I took a deep breath. *Dear God, I'm a disaster. Let Judy and Anna be happy. They deserve it.*

It had been a remarkable day for the family. I was happy, really, for everybody. I was glad I was there.

I came up with a little riddle: *How many beers does it take a thief to fall asleep?*

More than eight.

———

Saturday was the last full day of our trip. We menfolk would be heading out on the road before dawn on Sunday, and Mom and DeeDee would catch their flight that afternoon.

With our last day together, we drove up the mountain to the resort town of Breckenridge. We hiked. We had a picnic lunch, which Judy brought for us. We shopped. We talked. We laughed.

When we explored an area with incredible rock formations, Judy smiled. "I think of Anna when I come here, because of her special beauty," she said.

After an awkward moment or two of silence, Anna looked at Dad and asked, "Did you bring the bullshit machine?"

At the end of the day, Judy hugged each one of us good-bye. DeeDee and Mom searched for the Kleenex.

Judy wanted a reenactment of that family photo Anna had mentioned to me on the phone. Everyone took their position, but this time I extended my hand to Anna. And she took it.

Flash—it was night again. Uneasy thoughts returned to me. I told myself, *Get to sleep, Jake. Five o'clock comes early.* But I was still up at four. I decided to just get up and take a shower.

Next I headed to the kitchen to plug in the coffeepot. An envelope sat on the table. I picked it up, expecting it to be a nice letter from Judy to the family. But when I turned it over, it was addressed "Jacob Horton."

A feeling of dread prevailed. My first thought was that Judy had somehow, in some impossible way, found out why I really wanted to buy the company. Not only would the truth be exposed but I would also be responsible for ruining what had been, up to that point, a meaningful and happy family trip.

But then I opened it and found a typewritten letter, an agreement signed "Judy Morris," and a cashier's check for $250,000.

Judy wanted to buy 50 percent ownership of Sommer's Carpet and Tile with me.

All I can say is, I felt bewildered.

Timing. What were the odds of me suddenly deciding to call Jerrod when I did and having Judy walk in moments later?

And what had I said or done that would persuade her to invest $250,000 in me? How could anybody make a decision like that . . . and how did Judy have access to so much money so quickly?

I instinctively looked over my shoulder to make sure no one else was around. Ironically, while I faulted my family for their secrets and lack of candor, I wanted to keep this good news—crazy good news—to myself. Though I wondered if Anna knew. I stuffed the check and the envelope into my jacket.

Once the car was packed, we started to say our good-byes. Anna hugged everybody and gave an extra-long hug to Mike.

"Could we have a couple of minutes in private?" I whispered when it was my turn to hug Anna.

The little smile on her face instantly confirmed she knew. We walked to the kitchen.

"Anna, I'm shocked."

Her smile grew. "I was surprised as well, for a lot of reasons. Judy thinks you're a good investment, Jake. She knows people, and she says she trusts you totally. I think she did the right thing. At least, I hope so," she added with a nervous laugh. "That's a lot of money!"

I looked at my sister, understanding her completely. She may have phrased it as a joke, but what she was really saying was, *You damn well better be careful with Judy's money.*

"She will never be sorry—you have my word."

As I came back out to gather my bags, Mom eyed Anna and me suspiciously. "What was that about?" she asked.

"Anna can tell you about it. We have to get going." I leaned in for a hug. "Thanks, Mom, for convincing me to come along on this trip. It was a great time, a really great time."

Dad was at the helm. I took my seat on the passenger side. It was his turn to be suspicious—even more so than Mom.

"So, what was all that with Anna about?"

I wanted to say, "It's my secret. Be honest with me, and then I'll be honest with you."

Instead, I said, "Let me tell you something that's almost too good to be true."

I told them the entire story—again, omitting the embezzlement part. Hell, time has no limits when you have twelve hours of driving in front of you.

Dad shook his head. "Can you imagine being able to get a quarter of a mil' on a day's notice? Jake, are you sure you're not being screwed somehow? I would hate to see her lose that money."

Everything Dad had just said was wrong. I tried not to feel hurt or angry. Instead, I changed the subject.

"Okay, Dad, I have a question for you: How come nobody said anything about Mike's enlisting?" I turned to meet Mike's eyes. "Mike, if you're so proud to go, why didn't you tell them?"

This brought Mike's anger out into the open. He had been seething about this the entire time.

He yelled at me, his voice almost shrieking, "Because Dad told me it wasn't a good idea! He said he didn't know how Anna and Judy would feel about it. A lot of people hate people in the army."

I wasn't convinced. "What? Say that again, Mike."

"Jake, that's enough," Dad interrupted. "He answered your question. Stop badgering."

I rubbed my temples, then took a deep breath. As long as we were asking questions, I had a big one that I wouldn't ignore anymore.

"So, Mike, let's try this again. You mentioned Frank Nazar. And Pastor Lund. What's the story? Let's hear it."

Mike put his hand on Dad's shoulder.

"Can I tell him, Dad?"

16

EVER SINCE MIKE HAD MENTIONED Frank Nazar and Pastor Lund, I'd been waiting for someone to spill the beans. I asked for it, but I never could have prepared myself for the story that unfolded. My mind checked out with the very first thing that came out of Mike's mouth.

"I don't know about you, Jake," Mike began, "but Dad and I got really pissed off when we heard that asshole Frank Nazar broke your car window."

What the—? I thought. Frank did that? How do Mike and Dad know this? It's my fucking car—why don't I know this? Does Margie know? Has that son of a bitch been lurking out there to get me?

As these thoughts bombarded my mind, Dad sighed. "Mike, we've got nothing but time. Start at the beginning."

As the station wagon lumbered toward Lincoln, Nebraska, I sat in stunned disbelief as Mike told the whole story. It involved more people than just Nazar and Pastor Lund. Margie, of course, was in the middle of it. And Mike and Dad themselves.

As Mike told the story with remarkable clarity, I realized he had repeated the tale many times already. It was pieced together from other people's accounts and points of view. I felt worse and worse as Mike went on. Appalled. Totally clueless.

The story began the very night I met Margie at the armory dance. Frank's buddy Bronco Brocado had seen me leave with her. Once I left for the Cities Sunday night, Frank picked up Margie and drove to a closed mining well, a spot teenagers frequented for drinking and making out.

He never came out and said he knew she had been with me. He didn't have to say it. He just made it clear she was his girl—and he forced her to prove it. She had no choice. They were in the back seat about five minutes. No time for being gentle; no time for protection.

In the weeks that followed, Margie kept seeing me but, understandably, was worried Frank would find out about us. At last she discovered what she should have known all along: he was a no-good son of a bitch. But no doubt, she feared him, and for good reason.

Little did I realize that was why she moved to the Cities, so maybe he'd forget about her. She left a note breaking up with Frank and asking him not to contact her. But Margie felt only marginally safer once she moved to her aunt's.

Then came the phone call the weekend her aunt was out of town.

"You should ask your boyfriend about his car window," Frank told her. "I did it with a tire iron. And if you don't stop jacking me around, I'm gonna use it on Jake and then maybe on you too."

Margie didn't know what to do. She remembered me mentioning how Pastor Lund helped people with their problems. She left a message on the parsonage answering machine. She was crying so hard, she was barely comprehensible. She said she'd stop by the next day at ten.

By the time Pastor Lund heard the message, it was minutes before ten. He realized he was moments away from potentially breaking Pastor Lutz's commandment about meeting with women without another person being present. Roger never broke that commandment while he served under Lutz. He had no plan to break it now—or ever. With his two staffers off that day, he called in his backup—Colleen herself.

Margie explained the whole situation about Frank forcing himself on her, about being pregnant, and about him threatening her and smashing my window.

Colleen realized she was there only to witness the conversation—she was supposed to leave the pastoring to the pastor. Yet she couldn't help but be moved by the poor girl's story.

"Margie, what you experienced is rape," she said, to Roger's chagrin. "It's not your fault. This should be a police matter."

Roger did his best to curtail Colleen's more assertive approach, preferring instead a gentler approach himself. Knowing me as well as he did, he encouraged Margie to turn to me with the whole story.

All Margie could say was, "No, I'm not good enough for Jake. I'm stupid. He's better off without me."

At the end of the conversation, Pastor Lund told Margie, "Please, we want to help. I have some police friends in the Cities. Let me run this by them. I won't tell them your name. In the meantime, if Frank calls you, call me imme-diately. You can't see this guy anymore. It's not safe."

Before Margie left, the three of them held hands, and Roger began with the words of Psalm 121: "I will look unto the hills from whence cometh my help. My help comes from the Lord, who made heaven and earth."

While not an ideal plan on many fronts, the first thing Roger did was approach Dad.

When he heard about Frank smashing my window, apparently Dad's eyes squinted and his mouth clamped shut. After a long pause, he muttered, "He better stay away from Jake, the SOB."

What Pastor Lund maybe hadn't realized was that to Dad, Frank had com-mitted an act of war.

Just a few days later, Roger and Colleen were already in bed when the phone rang. Margie was visiting her parents in Mesabi and Frank had called the house. He never said a word, but she knew it was him.

Roger dialed Dad, and they were both on their way.

Roger quietly pulled up to the Kohler house a few minutes later, his lights off. Dad's pickup was already in the alley behind the house, as was another vehicle.

Movement caught Roger's eye. A man of somewhat smaller stature was walking up to Dad's truck. This had to be Frank.

Just then, Dad got out of his truck too. Roger's heart started pounding. Suddenly, he regretted bringing Dad into this. Roger had figured he and Dad would approach Frank together, carefully. Pastor Lund hated violence. He never meant for this to turn into some vigilante showdown. Yet there was Dad, barreling straight toward Frank. Alone.

Without thinking, Roger turned on his bright lights, gunned into the alley, then slammed on the brakes, sandwiching Frank's car.

Frank lurched back. He was outnumbered. He jumped into his car, ram-ming into Dad's pickup as he sped away wildly.

With all the commotion, Cy Kohler came out of the house. Dad and Pastor Lund did their best to reassure him it was just a little fender-bender. Margie stood behind Cy the whole time, her head down.

Once the Kohlers went back inside, Pastor Lund let out a long breath. "With the grace of God," he told Dad, "we may have saved a life tonight."

That was just the beginning. Now, it was war.

Dad had live-trapped some squirrels in our attic. He loaded the cages into the back of his now-dented pickup, then headed to Buck's for a quick swing around the parking lot to confirm Frank was there.

Fifteen minutes later, Dad parked his pickup in an alley down the street from Frank's house. Almost casually, Dad broke in, bringing the cages with him. He opened one cage in Frank's bedroom, then opened two cages in the attic. For the last squirrel, Dad opened the fridge. He relieved Frank of a six-pack of Grain Belt, released the squirrel, then quickly slammed the door shut.

But Dad wasn't done. He wanted to make certain Frank would know who had visited him. For the eye-for-an-eye effect, he took a tire iron to the glass in the back door, then tossed the iron on the dirt. He would have liked to have stayed to see Frank's reaction, but he had a hot date with a six-pack of Grain Belt.

That's what happens when you screw with Roy Horton's family.

Meanwhile, at the Lunds' home, Colleen pleaded with her husband to report Frank to the police. Pastor Lund knew she was right . . . but he didn't think he was wrong. He was becoming more of an Iron Ranger every day. He didn't want to hand the situation over to the police, who might do nothing. There had to be some way to get the police involved while still seeing it through for Margie's sake.

Both Pastor Lund and Dad assumed Frank wouldn't risk showing up at the Kohler house again. But that didn't mean he would give up. They decided to lure him to Margie's aunt's place in Fridley. Pastor Lund had a friend in the police department there. For bait, they spread gossip about Margie and me getting back together and having a party the following weekend while her aunt was gone. They knew Frank wouldn't be able to resist.

Pastor Lund planned to be in the Cities that weekend to coordinate with his friend on the force. Dad was to stake out Frank's place, watching for him to head out on the road to the Cities. He was then to call Roger at his in-laws' house to give the heads-up.

That Saturday evening, Roger was a bit surprised when his mother-in-law said a Michael Horton was on the phone for him.

"Pastor Lund," Mike said, "I'm supposed to tell you Frank's on his way. Bronco's with him too."

"Great work, Mike. You can go home now. Tell your dad thanks. I'll call him later."

But Mike stunned the pastor when he said, "Actually, Dad told me to pick him up. We're coming down there too."

Then Mike hung up.

Alarms clanged in Roger's head. His detective friend, Dan Kelly, stressed that the police would handle this. Once Frank was on his way, Roger was to give the signal from his in-laws'. He was to stay away from the scene. Otherwise, it would smell too much like a setup, and it might get dangerous.

But now the Hortons were on their way, putting the whole plan and themselves at risk.

Dad and Mike had borrowed a friend's car so Frank wouldn't recognize them. To be extra safe, they kept their distance on the drive down to Fridley.

Because of this distance, however, they didn't see Frank drop Bronco off a block from the house. Getting ambushed at Margie's house had rightfully made Frank wary. He sent Bronco in first to corner Margie.

When they arrived at Margie's aunt's house, Dad and Mike didn't see Frank's vehicle. They parked across the street and waited. They didn't see the cops either, but they assumed they would be on their way.

It was Mike who heard Margie scream from inside the house. Something was wrong.

Dad put his foot down on the gas pedal. With a loud screech, he pulled up to the garage.

The front door was locked. Dad tried to kick it open. To Dad's utter surprise, Mike took a pistol from the back of his belt and shot off the door knob. They burst into the house to see Bronco on top of Margie. He had spun around at the sound of the shot, yet he still tried to hold Margie down.

Before Dad could react, Mike slammed the pistol butt down on Bronco's head. Bronco instantly collapsed face first on the floor.

Margie scampered to her feet and collapsed in a recliner, hysterical with shock.

Mike watched blood drain from Bronco's skull for a moment or two before he pinned him down with his knee and held the pistol to his head. Blood oozed onto his hand and gun. Dad found a towel and tossed it to Mike.

The sound of sirens came in the distance, getting louder every second.

Bronco stirred. Even with a serious concussion, he sneered defiantly.

Dad and Mike exchanged glances. They now knew what had happened— Frank had sent Bronco in first. They figured Frank was already on I-35 heading north to Mesabi.

Dad reached down and took the gun. "Mike," he whispered so only he could hear, "this is my goddamned gun, you understand?"

Mike nodded as Dad set the gun and bloody towel on the table.

Moments later, Kelly and a few other officers were at the front door. As one officer went to check on Margie, Kelly cuffed Bronco. Even when Kelly pressed hard about Frank's whereabouts, Bronco kept his lips sealed.

He turned now to Dad and Mike. "You're the Hortons, I assume."

He motioned to the kitchen, where they'd be out of earshot. Dad filled him in on what had just transpired. He said, of course, that he had used the gun, which was his, to shoot the door and hit Bronco. Dad pieced together some flimsy lie about winning the gun from Charlie Osborne, an ironworker friend, in a poker game.

Kelly knew Dad was lying. And Dad knew that Kelly knew he was lying. Kelly glanced at Mike, then back at Dad.

After the police left, Dad and Mike stayed with Margie. She was scared. Frank was out there somewhere. She was embarrassed too. She alternated between thanking and apologizing to Dad and Mike.

———

Back in Mesabi, Frank pulled up to his house, where two officers waited for him with lights flashing. Kelly had called the Virginia police department, explaining that Nazar was wanted for his part in terrorizing and assaulting a woman in Fridley. Frank was well known by the Virginia police.

"They were more than happy to ship him back to Fridley," Mike told me, concluding his story. Mike waited for my comments and, really, for my approval.

I slumped back in my seat, spent.

"I'll tell you the truth," Mike added. "When I saw Bronco hurting Margie, I wanted to kill him. Wouldn't you have done the same thing?" he asked me.

Silence.

Mike had captured the essence of the whole matter. He had reacted decisively and intuitively to protect Margie, and now he had no regrets. Me? What *would* I have done?

The entire time we were dating, never once did I realize the hell Margie was going through with Frank. Never once did she feel I would protect and support her. She had me pegged right, I guess. When she told me she was pregnant, what did I do? I spurned her. Yet Pastor Lund, Dad, and Mike were willing to form a vigilante gang and risk their lives for her.

Dad broke the silence.

"Mike," he said, looking at him through the rearview mirror. "Why don't you tell Jake the rest of the story?"

Blood escaped from my face. There was *more*? What could there possibly be? Mike hung his head a bit, then sighed.

Even though Officer Kelly was Pastor Lund's friend, he still had to do things right. That meant following up on the gun. First he discovered Charlie Osborne, Dad's old drinking buddy, was deceased. Then he found that the gun had been part of a shooting in Chicago two years earlier. The perp was serving time, so Kelly knew Dad was in the clear. After speaking with the Mesabi police, Kelly learned that word on the street said Mike had been involved in an incident with a gun outside a bar. It was all messy enough to warrant a call to the Horton household to scare both Horton boys straight.

Only Mike was home when the call came in. When Kelly said he needed to talk to Dad about the gun, Mike confessed it was his. Kelly wasn't surprised in the least. He aimed his scare tactics at Mike, then.

"Not only did you have a gun that was involved in a crime, but you and your dad conspired to lie to us. Plus, I heard you had the gun outside a bar up there. You're in serious trouble."

"I hit that Bronco guy on the head because he was hurting Margie. Can you put me in jail for that? Can I still join the army if you do? I just signed up."

Apparently, that's when it all began to add up for Kelly. He softened a bit.

"Mike, we'll give you a break if you're going to fight for our country. Tell your dad to call me sometime. Good luck."

Mike sighed from the back seat. "So, even though people aren't happy about me going into the army, I have to," he said. "If I change my mind, I'll go to jail."

To Mike, it was a reasonable conclusion. To me, it made me feel sick about how I reacted when I first heard about his enlistment.

"Mike, I can be an asshole sometimes. I'm sorry I got so angry when you said you had joined the army. I didn't know any of this. And when it came to protecting Margie, you not only did the right thing, but you did a brave thing. I'm proud of you. I'm really sorry."

Mike gave a small smile. "It's okay, Jake." He reached over to hug me as best he could from the back seat.

His quick and complete forgiveness only made me feel worse.

Little was spoken the rest of the way home. I felt the envelope in my pocket. I had almost forgotten the check from Judy.

Mom told me this trip would be something I'd never forget.

My mind moved to my mother. "Dad, does Mom know about you and Mike playing like Eliot Ness and the Untouchables down in the Cities?"

"Well, Roger's cop friend kind of blew it when he called about the gun," he admitted. "But she doesn't know enough to get into any trouble. Roger, Mike, and I agreed to not say anything."

More secrets. Of course.

17

O N Tuesday, I completed the deal with Leo's son-in-law. The smug prick didn't seem too happy, but I sure was. I now owned Sommer's Carpet and Tile. Officially, I could quit worrying about going to jail.

The transition was fairly seamless, but there was still a lot to do. Once things settled down, I took Leo and Fern out to celebrate. A lot of nice words were sent in both directions.

Fern lifted her glass. "To Jake—you know you're like a son to us. God bless you always."

"And may my rent be paid on time every month!" Leo offered as a final toast.

I smiled and couldn't help but wonder how I had been so lucky to have learned so much from these people.

At nearly the exact time Fern and Leo were toasting me and my future, Dad and Mom were checking into a Saint Louis hotel with Mike. The next day, he would start his new life as Private Michael Horton at Fort Leonard Wood. As I watched the news that night, I felt a chill as they showed caskets recently arriving in Minneapolis from Vietnam.

In the weeks to come, sales at Sommer's Carpet and Tile continued to rock and roll. The cash balance grew to where I decided to get rid of my GTO and drive a car more reflective of a successful businessman—a Lincoln Continental. The business would own it, so I could write it off. I also started looking into buying my own home.

I called home, excited to tell Mom about the Lincoln. I didn't get a chance to speak because she immediately launched into updates about Mike. Apparently, basic training got off to a rough start.

On the very first evening, the recruits were dropped off in a remote area on the base and expected to find their way back to the post as a training exercise. In a way only Mike could manage, he got separated from the group, got lost, and spent the night in a shed on a firing range. After an all-night dragnet involving the entire company, they finally found him the next morning.

The experience placed Mike in the drill sergeants' sights. He unwittingly became the bad example to the rest of the recruits—living proof of what happened when you cross the drill sergeants. Basic training quickly went from miserable to almost intolerable. One drill sergeant in particular seemed to revel in terrorizing him.

Mike eventually made this jerk sorry for the bullying he had perpetuated from day one. Little did anyone realize, Mike was a natural boxer. Boxing had been a part of Mike since he was little. Dad loved boxing, and Mike loved to watch it with him. During the Friday night fights, they would be up and down. They'd whoop and holler. And if that wasn't enough excitement, they'd box together while the TV blared alongside them. When Mike got older, he joined the Golden Gloves program.

The other recruits discovered Mike's hidden talent in a pickup match in the training room one day. Suddenly the scourge of the drill sergeants earned some respect.

Unauthorized boxing matches were not allowed, so only a few guys knew of Mike's skills. That is, until this same drill sergeant tried to take advantage of Mike during a training exercise with pugil sticks. Pugil sticks are poles with padded ends. Mike trained with them often in Golden Gloves. In fact, his coach once told him, "Mike, it's too bad we don't field a pugil team—you would be the state champion."

Let's just say poetic justice was served. In a story worthy of a good novel, the miserable drill sergeant challenged Mike to a match. He berated Mike, calling him a coward. Almost with reluctance, Mike took him down . . . hard.

It was surreal listening to Mom recount these stories. I could hardly believe Mike was in basic training. I especially couldn't believe what was in store for him next, now that basic training was almost over.

"Your father, DeeDee, and I are going out to Missouri to attend the parade march ceremony on his graduation day," Mom said. "I know you're busy with the store . . ." she added.

While I appreciated her understanding, I still received it with a dose of guilt. I decided not to dwell on it. Instead, I used it as a segue about the Lincoln.

"About the store," I began, "things are going so well, that I—"

"Speaking of stores," she interrupted, "I stopped at Cy's bookstore yesterday. They're closing it down. Margie is back in town helping him. Mike has called her a couple of times, so she and I talked about that. She looks great—barely shows. She is due in late July, I believe. I'm a little worried about her, Jake. She seems terribly sad. I wanted to ask her about her plans, but thought better of it." She paused. "When will you see her?"

As always, Mom's intentions and intuitions were right. In contrast, I was beginning to think mine were always wrong these days.

"Mom, I know I need to talk to her. I just don't know what I'd say." I sighed. "I'll call her and try to get together with her next week. Will you be happy, then?"

Mom paused again. "Jake, I know it's complicated. I'm not trying to interfere. I know you're upset with her. But I just want both of you to be as happy as you can be."

Within ten minutes of hanging up with Mom, I called Margie. Granted, I picked up the phone, dialed part of her number, then hung up a few times first.

Mom thought I didn't call Margie because I was angry. The real reason was because I was afraid she wouldn't talk to me. After hearing how Dad and Mike had virtually saved her from Frank and his idiot buddy Bronco, I became more ashamed of my own actions or lack thereof.

When I finally dialed through to Margie, her mom answered. We visited awkwardly for a few moments, then she broke the conversation and said, "Here's Margie now."

"Hello?" Margie said, taking the phone.

Hearing her voice brought so many emotions to the forefront, so many conflicted feelings—and yes, so much guilt.

"Margie, this is Jake. I'm sorry I haven't called. I'm so sorry about so many things. I didn't know about everything that happened . . . and there's so much I don't know yet." I knew I was rambling. "How are you doing?" I finally mustered.

She started to answer, then she started crying. "Jake, it's good to hear from you. I'm okay."

"I'd like to see you," I ventured. "Maybe later this week?"

Her hesitation spoke volumes.

"What night works best for you—Thursday, Friday, or Saturday?" I pressed on.

After pausing some more to weigh her words, she said, "Jake, it doesn't have to be at night." She was making it known: this was not a date.

"Okay, then. How about I pick you up at the bookstore Friday afternoon around three?"

I didn't add it, but was thinking, *You can see my new car.*

"All right," she replied. "I'll see you then."

As the week moved along, I began to get excited about seeing Margie. I'll admit, I fantasized about getting romantic with her. Mom, Dad, and DeeDee would be in Missouri at Mike's ceremony, so we'd have the house to ourselves.

I can be shallow. Yes, I still cared about Margie. Yes, I was truly embarrassed and sorry for my lack of supporting her. But I was still excited by the possibility of seeing one thing lead to another and ultimately making love to her. Even after everything that had happened, my "little head" still pulled me around like a ring on a bull's nose.

As long as I would be in town, I decided to kill two birds with one stone. I finally returned Pastor Lund's call and made plans to meet for lunch at his house. Perhaps seeing both Pastor Lund and Margie could help me find some peace.

I pulled my Lincoln Continental up to Pastor Lund's house, then walked around to their front door. I was a bit disappointed they wouldn't see my car from the door. I wondered what Colleen would be wearing. I randomly remembered one Luther League meeting when we were making signs for a church celebration. I had my back to her while I worked at the table. Colleen came up behind me and admired my sign. I could feel her breast on the back of my arm as she leaned forward. It took a lot less than that to excite me.

Pastor Lund greeted me with a handshake.

"It's great to see you, Pastor Lund," I said.

"Please, Jake—you can call me Roger," he replied with an easy smile.

I nodded. As always, he had a way of making me feel good.

Colleen came over from the kitchen, smiled, and gave me a light hug.

"Jake, you look great. C'mon in and tell us what you've been up to."

She looked great as well. Those patched jeans looked like the same ones I remembered from a few years ago. She wore her hair a little shorter now, but she still looked like my age rather than hers.

We sat at the table, and Colleen eyed me as she filled the water glasses.

"Have you seen Margie yet?"

Mentally, I reeled. Now even *Colleen* knew I was a coward and needed my dad and brother to make things right.

Pastor Lund looked at Colleen, then quickly looked back at me. "Colleen has become friends with Margie. She's helping her through some problems." Once Colleen sat down, he added, "Could I say grace before you put our friend through the third degree?"

Colleen smiled. "Yes. If you keep it short."

I picked up my egg salad sandwich, my favorite, and took a bite. Some of the egg salad squeezed out on my fingers.

"Jake, do you realize what Margie went through?" Roger asked.

I brushed my mouth with my napkin. I hated to admit how little I knew, but I had to be honest.

"Really, the only thing I've heard is Mike and Dad's take on the story, especially the part about them pretty much saving the day when Frank's buddy attacked her. I still need to hear the full story from Margie. I really feel like I'm in the dark."

"Technically I shouldn't repeat any of this," Roger started slowly, "but you need to know, and I hope I'm doing the right thing for both of you. Frank forced himself on Margie multiple times after you started going with her."

I knew this from Mike's version of the story, but I still felt sick hearing it again.

Colleen felt she had heard enough dancing. "The word for it is *rape*. R-A-P-E. That's why he's in jail right now. Jake, you have no idea the courage Margie needed to press charges."

Rape? No one had used that word before, but she was right. I was speechless for a while.

"So, how come she came to you two and got you involved?" I finally asked. "Why didn't she come to me?"

Roger pondered while Colleen forced herself to stay quiet.

Roger met my eyes. "Well, Jake, let me answer your question with another question: Why haven't you come to see her before now? Why have you avoided her?"

I could see now—I was the bad guy here. I wanted to be anywhere else.

"Jake, nobody is suggesting you should maintain a relationship you don't want in your heart," Roger continued. "That would be a mistake for all concerned. But why have you not supported Margie? I'm not judging you. I'm just trying to understand."

"In hindsight," I said, "I wish I would have handled things differently when I learned she was pregnant—but I didn't know what was going on. A lot was going on in my life too at the time. I was trying to buy the business, and it was stressful. Mainly, though, when she told me it was Frank's baby, I just didn't know what to do. I was hurt."

There. I said it.

Roger looked from Colleen to me. "Just one last question, Jake: How could she know it was his baby and not yours?"

I squirmed. "I just figured she knew when she got pregnant and could trace it back to who she was with that night . . ."

My words trailed off once I realized how flimsy that reasoning was.

"You're right," I conceded. "I don't think she could really know. But who was I to question her?"

Roger sat back. "Well, I guess that's for the two of you to talk about."

I glanced at Colleen, who leaned toward me and made eye contact. She transmitted, "Ask me. Ask me. Ask me."

I returned my gaze to Roger and simply said, "I'm sorry for a lot of what I did and didn't do. I'm looking forward to talking to Margie."

There, I got the final word.

We visited a little more, then I got ready to head out. I needed to stop by the house before picking up Margie.

The conversation with Roger and Colleen ended as it started—with a handshake and a light hug. As I turned for the door, Roger stopped me.

"I almost forgot, Jake—Coll and I will be in the Cities this summer to celebrate her kid sister's graduation. You remember us mentioning Susan?"

I did remember her. They often encouraged me to hang out with her when she came to Mesabi for visits, but I always found some reason to decline. Considering how I was back then, she would have become one more embarrassing incident in my litany of incompetence with women.

"Where did she earn her degree?" I asked.

"She graduated from Northwestern Seminary with a degree in Christian social work." He leaned in a little. "She had a boyfriend, and it didn't work out. We would love for you to join us. How about it?"

This whole situation sounded like a disaster. "Maybe," I said a little weakly. "Call me when you get closer to the party date, and I'll let you know."

Roger grabbed my hand for a second shake. "I hope you can come, Jake."

As I drove to our house, I tried to figure out the conversation with Roger and Colleen. My emotions flew in every direction. How did Margie come to be so close to Colleen? I already felt like a rat about the whole, sad matter with Frank hurting Margie. It embarrassed me further to know Roger and Colleen were so invested in Margie's life. Given what Colleen knew about my relationship with Margie, I wondered why she would even want me around her sister.

Maybe Susan was messed up too?

When I arrived home, I straightened up my old room a bit, just in case Margie came back with me. I don't know whether it was optimistic or lame. I had to remind myself this wasn't a date. Margie made that clear.

But you never know.

I can only say I felt sad and empty when I drove up to the bookstore and saw the sign on the window: "Must Sell Everything, Wall to Wall." I parked and headed inside.

Hoping to avoid small talk with Cy, I found Margie. She was helping a customer. She gave me a nod, and when the customer wasn't looking, she signaled "five" with her hand. I nodded back. Before going out the door, I looked back to take another quick look at her. She was embarrassed to be caught doing the same thing, looking at me.

Mom was right—she barely showed. She looked beautiful. She wore a mini skirt.

My heart pounded, though I wished it wouldn't. I reminded myself, *Jake, this is not a date.*

When she came out of the store, she was wearing a coat. The mini skirt was now covered but still in my mind. She looked around and seemed a little confused. Then it occurred to me—she was looking for my old orange GTO. I gave a short honk and pulled up to the front of the store. She climbed in. I wondered if she was thinking about the first ride she took with me. I was.

"Oh, new car?" she asked.

"Yeah, just got it a couple of weeks ago. Gary says it looks like an old man's car. What do you think?"

Margie looked around at the interior. "I would say it's pretty nice."

"Do you want to go to the Loon?" I asked. "Or we could go over to my folks' place? Where would you like to go?"

Margie seemed prepared for the question. "Jake, I need to get back soon, so let's just drive around a little while we talk."

I looked straight ahead as I headed down the street. "Margie, you look great."

"You do too," she countered. "DeeDee stops by sometimes, and she told me you bought the carpet store. Good for you."

It became still again.

I finally broke the silence. "Margie, I had no idea about this stuff with Frank. I am so sorry, terribly sorry . . . I don't know what to say." I was babbling once again.

She looked sad. "I have regrets too, but I don't have hard feelings toward you. I want you to know that. I made some bad mistakes." She looked straight ahead.

I could see she was starting to cry. She went into her purse for a package of tissues.

"Will you stay in town or move back to the Cities?"

She hesitated. "I haven't told anyone except Pastor Lund and Colleen, but I want to leave before Frankie gets out of jail. Actually, I want to leave anyway. So I'm moving sometime this spring."

This was getting sadder with every sentence.

"Move to where?"

She dabbed at her eyes with a tissue. "I'm not sure, but far from here."

I couldn't leave well enough alone. "Tell me, Margie, did you ever think about us getting back together?"

She was direct. "At first, I thought it was the biggest mistake in my life not to ask you to take me back. I never felt I deserved you. Then the stuff with Frank just took over. My mom and I have really gotten close, and we talk a lot about this. We now know you and I just weren't meant to be."

I was finding this hard to grasp. This was not the "dreamer" Margie I once knew. She had thought the whole matter out, and now she was resolute.

I didn't know what to say, so out of my mouth came the question on my mind ever since that night at the concert and certainly since lunch with Roger and Colleen. It seemed unkind, almost harsh.

"Margie, how do you know the baby is Frank's and not mine?"

Margie straightened in her seat. "When I told you it was Frank's baby, I knew two things. First, I wasn't good enough for you. Second, I couldn't fight Frank. So, it was going to be Frank's baby."

I wanted her to tell me outright if the baby was a Horton or a goddamned Nazar. But then I played it out in my mind, and I knew it was immaterial. She was telling me "why" this was Frank's baby. But I knew it was mine.

I looked at her and tried to say something, but I couldn't help myself. I started to cry. I wiped the tears on my sleeve.

"I never was too good for you," I finally said. "I hated it when you said that."

Margie looked away, first out the window and then at her watch. "I should get back to the store," she said.

I turned the car back toward the bookstore. In the last minutes, we made some small talk about our families.

"Mike will be done with basic training in a couple of hours and on his way home for a while, right?" she said.

Embarrassingly, I had forgotten all about Mike. But Margie hadn't.

When we arrived at the store, I started to get out to open her door, but she took my hand and looked at me.

"Jake, I've come to know that I was wrong—you are not too good for me. And now I also know I can stop Frank. We both need to put the mistakes behind us." She squeezed my hand. "I'll let you know when I move. Thanks for the visit."

At that very moment, if she would have lingered just five seconds longer, I would have asked for a kiss. I wanted to kiss her so much. I cared for her right then more than ever.

But I didn't trust my own motives. She decided she didn't want me, and we always want what we can't have.

Rather, something inside me told me to do what was right for her. So as she climbed out of the car, I didn't try to stop her.

18

AFTER DROPPING MARGIE OFF, I headed back to the Cities. Not long after arriving, the phone rang. I figured it would be Mom calling to tell me how Mike's parade march had gone. It was Mom, all right. But she was nearly in tears. And she sounded angry.

"There was an accident. Your brother got hit by a car."

My God. Poor Mike.

She relayed a few details, but she couldn't talk long. I knew the full story would have to wait. Though I was swamped with work, and I didn't feel like driving back up there again, I promised her I'd make a quick trip on Monday to see Mike.

In the end, I was glad I made the trip. I walked in to see Mike sprawled out on one of those hospital beds set up where the couch used to be.

Dad had gone back to work, but Mom and Mike filled me in on the story. When Dad, Mom, and DeeDee first drove up to the gate about two hours prior to the ceremony, they were confronted by upwards of one hundred protesters waving signs and yelling obscenities. The signs screamed "More Killers Coming from Leonard Wood," "Stop the Killing," and "Learn Peace, Not War." The military police were doing their best to keep the protesters behind a barrier fifty yards from the main gate.

Mom had hoped they wouldn't ruin Mike's day. Little did she know.

In typical Dad fashion, he got out of the car and confronted some protestors blocking his way through the gate. One woman in particular was a nuisance.

Apparently, Dad warned, "I'm honking my horn three times, then I'm advancing whether you're in my way or not. I am not kidding, you coward assholes."

The people had the sense to move after the second honk.

Dad, Mom, and DeeDee made it to the parade area. Eventually, the band began playing and the parade march commenced. Company A marched first: in step, precise, crisp, turning in unison toward the officers and guests with a perfectly timed salute. Company B and C did the same.

Once Company C finished, they marched to the side of the street just south of the marching field. They maintained their formation for Company D.

Mike couldn't help but give Mom, Dad, and DeeDee a quick wave before the drill sergeant—the one Mike beat down in the pugil stick fight—called Company D to attention. He then ordered the road guards to halt traffic so Company C could march safely across the street.

Suddenly Mike heard yelling and saw the drill sergeant shove two recruits violently out of the formation. A second later, Mike saw a car speeding toward them. Tires screeched.

The car hit the drill sergeant squarely. His face hurled straight into the windshield. His body turned into a propeller, high into the air. He landed with a sickening thud on the street. He had put his own life at risk to protect the recruits in direct line of the car.

As heroic as he was, he couldn't protect all the recruits. As the car bore down on him, Mike hesitated only briefly, then pivoted quickly to his left. He thought the car would miss him. But everything was in fast motion. Bodies were flying like bowling pins. The car smashed into him.

"You know what went through my mind at the time?" Mike asked, chiming in on the story. "All I could think was, 'Holy shit—I just got hit by a car!'"

Next thing he knew, he was on his back. A bright light flashed in his mind, a reaction from hitting his head very hard on the pavement. Sharp pains ran through him.

Mike tried to pull himself up, but his left leg simply collapsed. He crawled over to see if the drill sergeant was still breathing, which he was. Motionless bodies were mixed with sounds of pain and cries for help.

The three other drill sergeants arrived to assess the injuries. Mike's dress slacks showed evidence of significant blood loss. Someone used a knife to cut the slacks so the wound could be treated. Mike's right leg was fractured.

Dad, Mom, and DeeDee tried to rush over to help Mike, but they were ordered back. At first, Dad wanted to argue the point, but looking and hearing the pain and grief around, he acquiesced. He didn't want DeeDee around this.

Dad was pissed. The woman driving the renegade vehicle was the same woman he had confronted at the gate.

There were only four ambulances on the base, and Mike was rated fifth for urgency. He would be sent to the infirmary instead. Dad, Mom, and DeeDee went straight to the infirmary and waited in the lobby. Someone promised Mike would be brought shortly.

Almost forty-five minutes later, Mike finally arrived. After a brief exam and a check of his bandaged leg, the attending doctor gave Mike a set of crutches and told him he could go.

A sergeant from another company overheard this and became outraged. Finally, somebody had some sense, it seemed.

But then the sergeant pointed to Mike's right leg and asserted, "He's out of uniform—he can't walk out here looking like this!"

Sadly, Mike was now discovering that the army was more concerned about the uniform than the well-being of the person in it.

Mom and Dad brought Mike to see a civilian doctor in Saint Louis later that afternoon. He was clearly less optimistic than the doctor at the infirmary. The Saint Louis doctor had Mike fitted for a neck brace. He said Mike's neck and back were of utmost concern, but he also told Mom and Dad to be sure Mike's knee and leg got the chance to heal completely.

From what I gathered, the trip back to Mesabi could be best described as somber. I could only imagine how Mike's entire body must have ached, not to mention how monumentally disappointed he must have felt. He wanted so bad to make his family proud.

As I drove back to the Twin Cities that night, I found myself alone with negative thoughts dragging me down.

Would Mike ever be whole again? How would Mom and Dad handle this? His physical therapy sessions were already set up in Duluth, about an hour's drive.

"We'll get Mike the treatment he needs," she told me privately as I was heading out. "I am not going to wait for the damn VA."

Mom swore very seldom, so when she did, it caught our attention. Mom didn't want Mike to feel victimized, nor did she want him to become an object of pity.

Mom didn't say it, but I know she blamed Dad for leading Mike to the army in the first place. She probably wouldn't ever forgive him. I'm quite certain Dad would never forgive himself either.

———

A few days later, Judy and Anna flew in. They headed to Mesabi for a few days, then they drove back to the Cities for a couple of days. I planned to have dinner with them, and Judy arranged a separate meeting with me on Monday to talk about the store.

We had been partners now for four months. I thought she should have been thrilled senseless at the first-quarter check I sent her. We had excellent results, a net profit of about $45,000. Per our contract, I sent her a check for $15,000. That was a pretty decent return already on her $250,000.

I just hoped she wouldn't interfere. We were doing great. What did she know about the flooring business, anyway?

Sunday night before the meeting, I was looking forward to having a couple of drinks with my friends. Trent, Gary, and I went to the Metropole Hotel bar where I had met Crystal—or whatever her name was. I hoped Ryan, the bartender, wouldn't be there, but I spotted him behind the bar. Like an evil reptile with a sixth sense, he turned and smiled.

"Mr. Player of the Week—it's been awhile."

We settled in at the bar. My skin crawled as I introduced him to Gary and Trent.

When Gary and Trent were conversing together, I leaned in to Ryan.

"Is 'Crystal' still around?"

Ryan glanced over at my two companions, unsure what he should say. He lowered his voice. "She's pretty much gotten out of her old career. She works for a travel agency."

I wanted to know more but decided to let it go, at least for now.

It was good to spend some time with guys. We were all so busy these days. Now that I had my own house, I missed our time together back at the old apartment.

Gary had a special announcement: he and his girlfriend, Linda Niemi, an elementary school teacher in Saint Paul, were engaged.

"No date set," Gary said. "Could be a year."

Trent was now in his second year of medical school. Despite some complaints about being in debt, he seemed excited about his future.

When I asked him how his dad was doing, he just shook his head.

"It's hard to believe Dad was a successful businessman five years ago. Now, he's a goddamned invalid. I want to be a part of finding a cure for fucking Parkinson's."

Trent's intensity surprised me some. But picturing my own father in that condition made me shudder.

The next morning, I watched Judy park a little rented Corvair next to my Continental. I watched her get out and straighten her skirt. While she couldn't be called attractive in my mind, she dressed well and always looked composed and professional. She possessed a certain classiness. Today, she was wearing a navy business suit.

I opened the door. "Welcome, Judy. Can I get you some coffee? Would you like to meet in my office or just at a table out on the floor?"

Judy didn't hesitate. "No thanks on the coffee. How about some water? And if it's okay with you, let's talk in your office so it's private."

I smiled. "Sure, Judy. That sounds ominous."

My humor seemed lost with her.

I motioned to the lounge chair across from my desk. She sat gingerly, not settling back as most would do. She maintained an erect posture as she sat on the edge of the seat.

"So, Jake, how do you think the business is going?"

"You weren't satisfied with the fifteen thousand dollars for the first quarter?" I knew I sounded a little annoyed.

She maintained eye contact. "We'll get to that. How do you think you're doing compared to our competitors?"

I didn't appreciate her aggressive tone. "I'd say we're doing fine anytime we have sales increases like we've seen. Really, more than fine. You disagree?"

Judy looked out the window briefly, mulling over my response. "Jake, when I invested in this store—really, in you—my father told me I likely would lose one way or the other. I respect my father as the best businessman I've ever known. What he meant was, if we go out of business and I lose my investment, I'd lose you. You'll avoid me at all costs. On the other hand, if the business is successful, I may lose you because you may resent that I've made a lot of money without the sweat equity." She paused. "I thought my father's advice through, yet I still opted to help you. I know our best shot is if I don't lose a handle on this part of our lives. I must do all I can to not have our relationship implode. So let's treat this as a real business . . . a business with a signed agreement. Jake, do you see where I'm at here?"

I felt diminished somehow. She had the upper hand because she was right. "Okay, Judy. Let me start over. I'm sorry I came across so defensive."

She nodded.

"To answer your question, I believe we're killing our competitors. My contacts tell me we are."

"Who are the competitors?"

I was warming up to the topic. "I would have to say, Springer Carpet for a local and Carpet King for a chain."

"What about Dayton's?" she mused. "I've found they sell more carpet than all three of you combined."

I couldn't help myself. "Well, Judy, Dayton's is Dayton's. If you have a charge card there, you're going to buy there. This is the way it is here in the Cities. Customers like that Dayton truck showing up in front of their house."

"I'm sure you have some good points there. Yet I have a friend here in town who needed carpeting. She and her husband didn't buy at Dayton's because it would have taken three weeks longer to get the carpet installed, and even with their Daisy Sale, they were the highest price."

What will she say to amaze me next? I thought.

"I hope she bought from us . . ." I ventured.

Judy shook her head slowly. "No, I'm sorry to say she didn't. And she didn't buy from the others either. She bought her carpet at Avalon Design. Are you familiar with them?"

"Sure, they're a decorating place maybe two miles from here. Was their price lower than ours?"

Judy anticipated the question. "Sommer's was the best price by almost two dollars per yard, but Avalon's matched the price."

She waited, ready to spring the trap as soon as I asked, "Why did she want to buy it from them and not us?"

"Two reasons. First, they offer a two-year warranty on the installation. Second, she liked the salesperson. She felt the salesperson at Avalon's helped her with her decorating."

I hated to lose any job. I tried to shrug it off. "Well, I guess we can't sell everyone."

At last, Judy presented her point. "Springer's, Sommer's, and Carpet King all have men only as salespeople. I think we're missing out on business with customers who want decorating assistance. I think we need a couple of good women salespeople."

I disagreed—but not strongly. "Could I think about that and let you know?"

"Absolutely, let me know what you come up with. I just hate to see us lose business. It would be a good thing to beat the others to the same strategy."

"Anything else?" I asked.

Judy opened a folder in front of her. She handed me a copy of the contract.

"Jake, is there any point on this contract you don't understand or you don't agree with?"

I started to respond, but then I realized where she was heading.

"You're ticked because I bought the Lincoln."

Judy turned up the heat. "Gee, Jake, I don't think you can say I'm 'ticked' because you bought the Lincoln. My personal reaction has nothing to do with it. The point here is that the contract says we need joint approval on any purchase over one thousand dollars involving capital expenditures beyond our normal business needs. That's plain. So, what made you breech the contract? Why didn't you call me?"

I thought briefly about protesting, then just stopped. Once again, she had the upper hand.

"You are totally right. Fact is, I forgot about the contract. I bought it because I thought we were doing well. And frankly, I deserved it. But I'm embarrassed now. What do you want me to do to make it right?"

Judy didn't answer my question directly. Instead she probed further. "I'm wondering how you planned on classifying the expenditure on our income statement. Do I assume correctly you purchased the vehicle instead of leasing?"

I felt trapped and couldn't look her in the eye. "Fact is, I never thought about it."

Judy folded her hands. "As you know, if you planned on a direct write-off, one-third of the money spent on the Lincoln would have come directly out of my next quarter's check. But then again, you also know you can't write a car off as a first-year expense, right?"

I nodded, then added, "I think it's five years write-off now, but I'm not sure."

Judy shook her head. "We won't be able to deduct the full amount because a Lincoln Continental is listed as a luxury vehicle for tax purposes."

I got up and walked behind my desk, suddenly thankful I hadn't also bought the Stressless Desk Chair. Judy had her hand on the money faucet. I leaned against the wall.

"I am sorry. Again, just tell me what you want me to do."

"Apology accepted. Keep the Lincoln. Be accurate with expensing the beast. Get somebody to do a better job of cleaning this place. And here's the most important: hire two women who can sell!"

"I will get on it this week. Anything else?"

Judy now was standing with her arms folded. "Yes. You and the employees should reserve the parking spots near the front door for our customers, don't you think? I think it's one small way of showing how important they are."

As we were leaving my office, I noticed Gary setting up a display of new samples. As we approached, Gary put some new plush samples down on the floor and looked at me, waiting for an introduction. He was wearing a black sweater that now had yarn of every color clinging to it.

"Judy, let me introduce you to Gary, our top salesman this month. Gary, meet Judy, my business partner."

Gary knew who Judy was. He played it straight, so to speak, which I appreciated.

"It's my pleasure, Judy. I love working here with my boss."

Judy smiled, liking Gary at once. "Let me ask you, Gary—do you think it's a good idea to hire a couple of women for our sales staff?"

I nearly fell over when Gary didn't even hesitate. "I think it's the way of the future. I lost a nice job to Avalon's because a customer assumed a saleswoman there knew more about design than me. Personally, I think I knew just as much as she did. But it's nearly impossible to overcome stupid gender stereotypes."

Judy started giggling, then broke into a full-fledged laugh. With that, she gave me a brief hug, smiled at a somewhat confused Gary, and walked briskly out of the store.

I went back into my office and closed the door again. I needed to ruminate.

I tried to remember a time in my life when I felt as overmatched. I kept going back to the same thought: What was I thinking when I bought the Lincoln Continental? Had I become so obsessed with looking successful that I willingly made a business move that was greedy and bad at the same time?

What about my poor analysis of the marketplace? How shortsighted.

And salespeople. Even before Judy mentioned it, I had been thinking about one specific woman. She had never sold carpet, but she did have a strong—if unusual—sales background. I decided to get on this right away.

I wondered if Anna knew about my stupidity. Shit.

19

A FEW DAYS LATER, I RETURNED TO the Metropole bar. It took me a bit, but I finally convinced Ryan I was looking for Crystal—not to have sex but to offer her a job.

I slid him a hundred-dollar bill and whispered, "All you have to do is tell me which travel agency she works for."

He pondered long enough to read the "100," then said simply, "Southdale."

Early the next morning, I drove to Southdale Mall, parked near the door closest to the travel agency, and waited. Sure enough, I saw Crystal walk confidently toward the entrance. She wore a heavy coat. I felt cheated.

If you handle this right, Jake, you'll be seeing a lot more of her, I told myself.

Back at my office, I called the agency with a made-up story.

"Someone recommended I work with a blond woman in her thirties who's an agent there," I said. "But I didn't get her name."

The receptionist responded crisply, "You want Marina."

I thought, *How right you are.*

The first part of my plan was set. Part two needed a go-ahead from Judy. If I knew my business partner well enough, she would be totally happy to go along with my idea. I could finesse it over the phone. I dialed her number with confidence.

When she didn't answer, however, my confidence dissipated. Now I had to leave a voicemail.

"Hello, Judy. I'm having trouble getting you on the line. I have some news about Gary, our top salesman you met while you were here. He recently got engaged. I was wondering if you'd agree to awarding him and his wife-to-be a Caribbean cruise to the island of their choice. Could you call me back and let me know if you're okay with this expenditure?"

As it turned out, Judy called back while I was away from my desk. Yet another voicemail. Thankfully, though, she was on board. "Let's set a cap of three thousand dollars," she said in the message. "If I don't hear more, I'll assume they're taking the trip and it cost three thousand dollars or less."

Okay, Jakester, I thought, *time for step three.*

Just before noon, Gary came in wearing his favorite coat and tie with a perfect smile to match. I gave him the signal we needed a private chat.

"Well, my good friend and great assistant manager," I began, "I am pleased to announce that you and Linda will be treated to an all-expense-paid trip to the lovely Caribbean island of your choice. Furthermore," I strung it out so we both could enjoy the moment, "Sommer's Carpet and Tile shall issue you a check for your dining expenses as well."

Gary usually knew what I was thinking, sometimes before I did. He put his hand on my shoulder and said quietly, "Jake, I just want to make sure I understand this. I don't want to see Linda get excited about this trip and then have to tell her later that I 'misunderstood' if there's a catch."

"Gary, there's no catch. I wouldn't do that to you. But I do have some specific instructions for you. First, go to any travel agent and check out their cruise packages. Get excited with your girl. After that, go to the travel agency in Southdale—first floor near the Dayton's entrance. Ask to work with Marina. If she isn't there at the time, make an appointment."

Gary smirked. "Looking for a saleslady, as Judy told you?"

"I'll have you know," I replied, once again acting hurt, "I was thinking about hiring women for sales even before Judy mentioned it. After all, who can relate best to women shoppers? Research shows over eighty-five percent of all carpet purchases are influenced more by the female rather than male shopper."

Gary's smirk grew.

"When you meet Marina, just don't mention my name," I added.

Gary was dependable, and he understood my plan. About a week later, we went out for cocktails so he could share his findings.

Gary took a sip of his Southern Comfort on the rocks. "Jake, even if you do have ulterior motives"—he winked—"you've been good to me. I truly do appreciate this trip. Linda and I are going to Paradise Island. She's so excited, she wet her pants."

I grinned. "That's great—I mean, the first part, not the part about wetting her pants."

Gary got right to it. "Do I think Marina could sell carpet? Absolutely. I don't know if you've met her, but she is *H-O-T*. Not sure of her age. Maybe late thirties. But she's taken good care of herself."

On to step four.

I sipped my scotch. "I need you to get her contact information."

Gary reached in his pocket. "You mean like this?" He handed me her card.

"Well done!" I said. "Next, give her a call. Tell her you told your boss about her, how great of a salesperson she is. Tell her your boss wants her to come in for an interview as soon as she can. Be prepared for her to ask how much we'll pay. Then just say, 'What would we have to pay?'"

It took Gary only two days to get Marina interested in accepting our offer. We set up an interview for later that week.

She may not even remember me, I thought. That would be good.

Marina wasn't the only woman I had in mind for sales. My other target was Rita Borgen at Avalon's Design. According to Judy and Gary, this was the woman who had taken several customers from us.

Recruiting her proved to be simple. I stopped by Avalon with my secretary, Sharon, posing as my wife. When a guy walks alone into a carpet store, it's like when a woman walks alone into a car dealership. In both cases, there's a strong chance of being ignored because the salespeople don't think you're serious. This is flawed thinking, admittedly. But I've seen it happen over and over—even in my store. Bringing Sharon along would hopefully mean we'd get Rita's attention.

Rita looked to be in her late thirties. She presented herself well. Tall women often slouch, but Rita stood tall at about five-nine and exhibited perfect posture. She just looked confident.

Keen on our undercover ploy, Sharon asked Rita, "Will you match prices if we find lower prices at Sommer's?"

Rita smiled. "Actually, they sometimes match *our* prices. We don't have to match theirs. We're lower."

"Are your installers trained and guaranteed? How do they compare to Springer's?" I asked.

"We take a lot of pride in our guys," Rita said confidently. "I'll tell you what, though: if you don't buy from us, you would get a better installation from Sommer's than from Springer's. Their installers are more like ours."

I knew right then. I glanced around the showroom. We were the only customers.

"Look, I'll level with you Rita. I'm the owner of Sommer's Carpet. I'm here to convince you to come work for us."

Sharon gave Rita a smile, then graciously stepped away so just the two of us could talk.

"What did you make here last year?" I asked.

Rita looked skeptical. "It's not about what I made last year. I was new then. But this year, if my trending continues, I will hit thirty-five thousand dollars."

I loved her transparency. "How about I guarantee you fifty thousand dollars?"

She opened her mouth as if to counteroffer, but then she said simply, "I could never make that here. Maybe it's a good time to make a change. When do you want me to start?"

"How about Monday?" I extended my hand to shake. "Rita, I hope this will be the best decision you've ever made. I know it can be. I'll be there to help you in any way I can. See you Monday!"

The next evening, Marina was due for her interview. A few minutes before she arrived, my phone rang. I didn't pick up. Soon the light blinked, meaning the caller had left a message.

As Gary escorted Marina into my office, I didn't dare to look at her too closely. If she recognized me, she didn't show it. That was good.

On the other hand, how could she not remember getting $300 from me that night?

Gary introduced us, then excused himself, just as the script called for. As I studied her resume, I looked up briefly and caught Marina looking at my football on the shelf. I remembered vaguely Ryan's comment in front of Crystal—um, Marina—at the bar: "Here's a drink on me for our football hero."

I changed courses. "I want to be honest with you, Marina. We already know you have what it takes to be our star salesperson. You came here knowing what our offer is, and I'm prepared to hire you right now if you want this job."

She glanced over her shoulder to make sure Gary had closed the door behind us. Then she eyed me suspiciously.

"You want to be *honest* with me? Let's be real, *Jake*." The emphasis on my name was clear. "You have been totally dishonest with me—sending your employee to do your dirty work while keeping yourself secret. What's your game? I need to know because I can't afford it. Please don't tell me this is all about having sex with me. What are you going to do, tell my travel agency about my former profession if I don't take this job and do what I'm told? What the hell?"

I thought I had the whole ploy figured out, but suddenly I felt cheap and stupid.

"Marina, there's no game. I promise. But I realize now I went about this all wrong. I'm sorry. I guess I just hoped you wouldn't remember me."

Marina shifted her position in the chair. She knew she now had the drop on me.

"I remember you because it was unusual for a young guy to have three hundred dollars. I know that was only a few months ago. But as far as I'm concerned, it was a lifetime ago. That part of my life needs to never be spoken about."

She stared me down. This was Marina, not Crystal. And if I thought Crystal was perfect for this job, Marina was even better.

"Absolutely," I said quickly. "I understand."

She nodded and settled herself a bit. "So, tell me exactly what my work here would entail."

I leaned back. "Have you ever bought carpeting for your home?"

"Yes, but it was just some cheap stuff. I like the high-quality rugs—it's just that I can't afford to buy the good stuff. Yet."

"The most important thing to remember about carpet," I assured her, "is that this is a long-term purchase. The customer needs to know you care and want them to make the right choice."

Marina took a deep breath. "Jake, I know I'd be good at this, and I like the money—especially the bonus possibilities. But once again, I need to make sure you're not expecting anything else from me aside from selling carpet. Can I trust my life with you?"

"Okay, I have to be honest—you will be called on to do more than sell carpet."

"Like what?" Marina said, unsmiling.

I had her this time. "I expect you to sell tile as well."

Marina threw her head back and laughed. "Well, then, there's a lot to learn. I accept if you accept."

I stood up, as did Marina. "Well, then, how about Monday for a start date?"

Marina smiled. "I'm looking forward to being your top salesperson. See you then."

I walked her to the door. As she got into her white older-model Chevy, I made a promise to myself: *I will do everything I can to make this the best decision of her life.*

20

AFTER MARINA LEFT, I CHECKED THE VOICEMAIL that came in right before the interview. It was Mom, filling me in on Mike.

Mom would leave me voicemails about Mike nearly every day for the coming months.

Mom and Dad fought for Mike's rights for better treatment. Medical bills began to pile up as they drove Mike to Duluth almost daily for physical therapy. But Mom and Dad had no other choice. The government still hadn't authorized treatment at the VA hospital. I shuddered to think what shape Mike would have been in if Mom and Dad hadn't taken his care into their own hands.

In what could have been a bad joke, Mike was ordered to report back to Leonard Wood for advanced infantry training just ten weeks after the injury. Apparently, the platoon leader hadn't been informed about the accident. "Are you fucking with me?" was the platoon leader's response when Mike explained why he couldn't don a heavy backpack and do the long march exercise.

Mike and five others who had been injured in the accident were eventually assigned to "light duty" in the training rehabilitation platoon. Essentially, this resembled a labor camp made up of four platoons labeled "Criminals," "Medical," "Disciplinary Problems," and "Undecided." This last platoon consisted of guys who, for whatever reason, just didn't fit into the other categories.

Despite Mike's obvious physical issues from the accident, he was placed in the "Undecided" platoon rather than the "Medical" platoon. It literally added insult to injury, and his attitude became unpredictable. Then Mike's problems compounded one night at the bar right off the base when he overheard somebody refer to the "Undecideds" as "Retard-Os." Bad memories of being called names at Mesabi came to his forefront. He hit the guy, who went down in a thud. Fortunately, this little fight remained unknown to the sergeant.

Before long, it became clear that Mike's injuries were severe enough to make him unfit for service. It took several weeks for the army to process him out. Mom and Dad once again had to fight—this time to ensure an honorable discharge.

Mike returned to Mesabi to a very quiet homecoming. He found himself back at square one as far as his future. He would fight severe headaches, neck pain, and depression instead of the Vietcong.

Although I knew it was silly, I suddenly thought about Officer Kelly, Roger's friend from Blaine who tried to scare Mike straight after the Nazar incident. Mike believed the only thing that saved him from jail was enlisting. Now that Mike was discharged, I knew Kelly would never follow up. But if he did, he'd probably take one look at the poor kid and realize he'd been punished enough already.

Sadly, the system had once again cheated Mike. After his medical discharge, the US Army would do only what it was forced to do. The flow of bills and the frequent and frustrating correspondence with the government added to the tension at home. While Mom had more skills and patience than Dad to deal with bureaucracy, she gave him the bills and the letters anyway. It was as if to say, "How do you feel about the army now, Roy?"

The one silver lining, though, was that Dad's guilt pushed him to create a closer bond with Mike. He harbored regrets for the times he hadn't stood at Mike's side while he was growing up. Now, Dad and Mike were best friends. They spent a lot of time playing pool, fishing, going to movies—making up for lost time. Dad wanted to prove Mike owned "normal" intelligence and more common sense than most.

Dad's ironworkers union provided help with the medical matters. With the union's help, Mom and Dad could get Mike into a more ambitious program of physical therapy in Duluth. After two days of testing, the head doctor said, "There's much to be done, but all of us recognize Mike's determination. My opinion is he can be much better within three months."

Dad's union also sponsored Mike in an apprenticeship while he earned his GED. Mike's progress became a source of family pride. If anything, the accident had shown the world Mike's ability to overcome obstacles.

Of all the reports Mom gave me about Mike, the one that rocked me the most was that Margie and Mike were seeing each other nearly every day.

It was DeeDee who called Margie and invited her over to see Mike. Margie's visits became the highlight of Mike's day. As Margie began to show her pregnancy, Mom and Dad began to wonder what Margie might be thinking in regards to Mike. They could see he was becoming too attached to Margie. But they also saw how she was giving him a reason to get better. She was helping him heal.

He was helping her heal as well. Considering what Margie went through with Frank and, honestly, even me, I realize Mike was the first man who cared about her but asked nothing in return. After all her visits to tend to him, he started visiting her as her due date grew nearer and nearer.

I was at my desk, going over the June month-end numbers, when Mom called me. Mike had just finished his final session of therapy.

"He really impressed his therapists," she told me. "He's now walking with almost no limp."

"That's great, Mom."

There was a silence on the other end of the line. Some might call it a pregnant pause, which would be fitting.

"Margie came to Mike's session today to help him celebrate."

Another pause.

"Jake, I will never forget how Margie supported Mike after he came home from the army fiasco. She came over nearly every day, helping him with his exercises. And Margie is due any day now, so Mike has returned the favor. He's visiting her and—"

"Yes, Mom," I interrupted. "You've said this before."

I could tell she was just stalling. She was dancing around something.

"Well, I'm worried he's deeply in love with her."

Visions of a crazy, mixed-up family came to my mind. People having to say, "Oh, Mike is married to Margie, but that's Jake's baby. Or maybe Frank Nazar's. No one knows." I felt sick.

"Mom, you don't think they're romantically involved, do you?"

Her response came too quickly. "How would I know, Jake? They're nineteen, you know."

Again, I sensed she was avoiding the real point. Finally, she took a breath.

"Today, they were waiting on the bench outside the hospital as I went to get the car. When I drove up, I saw them kiss."

I didn't know how I should feel. All I knew is that I wanted to end the conversation.

"Mom, after all the progress Mike is making, I'm afraid he could get hurt." Abruptly, I added, "I need to go, Mom. Love you."

I wasn't sure why this latest news about Mike and Margie caused me to recoil. Something inside me said, *I may still want her back.* I doubted the day would ever arrive when I didn't still lust over my first love—if I could call her that. But then my mind went back to the screwed-up family we would be: "This is Margie, Jake's wife. She and Mike were involved too. And we still don't know whose baby this is. The real father may be in jail. Might not even be a Horton."

I sat there staring into space until my phone rang again. It was Roger reminding me about the graduation get-together for Colleen's sister, Susan.

"Jake, the party is on Saturday. It's at their parents' home in Apple Valley. Come by and have a beer or two with me. I need somebody sane to talk to among all those Sundquists. What do you say?"

This turned out to be a classic example of my flawed inner decision-making process.

I first noticed this flaw when I took over Sommer's Carpet. I pretended to be thoughtful and analytical, when in fact, I made quick, intuitive decisions that often defied logic. Yet I had to sound reasonable and sensible as the owner of a company, especially if I expected others to follow me. Thus, I pretended I had weighed all the pros and cons and advice and input.

In these moments, I thought my dad might appear with the "Bullshit Meter" under one arm. Gary, especially, could see right through the sham. He would challenge, "Why are you even asking me about this when your mind is already made-up?" The only person I deluded was yours truly.

I also used this same flawed process to fool myself when it came to decision-making in my personal life. I sat there, pretending to contemplate Roger's offer to attend Susan's party.

I said to myself, *Jake, you shouldn't go. Your relationship with Margie is too complicated—there's a baby on the way.* I also told myself, *Susan herself just emerged from a broken relationship.* And then I said to myself, *Jake, Susan graduated with some kind of theological degree—what would she think of someone like you?* And more yet, *Jake, you already have questions about Roger and Colleen. First they're getting involved with Margie. Now they're practically pushing you off on Susan.*

All these points should have clearly made me decide to pass on this gathering, where I would feel out of place, anyway.

Yet I had already made up my mind.

"I'll be there," I told Roger. "I'm looking forward to it."

I wanted to know what Susan looked like.

Embarrassingly, it came down to that.

21

AS I PULLED UP TO THE SUNDQUISTS' BEAUTIFUL SUBURBAN home on a very sunny afternoon, I thought of the old saying, "You can't please everyone, so you might as well please yourself." I took a deep breath, gathered the bouquet and candy I brought, and joined Susan's graduation party.

I had never been so happy to see Roger. There, on the front lawn, he introduced me to Colleen's two uncles plus two guys from the neighborhood. One of her uncles raved about my Lincoln. I could tell he was sizing me up.

It took about two minutes before the other uncle asked, "Jake, what do you do for a living?"

With a little false modesty, I said, "I sell carpet and tile."

Roger jumped in. "Jake, give yourself due credit." He put his arm over my shoulder. "Jake is the owner of Sommer's Carpet. Coll and I just purchased two rooms of carpet from him, and his installers did a wonderful job. By the way, Jake, Gary is an excellent salesman. He really took care of us."

With that, I was unofficially invited into the fraternity out there on the lawn. Roger opened a can of Heineken for me. I sat down and settled in, feeling comfortable. One of the uncles was hilarious. He also was a little drunk.

The first sign of female life was the funny uncle's wife, Rachel. She came out to see what the guys were doing. Roger introduced us. She asked me a couple of questions, then fulfilled her mission by moving her husband out of the group and suggesting that perhaps a coffee would be a smart replacement for the beer in his hand.

Whether in Mesabi or Apple Valley, the same thing always happens when a man receives that suggestion from his wife while in earshot of other men. The uncle guzzled what was left in the can and opened another.

Just then, another neighbor stopped by. He possessed one of those contagious laughs. His loud and deep voice and his ability to find most anything funny provided the perfect background for Mr. Drunk Uncle's questionable comments.

Sporting fresh cans of cold beer, Roger and I walked toward the house together.

"Say, Coll will want to say hello, and you can congratulate Susie."

Roger led me to the kitchen and introduced me to all the women. I noticed most were drinking wine. He turned to MaryAnn, his mother-in-law, who looked a little frazzled as she tossed salad in a huge bowl.

"Hey, where are Coll and Suzie?" he asked.

"I think they're hiding out downstairs. Why don't you go tell them to come back up and be a little more social—and maybe give their old mom some help," she said with just a little attitude. "Glad you could make it, Jake," she added. "You're a darn good-looking young man."

I smiled. "Very happy to be here. Where should I put these flowers?"

"What a sweet guy. Good-looking and sweet. Yes, where is Susan?" she said a little too loudly.

Aunt Rachel, having failed at cutting off her husband from his beer, succeeded in making me more comfortable by taking the flowers and finding a vase.

Roger gave me a quick head motion, and we headed downstairs to the family room. The room was decorated in the "barnwood" look—very rustic, very warm, but a bit dark. They could have used one of our nice tartan-plaid plush carpets to liven up the room. The furniture was comfortable and oversized but too large for the room. *Listen to me, Mr. Interior Decorator.*

At the far end of the room, I spotted Colleen. She was having an animated conversation with the young lady next to her, presumably Susan. They were seated on rustic wooden bar stools with John Deere tractor seats. Cocktails accompanied the sisters.

They were enjoying a good laugh when Colleen noticed us—or at least noticed me. While swinging around on her stool, she smiled radiantly and outstretched her arms to me.

"Jake, it's so incredibly great to see you. Give me a hug."

Colleen wasn't drunk, but I guessed she had enjoyed more than just the one "Tommy" in front of her. I felt a little awkward for a moment—I thought she was going to kiss me on the lips.

Roger had disappeared to the bathroom, so I turned to Susan to introduce myself. She was already eyeing me with a mixed expression after watching Colleen hug me. She sat at the corner stool with her legs crossed and her hands in her lap. I noticed her outfit looked kind of Western, with brown boots, a gaucho skirt, and a soft cashmere-looking cream sweater.

I extended my hand to her. She put both of her hands on mine.

"Thank you for coming, Jake," she said a little nervously. "I've heard many good things about you."

Roger was back, and he took his place behind the bar. "Susie will be Pastor Susie someday—she just doesn't realize it yet."

They bantered for a bit, giving everyone a chance to get more comfortable.

Yes, indeed, Susan was pretty. Very pretty. Her hair was a sandy color, and she tied it back in a sort of ponytail, exposing both ears. She wore a pair of tiny emerald earrings to match her green eyes. At first I thought her freckles appeared a little dark, but they only looked that way because of her light skin. She hadn't gotten up from her stool, but I liked the rest of the package, based on what I had noticed so far.

When I noticed Susan's perky little nose, my mind drifted back for just a moment to Leo and Fern's daughter Cynthia. I quickly pulled my mind back. That story didn't end well in my self-critical mind.

For two sisters, they had very different looks. While Colleen liked to wear makeup and looked good with it, Susan wore none and didn't need it.

But they both looked pretty darn good.

My eyes moved back to Susan's ears. The weird thing was that I had never noticed a woman's ears before, yet I had this urge to give the ear closest to me a little nibble.

That's enough beer, Jake, I thought to myself.

Both the clock and the alcohol did their work. Between eight and nine o'clock, the crowd thinned and cleanup activities commenced. Colleen and Susan's father, Albert, held court reminiscing how he and MaryAnn had become a couple. While Al tended to brag a little, I couldn't help but like him.

I also couldn't help but compare him to my dad, who was far more likely to put my mother down with his sarcastic humor rather than express kindness. I always held the feeling Dad stored his affection in some secret compartment of his brain, saving it for who knows what.

Al was rubbing MaryAnn's back as I opened my final-final beer. He was getting a little playful with her. Up until that point, I hadn't noticed that even MaryAnn looked good for her age.

Susan got up from her stool and leaned on the bar. I wandered back over to the bar, pretending I wanted to visit with Roger. But I found myself near Susan's empty stool.

"Are you going to sit here?" I asked.

She shook her head. "I need to stand and stretch."

As I sat down, Roger grinned. "Suze, I think Jake was inviting you to sit on his lap."

Looking slightly embarrassed but smiling, she pointed her finger at Roger. "These stools wouldn't take that kind of weight."

I seized the opportunity. "I bet they would. Here—jump up."

Both Susan and I knew instinctively that her reaction at this moment would determine whether we were interested in a relationship. I cursed myself for being prematurely forward.

To my relief, though, Susan turned around with her back to me. I lowered my legs, and she hopped on my lap. The stool swayed slightly, and she grabbed my arm for balance. I leaned comfortably against the bar, and she giggled as she relaxed next to me.

I caught the expression on MaryAnn's face: a little surprised, a little pleased, a little too much wine. Perhaps fifteen minutes later, the attention had moved elsewhere.

"Seriously," Susan whispered, "I know this can't be comfortable for you. I'll get off."

With that, she slid off my lap, taking my hand when she stood up.

"It's still nice outside and it's so hot in here. Do you feel like taking a little walk?"

Before I could answer, Colleen piped up. "Can we come? A little walk would feel great."

Roger, thinking on his feet, got Colleen's attention. "Why don't we go a little later? Your dad wanted to talk with us about something upstairs."

Colleen led the way up the stairs. Roger couldn't resist pinching her from behind. She laughed as she admonished her husband for being fresh.

I hadn't walked hand in hand with a girl for a long time. The last time would have been the night of the stupid Herman's Hermits concert.

My mind turned to that evil evening. *Margie, how could you do that to me?* But then I shook my head and thought, *How could I be such an asshole?*

As if by some script, we arrived at a playground. Susan let go of my hand and walked to a swing.

"I came here often when I was a kid. Sometimes my dad would come over and push me on the swing."

I sat on the swing next to her.

She paused, then surprised me by asking, "Do you feel sorry for my dad, being married to my mom?"

It kept the moment from becoming the moment I wanted, but I went with it.

"Honestly, Susan, I don't know what you mean."

"Doesn't it bother you, the way she talks to him, the way she treats him like he's stupid?"

I searched my memory of the day. I kept thinking about how he had touched her affectionately and how she had liked it.

"I must be clueless. You of course know more than I do. But I didn't hear or see anything like that today. Actually, I noticed your dad got a little playful with your mom. If anything, they seem far more in love than *my* parents."

Susan slid off the swing and stood in front of me as my swing came to a stop.

"Jake, do you think men and women just get bored with each other after a while?"

She remained standing in front of me. She slipped her hands down around my neck. Her gaze looked down a little at me. I remember thinking, *She's going to kiss me. She's going to kiss me.*

I smiled. "You mean like Roger and Colleen?"

"Good point. Maybe there is hope."

She took my head and pulled me close to her soft sweater, which couldn't have felt more amazing. She kissed the top of my head. She held me close in that awkward but wonderful way. Then she stepped back so I could stand up too. We kissed for a few minutes.

As we headed back, I tried to come up with some excuse to take her some-where—anywhere—or for me to stay longer. I just didn't want to lose what we had started.

"Do you think your parents are still awake?" I asked. "I should thank them for everything."

Susan looked toward the house. "I'll let them know you said that. Jacob, it's been a fun day, a special day. I'm so glad you came."

I was being dismissed. Still, I asked, "Can I call you?"

She kissed me softly and whispered, "You damn well better!"

I started my car and drove away slowly. This was a special woman. A little like Colleen, yes. But kind of a mystery.

22

I T'S FUNNY HOW LIFE WORKS SOMETIMES—the way seemingly random events change everything. A few days after Susan's party, Blaze Hart, my quarterback friend from Mountain Iron High School and the U of M, dropped by the store to say hello. It turned out to be serendipitous timing.

Blaze and I had stayed in touch over the years. While I will never forget what he did for me that beautiful fall day when the Gophers beat Michigan, I could never tell what his agenda was each time I saw him. This day was an exception, though.

He point-blank asked, "So, Jake, where you hiding your Mesabi woman?"

No way would I tell him everything, so I kept it simple. "Blaze, you mean Margie? Why do you ask?"

He looked embarrassed and mumbled, "It's just that I haven't seen her for a long time. I was wondering if you and she broke up."

I don't know why I lied, but I said, "I really don't want to talk about it, but she's going with my brother now."

We exchanged some banal chatter for a few minutes and then he left.

Blaze's visit took just long enough for me to miss two calls. I checked my messages.

"Hello? Hello? Hello? Jake, are you there?"

No matter how many times Mike left me a message, he sounded confused every time.

"Jake, I'm at the hospital and calling long distance. Margie just had her baby. It's a boy. Everybody says he's beautiful and looks just like—"

I gasped before Mike added, "Like Margie."

Mike hurried a final thought: "I hope you can come and see him. And oh, this is your brother, Mike."

I listened to my next message. Not surprisingly, it was my mother. She and DeeDee had just returned from the hospital.

"We just saw the most beautiful grandson anybody has ever seen. Margie is good. When DeeDee and I left, your father was still there, trying to make the little guy smile. DeeDee was so happy she got to see the baby before she leaves tomorrow for Anna's. She'll be staying there a week, you know. Are you coming to see the baby soon?"

Thankful sometimes for small things, I felt relieved Blaze had stopped in. If he hadn't, I would have taken those calls and been put on the spot. This way, I had a chance to think this over before I talked to Mom or anyone.

My mind felt like a mug, and somebody kept pouring beer into it until it overflowed down the sides of the glass. I needed to take a deep drink to regain control.

No good could come from procrastination. I needed to head north tomorrow. But I had just made dinner plans with Susan for tomorrow night. I'd have to reschedule.

I dialed, and her mother picked up. I visited with MaryAnn for a couple of minutes, then she turned the phone over to Susan.

"Hello, Jake. It's good to hear from you. How are you doing?"

I decided to just be upfront with her. "Well, I'm a little overwhelmed, actually. I have some personal matters to address. I have to drive up to Mesabi tomorrow, and I'll head back late. I know we had plans. I'm sorry. I still would really love to take you to dinner. Are you available on Sunday night instead?"

It seemed like 30 seconds before she spoke, though I'm sure it wasn't. "Sunday works. May I ask what kind of personal business you have up north?"

There was something in her tone. Her tone wasn't accusing or suspicious. But it wasn't merely curious either.

I sighed. There was no use keeping secrets. I had to tell her—whatever the consequences. I genuinely liked her, and when all of this came down, I hoped Susan would still like me. I hoped our relationship could continue.

"I can fill you in about this whole mess on Sunday night if you really want to know. But it's not a phone conversation."

Then she surprised me—and I think surprised herself. "Or I could ride up north with you tomorrow to keep you company, and you could tell me then. You could drop me off at Roger and Colleen's while you do what you need to do."

I didn't really think it through either. I just said, "Well, sure. That sounds good to me, if you're up for it. How about I pick you up at eight tomorrow morning?"

"I'll be ready. Good night, Jake."

I pictured that no-need-for-makeup face. "See you then."

When I hung up, the mixed feelings rushed in. On the one hand, I liked the idea of having company on this particular trip. And it was a good time as any to come clean. I figured sooner or later, it would come out anyway.

But on the other hand, the situation could be volatile. Lots of emotion. It seemed unfair to even include Susan in this mess. Then again, she asked to come.

As I turned my pillow for the umpteenth time, I smiled to myself. *I can't wait to see Roger and Colleen's reaction tomorrow when they discover Susan had come along with me.*

The next morning, I pulled up to the Sundquist house a few minutes early. I opened my door slowly, and Susan exited with a quick wave to her dad. I wasn't sure whether I should hug her, but then she came and put her arms around me.

"Thank you for letting me come. I'll try not to get involved. I'm going to be there as your friend, Jake."

I almost cried. I just needed somebody to show me I could still be redeemed. As I got back in the car, I stopped and looked at this beautiful woman.

"You can't imagine how good that makes me feel. Thank you."

She smiled, I put the car in drive, and we headed north to another world.

Mainly, we talked about our families and what it was like growing up. She surprised me by telling me she felt hopelessly awkward whenever Roger and Colleen had prodded her to go out with me during her visits to Mesabi as a teenager. I told her I had felt the same way whenever they prodded me about meeting her. She literally threw her head back and laughed when I told her I always assumed she was out of my league.

When she stopped laughing, I added, "I still do . . . I still think you're out of my league."

With that, she put her hand on mine and rested her head on my shoulder. I think we both were thankful for the quiet.

Really, I didn't know if I wanted to involve her with the nasty details of my current mess. I got the sense she didn't really know if she wanted to know more. It seemed Susan wanted to like me, and she hoped whatever may unfold wouldn't change that.

But then when we pulled up to Colleen and Roger's, she grabbed my arm before I could get out to open her door.

"Jake, wait. I have to be honest with you . . ."

I froze, unsure of what she would say next.

"Colleen told me about your former girlfriend and the baby." She put her hand over her face to cover her embarrassment. "It all came out in a stupid argument—about you, actually. She told me she was 'surprised' that I sat on your lap the night of the party. I then said to her, 'Well, that was quite an embrace you gave him. I had to do something to remind everyone which one of us is married and which isn't.'"

Shock and anger were mixed with curiosity about Colleen and Susan going toe to toe over me. Before I could open my mouth, Susan quickly continued.

"Colleen was so miffed, she let it all out. She put her hand on my shoulder and said, 'I'm sorry to tell you this, but an eighteen-year-old in Virginia is having a baby any day now, and there's a strong chance it's Jake's.' She told me all about Margie and the other boyfriend who was raping her. She said Margie told you the other guy is the father but that she can't really know."

I felt my hand clench the steering wheel. No wonder Susan had been so interested in coming today and hearing about my "personal business." But then I quickly realized Susan wasn't to blame here. That honor went to Colleen. I felt as though I had been shot in the back.

"I'll admit the news surprised me at first," Susan said, casting me a sideways glance. "But I want you to know I'm not angry with you at all. It's not like you've been deceitful by not mentioning this. You and I just met. And it's not like we're dating or anything. If Colleen hadn't told me, I know you would have, if and when the time was right."

I let out a long sigh and relaxed my hands from the wheel. I looked into Susan's eyes. Even though she already knew the sordid details, Susan still chose to drive up with me, to support me when I needed it the most.

"Well," I said, "maybe it was better this way. I honestly don't know when the 'right' time would have been to tell you about this whole mess."

"I hope you don't think I'm simple, Jake, but always remember that God can take a *mess* and make a *message* out of it."

With that, she kissed her hand, brought the kiss gently to my lips, then exited the car.

In a mental fog, I headed to the hospital. Thoughts of Susan flashed through my mind. Thoughts of Colleen. Of Margie and now the baby. I had to force myself to keep putting one foot in front of the other as I walked to the maternity ward.

When I stepped into Margie's room, everyone was crying. There was Margie's mother, Alice, and my mother sitting alongside the bed, tears streaming. Margie was propped up holding the child, crying as well. Roger was sitting next to Margie on the side of the bed, holding her hand, sobbing.

It was as if I had walked in from outer space. I had no clue why all three women, plus the parson, were weeping. Honestly, had I not seen the baby stir with my own eyes, I would have guessed he had passed away, bringing this heavy sadness to these people.

I didn't know what to do. "Should I come back later?" I asked.

Margie looked up at me and managed a smile through the tears. "Jake, come in. I have something to tell you."

I took a few tentative steps closer but kept my distance.

"Before you came in, I was just telling everyone that Mom and I have been talking for months about what I should do with my baby." Tears formed again in her eyes. "I don't think it's fair for me to keep him."

Roger's face conveyed an almost-overwhelming sadness as he squeezed her hand.

"Of course, I'll have regrets, but I want my baby to grow up in a home with a mom and dad. A mom and dad who love him and raise him to be a good person. Jake, I just now asked Pastor Lund if he and Colleen might consider adopting him. Colleen told me they haven't been able to have kids."

My own emotions and reaction didn't even register. Instead, I just looked at the faces of everyone there in the room.

I know Roger had heard Margie say these same words before I walked in. But now, hearing them a second time, he still couldn't help himself. I could tell he didn't even understand why he found himself sobbing.

"I'm sorry," he managed to say weakly. "It's just that I've never witnessed such love." He wiped his eyes.

As suspicions grew in the back of my mind, I realized I didn't care about his tears. I looked instead at the women.

Alice, given her faith, was crying with pride, yet I knew she also felt as though her grandson had been given away. I'm sure Mom felt some of the same, seeing as she was convinced I was the child's father. I hoped both women felt some relief in knowing the baby would be with a good family and, at least for now, live nearby.

Margie, well, I knew she was giving up nearly everything.

Roger was, fittingly, the first to flit as the group began to compose themselves.

"Let's give Jake and Margie some time, shall we?"

Mom moved a little quicker than Alice. She came and gave me a hug, then went back to hug Margie.

"I love you," she told her.

Finally, Alice walked toward me, and we exchanged one of those "I guess we need to hug" hugs. She seemed confused, as if she didn't understand what had just taken place.

As he made his way to the door, Roger offered his hand to me. I pretended not to see it.

"Mind if I close the door?" I asked Margie when everyone left.

"Sure. Whatever you wish."

She looked good despite the wet face. She looked older for some reason.

I felt no resentment whatsoever from her.

She looked so content holding the baby. I felt bad for her. I didn't have to pretend.

I sat down next to her in the chair where her mother had been sitting moments before. I started to speak, but she stopped me.

"Jake, you need to stop feeling guilty—or at least stop looking like you feel guilty. There's no reason for it. You never said you wanted to marry me. You certainly never said you wanted a baby. Yes, that's on both of us. Maybe, if there was no Frankie, we would have had a chance. I don't know. Maybe we never had a chance at all. You expect more in life than I do, and you'll get it. It's not that I'm stupid or was stupid. I was immature. When talking with Roger and Colleen, they've pointed out that maybe the difference in our ages meant more than I thought."

I bristled at hearing her mention the Lunds once again. It always seemed to come back to them. They always seemed to know all the answers.

As it turned out, Colleen obviously had the perfect answer for Margie all along. She probably had the answer the moment they met her.

I never knew they were unable to have kids. I never gave it a thought—I just assumed they didn't have kids because they were so young and carefree.

Margie noticed my reaction. "I heard you're angry at the Lunds. I don't know why." She looked at me carefully. "Jake, don't you agree it's my right to make the best decisions for my baby? Because if you do, and I think you do, I'm going to offer him to be adopted by Roger and Colleen. I need to know now, right now, if you have a problem with this."

How could she be so wise and so unselfish and so good?

"Margie, my problems with them aren't about the baby," I answered. "It's something between them and me."

Margie redirected the question. "Then you have no problem with the Lunds adopting the baby?"

Actually, I did, but it wasn't about their ability to be good parents. And again, that was something between me and them.

"I think it's a tough but good decision. But, Margie," I said gently. "Have you thought about how hard it'll be to watch him grow and not be his mother?"

Margie started to weep again. "What do you think? Of course I've thought about that. But I know I'll still be part of the child's life. That's the best deal for both my baby and me."

"But didn't you say you wanted to move far away from here?"

She nodded. "Yes, but I can still write and call, and I can visit. I know Roger and Colleen will do everything they can on their end too."

We both sat in silence. Then she handed the baby over to me. I could see the similarities to my own baby pictures.

"Jake, please meet Cyril Alex Kohler."

I have no idea why this name rubbed me the wrong way. But I said, "Your dad must be pleased."

"Mom too. Alex is the boy version of Alice."

She didn't even ask me about the name, I thought. *No trace of the Horton lineage. But I guess that's what she's been saying all along. And that's what I wanted. Or is it?*

I looked at Margie, at this girl-turned-woman and into those eyes. Was this the end for us? It seemed cheap and unfair. Unfair to Margie, I could now see.

My brain spoke to me: *Don't do it. Don't do it, Jake.*

Much to my own shock, I wanted to say, "Margie, let's give it a try. What do we have to lose? We're two different people now. And Frankie's never getting out of jail. Let me marry you and take responsibility for my child."

Don't do it Jake. Don't do it to her. She's resolved. She's at peace.

With that, my mind shifted. *This may be my baby,* I thought, *but I sure don't feel like it's my baby.* I didn't feel love for the child. Life would be simpler if he were given to some needy couple in California. I handed him back to Margie.

As she settled the baby in her arms, I asked her another question with some trepidation. "Could you tell me about you and my brother?"

Margie's expression told me what I expected. She answered slowly, "Mike has been so good to me, so caring. I know he loves me, but I've told him I can't love him the same way."

"Mom said you kissed."

Margie nodded. "It was his last appointment. We were waiting for your mom to pick us up, then Mike suddenly asked, 'Margie, can I kiss you?'"

Immediately, I imagined how Mike had to build the courage for several weeks to ask her that single, simple question.

"I took his hand and said, 'I'll kiss you if you want me to. But first, tell me what the kiss means to you. If it means we love each other as best friends, then I'm happy to kiss you—only this one time. But if it means you want to be lovers or husband and wife, then I won't kiss you. Because then I wouldn't be telling you the truth. And I would never do that to you.'"

Margie paused. "He said, 'I want to kiss you because I love you, even if you won't ever marry me. It makes me sad that this will be the only time. But okay.'"

With that, I pictured Mike slowly moving his face toward hers and Margie closing her eyes. I know they kissed each other fully realizing the kiss would be one of true love.

But only this once.

I sighed. "Let me see if I can help Mike through this," I said.

I kissed her cheek, and she put her arms around me and hugged me.

"Now stop looking guilty—I order you." She laughed.

As I reached the door, I looked back at her. She was smiling at the baby. Peace. She felt peace with her decision.

23

A COUPLE OF HOURS LATER, I STOPPED BY Roger and Colleen's house to pick up Susan. On top of my unreasonable anger toward the two of them, I felt frustrated because I hadn't been able to connect with Mike. I knocked, and Roger opened the door. He started to offer a handshake, but then pulled it back with a sad frown when he realized I once again would not accept it.

He led me into the kitchen, where Colleen and Susan sat at the table. Colleen began to stand, but Roger gestured for her to stay.

I didn't want to sit down. I wanted to just get the hell out of their house and get the hell out of this town.

"Susan," I said as calmly as I could, "can we get going, please?"

She looked at me with some sympathy. "Sure thing."

Colleen couldn't stop herself as Susan got up. "Jake, I'd like to know how you'll feel if Roger and I adopt Margie's baby."

In the back alleys of my mind, I still wondered whether Colleen had plotted from the start to get this baby, one she couldn't get on her own.

"Do you mean the baby who looks so much like me?"

Colleen pressed on. "I want you to know, this generous offer of Margie's came as a complete surprise to us. But how do you feel about us accepting it?"

I was beginning to feel fire in my chest. "Who cares what I think? Why don't you guys just go over to the hospital and tell Margie what to do?"

I turned my back, and Susan said a quick good-bye to the two of them. Roger followed us out the door.

"Jake, please. Colleen and I made mistakes in this whole situation—I agree and I apologize. But we're trying to do the right thing. Please, let's talk about this some more."

I didn't want to talk more, and I could tell I had an advocate in Susan. We got in the car.

We traveled in silence for quite a while. It didn't feel awkward. The events of the day seemed well beyond trite or even normal conversation.

Below the surface of the silence, however, I knew both of us were wondering about our future relationship. Susan had inadvertently boarded—or, as you could argue, been shoved onto—a train wreck. Me, I felt I had revealed to everyone who counted in my life that I was morally questionable at best, morally decrepit at worst.

"Susan, I need a favor," I finally said, breaking the silence. "I'm trying to sort out the day. I'm trying to make some sense of what's happening and how I should feel. Would you mind just telling me, given what you know, what your thoughts are?"

Susan moved just a little closer to me. Perhaps to hear better. But either way, the gesture made me feel she was not abandoning me.

"Well, for starters, you should know your mother stopped by the house while you were still at the hospital. I really like her. Colleen just introduced me as her younger sister, without mentioning why I happened to be there or that I had driven up with you. Maybe that was smart. It probably would've added another complication. Your mother was telling Colleen how she believes, with no reservations, you are the biological father. She might not have spoken about that if she knew about you and me.

"On the other hand, it was deceitful for Colleen to not be up front about me. Usually, these things come out. I mean, it sounds like you talk to your mom often. So someday you'll tell her about me being with you today. And then, naturally, your mother will wonder what our relationship might be and why Colleen didn't tell her."

She paused. "Say, are we going to stop somewhere for a bite to eat?"

I, again, was heartened by this small return to normalcy. "Sure, we can stop in Hinckley in about a half hour. Or if you can wait, we can go to a better place in less than two hours."

"Which do you prefer?"

I looked at her. "Your call."

She thought for a moment. "Let's wait and have a nice dinner—maybe a glass of wine. Now, where was I? Oh, you wanted my view of everything." She took a deep breath. "So, I'm only going to say what I've heard and what I know. I realize I'm missing important pieces."

"Understood," I assured her.

"So, the bottom line as I understand it: Margie wants Roger and Colleen to adopt the baby. From what I can sense and from what I know about pastoral ethics, Roger's in somewhat of a dilemma because, professionally, Colleen should not have been involved. The fact Colleen told Margie they couldn't have kids is troublesome, at the least."

Susan glanced out the window, then back at me.

"I know Colleen can be a bit much sometimes. As my mother likes to say, '*Father Knows Best* may be a popular show, but we have *Colleen Knows Best*.' And Roger once told her, 'Gosh, Colleen, it's too bad we're not swinging by the Middle East tonight so you could solve Egypt's and Israel's problems.'

"Yet I know my sister, and I believe her intentions are always good. Even in this case with Margie. No doubt, they—Coll especially, and Roger as well—want the baby. But I can see why this would be an uncomfortable development for you."

I didn't say anything. I didn't need to.

"On top of it all," Susan continued, "your mother also said Margie is moving away, and your brother, Mike, will be hurt and upset. He seems to have feelings for her." She caught her breath. "That's all I know. Correction—that's all I think I know."

Susan's synopsis was quite accurate and helpful. I needed to break the story down in pieces, then figure out each piece. That's what my business education taught me.

This, though, was far more complex than business. This drew from emotions—and emotions are subjective at best, notoriously detrimental to logical conclusions. In particular, women have deeper passions than men and therefore have deeper emotions. This means that if women are involved, the process will be more painful. Second, women and men will differ in how they view and report the issues.

I kept these last two thoughts to myself.

I knew Susan wanted to know more about my relationship with Margie—more than Colleen's version. I decided it couldn't hurt to tell the whole sad story, or at least most of it.

So, I started from the beginning: how we met at an armory dance and how we soon came to realize we were growing apart. I shared my recollection of the strange and painful evening Margie told me she was pregnant and that

Frank was the father. I told her about giving Margie the car keys that night because I was so angry.

I edited out Marina's role that evening. Happy for small favors, I felt relieved Roger never knew about her. Because if he did, it's hard to know who now wouldn't.

I finished up with my guilt for not supporting Margie more, but I tried my best to explain my actions.

Susan waited a few moments, soaking it all in. "Jake, you haven't said how you feel about Margie's choice with the baby."

People kept asking me that question, and they would keep asking it. I didn't have an answer. I didn't know how I felt.

When Margie handed me the baby, I didn't feel anything special. I didn't feel any bond. Margie and her baby represented an old part of me I hoped to shed. They both made me feel as if I had let them down, let my parents down as well.

"How do I feel about Margie's choice? I think your sister and Roger will be exceptional parents. I really do. I'm surprised Margie didn't choose to keep the baby, but it's her choice and likely the best for the child."

I hesitated, then let it all out. "Most importantly, I'm afraid that if I spend time with Roger and Colleen down the road"—I quickly but knowingly glanced at Susan—"it may be awkward. Seeing him grow up with them—I may feel like I've abandoned him. It'd be like a permanent reminder of my failures."

Susan tried to make me feel better. "Jake, you're acting honorable in a tough situation. Don't be so hard on yourself."

I drove us to Kozlak's in Shoreview, one of my favorite restaurants. We enjoyed a nice dinner with a glass of wine.

When I took out my wallet to pay, I noticed the note I made about calling Mike tonight. It'd be too late by the time I got home. I'd call in the morning.

Back on the road, we had a half-hour drive ahead of us to Apple Valley. Susan moved just a little closer to me.

"So, I've told you my tales of misery. Now how about telling me the 'Susan Sundquist Story'?"

She smiled. "Let's wait and do that when we have less time."

I smiled back. "Okay, how about just the chapter where you decided to be a minister?"

She looked straight forward. "That decision has never been made."

I didn't know if it was me, or if she didn't want to talk about herself, or if she was tired. I just let it go.

Her parents' house was dark. I shut the car off and started to open my door. Susan almost said something, then changed her mind. I opened her door and walked her to the house.

"Thank you, Jake, for taking me, and thank you for the nice dinner too. I'll buy next time." She kissed me, then kissed me again.

I wasn't sure where I stood with her. I knew the drama with the baby, Margie, and the Lunds wouldn't end anytime soon.

My phone rang at just past seven in the morning. It was cloudy so my bedroom was dark. I felt like staying in bed, but I forced myself to roll the other way and pick the phone up.

"Hey, Jake. This is Mike. I hope I didn't wake you up."

I was glad he called. "It's fine. Actually, I'm really sorry I didn't catch you when I was up north. I wanted to call you last night, but I was just too tired to think straight when I got home."

"I can't talk long," he said. "I'm meeting Dad today at work. We're doing structural steel for the new hotel. The union is allowing him to teach me because I'm an army veteran. And after work tonight, Mom and I are taking Dad to Duluth to meet up with some friends and celebrate Dad's birthday— the big five-five! It should be fun."

I forgot it was Dad's birthday. Shit.

I decided to lead the conversation. "Say, I've heard that you and Margie have become pretty close."

I gave Mike some time to get his thoughts together.

"I really like Margie," he replied, a bit defensive. "She has been really kind to me. Do you still like her, Jake?"

"I always liked Margie, and I still do," I answered cautiously. "She was a special part of my life. But I don't think we were meant to be married."

"Are you mad she's giving her baby to Pastor Lund and Colleen?"

"No, I'm not mad. They will be good parents for the baby."

I shifted the focus back to him.

"Mike, Margie is thinking of moving to a different part of the country. You might want to prepare yourself for that."

"I know she's going to move. I'd like to go with her. What do you think?"

"It doesn't matter what I think. It's between you and Margie. Have you talked to her about it?" I asked, already knowing what Margie would tell him.

"No, because I thought you might be mad at me if I did. She was your girl."

Why did I always feel like an asshole after talking to Mike?

"Well, Mike," I said gently but honestly, "I don't think it would work out for you to move with Margie. I know she's your friend, and you care about her very much. But she needs to start her own life now. Plus, would you really move away from Dad, Mom, and DeeDee?"

Mike didn't answer. Instead, he hurriedly said, "I'm going to be late if I don't get to the job right away. Bye."

Maybe, I was becoming paranoid, but Mike's tone made it sound like he was annoyed with me. Join the club.

24

I T WAS 4:00 A.M. WHEN THE PHONE RANG from the top of my night stand.
"This is Officer Fairchild, Duluth Police Department. Is this Jacob Horton?"

My mouth was dry. "Yes, it is."

The officer lowered his voice. "I'm sorry—I have some bad news. Your father, Roy Horton, died in a vehicular accident earlier this morning. He was alone in his vehicle. I have no further details. The accident remains under investigation."

My mind refused to accept this information. Honestly, as soon as I hung up, I started to believe I had imagined or dreamed the whole thing. I paced the room. I wondered if the call had been a terrible practical joke. I hoped it was.

Then the phone rang again at 5:00 a.m. I knew it would be my mom.

This was no joke.

She was crying. "Jake, did you get a call from the Duluth Police Department?"

Hearing the deep pain in her voice made me feel as if I were choking. I spoke in a raspy, broken sound, which didn't even sound like me.

"Mom, I can't believe it. I just talked to Mike yesterday—he said you guys were going to Duluth for Dad's birthday. What happened?"

"We got a hotel and went out to celebrate . . ." Her words fell apart.

"I can't believe it," I repeated. "Are you okay? Where are you? Are you still at the hotel?"

I could sense she was trying to reclaim her composure. "Yes. Mike is here too. You know, he was the last to see Dad. They stayed at the party after I came back to the hotel . . . Only fifty-five years old. Just yesterday." She sobbed. "Oh wait—the police are here. We need to talk to them. Dear God, it's terrible. I'll call you back."

I heard the click signaling the conversation was over, but not done. I sat at the edge of my bed, drowning in profound loss—and an unmistakable, ominous knowledge that there was much more to this story.

I wanted to call Mom back, but I didn't know which hotel they were at. All I could do was to wait for someone to call me again.

I rarely drank alone, but I did so now. I did it not for the emotional or escapist need. I poured it because I simply couldn't think of anything else to do. I turned the TV on, though I knew there was nothing to watch.

I wandered around, thinking of Dad. I tried to remember the good memories. I thought about the tenderness he seemed to reserve for DeeDee. I wanted to remember the good stuff. Yet my mind drifted to conversations that led me to doubt, frustration, and anger.

Dad and I loved each other, but we never quite got it right. Now we never would. I wanted one more chance to talk to him—to tell him again how I loved him and to have him tell me he loved me.

I poured more Southern Comfort and decided to stop pacing. I sat down at my kitchen table.

Focusing now on the good memories, I thought about my final football games both in high school and at the U. I thought about the pride Dad had shown in my accomplishments.

Then my mind switched to the trip to Denver and Mom's happiness in her "three men" spending time together. It was a trip for the ages, no doubt about that.

But then an old question popped up, the troubling question that had been nagging at me for a long time: What actually happened between Dad and Anna to cause Anna to leave Mesabi and move to Denver?

Anna would be coming for the funeral, I guessed. I decided she would not leave without ending this mystery for me.

I thought about Mike and how close he had become to Dad—the conversations they enjoyed. And the conversations I didn't have with Dad and never would.

Then I thought of Baby Cyril. Now I knew why I didn't like Margie's choice of names. My dad had been a man of action, brave, and strong, while Margie's dad seldom expressed a strong opinion, liked to daydream, and described himself as "passionless." Should I have fought for my dad's legacy?

I laid my head down on the table and wept and prayed. I prayed for forgiveness. I prayed for Mom. I prayed for Mike and DeeDee and Anna. I prayed something good would come out of this tragedy.

For a moment, peace came to me.

The phone rang.

"Jake, this is Mike. Mom wants to know when you're coming home."

I felt a bit annoyed Mike apparently had graduated to Mom's spokesperson. All I wanted was to talk to Mom, but apparently she didn't want that right now.

"Ask Mom when she would like me to be there, would you please?"

Mike put the phone down. I could hear voices in the background.

"Mom says it depends on when you can make it. What works for you?"

Now I was more than annoyed. "The hell with this, Mike—get Mom on the line."

Mom sounded very tired. "Jake, this has been the most terrible night of my life. I'm sure glad I have you kids. I know it's terrible for you too. Please come home when you can. I know you're busy."

I liked Mom's "I know you're busy" favorite little saying about as much as I liked Margie's "You're so smart, and I'm so dumb." What this seemingly innocent comment really meant was, "You self-important little twit, I don't ask you to do much, so step to it."

"I'll be there around noon, Mom. I love you. Try to get some sleep. Let me talk to Mike again, please. Love you," I repeated.

Mom returned my sentiments and gave the phone back to Mike.

"So what can you tell me about Dad's accident? What did the police say?"

"The cops have already arrested that worthless creep Nazar. He's being charged with attempted murder."

What the fuck? I felt as if I were watching the final act of some tragic play after missing the earlier acts. And now a villain from another play just appeared on stage, a character whose name would always remind me how worthless I could be.

"Mike, what the hell are you talking about? Nazar?"

"I already told you—the sonabitch killed Dad!" Mike said, now crying and sniffling. "Weren't you listening? I told you he smashed Dad's head with the cue stick, then Dad tried to drive back to the hotel."

"What the *hell* are you talking about?" I repeated.

My brain had been struggling with reality since the phone call arrived from the police. But it absolutely couldn't compute what Mike was saying.

"You never told me anything about Nazar. Frank hit Dad with a *cue stick*? Did you see it? What happened? Start at the beginning."

I could hear Mom in the background asking for the phone.

"Jake, I'm sorry," she said when she came on the line. "Your brother is just shook up and confused. He thought he had already told you the whole story about Nazar. But he told Pastor Lund about it."

That just about set me off. "He's talked to Lund but not me? When?"

"Really, Jake, does it matter? Pastor is here trying to help us through this disaster."

Blood rushed to my head as if I'd burst. I was sick and tired of Roger Lund meddling in my personal life. First, Margie gave him the portal. Now, my mother. As angry as I was, I knew this would be the worst possible time to show my deep ingratitude toward him.

"Okay, okay. Yes, Mom. That's good. I'm glad Roger is there. He's trying to help. As I said, I can be up there by noon. I'll get ready and leave shortly. When will you be back at home?"

"Well," Mom said slowly and quietly, "it's bad enough losing my husband and you kids losing your dad—you know he loved you. But there may be legal problems as well. I need to get a lawyer."

I wanted to scream, "For *what*?" I felt less sure of myself with every word coming from Duluth.

I rephrased my question. "Can I help? Do you want me to meet you in Duluth?"

Mom sounded like a robot now. "I'm so tired of questions. I'm going to go back to the house with Mike and just sleep. Why don't you come tomorrow? There's nothing you can do now."

That hurt.

Before I could respond, she added, "Actually, do you want to do me a big favor?"

I brightened. "Of course, Mom. What can I do?"

"Could you call Anna and DeeDee and let them know what's happened?"

Silently, I shook my head. I almost told her no. She should be the one to call them.

But instead I said, "Sure. I'll call them right now. I feel so bad for you, Mom. Of course I feel bad for the rest of us. But you especially. I love you."

Mom quickly replied, "I love you, Jake. I'm sorry I'm so shook up. Do you want to talk to Pastor?"

I replied back quickly as well, "Not now, Mom. Bye."

I hung up and stood there frozen for a moment. "What the fuck?" I asked myself out loud.

I tried to piece together what may have happened. Mike said Frank Nazar hit Dad with a cue stick, so that meant they were at a bar. How in the world did Frank end up at the same joint in Duluth as Dad? Did Frank ambush Dad out of nowhere? Was there some sort of brawl first? Who jumped who? Mike said Dad tried to drive back to the hotel. What happened? Did he black out behind the wheel? How did the accident happen? Where was Mike the whole time?

Of course, I was missing many facts. All I knew was that this was a nightmarish sequel to Mike and Dad's vigilante incident—yet another story I was the last to hear. I was always in the dark because that's what they wanted.

I couldn't get answers to my questions, yet Roger had them all. Apparently, he was in charge. Pastor Roger Lund had become the consummate insider in all matters Horton.

I was pacing. I noticed my fists were clenched. When it came to protecting Margie in the first go-around with Nazar, Dad and Mike considered me an outsider. Indeed, Roger became the third musketeer. Now, there he was comforting Mom when she should have been leaning on my shoulder. Like everyone else on the Iron Range, my own family now saw me as somebody who wouldn't understand.

Then my thoughts moved back to my dad. The reality began to set in. Dad was dead. All these other complaints were selfish and insignificant. My sense of loss hit me. I collapsed on my bed and simply cried.

The one thing I had been put in charge of was breaking the news to my sisters. No time like the present. I got up and dialed Anna's number. It was about eight in Denver. I imagined Anna and Judy enjoying coffee at the kitchen table where Judy and I had our special talk.

Immediately she could tell by my voice this wasn't a happy call. In a blur, I gave her the information I knew. She gasped, then just bawled. I could hear Anna repeating the news to Judy, who took the phone.

"My God, Jake. I am so sorry for all of you. What happened?"

"Honestly, I don't really know," I said. "Is DeeDee there too? Can you put her on the phone?"

Judy guided me. "She's still sleeping, actually. Let Anna and me talk to her, Jake. I'm sure you have so much to do. I know we'll all be in touch once more details come in. We'll fly out as soon as we can. You just take care of yourself."

The selfish me wanted to share the awful news with DeeDee, but I could understand Judy's thinking.

I thanked Judy. Did she ever not know what to do?

I felt as if I'd been force-fed through the ringer. I played the conversations back in my mind. I couldn't get the straight scoop from Mike nor Mom. I thought about ignoring my mother, packing a bag, and driving to Mesabi. But I put it aside. Mom had made a point of saying there was nothing I could do.

In a fog, I headed to the store. It was my day off, but maybe I just needed some normalcy on that abnormally shitty day.

I knew Rita and Marina would be working. I loved seeing them in action. They competed in a friendly way, much to my relief. Women as well as men seemed captivated by both. My salesmen had gone from pessimistic, to amazed, to fearful. After only a few months, Rita and Marina were consistently out-selling the men. Actually, it had taken them only a few weeks to eclipse the guys.

I was thankful no customers had arrived yet.

"Jake, what are you doing here?" Rita asked with a smile as she and Marina headed toward me. But then they saw my expression.

It was hard to speak. "I just found out my dad died in an accident."

"Oh, Jake," Marina said, putting her hand to her mouth. "What happened?"

"I don't know," I said with a sigh. I was getting tired of not being able to answer that question. "I just wanted to stop in to let you know I won't be around for a few days. I'm heading up north tomorrow morning."

They both hugged me and seemed genuinely sad.

It's hard to explain, but the store just seemed like the place *not* to be doing this. I gave each an extra squeeze, then retreated.

Back home, I knew I had to call Susan—though Colleen or the all-knowing Roger had probably already taken care of that job too.

Susan could only say, "Jake, that is absolutely terrible, I'm so sorry."

She seemed shocked. Maybe Colleen hadn't contacted her after all. I thought briefly about telling Susan my concerns about Roger, but didn't.

"When are you heading to Mesabi?"

"Early tomorrow morning."

A quiet moment passed as I contemplated asking if she wanted to go with me. She may have been wondering if I would ask.

"I'll stay in touch—I promise," I finally said.

By the time I got back home, there was a message from Mom. The funeral was set for the day after next. I once again resisted the urge to drive up there rather than wait until morning, even though it would have given me something to do.

Mom's lawyer comment popped up in my mind. Little doubt, Dad had been drinking, likely too much. I shut my eyes, wanting to shut out the world, and thought about that little Christmas tree in the bar on that very sad Christmas Eve. I wanted to pray but the words didn't come. My mind felt empty. I slept.

25

B<small>Y THE TIME</small> I <small>ARRIVED THE NEXT AFTERNOON</small>, Anna, Judy, and DeeDee were home too. When I walked in the house, I heard Mom and my two sisters practicing in the living room for a song they would be singing at the service. I listened from the kitchen while Mom played our old piano and the three of them sang. Mom's playing and singing sounded even more beautiful than I remembered.

When they finished, I walked into the room clapping. Anna and DeeDee smiled at Mom and clapped with me. Mike and Judy, who were sitting nearby, joined in applause.

I wondered if Mike remembered what he had done that fateful Sunday when his five-year-old antics forced Mom to announce she would never sing again in church or anywhere public.

Anna seemed to be recalling the same memory. She turned to Mike with a big smile on her face. "Can we count on you to behave in church while Mom's up front, Mikey?"

Mike looked a little confused but rolled with it. "Scout's honor."

We all enjoyed a good laugh, including Mike.

Planning a funeral for a parent is both tedious and healing. The details seem daunting and in some ways trite, but the diversion from grief can be welcome. Mom asked me to deliver the eulogy, and I agreed without hesitating.

I kept looking for an opportunity to take Mike aside. I had to hear the whole story about Dad. But given everything we had to do for the funeral, we never had a moment's rest. It was not unlike our trip to Denver, when I tried so hard to get him to talk about the first Nazar story. But that story had to wait, and apparently so would this one.

At last, there seemed to be a lull after dinner. Mom was ready to call it a night. Anna and Judy headed out for the nearby Holiday Inn, where they were staying. Before they left, they extended an invitation for me to join them in the hotel bar for a drink. As they left, Mike sat down to watch some TV—it looked like the perfect time to fill in the blanks.

Just then, DeeDee came over and whispered, "Jake, can I talk to you?"

I guess I wasn't the only one who thought it was the perfect time to talk. She motioned me to follow her to the kitchen.

"So, what can I do for you, little sister?"

She looked up at me and touched my cheek. "Jake, I'll understand if this would make you uncomfortable, but I'm wondering, would you have a problem if Margie hung out with me at the funeral? I think you know Mom and I always liked Margie. I got to know her really well during her pregnancy. You know how Dad cared about her too. And then there's Mike." She evaded my eyes for a moment. "Anyway, she just feels like a part of the family to me. But if it would be uncomfortable, she can just keep her distance . . ."

Truth be told, I didn't even stop to weigh how I actually felt about Margie being with the family during the funeral. Instead, something inside me just lashed out as I realized my little sister was so nervous about my reaction, so certain I'd say no.

"So, DeeDee, you must think I'm a real asshole."

She straightened up. "How can you even say that?" She looked hurt.

I shook my head at myself. "I'm sorry. I didn't mean anything by it. Please make whatever decision is best for you." I added, "I think it's good you're her friend. She couldn't have a better one."

DeeDee hugged me and held me tightly. I could never say no to her. And why would I?

By the time DeeDee and I wrapped up, Mike had gone into his room. The moment was gone. I decided to take up Judy and Anna's offer for a drink.

When I got to the hotel bar, I found them in an affectionate moment. I was glad Anna had someone like Judy during this sad time.

I hated to interrupt them, but an older man at the table next to them felt otherwise. The guy went about three hundred pounds. As I approached, he was giving them the lowdown on what the Bible says about homosexuality.

"You know you'll go to hell if you don't change," he told them.

Judy and Anna eyed the man.

"May I respond?" I asked.

Judy arched her eyebrow and nodded. Her expression read, "Sure, if you want. But who cares?"

I asked the man, "Do you know the book and chapter in the Bible where it says homosexuals will go to hell?"

He didn't.

"Then you may want to worry about your own salvation instead," I continued.

He held a look of contempt toward me. I'm not sure if he thought I had stuck my nose in a place it didn't belong or if he just put me in the same sinful category he considered these obviously gay women.

"Sir, the Bible contains multiple verses calling our attention to the sin of gluttony."

I glanced suspiciously at the oversized plate he had used to heap his bounty from the all-you-can-eat buffet. In a second plate sat enough rib bones to construct a small dinosaur.

"But I do not judge you," I said. "I'm a sinner myself, and I need God's forgiveness. None of us here needs *your* forgiveness, however. I hope you agree."

With that, I sat down with Anna and Judy.

The waitress appeared. She was an attractive blonde. Then I looked at her again.

"Hey, you're Roberta from high school. Remember me—Jake Horton?"

Roberta leaned in close. "Of course! Jake, you're not one to forget." Her smile faded a little. "I'm sorry about your dad. He came in here sometimes."

"Thanks," I said.

Roberta was still leaning close. I vaguely remembered she had gotten married the summer after our senior year. My gut told me she was no longer married. I could see the smirk on Anna's face as she looked at me and back at Roberta.

"So, what are you drinking?" I asked Anna, trying to keep my cool.

Anna shook the ice in her glass. "Ginger ale on the rocks."

I turned to Judy.

"House merlot."

"And I'll have a Dewar's and water."

"Sure thing, Jake." With that, Roberta winked and headed for the bar.

Anna gave me a sly look. "Did you date her or something?"

I shook my head. My mind drifted—I remembered fantasizing about Roberta. I think she liked me, but I was timid with girls back then. As she brought our drinks, she touched me gently on the shoulder.

"Let me know if you want anything else." She smiled at me and added, "I'll be right around the corner."

The three of us were alone now. Anna sipped her ginger ale. "Got your eulogy done?"

I thought for a moment. "Pretty much, yes. I still have a couple of ideas to nail down."

We chatted for a while. It was nice to unwind. After a bit, Judy looked at her watch.

"I'm calling it a night. See you tomorrow, Jake. Come up whenever you're ready," she added to Anna.

"I won't be long," Anna replied. "See you in a few minutes."

Sitting there with Anna, I realized that, once again, I had found myself in a perfect time to talk. In this case, to ask Anna what I needed to know now more than ever.

"I know it's been a long day with a lot of memories. If you don't want to talk about this, just tell me—but I have a question I really need you to answer."

Anna put her glass down. She seemed to understand.

"I'll tell you what, Jake: I'll answer any questions you have after the funeral. Can you live with that?"

"I can," I said.

She stood to give me a good-night hug. "I am so happy to have you as my brother. I love you," she whispered.

"And I love you, Anna."

Sitting down after Anna left, I noticed Roberta bend down to clean under a table. I opened the folder to pay the bill. Inside, a note read, "Buy me a drink in the lounge after 10pm—Bert."

Roberta glanced over.

There's been too many surprises already, and tomorrow is a big day, Jake, I told myself. I smiled and waved her good-bye.

When I headed back to the house, I was surprised to find Mike back in front of the TV. Mom and DeeDee were in bed. Here was my chance.

"Hey," I said as I sat down across from him.

"Hey," he replied. Then he added, "Looks like we're the only two still up."

I started slowly. "Mike, I need you to tell me more about the night of the accident."

Mike got a stricken look in his eyes. "Will you be talking about this at his funeral service?"

I shook my head. "No, I won't repeat what you tell me. But Mike, you were the last person with Dad, and it's important for me to know."

Tears welled in his eyes. "It was his birthday."

I waited as he gathered himself.

"We were at this bar—me, Mom, Dad, and some guys from work. The guys were ready to head out around twelve thirty or so. They drove Mom back to the hotel first. You know how her eyes hurt when she's around cigarette smoke."

I could picture a pool parlor adjoining a bar lounge. I imagined the moldy smell of countless cigarettes from past and present patrons in the poorly ventilated room. Above each table, flickering fluorescent lights lent a bluish color to the haze.

"It was last call, so Dad ordered another pitcher. We found an open pool table. I told Dad we had time for only one game. I asked how much he wanted to bet. He said, 'Whatever amount you want to lose.'"

I smiled.

"We had just put our quarters in the table when Dad said, 'Who the hell does that look like to you?' He pointed at a guy at another table in the back. It was that no good sonofabitch Frank Nazar. I couldn't believe it. I didn't even know he was out of jail. And what are the odds we'd be at the same bar as him in Duluth?"

Mike paused. I knew the difficult part was coming. Telling this story was much different than telling their "Untouchables" story.

"Before I knew it, Bronco was charging right at me, out of nowhere. He swung at me like he wanted to take my head off. I slammed my knee into his groin. Then I drilled him in the nose with a right hook."

I now pictured the flesh of Bronco's nose smeared against his face, a bloody mess.

"All I could think about was Bronco on top of Margie. I hit him with a left, a right, a left. He went down and stayed there."

It sounded like the match initiated by Bronco Brocado lasted less than twenty seconds and ended not with a bell but with the waitress yelling, "Somebody call an ambulance!"

"I turned to find Frank," Mike continued, "and he was running out the back door with his cue stick. Dad saw him too and ran after him. I went after them both. The alley was really dark."

Mike's voice dropped to a hush.

"It took me a bit to see, but finally I saw Dad standing there, his back to me, listening for Frank. Then I saw it. I saw Frank come out from behind a dumpster and go right up behind Dad. Before I could yell out, he brought his cue stick down on Dad's head with all the force he could. There was this thud. Dad went down."

I was glad I was sitting. My muscles went weak. If I didn't already know Dad died in a car accident, I would have thought that was the end of the story.

"I ran to Dad, and Frank took off. There was blood everywhere, but he was breathing. I guess it was one of those wounds that looks worse than it really was. Somebody came out of the bar and brought me some towels. We stopped the bleeding, and Dad sat up. He seemed okay. He was going on about wanting to 'kill that coward asshole.'

"He wouldn't let us call an ambulance, and he wouldn't let me drive him to the emergency room. He just said, 'This'll just be a little bump on my head tomorrow.' All I could say was, 'Dad, I'm sorry this wasn't a great birthday.'"

Even now, as he repeated these words, I could hear Mike taking personal responsibility for the guilt.

"Mike, you didn't do anything wrong. None of that was your fault."

He eyed me. "That's almost exactly what Dad said." He sighed. "He said we had to get out of there before the cops came. Dad's truck was parked in back, but my car was parked out front. He said he'd see me at the hotel."

Mike once again paused. He was remembering those last words.

"I got to the hotel, and Dad wasn't there yet. I went to my room. I just assumed he made it back. Next thing I knew, the cops were calling Mom. They said Dad had been only a few blocks from the hotel, at the stoplight for Mesabi Avenue."

I knew the street. In a town known for its hills, Mesabi Avenue was the steepest of all.

"They said Dad turned up the wrong side of the median. A gas tanker going fifty miles per hour couldn't stop in time. Dad's pickup looked like an accordion—squashed to half its size. Pieces of glass in every direction. And the blood . . . But the truck driver didn't even have to go to the hospital."

A concussion, I thought. I'd seen guys get their bells rang on the football field and not even know what day of the week it was.

"I know I should never have let him drive," Mike said, "but you know how Dad was."

"Of course I know. I would have done the same thing."

Mike dropped his eyes for a long moment. When he looked up, I met his gaze and saw real hatred, even cold hatred.

In a measured, robotic way, he said, "I wish I would have killed Bronco the first time. I may yet. Frank too."

I swallowed and responded like the older brother I was. "Mike, I can understand how you feel. But whatever you do, stay away from those idiots. I don't want to be visiting you in jail somewhere. Speaking of jail, I sure hope the DA goes for a murder charge on that worthless piece of shit Nazar."

Mike again got a grim look over his face. "You maybe think I'm a nutcase or something, but if he gets out, I promise you I will, at the very least, break a cue stick over his head. I hate that motherfucker."

I couldn't believe this. It reminded me of the feeling I had when Mom mentioned Mike owned a gun. This conversation shocked and scared me. I had to change the subject.

"So, you planning on living at home with Mom?"

He chewed on the question. "I wish Margie would let me go with her when she moves. That's what I want—to just to be near her. I wish I was you sometimes, because if I was, she would marry me."

For the first time, I realized he carried the profound weight of losing not only Dad but Margie. No words could change his love and loss.

"Mike, you've been the best friend Margie has ever had. I hope you know that. But you can't go with her."

Mike knew the reality of it all. "I guess I'll go on with life, but I won't care." He looked tired.

"Mike, we better get some sleep. Just know you are one terrific guy. Dad knew that. So do the rest of us."

I reached out for Mike and hugged him like I meant it. Because I did.

26

THE NEXT MORNING, THE FAMILY RECONVENED at the church just prior to the visitation. We engaged in small talk as we waited for Roger to join us. He showed up right on time. He lifted a prayer and then, starting with my mother, offered each a sympathetic hug.

As he came to me, I reached out my arm—partly to offer a handshake but partly to block any embrace. It occurred to me: I wanted to be angry at him. I was giving it my best effort. We both now were officially uncomfortable around each other.

As we gathered in the church basement for the visitation, my mouth went dry and my hands trembled slightly. I just wanted to get through the visitation, but it turned out to be okay. It was overwhelming to see so many people showing their support.

Many of Dad's ironworker friends and their families attended. It made me proud to see how Mike interacted with them. He introduced me to some of the guys and several repeated the stories of Dad's legends.

For the most part, no one discussed what happened the night he died. The details had spread through Mesabi like a bad cold, but the whole topic seemed surreal even now.

I never realized the day would be like a trip down memory lane. Coach Lyttinen and his wife greeted me and shared their sympathies. Seeing Mrs. Demming was a wonderful surprise. She looked her age, whatever number that may have been. It touched me that she came.

Margie's Dad, Cy, stopped by, and we shook hands. We visited a little about the store, now closed. The small talk was awkward and superficial, and we both knew it.

"Alice sends her greetings. She's home with the baby," he added. Then he paused before saying, "Jake, we'll always wish the best for you. Your dad saved Margie's life. He's a hero to me."

"And to me, Cy."

Gary and his fiancée, Linda were a nice diversion. "Everything's fine back at the store," he assured me. "The Good Ship sails toward another record month."

Trent surprised me by showing up. He introduced me to his girlfriend, Belinda, and we enjoyed some banter.

"How's your dad?" I asked.

Trent shook his head. "He gets worse every time I see him. We placed him in a nursing home. Dad didn't want that, but what else could we do? He fell three times in one week."

Belinda, trying to soften the moment, took Trent's hand. "Well, when you find the cure for Parkinson's, that will help." She added, "Trent is specializing in Parkinson's research."

I smiled. "Why am I not surprised?"

I gave him a man-to-man hug. You know—the one where you pat each other's back so you know the hug will be over quickly.

Then I saw Margie. She was standing with DeeDee and some of her friends. Even though I had just seen her in the hospital, she somehow looked even more mature and classier than before. I liked the look of her black-and-white houndstooth skirt and jacket. She wore a black sweater underneath the jacket. She looked beautiful, really. Especially considering she had just been released from her maternity stay.

My mouth felt parched like a desert. I needed more water. As I headed to the water fountain, there stood two people I wanted to avoid, Roger and Colleen. Roger was looking my direction with a small smile. Colleen made sure to look anywhere but toward me.

Just before I moved past them, Roger stepped over and stopped me. "Jake, you and I are meant to be friends. My door is open."

I didn't like that. Or perhaps I just took it wrong. To me, it sounded as though he was forgiving me for something but not apologizing for his role.

I simply nodded and said, "Thank you for being good to Dad and Mom."

In the back of my mind, I knew my feelings toward Roger and Colleen were dubious. Still, I wanted them to suffer a little. I shook my head. It was almost time for the service to begin. I needed to focus on my eulogy and get the Lunds out of my mind.

When visitation was over, we lined up behind the closed coffin in the back of the church. As the pallbearers rolled the coffin forward, we followed behind. Mom and me. Judy and Mike. DeeDee, Anna, and Margie. Assorted relatives followed behind.

The service—typical Lutheran with a few good hymns—provided a fitting funeral. When Mom and my sisters sang, you could sense an overwhelming feeling of love and reverence fill the space. I knew that if one person would have clapped, there would have been a standing ovation. That didn't happen. Remember, these were Lutherans. And without the Charismatics. But clearly, the Horton women caused many to wipe tears from their eyes.

Giving the devil his due, Roger's sermon couldn't have been better. He emphasized the positive side of Dad and reflected on the times he observed him being a caring father and husband. And loyalty. Roger talked about the loyalty Dad held for his friends and family. He got some good laughs when he talked about Dad's expectations with his fellow ironworkers. He had even gotten permission from one of the young guys to share a story about how Dad had dressed the kid down for being careless, but then requested that the young man be part of his team the next day at a new worksite.

Roger ended his sermon by saying, "The family would like Jacob, Roy's eldest son, to share some thoughts."

Of course, I had been dreading this moment all during the service. Though my last public speech, my graduation commencement address, had been a success, and though I had read several books on how to become an effective public speaker, my nerves were still getting the best of me. My mouth felt dry again, and the tremor in my hands reminded me, "Jake, you're scared."

I smiled slightly at my mother; she smiled back at me. I worked my way through my family, Judy, and finally Margie. She looked so profoundly proud of me. I couldn't help it—I thought back to the first time we were together in my old Pontiac GTO Judge.

I looked briefly at Margie again, then focused on the task before me. What I would quickly learn is that a public speaker will never enjoy a more receptive audience than at a funeral.

I began slowly.

"Some people say God is a myth." I paused. "I am not one of them." I paused again. "And neither was my father, Roy Horton. God forgive me for taking him for granted. Please forgive me for taking the people I love in my life now for granted.

"And I've taken God's promises for granted. My father once showed me a special tool he carried in his toolbox. He told me the tool could be used to separate tangled pieces of wire. He said, 'It's an important tool when you need it, but because I use it so rarely, I forget I have it when I need it.'

"I'm feeling that way about my Bible. But I'm thinking of and counting on Revelations 21:4, 'And God will wipe away every tear from their eyes, and there shall no longer be death; there shall no longer be mourning; or crying or pain. They have passed away.'

"There exists a terrible emptiness we feel with the loss of my father. Within that emptiness, I believe in the promises of God, and I believe Dad has left this world, where people are so often judged by their poor deeds rather than measured by all the good they've done."

Here I paused and looked up. We all knew what I was talking about. I noticed some people nodding in agreement. The unspoken point was, *Let's not judge Roy Horton, a good man, by this one terrible mistake, which never would have happened except for that asshole Frank Nazar.*

And the unspoken point behind that, which maybe only I knew, was, *And I'm the one who brought Frank Nazar into my dad's life.*

I was ready now to return to my text. I straightened up.

"Roy Horton did a lot of good while he was with us."

I went on to talk about Dad's loyalty to his friends, especially his work brotherhood. How he could be a bit of a curmudgeon—well, a lot of a curmudgeon. How he would do anything for his friends and his family. How he gave me only begrudging credit for my football record at Mesabi when he told me, "Yeah, well, I still believe you could have played hockey."

I brought each member of the family into the eulogy, including Judy, then I finished with the story I knew would pull their heartstrings the most. Out of sorrow comes the desire not to grieve, which is best achieved by laughing.

"This story, I think, shows a side of my dad people often didn't see. Occasionally on Sundays, our family would eat lunch at the Holiday Inn after church. On this occasion, DeeDee was maybe about five or six. Mom had put DeeDee's hair up, and she proudly wore a new lacy dress with a matching ribbon. People walking by would stop to comment how cute she looked. Dad ordered chocolate ice cream for all of us, except he ordered peppermint for Mom, her favorite.

"Remember, DeeDee, what happened next?" I asked, looking at her.

She grinned.

"Yes, you spilled ice cream on your new dress." I addressed the audience now. "DeeDee tried to hide the chocolate stains, but then she started to cry because she thought she had ruined her new dress. Mom tried to console her. But what had started out as a special family dinner was now in danger of being spoiled.

"Dad got DeeDee's attention and smiled at her, coaxing her to smile too. Then in a conspiratorial voice, he said, 'I understand, DeeDee. It really is sad when you spill ice cream on yourself. Like this . . .'

"With that, he took a spoon of chocolate ice cream and dropped it on his shirt. He sighed. 'Oh no—look what I've done.' Then he did it again. Mike, of course, got into it and even started throwing ice cream. Finally, all of us, including Mom, had ice cream stains.

"I'm not sure everyone who witnessed this in the restaurant that day approved. But we left laughing. Life isn't always a joyride—sometimes we spill our ice cream. But Dad changed what could have been a frustrating experience into a family memory. A good family memory. Dad did not consider his cost when he saw a need to help those whom he loved. If you knew my father, Roy Horton, then you know this."

I made my way slowly to my spot in the pew. But before I could sit down, DeeDee got up and hugged me, just sobbing. Now I was crying. We looked at each other.

"Jake, thank you," she whispered. "It was wonderful. And so are you."

As DeeDee released me from her hug, I looked at Margie next to her. Tears were flowing. She couldn't restrain herself, and neither could I. We hugged each other, maybe a little longer than we should have. Despite the context of a funeral, a quick thought invaded my mind: *Maybe I should try to get together with Margie afterwards.* At last I sat down, drained.

Roger rose to finish the service. He too was weeping. I wondered what thoughts bounced around in his mind now. He ended the service with instructions regarding the burial, then invited everyone back to the church to share lunch afterwards.

The burial service at the cemetery finalized Dad's transition from the living to his return to the dust. The crisp, sunny day provided both a bright background for a sad event and a conversation starter for those who liked to talk about the weather. I often wondered what people thought as they exchanged such inane details of a topic no one cared about. Well, at least I wasn't hearing about the "terrible" traffic back in the Cities.

We filed back into the church basement for a lunch. It makes sense to serve a lunch after funerals. Many people had driven hours to be here, so this saved them both time and money. The lunch also provides people a time to unwind from the tension of the funeral and have one last chance to share their sympathies with the grieving family.

I smiled as I saw the spread the habitually underappreciated Ladies Aid had put out for us. I've always loved those sandwiches with the bologna spread as well as the egg salad. The proverbial main feature typically was casserole with tater tots.

I smirked as I saw Mike load one huge scoop onto his plate. My memory took me back to the time young Mike used a spatula to lift the entire tater tot layer onto his plate, thereby depriving everyone else of the golden little tots.

All the Hortons stayed until the last guest left. Even the Ladies Aid members had called it a day.

We were tired when we decided to finish at the house. Mom smiled at us kids and said simply, "I couldn't be prouder than I am of all of you. Jake, that speech—" She paused as if reflecting. "I agree with your Dad: I think you could have played hockey."

We grievers enjoyed a good laugh.

Anna and Judy got ready to head out to the hotel. When we exchanged hugs, Anna said to me, "We're heading down to Minneapolis for a couple of days to visit some friends before we fly home."

Judy seemed a little surprised by the announcement. It might have been the first she'd heard of these plans. In an instant, though, she decided to make the most of it.

"Can I stop by the store on Friday for a moment or two?"

I'm sure now I seemed a little surprised. "Of course—but I just want you to know, the store may be a little bit of a mess, and I'll be swamped after being away like this."

Judy smiled. "I can imagine—or maybe I really can't! I won't take a lot of your time. Actually, I would love to review the salespeople's numbers and see who sells what."

After they left, it was just Mom, DeeDee, Mike, and me sitting around a folding table, nibbling on lemon bars and date bars. God, I love those date bars. Mom took my hand, then took Mike's hand. Mike instinctively reached for DeeDee's hand, and she reached for mine. We formed a circle as we sat there. For a while, nothing was said, but we were all thinking the same thought: we had gotten through this day, and we had done it together. A perfect family? Are you kidding? Still, we possessed love, and we held the strength to overcome what we needed to overcome. Roy Horton lived his life in just that way.

We each sent a prayer, then prayed what could be called our family prayer, one Mom learned from her mother.

Father, we thank you for the night
And for the pleasant morning light.
For rest and food and loving care
And all that makes the world so fair.
Help me to do the things I should,
To be to others kind and good.
In all I do in work or play,
To love you better day by day.

We squeezed each other's hands and finished, "Amen."

27

I STAYED ANOTHER DAY WITH MOM, then drove back to the Cities on Thursday. The first thing I did was call Susan. We engaged in a warm conversation. I shared the basics about the funeral but couldn't push myself to wade into the deeper emotional waters over the phone. She sensed my struggles and suggested getting together Friday evening at my place.

After we hung up, I couldn't help but picture those cute ears of hers, then I shook my head at myself.

I had hoped being back to work would make life feel "normal" again, but everything still felt surreal. I realized it would take some time. I wasn't ready to head to the store yet, but I also didn't want to stay home and stare at the walls.

On a whim, I drove over to see how Jerrod Springer was doing. I noticed his car in the lot. As I walked in, nobody came to help me. The same thing happened the last time I was in. The place felt deserted. Two salesmen gossiped over in the far corner, not even turning their heads toward me.

A customer mistook me for a salesman and asked me, "Do you carry Persian Luxury?"

Had Jerrod not been there, I would have sent them to my store—I had done that before. But I just said no and walked toward the office, where Jerrod immersed himself in whatever busywork he could find so he wouldn't be forced to help any customers.

Jerrod seemed happy to see me. We made small talk for an hour out on the floor. During that time, three customers received no help while the salesmen continued to gossip. Jerrod either didn't notice or didn't care. It didn't matter which.

At last, Jerrod looked over at the salesmen. "Worse than women, don't you think?" he commented with some distain. He was always smarter than he seemed.

"Way worse," I replied. With that, I checked my watch. "I suppose I better get going. It was great seeing you, as always."

Just as I turned to leave, Jerrod spoke in a low, conspiratorial voice. "It's funny that you stopped by today. Your partner and her girlfriend stopped by earlier this morning. Did you know that?"

"I did not know that," I admitted. My face surely showed my surprise. "How do you even know she's my partner?"

"I know them because I make it my business to know what's going on with my competitors." He paused. "Plus, she came right out and said it. That Judy has balls."

I smiled. "Yes, she does. What did she say to you?"

"Well, I was bitching about the rigors of a retail store and she said, 'Jerrod, you shouldn't do what you hate. We have some extra cash. If you want to talk to Jake or me in the next thirty days, we'll buy this business—what's left of it—and rent from you, if you're in the ball park.'"

Balls indeed, I thought.

"So, is that thirty days from today or Monday?" I asked as I winked at Jerrod and headed to the door.

I could hardly wait to see Judy tomorrow. I could be the coy one this time.

True to form, Judy arrived at exactly 2:00 p.m. I fought to keep from grinning as I held my nugget of secret information from Jerrod. Not that it remained a secret for long.

"Let's talk about expansion," Judy said.

With that simple comment, she led me to my office and proceeded to lay out her plans. We would present an offer to Jerrod to buy his business and let him collect rent from us, much like the Sommer's collected rent for this building. If he didn't agree to our offer in thirty days, we would simply open a new store near him. She even showed me pictures of three possible locations. And then she went further. Once the Springer location broke even, we would open another location near one of the most successful malls in the Twin Cities.

After twenty minutes of presentation, she asked, "So, what would you do for a store manager at our second Sommer's location? Could you manage both stores?"

"I think it would be better to have a different manager at the new location." I paused to consider who would fill the position. "Well, Gary has a teaching degree, but he seems to love working here. He may consider staying if we offered him a salary he couldn't refuse. Linda wants to start a family, but that won't happen with what he'd make teaching. I think Rita has the capability to manage as well."

Judy reflected. "Interesting. What about Marina? She's been outselling everybody."

I had anticipated the question. "Marina would be a better-than-average manager, but I think she has some rough edges when it comes to dealing with people."

Judy nodded slowly, thinking. "All right," she said after a bit. "I'd like to meet alone with Marina first and then Rita."

"Sure," I said.

I kept a straight face as I walked out to call Marina into the office, but inwardly, I didn't understand why Judy wanted to meet them without me present. In the end, I just assumed she had her reasons.

Marina headed into the office. Thirty minutes later, she emerged, smiled at me, and mouthed, "Thank you." She apparently thought I knew what the meeting was about.

Then it was Rita's turn. She wore a positive expression as well when she exited the office, but she seemed just a little flustered.

While I was waiting out on the floor, I saw Gary. Even though it was his day off, he was in to check on a couple of matters.

I stepped into the office. "Do you want some 'alone time' with Gary as well?" I asked Judy.

She thought for a quick moment. "That won't be necessary. But I would like to say hello before I head out." She gathered her things, then we headed over to Gary's desk as he worked on a blueprint trying to figure out how much carpeting his customer needed.

Just as Judy impressed me to the point of scaring me a little, I knew she had the same effect on Gary. She thanked Gary for his good work, mentioning his specific sales number for the last two months. Then she asked, "How much longer will we have your services here?"

Caught off guard but always honest, Gary grinned. "I think Jake would have to fire me before I'd leave. My fiancée says I'm addicted to the business. I'm conflicted about whether I should go into teaching, yet here I am on my day off. I can't resist."

Judy reached to shake his hand. "Well, the kids' loss is our gain."

I escorted Judy out to the parking lot, then a thought came to me. "Say, how much time do you have before you leave for the airport?"

Judy looked at her watch. "Well, I'm meeting Anna at a diner near the airport in twenty minutes, and I already have the suitcases in the car. We likely have at least an hour."

"Judy, how about I ride along with you? The drive over will give us more time to talk. I can call a cab or have someone come pick me up afterward. I'm interested in your thoughts about Rita, Marina, and Gary." I hesitated. "That, and I want to have a conversation with Anna—a conversation she's been avoiding."

Judy stopped by her car and eyed me knowingly. "That last part could be tough," she said. "I'm not sure of the details, but I know it's something that still hurts her. But you can try. Hop in."

As we took off, Judy wasted no time in getting back to business. "You've done an excellent job of bringing in three good employees, each who would likely excel as the manager at the new location. My choice would be Marina."

"Really?" I said. "More than Rita?"

"Marina has the killer instincts and seems to have the most to prove. I think she can smooth out those rough edges if given the chance. She says she learned a lot in the travel business. But what I'm looking for can't be taught. The more I think about this, the more I realize something: Our competitors still run their stores like they were a pair of comfortable old slippers. We need to be like ruby high heels. Rita would look good in them, but Marina could make you *want* them."

I saw her logic, but I had to ask, "And you believe Marina is a better choice than Gary?"

Judy glanced at me. "Did you see his shoes, Jake?"

Gary wore penny loafers. I got her point.

"Currently," Judy continued, "Springer's has five salesmen and two saleswomen. We could keep one or two men, if you wanted. The rest of the staff should be women. Rita would be excellent to train in the new employees. We could add to her title and even give her something extra. But we can discuss that later," she said.

We had arrived at the diner. I took a deep breath.

Judy reached over and put a hand on my shoulder. "I'll be back in a half hour. Good luck, Jake."

I went inside and made my way to Anna's table. Other than her and an older couple sitting in the back, the diner was empty.

Anna looked up at me with surprise. "Jake?" For a moment, her face tightened. "Is everything okay? Where's Judy?"

"Everything's fine. Judy is picking you up in a half hour." I reached for Anna's hand. "But first, I need to hear what you promised to tell me. I'm not letting you out of my sight until you do."

She squeezed my hand, then removed it to open her purse for some Kleenex.

"Okay, Jake. I guess I can't avoid this any longer. But you may wish you hadn't heard it, once you do."

She stopped, probably hoping I would change my mind. When I didn't say a word, she looked down at the Kleenex in her hand.

"It was late in my senior year. Do you remember the Bacig family, who lived by the park? Patty Bacig was a junior and a friend of mine. She had those fainting spells, where she would pass out sometimes. I helped her babysit her little sister sometimes because she couldn't do it alone."

Her hand gripped the Kleenex.

"Patty and I were attracted to each other. We found comfort in finding somebody with the same 'sickness.' You know, the so-called sickness of being born with an attraction for girls instead of boys."

She paused giving me an opportunity to say something, but I didn't want to stop the flow.

"So, one Saturday night, we put her sister to bed around nine. We watched wrestling matches on TV, then Patty shut the lights off, and we fooled around with our own wrestling match. We made out on the living room floor. Some of our clothes ended up scattered about. We fell asleep in each other's arms.

"But then suddenly we heard the backdoor slam. We both thought it was her parents coming home. Two people were talking in the kitchen. We could hear it was Patty's mom, but the male voice was not her dad's.

"There we were, mostly undressed and on the floor right by the kitchen doorway. We didn't dare move nor make a sound. Then we could hear heavy breathing and Patty's mother moaning.

"Patty slowly crawled over to try to retrieve her panties, but her mom saw her through the doorway. She stormed into the room with her blouse open and saw me pretty much naked except for the guilt on my face. Right behind her came the man." Anna hesitated. "Standing there, looking down at me with a mixture of hatred and fear, was that pillar of righteousness, our father. And then Patty's mother kicked me. Hard. Right in the stomach."

Tears slipped down Anna's cheek, though she didn't use the Kleenex to dab them. Her hands clutched the tissue even harder.

"All I remember is somehow I got dressed, and Dad and I drove home. Not a single word was spoken until we got to our driveway. Then Dad looked at me and said, 'Let's hope the Bacigs can keep their mouths shut, just like we will. You understand?'

"I couldn't stop crying for days. I cried because I thought I was a worthless sinner. I cried because my father was now a stranger. I cried because he must have believed I deserved to be kicked by a woman cheating on her husband— with him."

Anna lifted her hands over her eyes and sobbed.

I looked at her, my own face covered with shame. I cursed myself for being so persistent in demanding she tell me this story. I felt shattered somehow. She was right. Now that I'd heard it, I wished I hadn't.

It was also the shame of discovering what kind of man my father was. My mind whirled. All the times he railed about married people who cheated or got divorced. Then my thoughts moved to the eulogy, which all of sudden felt cheap. Like a lie.

I could hardly speak, but I held her hands and said the only thought on my mind. "I am so, so sorry, Anna. What a goddamned hypocrite."

After a moment, she wiped her eyes and sat up straight. "When you guys came to Colorado, Dad and I went for a walk. We sat down on a bench to talk. I waited. He looked at me and shook his head. He started to talk, but then stopped. When he started again, he said something like, 'Words never have been my strength. But that doesn't matter, anyway, because words can't express what I would like you to know. Every single day, I regret what I did. I don't expect you to forgive me. I don't expect God to forgive me. Just know what I did that day is the worst thing I ever did in my life. Anna, seeing you now, I'm so happy you survived me.'

"Then he stood and looked up, trying not to cry. I took his hand, and we walked around the park holding hands. We both knew words couldn't change what had happened, but I also wanted him to know he had never stopped being my father."

I thought back to when she and Dad hugged and cried when we first arrived in Denver. I understood it now.

"Jake, I promised Dad I'd never speak a word about that night. I kept my pledge until now. Don't tell Mom or Mike or anybody. You promise?"

Before I could speak, I looked up to see Judy's car pulling into the parking lot. Anna waved at her through the window, then took my hand.

"Jake, do you promise?"

I didn't hesitate. "Of course, Anna. I won't say a word." I sat there shaking my head. "I know you're the one who got hurt the worst, but the rest of us were hurt too—we lost you those years because of him. And all his speeches about fakes. It just makes me sick."

Anna nodded. "I know, I know. But Jake, consider this—I truly believe Dad paid a heavy price for what he did. He paid a very heavy price. He was like someone who served prison time for a crime. But as you said in your wonderful eulogy, we shouldn't judge a person's life by his worst deeds. I know you didn't know my story when you said that, but it still has much wisdom. So let's not be bitter about the past. Let's take the best and leave the bad behind. Can you do that, Jake?"

I tried to reflect upon my own wisdom. It was true. I did say we shouldn't judge Dad on his poor deeds. For that matter, I had to remind myself of "judge not, lest ye be judged." Here I was condemning Dad when I'd done plenty of crap that I hoped would never see the light of day. There was more than enough to convince those closest to me I was not the Jake they thought I was.

Judy joined us at the table. She held Anna's hand and touched my arm, saying nothing out loud because words were not needed.

We chatted for a bit before we said good-bye and they headed out for the airport. I knew I still had to call for a ride, but I was drained. I needed to get back to the store and, hopefully, leave work early. Susan was coming over to my place tonight, and I hadn't had the time to clean up.

I got up and made my way to the pay phone.

28

A LITTLE BEFORE SIX O'CLOCK, I sat at my kitchen table. I felt a little nervous. I didn't know why.

Maybe it was because I was peering into my empty living room. I had gotten rid of my old hand-me-down couch and chairs from college, but the new furniture hadn't been delivered yet. This wouldn't impress anyone.

I turned on the radio and found a classical station. Susan liked Lancer's red wine, so I had picked up a couple of bottles. A glass of wine sounded good right now, but so did a Southern Comfort old-fashioned. I grabbed the Southern Comfort. I needed to find that corkscrew for the wine, but it could wait.

Outside, the wind picked up. The clouds were getting darker, promising some much-needed rain. Susan's car turned into my driveway, and I watched her step out into the windy night. I put my glass down and opened the door for her.

The wind and humidity had done a number on her hair. She wore her hair in a different style every time we got together, as if she couldn't find a style she liked. I decided I liked this way the best—long and free with a few strands pulled back over her right ear.

We kissed quickly, and I invited her in. I helped her with her coat and commented on her beautiful purple sweater. She wore a gray skirt just above her knees. I wasn't sure about the milky-colored stockings, but what do I know?

"Mind if you give me a tour of the house?" she asked.

We headed to the kitchen, where she accepted my offer for some wine. Then I quickly ushered her through the living-room-in-waiting.

"I'm sorry," I said with some embarrassment. "I have new furniture on its way. I realize that means there's no comfortable place to sit."

"Well," she replied, "what about your bed? Is that comfortable?"

I eyed her carefully. When I first met Susan, and even after the second time we were together, I couldn't tell whether she knowingly made these types of comments to bring a guy's mind to sex or if she was naïve. Now, I knew she was a little naïve, perhaps. She wasn't trying to be sexy or suggestive at all.

Still, I answered a bit too enthusiastically, "Why don't you test it out?"

When we got to the bedroom, Susan very deliberately climbed onto the bed and propped herself against the headboard.

"Jake, come join me. I think this is the most comfortable seat in the house right now."

"Let me get some extra pillows first," I said. I got them from the closet in the second bedroom—then took a detour to round off my drink at the same time.

Returning, I positioned myself next to her on the bed. We looked at each other. I couldn't help but say, "Susan, you are always more beautiful than I remember from the last time I saw you."

She set her glass of wine on the nightstand and moved toward me. She climbed on top of me and kissed me. I kissed her back. The whole scene felt like a dream.

We held each other and she asked, "Tell me about the funeral and Colleen and Roger and Margie and your family. Tell me everything."

I held her and kissed her. "I will," I whispered. "But remember, you promised to tell me more about yourself, so you're first."

"All right. What do you want to know?"

I thought about starting slowly, but instead, I went right to my biggest question.

"Susan, you went with a guy named Bob for over two years, then you broke it off. What happened? Do you still care for him?"

For a few moments, I wondered if she wouldn't answer. Then at last she spoke.

"As I look back, I think mostly I wasted those two years on him."

I was taken back by her cold honesty. "So what happened?"

"Bob is a devout Christian. At first, I thought that by following Bob, I could more closely follow Christ. He claimed to love me and we talked about marriage, but . . ."

"But what?"

Susan sighed. "I've never told anybody except Colleen this—the 'but' is that he wouldn't make love to me. I asked him about it. I asked him if he wanted me. He assured me he did, but he said sex before marriage was wrong."

As you can imagine, I couldn't relate to this guy. Here was this beautiful woman telling me her boyfriend wouldn't sleep with her.

"After two years," she continued, "I got to thinking about what marriage would be like with a man with that much self-control. I concluded, there must be more. Maybe I'm not realistic—I don't know." She ran her hands slowly up and down my thighs. "I want a good man, yes, but I want passion too."

I didn't care, but I asked anyway, "What's Bob doing now?"

Susan's fingers were beginning to find their way around to some arousing destinations. "He's a minister for a strict, conservative Missouri Synod congregation in some town in central Wisconsin. Word is, he isn't married and spends a lot of time with a young man he met at the seminary. To tell you the truth, I don't care what he's doing, and I'm quite sure, he feels the same."

I leaned in to whisper in her ear. "I promise I will never make the mistake he made."

We made love and talked into the early morning. It was her first time. I will admit, I was glad I had some experience. She made me feel as though I was her perfect lover. I couldn't imagine wanting to sleep with anybody else.

At least, that's how I felt at that moment.

PART 2

29

PEOPLE OFTEN BEGIN TO REFLECT UPON their lives at forty. I was no exception. It was 1986, and I had much to be thankful for. And while I felt I had put miles between me and my worst behavior, it still felt like old graffiti painted on a cement wall, faded but still readable.

Less than a year after our first night together, I proposed to Susan. We married in 1971. We celebrated our fifteenth anniversary the year I turned forty.

We had two children. Our first born, Jacob Junior, age twelve, won people over with his vigor and good nature. Competitive in nature, JJ excelled in soccer and hockey while making the honors list. Lindsey, age nine, looked a lot like her beautiful mother. She also shared her mom's independence, intelligence, and kindness.

Susan and I felt a deep sense of gratitude for our family. I often expressed my appreciation to Susan because I really and truly believed it was she who deserved nearly all the credit for how our kids had turned out. When I said this, though, she would respond passionately with a list of good traits the kids had gotten from me.

Now with five locations, Sommer's Carpet and Tile had outlasted almost all its original competitors and couldn't be touched by any new competitors. The company proved to be a money machine. Success takes inspiration and perspiration, as the saying goes. But it also takes a little good luck plus discipline and direction.

The fruits of the business provided the funds to build a "wow" house near Susan's parents' home in Apple Valley. The success also provided opportunities for several family trips. We lived very well, and we knew we were lucky.

I gave credit to Judy for much of my success. She decided to cash out of the business when she was diagnosed with cancer in 1983. Surgery successfully removed it, but her surgeon gave her no guarantees she was cured.

Judy could have asked for more money with the buyout, but she did double her investment—in addition to the quarterly dividends she had received over the years. Financially, our relationship had paid off well for both of us. I hated to see her leave. To this day, I've never met a smarter businessperson with a greater penchant for well-thought-out action.

She called it right when she identified Marina as the "number two cog," as she put it. (Thankfully, she considered me the number one cog.) Marina thrived as manager at the former Springer location. She knew how to read people, and she proved fearless. We eventually made her my general manager overseeing all locations. She got that job done as well.

Rita managed our third location, and Judy and I were right about her too. She's excellent at training throughout the company, but she'll never be a Marina.

I offered Gary a store to manage, but he chose to accept a teaching position after all. He augments his salary with part-time sales. Could there be a better part-time salesperson than Gary? I don't think so. And Gary remained a true friend—loyal, encouraging, and present.

The Horton family experienced change as well. With Dad gone, Mom spent a lot of time in Denver. She loved to help Anna with her art showings at the museum.

During one of those shows, she met Devin Whiteman, a University of Colorado professor. His wife had been bedridden for several years. He had spent most of his time at her side before she passed.

With wild white hair and a short five-four frame, he reminded me of a whirling dervish. Mom would ask, "Devin, can't you just sit still for a moment?" He would respond, "There'll be plenty of time to rest when I die."

When he proposed to Mom, part of her wanted to accept, but part of her simply couldn't imagine being married again. Devin didn't give up, though. Ultimately, Mom asked each of us kids what we thought.

She became Eva Horton-Whiteman.

A philosopher, Devin's politics were even further left than the liberals I had known on the Range. I liked him from the first. He was younger than my mom, and he gently pushed her to explore new ideas. Through a program at the university, my mom attended classes free. She earned her bachelor's degree and accepted a teaching position at a local elementary school.

DeeDee married Trevor McCarver, her long-time boyfriend. He served as pastor at an Assemblies of the Lord parish in the northern part of the Cities. DeeDee served as a minister of sorts herself. She was a fundraiser with Billy Graham Ministries. They have a son and a daughter—good kids. We saw them often.

And then there was Mike.

For years, Mike never lost hope he and Margie would end up together. Not long after Dad's funeral, Margie moved to Montana. She had an aunt out there. Mike would save his money, visit Margie in Montana, then return wearing a sadness he couldn't shake off. Mike would call me and give me a "Margie Report."

With a little embarrassment, he once told me he secretly hoped she would realize nobody could love her like he did and that she'd come home to marry him.

"Jake, am I stupid for that?" he asked.

"No, you just love people deeper than the rest of us," I said with sincerity.

A few months after that conversation, Ryan Lofald, one of Mike's iron-worker friends died when a twenty-story-high section of scaffolding gave way. He left behind a wife, Sharri, and two young boys.

Sharri knew Mike well. She already loved him as a friend. He and Ryan had been brothers in the union. The two could also be described as drinking buddies. More than once, Mike had spent a night on their couch after an evening of frolic.

As Ryan's friend, Mike was always respectful and kind with Sharri. She noticed how much her boys enjoyed playing around with him. Mike would tell her about his trips to visit Margie in Montana. She told him never to give up, that Margie would one day see what she was missing.

Following the funeral, the two of them began spending more time together. Sharri's house—actually a cabin on a lake near Mesabi—frequently needed attention, and Mike wanted to help.

About six months after the funeral, Mike was tuning up her boat engine and fishing for walleye on the lake with her boys. As the three of them brought the boat to the dock, Mike could see Sharri sitting with some guy on her swing in front of the cabin. As he got closer, he could see the guy's arm around her neck. It looked like he was taking some liberties with his hand near her breast.

He didn't think the boys should see this, so he yelled a little louder than necessary, "Sharri, come and see the fish your kids have caught!"

Sharri and the guy quickly broke apart. As Sharri hurried away, she gave the guy a wave to signal him to leave.

Mike cleaned the fish with the boys and made dinner. Mike was just about done with the dishes when Sharri returned from tucking the boys into bed.

Mike, always an easy read, had something to say but was holding back.

"Mike, do you think it's wrong for me to start spending time with men who like me?" She noticed tears in his eyes, but she demanded an answer.

Still, he couldn't speak.

Sharri finally took Mike into her embrace. Now with tears in her own eyes, she told Mike she had loved him from the first time she had met him, years ago. They kissed. They loved each other.

When Mike told our family he was marrying Sharri, he said with a wink, "I'd marry her just to get the two boys, but I'm glad they threw her in too." Mike loved those boys and he spent more time camping and fishing with them than he did working.

As for Margie, she stayed in Montana for a few years, then returned to the Cities. She knew she'd never move back to the Range. She told DeeDee, "When I'm up there, it makes me realize how lost I feel. And how much I've lost."

Then her life took a turn none of us expected when the old man, Frank Nazar Sr., passed away. Margie attended the funeral. Perhaps it was out of curiosity or perhaps it was out of some compassion for Ina, the long-suffering wife.

To many people's surprise, the Virginia chief of police escorted Frank Jr. to and from the funeral. He was in handcuffs and an orange prison uniform. Ina tried to hug her criminal baby, Frankie, before they took him away. The police wouldn't allow him near her. Thankfully, they didn't allow him near Margie either. He had been coached to just keep his head down. My old buddy Clay Fortson, of Fortson Welding where Frank once worked, attended the funeral and kept a watch on the jailbird. He told me he saw Frank looking at Margie with an "evil countenance"—whatever that is.

Also to many people's surprise, Frank's brother, Vince, attended the funeral. Having never married, he lived in Washington State and made good money building log homes.

Being home brought him back to that night in the store basement, when he'd punched his kid brother, Frank. That night, he promised himself he would never hit Frank again. He promised himself he would do whatever it took to get by on his own. In the darkness, while fearing for his life and the lives of his mother and brother, he formulated a plan.

After the funeral, Vince visited his incarcerated brother. Frank hadn't lost his volatile temper. Frank railed on about the "bogus rape charges" and his hatred for "those damn Hortons." It was everyone else's fault, he claimed. He'd been railroaded.

All Vince heard was a victim mentality reminiscent of their father's. Leaving the prison, Vince hated his father that much more.

Realizing Frank's side of the story was far from complete or reliable, Vince called Margie. As he put it, "I need your help to connect the dots with my family."

They met in the Cities and Margie repeated her story. As she quietly spoke, Vince wondered how such a beautiful, classy, compassionate woman had gotten involved with Frank in the first place. Well, this Margie hadn't. The Margie who had gotten involved with Frank was an insecure sixteen-year-old girl who had never dated anyone else. Vince shuddered when he pictured his brother treating Margie as his father had treated their mother.

Vince shared his own story about how he had left home with stolen money. With some earned pride, Vince showed Margie pictures of the houses he had built. Margie asked questions about Washington and mentioned she would like to see the beauty of the state someday.

A couple of weeks later, Margie received two airline tickets, $500 cash, and an invitation to visit Vince in Washington. His note said, "The second ticket is for you to bring anyone you wish." Cy, Margie's father, had never been on an airplane, so he happily accepted her offer to travel with her.

Margie and Vince, two broken people in need of healing companionship, were attracted to each other. Two months after that first visit, she returned to Washington by herself.

Three months after that, the announcements column in the *Mesabi Sentinel* reported "Margaret (Margie) Kolar married Vincent (Vince) Nazar in a church near Tacoma, Washington."

Mike stumbled across the announcement as he sat at the counter of the Loon, eating an omelet before work with a car-pooling ironworker friend.

Though he'd been married to Sharri for quite some time, it hit him hard. A wave of sadness overcame him. Mike felt a choking sensation in his throat.

He excused himself, and once in the men's room, he broke down and cried. He stayed in the restroom until he had regained his composure, then he joined his bewildered friend back in the diner.

Mike called me at work that afternoon and shared the news. He usually called me at home. I realized he called at work this time because it wasn't a conversation Susan or Sharri would want to know about.

We both grieved for our losses. In retrospect, that phone call may have been the closest we had ever been.

I had a nagging feeling this wouldn't end my feelings for Margie. This wasn't closure. I also worried whether Vince had his dad's or his brother's violent tendencies. But I had to remind myself none of this was my business anymore.

"I'm gonna do my best to be happy for Margie," Mike said with sincerity and determination. "It might take a while, but I'll get there."

I already had tears forming; now they fell freely. Mike had always been a lot smarter than I gave him credit for. There he was, challenging himself to stay positive and think of Margie first.

Once again, I thought, *Nobody can make me feel more like an asshole than Mike can.*

———

Long ago, I presented myself with a personal challenge. My challenge was to overcome my resentment toward Colleen and Roger. With Colleen and Susan being sisters, we would often cross paths. And while we could never know for sure if he was truly my son, Cy looked more like me every year.

When my mother-in-law's health worsened, Colleen wanted to move closer to her—and to Susan as well. Roger applied for a transfer to a congregation near Apple Valley. But to his disappointment and to Colleen's consternation, he still didn't get assigned to a congregation in the Cities.

Instead, he became pastor at a church in southern Minnesota, about a hundred miles from Apple Valley. The parish was somewhat larger than Saint James in Mesabi. So when Roger, Colleen, and little Cy packed up and left Mesabi, they drove right through the Cities and continued for another two hours to reach their new home.

Colleen asked Roger, "Have you ever wondered who you pissed off at the synod office?"

Roger said nothing. He needed to block out those kinds of negative thoughts.

The Lunds experienced much uncertainty as to what and when they should tell Cy about his birth parents. They decided to wait until he was older to share the truth. Whether their strategy was wise or not, it didn't make things any easier.

Colleen and Susan remained close over the years, so we were with their family many times. I always felt a little awkward, even if I shouldn't have been. I don't think I was alone in this.

Roger and Colleen did encourage Margie to remain an important part of Cy's life. But Margie lost out in those early years when Colleen did not want Cy to know who his birth mother was. Margie was relegated to being their "special friend." She visited often. Yet this was another disadvantage for Margie because her finances were limited and sometimes she was out of state.

When Cy turned twelve, Roger and Colleen finally sat down and told him the truth. Understandably, Cy expressed some questions. So, his birth mother was "Special Friend Margie." And Uncle Jake was his birth father. And his birth father was married to Aunt Susan—who really wasn't an aunt by blood at all. And what went on between his "other mom" and his uncle-slash-birth father? You get the idea. And that's not even adding in that Cy's birth mother was married to the brother of the man who could, however unlikely, be his actual birth father because he was raping her at the time she was also sleeping with Uncle Jake.

After the truth came out, I agreed to meet with Roger, Colleen, and Cy. I found it difficult to sit there and at this stage tell him, "I already love you as my nephew." It sounded hollow. It was hollow.

Cy, JJ, and Lindsey had always gotten along very well. That didn't change once the truth was revealed. Lindsey thought of Cy as her other big brother. Cy seemed more serious than JJ, which wasn't surprising. Susan's playful spirit was so present for the kids every day. When I turned forty, Cy was seventeen, and he seemed ten years more mature than JJ at twelve.

There was very little I could ever complain about when it concerned Susan. Considering how she'd been thrown into this mess in the first place, she handled it with compassion and grace. Unlike me, she never resented Roger and Colleen. A forgiving nature is a hallmark of those who hold the teachings of Jesus. And this described Susan Sundquist. She was, after all, the one to tell me that God can take a mess and make a message out of it.

That said, Susan was often protective when it came to my relationships with JJ and Cy. I do and I don't understand why she tensed up whenever I made positive comments about Cy. In my mind, I was never comparing the two boys. We had plenty of love in us for all three of the kids.

Susan was also territorial toward Margie. I made it my business to avoid being around the Lunds when Margie was visiting. However, Susan always "happened" to be at the Lunds' home when Cy's "other mom" was in town.

A few weeks before my birthday, the issue came to a head. Cy told me he was thinking of attending the U. He expressed interest in a part-time job at our original store. When I shared that with Susan, her response was so unlike her.

"I fail to see why that's a good idea. Jake, he is *Roger's* son. You need to remember that."

I didn't like the tone at all. "Susan, do you want to talk about your attitude toward Cy? I'm starting to wonder if you still see him as the product of my relationship with Margie, not your nephew."

Susan denied it and quickly moved on to another conversation. But in this case—albeit, rare case—she knew I was right.

Looking back, I think Susan understood I had experienced a passionate relationship with Margie. She suspected I still held potentially destructive feelings and desires toward her. Outwardly, I denied that very thought, but inwardly, I wondered. Time had done nothing to diminish Margie's looks. Or my attraction to her.

———

The whole matter brought a very important truth to light. As I reflected upon turning forty, I knew two things: One, I couldn't have been married to a better wife. Fifteen years of marriage did nothing to diminish my love and passion for her. I could honestly say I looked forward to seeing her every single day.

But two, I still fantasized being with other women.

Had it stopped every time with "fantasy," I would have nothing to be ashamed about.

But sometimes I did more than look. I'm glad I wasn't caught.

How I could not see the incongruity when I said I loved my wife in one sentence yet talked about my infidelity in the next sentence, I don't know.

For the most part, my "big head" did the thinking. I loved my wife and our life. I didn't want to lose everything. But sometimes I still let my "little head" make the decisions. Dad warned me years ago. Not that he was one to talk. It turned out I didn't *really* know my dad.

Again, it wasn't because I didn't love my wife. When most people act out with affairs, it's because they're discontented with their spouses or anxious about their life in general. If my marriage had been the problem, I would have simply ended it.

People lament the divorce rate. I lament how many bad marriages last until "death do you part." Some of those long-time marriages are nothing to emulate. The passion, the surprise, and the love burned out a long time ago. A man in an unhappy marriage bears a similarity to a man who hates his job. In both cases, he fears the unknown so much he willingly wastes a big part of his life doing something he's not meant to do and being with someone he's not meant to be with.

Excuses for not leaving an unhappy job or marriage can be simple or elaborate, but they remain excuses. Meanwhile, you not only drain your chance for true happiness in life but you make the people around you suffer for your lack of guts.

But I wasn't one of those men who had trapped himself in a bad marriage. I wasn't seeking out other women to mask some sort of indecisiveness. For me, the need to experience sex with other women came from the simple lust I held for good-looking women. It was nothing more than that.

Sometimes I wondered if I was still trying to prove I was "good with girls." Memories of being an awkward virgin through high school and college haunted me. Granted, then I won over a knockout like Margie, and I never looked back after that. What was left to prove? And to whom did I need to prove it?

It seemed the devil had mixed up the perfect brew for trouble: my love of women and my love of work. As my business grew, I still held that Iron Range trait of "Work hard—play hard." There were plenty of conferences and expos to attend out of town, creating opportunities to do more than just mix and mingle in the hotel bars at night.

Even back at home, Marina had a penchant for hiring attractive women. She told me how middle-aged men would just nod along with their wives' expensive flooring choices as they mentally undressed the saleswomen. I scoffed at that, but I knew there was at least some truth to it. I certainly knew what effect these women had on me.

Of course, there was Marina herself. And Rita. Both were temptation on heels. They threw a *Wizard of Oz* party once. Rita came as Dorothy with pigtails and a gingham dress. But the dress had been altered with a low-cut top that showed more than I'd seen before and a slit that showed her absolutely stunning legs.

And Mother of Jesus, Marina came as the Wicked Witch. She looked like, well, a hooker, with a tight black sweater, a cape, black leather shorts, and black boots. She was crazy intriguing with heavy black eye makeup. Her lips, though, were heavily covered with a deep red lipstick. You can't even imagine how sexy this getup looked. Trust me.

Me, I was the Wizard—the man behind the curtain. You get the idea.

I tended to absolve myself by thinking all men have these same feelings, but because they *can't* act on them, they just sweep them under the carpet. Nobody knows.

Well, hardly nobody.

30

I SPENT A LOT OF TIME DENYING my fortieth birthday meant anything
special to me. The big day finally emerged in the form of a birthday
party Susan described as "mandatory." When the guests started to arrive
around six, I had gone from being skeptical about the need for this
party to downright wanting it to be over.

Roger, Colleen, and Cy were staying with us. Most of Susan's relatives
were coming. Judy and Anna had arrived two days earlier and gotten a room
at the Embassy Suites hotel. Mike, Sherri, and their boys roomed there as well.
Mom and Devin were staying with DeeDee and Trevor.

I was content to just observe this odd mixture of people, but I knew I had
to circulate regardless of my feelings. Many people from work were there. Susan
had originally suggested we invite only management and salespeople, those
who had personal relationships with me. But I demurred. Some people get so
jealous in situations such as this, so I invited everyone at my store. Now as I
listened to my biggest bellyacher, a tile installer, attempt to wow Susan's doctor
with his opinions on where the country was going, I regretted my decision. I
figured the doctor would sneak away at first chance, and that's what she did.

A continuous stream of well-wishers came at me. I so wished Susan would
have specified no gifts. It's hard to describe the assorted junk people paid good
money to wrap. Early in the evening, I stopped pretending "Oh Lordy, you're
forty" was amusing.

After a couple of drinks, I finally started to get into the spirit. The party
had just begun when I could see, booze was the glue in this event. A cake with
forty glowing candles presented the backdrop for the dreaded but necessary
"Happy Birthday to You" song. I passed up some offerings for birthday spank-
ings but gratefully accepted offers for drink refills. The party got loud.

Around ten o'clock, Mike and his family decided to head back to the Embassy Suites to go swimming before bed. JJ, Lindsey, and Cy asked if they could join them. Roger agreed to take them so they could swim for a few hours before returning back to our place.

Finally, it was near midnight. Susan needed to bring her mother and father back to their house. That left me and Colleen.

She sat down on the couch and invited me to get a drink before joining her.

"Jake, maybe we should have that talk we've never had?"

She kind of slurred the "never had." I didn't say anything, but for a moment, I felt like the kid back in Luther League, entranced by this attractive woman. I figured, *What harm could there be in talking?*

"So what's the talk we've never had?" I asked.

"Just think, Jake—back in Mesabi, who would have ever thought you would be my brother-in-law, married to my kid sister? I sometimes get jealous of Susan. I mean, wow—look at this mansion." She gestured around the room. "Plus, I always had kind of a thing for you. Did you know that?"

I should have been uncomfortable. I should have wanted to change the subject. Rather, I found it strangely and perversely alluring.

"Really? No, Colleen, I never knew that. But back then in Luther League, seeing you there was always a highlight. And you're still a sexy dish."

"You're making me blush," Colleen slurred.

Common sense told me to brew some coffee and move the conversation from the couch to the kitchen. But I ignored the inner voice of reason. Instead, I took another swig of my scotch.

Colleen stood up, albeit shakily, and made her way to the stereo system. She turned up the volume on the Yanni cassette playing softly.

"Can I have this dance?" she asked.

I tentatively took her hand, and she brought me close. I was conscious that Susan or Roger could return any moment, so I swayed with her, leading us away from the living room entrance.

Colleen moved even closer, wanting me to kiss her. I wondered how far she would go. I found myself bridging my past fantasies with a possibly disastrous future.

I kissed her. The kissing became passionate. She took our held hands and brought them to her breasts.

"Jake, love me."

I thought I heard the front door opening.

Suddenly, I moved back from her. She almost fell, but she grabbed the fireplace hearth to restore her balance. She looked at me with her eyes half closed. She was beyond pale.

"Colleen, what are we doing? I'm married to your sister, for God's sake."

She put her hands over her face and walked toward the sofa. I took her hand and guided her to her seat. She slumped down on the couch and started to cry.

Apparently, my ears had deceived me, because no one was home. Still, I knew Susan was on her way, as were Roger and the kids. While better than being caught in an embrace, I didn't want to get caught sitting on the couch with a sobbing Colleen.

I took her hand again. "Why don't you go to bed? I'll wait up for Susan and Roger."

With that, she mumbled an apology and headed for the guest room. I could hear her fumbling for the light switch, crying, so I went in to help her.

Before I even knew what I was doing, I drew her close. We kissed passionately once again. My primal instincts were to screw her right there.

Instead, I whispered, "Not here, not now."

I turned the lamp on, closed her door, and left her alone. I wondered how she would act in the morning. I thought about the repercussions if she confessed to Roger—let alone Susan. I sat there with my drink, angry at myself.

"Jake, what was that about?" I literally asked myself as I sank back into the couch.

Was I just being a guy? That wasn't the first time—nor the last, likely—that I'd put my marriage at risk. Or was it more than that? Maybe I was acting out the anger and resentment I still harbored toward Colleen and Roger.

I wanted to be honest with myself. Yes, I still resented Colleen's role in the whole Margie saga. Nobody cared about the ongoing discomfort I endured because she and Roger were raising my child. Perhaps our tryst was a way to knock her down a peg or two as payback.

But I really wasn't a payback kind of guy. Would any revenge be worth hurting Susan, who would lose not just me but her older sister? Hell no. So maybe it wasn't out of anger.

Maybe I just got turned on, and that was all there was to it.

I decided to start cleaning up the place. I needed to do something positive to balance my guilt for the shit that just happened. I gathered up my drink and read some of my birthday cards until the others returned. I pledged to never utter another word about this to anybody, including Colleen.

Ten minutes later, Roger arrived with the kids. After quick hellos, they all headed to their beds.

Susan came home shortly after that. She peeked in the living room looking for me.

What a lucky man I am, I thought as she sat next to me and kissed me. I put my hand gently on her inner thigh.

"You are a bad little birthday boy," she whispered.

I couldn't help but smile inwardly at a little twisted humor. *Well, maybe I am bad. But I'm not as bad as your big sister.*

"It's been a long day, but if you're up for it, I am," she said as she kissed me again.

I pretended to look hurt. "What? You think I'm too old now? And here I've been, praying you would be loving me tonight."

"Well, then, prayer answered."

The next morning, Susan was surprised to find a note on the kitchen table. Roger, Colleen and Cy had decided to leave early. Apparently, Colleen needed to get back for some reason.

———

With my birthday being in November, it always felt like the official beginning of the Horton holidays. From my birthday to Thanksgiving and then Christmas, celebrations were right around the corner.

Christmas always gave us a reason to celebrate and to be thankful. In the days leading up to Christmas Eve, Susan poured herself into gift-giving. The kids rarely asked for specific things because they knew their mother liked to surprise them. Her gifts were always better than what they would have asked for, anyway.

The only gifts I needed to buy were Susan's. But even that I struggled with.

Two days before Christmas Eve, I told her, "I have no idea what to buy you, Susan. What do you need?"

She smiled as she straightened my shirt collar. "I know you like to get me clothes, but you don't have to. At the very least, make sure you keep the receipts so I can exchange them." She smiled again. "But if you want to give me something I would really love, give me a gift certificate that says you'll try Bible study with me for one quarter. I would love to have you go with me, Jake."

With her degree in Christian social work as her foundation, Susan had long been committed to working within the church, but she was also open to applying her faith outside the church. Because she didn't need to work for income, she was more than happy to volunteer in various church and community affairs. She often participated in Bible studies, and she always encouraged me to join her.

Bible studies weren't anything new for me. Growing up in Mesabi, my church experience at Saint James could be called typical Lutheran. I participated in youth Bible study and, of course, Luther League. Then again, I rarely enjoyed church activities nor that crowd of people, for that matter. But my parents made it mandatory to attend.

Once I was on my own in the Cities, I never attended any church on a regular basis. So when Susan and I married, it only made sense that I join her church. She loved Family of the Risen Lord, which belonged to a loose confederation called the Assemblies of the Lord.

The decision to join her church rather than seek my own Lutheran church was simple—it meant a lot to me to worship nearly every Sunday with my wife and later with our kids. It pleased me that JJ and Lindsey were both sincerely committed to the faith and active in church activities. I gave Susan most of the credit for the kids' dedication.

Joining a new church took some give-and-take. I was more accustomed to formal worship at Saint James, compared to the Christian contemporary style at Family of the Risen Lord. I wouldn't say I was troubled by the guitars and drums and the modern songs, but I still preferred the traditional liturgy. I missed the old hymns my mother used to sing with us.

But on the plus side, the membership was clearly more engaged at Family of the Risen Lord. The main message came through loud and clear: You need a personal relationship with Jesus Christ. That said, some of the people at Family of the Risen Lord seemed too in-your-face and too demanding—which provided me a good excuse to not get involved much.

My involvement came from my financial contributions, I figured. I understood that each church has a budget and that it's important to pledge a certain amount of money for the operation and mission. Still, I never committed to tithing—giving 10 percent off the top. Susan and I mildly disagreed on this matter.

When my income increased substantially, I "tithed" by calculating the percentage of my income taxes that went to social welfare in general and adding that to my own contributions to the church. Regardless of the exact percentages, I knew I was one of the top contributors in the church. That seemed quite enough. Of course, I never discounted the message of the "Widow's Mite" parable. I heard that story many times at Sunday worship and always during stewardship campaigns—or in my lingo, "pledge drives."

With all this in mind, I gave Susan a quick kiss on the cheek. Her "gift certificate" idea was perfect. With some chagrin, I had to admit she was the best gift-giver—even the best at giving herself gifts.

At the last minute before Christmas Eve, I rushed into Dayton's department store. My typical buying technique was to find an outfit I liked on a featured display, buy it along with some jewelry, have it all wrapped, and place it under the tree in the nick of time. I truly liked to surprise and delight her. But these days, I had no idea what to buy. She returned more than she kept.

While I was proud that my business success allowed Susan to get the kids whatever they wanted—or more to the point, whatever she wanted to give them—I still felt out of the loop. The presents, the wrapping, the decorations—it was all Susan.

Thankfully, Susan realized this and asked me to read the story of the birth of Christ by our tree every year before we opened gifts. We somehow made it through the years when JJ and Lindsey didn't want to sit and listen while their gifts sat unopened. But now they waited for me to read the tale from our Bible as if the words were magical.

No doubt this was my favorite part of Christmas. I was proud to bring the "true meaning" of Christmas to the family. What I loved most was that Susan had purposefully given me this role in our family tradition.

After the gifts were all opened and after the kids went to bed, Susan and I tidied up around the tree. She laughed and shook her head as she ran her hand over the clothes I had bought her.

"I like the outfit, but I'm not twenty-one," she gently reprimanded me. "This may surprise you, but I don't shop in the juniors' department anymore!"

I knew what she meant, but I disagreed silently. Her seeing me as clueless hurt a little.

I decided to be honest. "Suze, I know you think these clothes don't look good on you. But you're wrong. You still look great in tight clothing—I love it when you show off your figure. That said, I think I'm guilty of buying for me instead of for you. Next time, I'll try to buy something more like what you wear these days."

Her expression told me I had surprised her. She came over and hugged me tightly.

"Jake, I love you for trying."

As quickly as she hugged me, she disengaged.

"I do love the earrings, though," she went on. "The emeralds and diamonds are stunning. I'm glad you still like my ears. Considering all the body parts I need to turn on my husband, my ears have held up the best, I guess."

Susan was silent for a moment. I'm sure she was contemplating whether to say anything about the certificate—the one thing she had asked me to get her. Just as she opened her mouth and turned to face me, I handed her an envelope. Inside was a simple handwritten note that said: "I will attend Bible study with you."

With tears, she held the certificate her to heart. "I think you'll love going to the study with me. I really do. And I love you most for doing this."

———

We made our way to the living room to watch some TV before winding down for the evening. Or actually, I watched the news and Johnny Carson while Susan read from her Bible and study guide. I looked over at her once, with her specs down on her cute little nose. She glanced up and met my gaze.

"Jacob"—she never called me that—"do you know what your name means?"

I thought for a couple of moments, trying to remember what Mom had once shared with me.

"Well, I know Jacob was the twin brother of Esau. His parents were Rebecca and Isaac. I think Jacob means 'favored one' because he was his mother's favorite." I paused. "Then again, I think I heard Jacob and Esau struggled in the womb. So does Jacob mean 'one who struggles'? Which is it again?"

She looked at me thoughtfully, took her specs off, and closed her Bible gently. "The study guide says it means 'one who manipulates.'"

Immediately I didn't like the inference, but I kept a poker face.

"I wonder if the interpretation comes from the story about when Jacob and his mother stole Esau's birthright," I speculated. "Is that the only possible meaning listed for the name?"

Susan opened her notebook. "It says here other variants may be 'circumvent,' 'assail,' 'overreach,' or from the word *heel*, like the heel of a foot. That likely came from during childbirth—Jacob was grasping Esau's heel, or something like that. I can look it up."

"Don't bother," I said, then quickly steered us in a new direction. "By the way, what does Susan mean?"

"That isn't so clear because my name is a variant of another name, which means 'lily.' Apparently, women accompanied Jesus in his ministry, and Lily referred to women bringing gifts."

She again closed her notebook. She was quiet for a while, but I could see she had more thoughts on the matter.

"Wouldn't it be nice if people's names described what they really were like? 'How are you doing today, Violent in Nature?'" she play-acted. "Or 'Hey there, Talks Too Much.' Or 'How are things going, Known To Be Infertile?'" She couldn't resist adding, "Tell me again where you were last night, He Who Manipulates."

I almost asked straight out if she had something to discuss. Instead, I opted for a nod and light laugh, pretending I was taking her comments at face value. When somebody makes a soft challenge, a thin skin often indicates guilt. The person sending the challenge does so with the idea of watching how you react. They hope you'll tell them something they don't know for sure.

Perhaps Susan wanted a bigger conversation but lacked the courage or desire to bring it out in the open. Perhaps it was a simple observation about names. Either way, it troubled me.

Did I consider myself "one who manipulates"? Yes, I did. What is the difference between motivating and manipulating? Very little. What's the difference between manipulation and persuasion? Also very little. Can you motivate and persuade and not manipulate? I don't think so.

Did Susan now regret JJ's name? Was she worried he would grow up to take on some of his dad's characteristics?

He was twelve now. We were beginning to discuss the emotional and physical dangers of sex outside of marriage. More importantly, he knew my actions with Margie had resulted in his cousin—his half-brother, more accurately.

With his teenage years right ahead of him, I hoped he was on the right path. It pained me to think his morals could be as disappointing as mine.

But were they "my" morals? Or was I just like all other men? Are we all the same, only that some of us have more opportunities, less fear, and the means to act on the fantasies we all create?

One thing for sure, Susan's approval meant a lot to me. I went to sleep that Christmas Eve night wondering if Colleen had told her about what happened at the birthday party. Hell, what would Colleen's version of the whole story even be? Who knows what she told Susan, if anything.

Then again, I doubted Colleen would ever share the details. After all, she had made the move on me, not the other way around. For her to repeat the story in any form would surely result in an end to Susan's friendship. And things would never be the same between her and Roger. She wouldn't risk either one, I thought.

I wondered now what the name Colleen meant.

I checked it out the next morning. It meant "victory of the people." I wasn't sure how that would play out.

31

SOMEONE ONCE SAID, "LIFE IS LIKE a roll of toilet paper—the closer you get to the end, the faster it goes."

Like the hour glass shown at the beginning of the popular soap opera *Days of Our Lives*, life goes by little by little, almost invisibly. But goes by it does.

Susan hadn't been feeling well, so we quietly shared my forty-ninth birthday at home, just the two of us. I cringed when she said we would really celebrate next year, for my "big five-oh." I made her promise me she wouldn't plan a big party. Not even a little party.

Thinking about parties made me think, *It's been nine years since that crazy fortieth, when I almost had sex with Colleen.*

Sadly, in some ways, I had gotten older but no smarter.

There was still the Jake Horton who deeply loved his wife. And then there was still the Jake Horton who continued to look for the excitement of intimate relationships with other women.

These two worlds were about to crash and change almost everything.

It began with a surprise phone call from our lead pastor. As it turned out, that Bible studies certificate I gave to Susan had led me deeper and deeper into church involvement over the years. With JJ now twenty-one and Lindsey eighteen, both were in college, leaving us more time to devote to our church.

"Jake," the pastor said, "you've become such a positive force here, I would like you to consider leading our Growth Ministry."

This unexpected request flattered me. While my first thought was to just say no, I found myself interested as well as flattered. I later discussed the topic with Susan, and she encouraged me to be open to the call of the Spirit.

The more I immersed myself in the church, the more Susan suggested I had missed my calling for parish ministry. She once made comments of this nature when we were with Colleen and Roger. Colleen looked at me briefly, her eyes filled with shame, while Roger launched into a wordy discourse about how selling rugs was like bringing people to Jesus. Interesting how one look can say more than ten minutes of words.

I accepted the position to lead the Growth Ministry. My orientation would begin with Susan and me attending a Billy Graham rally the next week with the lead pastor and his wife.

A few days before the rally, however, Gary and I would attend the Floor Covering Market in Dalton, Georgia. I was anticipating the trip a little more than I should have been. And for all the wrong reasons.

After buying carpet for over twenty-five years from men, I got a call—several calls and a visit, actually—from Tanya Jamison, a persistent female carpet wholesale rep from New Horizon. She stopped in the store once to present her "Hot Favorites."

Tanya looked to be in her early thirties. A striking brunette, just a bit overweight, she carried herself in a manner that seemed to say, "Here I am, boys—you should be so lucky." Working in a "man's world," her language could be tough, and she laughed a little too long and too hard at some questionable jokes. She liked to touch people when she talked. Fact is, though, she was a damned good rep and knew how to get the order.

Her carpet line didn't interest me, but her body lines did. And she was one of those women who would know.

Marina happened to walk by when Tanya leaned in real close, put her hand on mine, and said, "I would do *anything* to get you to try this in your stores."

Marina gave me the eye.

Tanya invited me to meet up with her at the wholesale carpet market in Dalton. We made plans to connect on Wednesday. She said her company paid for a handful of rooms at the Holiday Inn, and she wanted to pay for mine and Gary's.

"I like to stay on the seventh floor," she added. "They have a hospitality bar. It can be a lot of fun. What do you think?"

Gary and I had attended the market for over ten years. In the past, I always booked two adjoining rooms. But this year, I booked my room on the seventh floor and Gary's on the first. I even planned an excuse to explain how I wound up alone up on the seventh floor.

As I packed my suitcase, I felt an odd combination of guilt and excitement. Adding to the guilt was the fact that Susan was relaxing on our bed as I packed.

"Do you think you'll ever get tired of markets?" she asked.

I paused. "I hope not. But I'll miss you."

She opened her arms as she lay there on our bed. I embraced her.

"I'll be back on Thursday," I said.

"Don't forget I have that doctor's appointment on Wednesday," she added as I gave her one last good-bye kiss and headed for the door.

———

Gary and I worked hard on the first day, "Market Tuesday," as it was called. We found several new carpet styles from existing suppliers to fill gaps in our selection. Neither of us liked the new "sculptured plush" style. We wondered if it would be a service nightmare when it began to flatten in peoples' homes.

We enjoyed a nice steak dinner and a couple of beers before turning in. As Gary turned down the hall toward his room, I turned for the elevator.

"Isn't your room next to mine?" he asked.

"No, I'm on seven," I said with a look of disappointment. "All the first-floor rooms must have been taken. Good night," I added as slipped inside the elevator.

Day two, we liked to look at new potential brands. Even if we didn't buy them, it could be helpful knowing what our competitors were selling.

When I nonchalantly mentioned I had promised to look at the New Horizon introductions, Gary grinned and laughed.

"Marina said I better put a muzzle on you if you visit New Horizon."

I resented the comment on many different fronts. Mostly, the comment ticked me off because Marina knew what was really going on, and now so did Gary. Here I was, the owner and the leader, and they thought I was willing to put so-so products on display just because I wanted to jump Tanya's bones.

"Well, what if they have something to fill our needs?" I asked. "Should we not buy because Marina thinks the rep is too sexy?" I held my hands up. "Okay, smartass—I'll let you make the call here. If you think it's a waste, we'll move on."

Gary laughed but did in fact take the lead when we met with Tanya. Surprisingly, she showed us three exclusive carpets we both liked for look and price. Both Gary and I were happy to place an order, though I'm sure I was happier. As we were leaving, Tanya shook our hands—and winked discreetly at me once Gary turned.

I knew what the wink meant. She'd meet me at the seventh-floor lounge that night. I was excited with anticipation. Unaware, Gary headed off to his first-floor room.

I went to the lounge, ordered a tap beer, and found a booth. As I glanced around, my inner voice started up. *Who are you kidding, Jake? You're nearly fifty, and she's in her late twenties or early thirties. Don't make a fool of yourself. What are you doing, getting all excited about having sex with this woman? It's just business to her. You're still screwing prostitutes. And what if she doesn't show? Or what if she shows up with some guy twenty years younger? What then? Do you cancel the carpet order?*

Those worries flew out of the window when Tanya not only showed up but also squeezed in right next to me in my booth. I still wasn't convinced, so I tried a technique I had read about in some second-rate novel: I moved my leg right next to hers. According to the novel's theory, if her mind was on the same horny wavelength, she would keep her leg next to mine.

Well, my overperforming rep actually moved her leg over and between mine.

With that settled, she pulled my face toward her and kissed me. "Your room or mine, Jakester?" she whispered.

"How about both?" I replied.

I quickly paid the tab. As we got up, she grabbed my butt. I jumped, providing entertainment for both my new friend and the others trying to enjoy their drinks in the lounge. We carried on like eighteen-year-olds with bad judgment as we proceeded down the hall toward my room.

When we came around the corner, there was Gary. His face was flooded with disapproval.

"Hey, Harry," she said, getting his name wrong. "Do you want to join us for a drink?"

Gary just put his hand up for silence. "Jake, can I talk to you in private?" he said crisply.

We moved to the other side of the hall as Tanya slipped into her room next to mine.

"First of all, you idiot—what the hell are you doing? If you fuck her, don't ever think of me as a friend again. You're married to a wonderful woman—an all-star. And you're willing to risk it for a minor league bench-warmer? You're a fucking idiot. You're an almost fifty-year-old fucking idiot. Right now, I can't stand to look at you, Peter Pan."

Something else was fueling Gary's anger, though.

"And to think I came up here to tell you something serious is happening back home with your family. JJ called me. He's been trying to get ahold of you all day. He said Susan got some bad news at her doctor apppointment today. You need to call home right away."

I tried to explain away what Gary had seen, but he once again put his hand up. "Stop. Jake, go down to my room and call home—now."

I called the house. JJ answered. He was upset but didn't know what to say except, "Dad, where have you been all day? Mom has cancer. It's spread through her. Please come home."

With all my planning to get with Tanya, I had forgotten about Susan's appointment. I squeezed the phone, wanting to squish it to powder.

I asked to talk to his mother. Susan came on the phone.

"I hear we had a lousy appointment today," I said.

She wept softly. "Jake, come home as soon as you can."

I've hated myself before, but this was extreme loathing. It cut deeper.

I took the first flight available, arriving home Thursday afternoon. I hesitated briefly before I got out of my car. Would this place ever be the same after this? I picked up my bag and walked in.

I could hear the TV in the living room. I just about broke down when I saw Susan with Lindsey on the right and JJ on the left, all sitting on the couch with a blanket over their legs.

"Hey, it's good to have you home," she said quietly. "Sit with us. We've decided to not talk about our worries right now."

I liked that plan. I crawled in between the two girls.

Eventually, we did talk. From what I understood, Susan had gone to the doctor to check out a lump under her arm. Cancer had invaded her lymph nodes and then from there had likely spread to the intestines and appendix. Susan had the impression radiation was perhaps an option but unlikely to work. She would be seeing another specialist on Monday.

———

I assumed we wouldn't go to the Billy Graham rally in two days, but I assumed wrong. Susan was determined to attend.

The rally sold out. The convention center rocked with enthusiasm, building in fervor through several gifted preachers and through wonderful music and beloved hymns.

Then Billy Graham, without an introduction, walked briskly to the pulpit. The crowd cheered. The musicians led us through a spirited version of the wonderful praise hymn "Crown Him with Many Crowns." Reverend Graham began his message by reading from the Gospel of Mathew, chapter 27, verse 28: "They stripped him and put a scarlet robe on him, and made a crown from long thorns and forced it on his head . . ."

His voice dropped very low as he prayed, "My Savior, forgive me for reading this so many times and not coming close to grasping the sacrifice you made for me."

One of Reverend Graham's assistant pastors brought what looked like a nest of sticks to him. A close-up of the piece appeared on the large screen behind him, and I could now see it was a crown of thorns. Reverend Graham described how he had made the crown with the help of his daughter. He showed us his hands—a Band-Aid on nearly every finger. His voice became quiet again as he described how difficult it was to handle the thorns without cutting himself.

"I realized, to my shame, the pain brought upon Jesus when those soldiers forced that wicked crown on his innocent head. How the blood would have drained down his face and neck. Yet Jesus himself beseeched his Father, 'Forgive them, for they know not what they do.'"

Reverend Graham lifted his head. "Dear friends, our forgiveness did not come cheap. Our God is a big God. And believe it—he wants you to know that no matter what sins you may be bearing, they are not too big for our God."

If I live to be a hundred, I will never know what came over me at this moment in my life. Time stood still. It was God and me.

My tears flowed uncontrollably, inexplicably down my face, just as the blood had drained down Jesus's innocent head. I closed my eyes, and Jesus came to my mind with the awful picture of that torturous crown inflicting unfathomable pain on him. Then with my eyes closed tightly, that awful face of pain changed to a kind and loving face. God smiled at me as if I were a child who just didn't know better.

I sometimes wondered about the sanity of people who claimed God had spoken to them. Not anymore.

God said softly, "Jacob, if you are tired of sinning and tired of squandering what I've given you, come to me. It's up to you. You have to choose. You can't have both. You can pick up my cross and follow me, or you can continue to be burdened and eventually crushed by the weight of your sins."

I'd been so transfixed that I didn't even feel Susan's arms around my neck. Now I realized she was sobbing with me.

Reverend Graham pleaded, "God wants you to live your life without the awful burden of sin. He stands ready to forgive you. Come forward if you are ready to give your life to Jesus."

I hesitated for only a moment. I had never professed my faith in public. But I didn't want to waste this moment. I took Susan's hand, and we walked together to the altar and knelt with the other sinners. Perhaps twenty-five people had come forward like us.

I wept. I wept for the past. I wept for the woman I loved kneeling next to me. Talk about undeserved love.

My mind began to move down from the mountain of emotion to a place of honest reflection. I thought of the people I had treated badly. After all these years, Margie came to mind. Was I to blame for the sadness she had experienced in life? *God forgive me*, I thought, *and let her find the joy you want for all of us.*

Then my thoughts moved to Susan. *God, you sent me an angel, and I've treated her with calculated deceit. Don't let me ever do that again.*

And you blessed me with parents who loved me. And what did I do? I deceived them too, growing to be the fake they never wanted me to be.

People around us were now getting up from their knees. Now, only Susan and I plus one other person remained kneeling before Reverend Graham. Susan and I held each other's hands tightly. I felt her give me a quick squeeze, and we rose slowly.

As I stood, I felt exhilarated. God had spoken to me. I couldn't help but thank him. He forgave me for my selfish and disloyal ways. I felt like a man who had been convicted of a heinous crime and had been given a fifty-year sentence, only to receive a pardon and a chance for a do-over. And nobody knew except God and I.

Nobody knows.

By the time we got back to our seats, though, reality began to tap on my shoulder. I had been living in sin for a long time. This wouldn't be easy.

I thought about my mom, who frequently referenced Psalm 121, her favorite: "I looked unto the hills, from whence cometh my help. My help cometh from the Lord, who made heaven and earth."

God sought me out. Now, I would seek him out for his help.

I had been looking in the wrong places.

32

In church the next morning, Susan stood with me as I declared my intentions to become an Assemblies of the Lord parish minister. I believe it was my goofball son who stood up yelling and clapping. Within moments, the entire church was standing and cheering.

I felt the hand of God. I felt blessed. I felt scared, yet I felt loved by this group of Christians. I felt this was what I was meant to do.

We stayed after the service to speak with our lead pastor, who was thrilled to hear of my decision. He too had felt the power of the Spirit at the Graham rally. He was so happy that we hated to tell him about the other news in our life—Susan's cancer.

"I'm so sorry," Pastor said, reaching out for Susan's head. He turned to me. "I assume, then, you'll be postponing your studies for now? A commitment to ministry would call for you to spend about three months at the Ministry Learning Campus in Greensboro, North Carolina."

Susan reached out with her other hand to take my own.

"We've talked about this," she said, "and I'm adamant that he not postpone anything. I want to see him ordained."

Pastor prayed with us and pledged to help us in any way. Through his connections at the school, and given the special circumstances, perhaps we could arrange for a combination of study at campus and at home.

Clearly, both the pastor and my wife were prepared to do what was necessary to make this happen. Susan couldn't be clearer of her wishes. When we prayed, she asked God to allow her to live long enough to see me preaching at the pulpit.

First thing Monday, I met with Gary, Marina, and Rita and told them I was selling the company. While this seemed sudden, spurred on by the events of the last few days, I actually had been thinking about this for a while. I knew too many successful businessmen who could never let go. I had been thinking about a succession plan for a while, but I never imagined this would all happen at age forty-nine—with plans to become a pastor while my wife battled cancer.

Cy, JJ, and Lindsey would each own one-third. If any of the three opted out or had to be let go, they would forfeit their ownership, but they would be paid a portion of the net worth.

I told Gary, Marina, and Rita I wanted them to be part of the company board along with the kids. I assured Gary, Marina, and Rita they would be well-paid for their roles. The board would distribute profits based on income and contributions to the success of the company. On my end, I would get a significant amount of money up front and then a percentage of the profits for ten years.

What I didn't tell Gary, Marina, and Rita was that I had arranged for each of them to receive a significant bonus if they signed on. I kept that quiet because I didn't want them to agree to serve on the board because of the money.

As I stood to leave, a sharp pain moved raggedly down my right leg to my ankle. I grimaced. Recently, this was the result of sitting too long. I reminded myself to make an appointment with a nerve specialist at some point. But not now. Whatever this was could wait while we focused on Susan's cancer. And our future—whatever that might be.

Susan invited Colleen and Roger to join our family for dinner that evening. She wanted to share the terrible news about her life-threatening cancer as well as my life-changing call from God. I had many reasons for feeling uncomfortable about this plan.

"Are you sure you don't want to just tell them about the cancer?" I asked. "I don't think we should discuss my plans with them now."

Susan held my hand. "Jake, you mean *our* plans, not *your* plans. Plus, I'm so proud of you—I can't hold it in."

The dinner discussion didn't begin well. Before we could share any of our news, Roger and Colleen expressed their "concerns" that I had recently increased Cy's responsibilities at the store without their knowledge. We both resented their attitude, which we translated as Cy being too intelligent to work as a rug peddler.

Susan and I exchanged glances, steeling ourselves for what would be coming once we told them about my plan to sell the company. But it wasn't time to discuss that yet.

"Speaking of 'concerns,'" Susan interceded, "we want to let you know about some important stuff going on here at the Horton's. There's what seems like bad news, and then there's what seems like good news."

I didn't even hear her words as she gave her distressing news to her sister and brother-in-law. I checked out mentally, lost in my own thoughts. I had a fuzzy sense of Roger crying and Colleen wailing. I think I heard Roger inviting the six of us to hold hands and pray.

My thoughts went back to a Luther League meeting at Saint James. A friend at the meeting had lost his dad in a car accident a week before. This was well before I would lose my own father in a similar way. Roger asked the boy if we could pray about it together.

I remember the kid looking down, mumbling, "Maybe pray on your own later, if you have time."

But Roger saw the time was now. He saw an important learning experience for the group.

"If you haven't been touched with tragedy yet in your life, you should build your faith because that's how you can deal with the tough moments that are sure to come." He added with emotion, "Prayer is how we communicate with God. There is nothing God can't do."

All eyes turned to the guy who had just lost his dad. He looked somewhat defiant as he responded, "I'm glad to hear, Pastor, that God can do everything. I would like God to just bring my dad back."

Then—and many times since then—the conversation ended with, "*Thy* will be done. God can do anything but chooses not to for reasons we cannot understand."

Here and now, I wanted God to remove Susan's cancer. I knew he would, if he willed it. Only time would tell what he had willed for us.

Earlier that day, I had called Mom to tell her the news. More assertive and confident in her later years, she came right out and said, "Jake, you have nothing more important in this world now but to make every single day of Susan's life the best it can be."

Perhaps that was why Susan and I both agreed I needed to complete ministry training now, rather than stay home to support her. I knew my limitations, and so did Susan. I had trouble being with sick people. I already felt the loss of the life we experienced before the cancer. I didn't want to think about life without Susan.

I shared this thought with Judy, whom I called after talking with Mom. Judy had faced cancer with Anna's love and support. She asked if I thought denial was part of the equation.

I suddenly realized a question had been directed at me. Everyone was waiting for my response. Susan's hands were gently massaging my shoulders.

"I'm sorry," I simply said. "I'm just having a tough time."

Susan chose this moment to make our second announcement. "We also have some good news. It began when Jake and I committed ourselves to Christ at the Billy Graham rally—"

"Both of you committed yourselves to Christ when you were baptized," Roger interrupted with some skepticism.

Susan ignored it. The pride in her eyes made my heart melt. She nodded for me to continue.

"I'm going to sell my business and begin serving God as a parish minister. I'll go wherever God leads us."

When Roger said, "Gee, that's great," it was one of those moments when it was clear to everybody, including Roger, that he didn't think it was great at all.

Colleen, trying to take Roger off the hook, added, "Well, that's amazing news, Jake. But it takes, what, four years to get through seminary? Doesn't that concern you at all, especially with Susan's news?"

I knew sooner or later things would get unpleasant. It might as well be now.

"I'm not going to be a Lutheran minister. I'm going to be an Assemblies of the Lord minister."

Roger immediately launched into a series of statements expounding how I would be less of a minister than he was because I was taking the easy way via the short course from the Assemblies.

Susan, who of course owned the credentials already, broke into the conversation. "Roger, how many times over the years have you said that most of what you learned in the seminary turned out to be worthless? Now you're trying to say you're more qualified to serve Christ than Jake will be because you spent time learning that worthless information? I can't believe this."

"Who are you selling the company to?" Colleen suddenly blurted.

And here was where it would get really unpleasant. I sat back in my chair.

"To the kids—Cy, JJ, and Lindsey. They will be part of a board along with my right-hand people."

JJ, recognizing a great opportunity coming his way, jumped in. "Dad, that's awesome! Thank you!"

Lindsey just sat there with a stunned smile.

They were the only happy ones, however. If Roger and Colleen didn't like the idea of Cy getting more hours at the store, they really didn't like the idea of him being a part owner. Here I was giving—free—the same equal share of the business as I was giving to JJ and Lindsey, yet they went on and on. Why wouldn't any parent just take this gift on behalf of their son and say thank you? I had about all I could take.

Roger asked for a copy of the agreement so he could analyze it. He actually said "analyze." That didn't impress me. His business acumen was limited to discussions about church budgets.

It occurred to me one or both of them simply did not trust me nor my motives. Did they think I was taking advantage of Cy? I couldn't see how. It made me angry, yes. But it hurt me more. I was giving Cy's future a huge boost that few young people get. And instead of thanking me, they acted as if I had conscripted Cy to some form of service in the lowly flooring business.

Before I could formulate these thoughts into a reply, Susan did it for me.

"I find it hard to believe you're criticizing Jake—for what? For supporting that kid like he has? Isn't Cy old enough to make his own decisions? Geez, Jake pretty much put him through college, and this is the thanks he gets?"

Susan's anger surprised me. She typically felt I went overboard in mentoring Cy and providing for him. In fact, I still wondered if she was comfortable with my decision to include Cy along with JJ and Lindsey as owners. Yet here she was, going to bat for me now.

"We just have hopes for Cy beyond working in a carpet store—that's all I'm trying to say," Colleen said. "It's been a good job for him. Nobody questions that. I just think, given Jake's relationship with Cy, that this is a blurry line."

Roger, of course, added his ditto.

"I too want the best for Cy," I immediately responded. "And I agree it's not all business. When I see how Cy and JJ work together, I like it. I'm proud of them both." I looked at JJ, who was all but biting his tongue. "What do you think, JJ?"

"Well, Dad, you always say the important thing is not what your title or your work may be; it's the honor you bring to the job. Couldn't God call a person to work in retail?"

Roger smiled at JJ. "You are right, and that's well put. But we're speaking from a parental viewpoint. You'll see someday."

My son didn't back down. "Even when I'm a parent, I'll always feel God gives a blessing to people who provide meaningful work—and owning a carpet store with five locations is as meaningful as anything."

"Amen," I said with a sigh.

JJ became very serious. I could see he was mad.

"It appears to me there's way too much jealousy at this table. I can't take it."

JJ got up and left the room; Lindsey followed him.

Right on cue, Roger stood up and Colleen followed.

It was Colleen who made the Lund family's final pronouncement: "This has been a tough night for all of us. I just want to say, never forget we love you both, and we love your kids too. And Susan . . ." She then broke down and wailed as they left.

We each sat there for a moment, shaking our heads. Then Susan came over, and I put my arms around her.

"I am so pissed off, I don't even want to talk about it," she said. "And," she went on, her voice raising, "I'm pissed at you right now."

"Really? What are you upset about? Something I said?"

"No."

I kissed her, but she didn't kiss me back. I was stumped.

"Something I did?"

She looked at me, still in my arms. "No. It's something you *haven't* done. You haven't fucked me since you found out I have cancer, and it's pissing me off."

With that, she grabbed me with mock anger.

"Take me into that bedroom and show me you still love me. Then when you're done, you can show me you really, really love me."

I was already well on my way. "How do I show you that?"

She smiled. "You do the dishes."

33

BEFORE I KNEW IT, I WAS A STUDENT in the Ministry Learning program. Thankfully, they granted me the ability to split time between Greensboro and home. I was on my way to becoming an Assemblies of the Lord parish pastor. It was really happening.

Susan's cancer was really happening too, though. As I began the program, she reached out to cancer specialists to learn more about the fight in front of her.

Right away, I realized the program in North Carolina was more difficult than I had imagined. At forty-nine, I found memorization difficult. And we were told, or possibly warned, we needed to possess a working knowledge of Greek to better understand the New Testament. Susan could help me with this some, but clearly I felt overwhelmed. I was relieved a bit that I wasn't the only "encore" student. With thirty-five of us in the program, several were even older than me.

I was thankful the school allowed me to split time between campus and home. I made many flights back and forth over the weeks. I tried to make the most of my time in transit, bringing my books and notes to study. But as I sat belted in my seat, that throbbing pain would shoot up my right leg. It seemed to yell for attention. If I didn't get up and at least stretch a little, the pain would then shoot down to my ankle and sometimes up my back.

I kept postponing making an appointment. Again, nerve pain was nothing compared to what Susan was going through.

I was in North Carolina when she found out her choices were to either fight the cancer with chemo or plan on dying within a few weeks. She called to ask me what she should do. Of course, I told her no choice existed—she had to try everything to stay alive. I wanted to add "For the kids and me" but didn't. She knew me well enough. She knew that was implied.

"Let me quit my studies so I can be with you as you go through chemo," I pleaded.

At home and in North Carolina, I felt the sadness and burden of Susan's cancer. Even when I had moments of happiness, my mind would quickly remind me: we were losing Susan.

"Jake, you are with me whether you are physically here or not. Please promise me you won't ask this again," she said defiantly.

I didn't ask again. My top priority became to finish my studies; Susan's priority was to fight this cancer with every ounce of energy she could muster.

The next time I was home, Marina called and said we needed a face-to-face.

"Could you come by the house?" I asked.

I knew she understood that my time at home was precious. Chemo was hitting Susan hard.

Nonetheless, she responded, "Jake, it's not that kind of conversation."

I went into the office the next morning. I listened in disappointment as she documented Cy's lack of judgment and immaturity.

In the few months since I had sold the business, the harmony and sense of shared mission I had pictured was nowhere in sight. The six-person board had settled into Marina, Rita, and Gary on one side, and Cy, JJ, and Lindsey on the other. They disagreed on most important matters.

Marina could already see that Cy at twenty-seven was "power hungry"; JJ at twenty-two seemed more level-headed, yet he still linked up with Cy; and Lindsey at nineteen owned the ability to someday succeed but found herself in the middle of the power struggle. I had looked forward to Lindsey learning from Marina and Rita, but Cy had persuaded her to distance herself from them.

"Jake, we've given Cy every chance," she said matter-of-factly. "He's twenty-seven, now, not a child." She handed me the latest sales reports. "Look at these numbers. We're not the fine-tuned machine we were when you were here. I'm working a lot of hours, and I'm just getting more frustrated."

Marina reached over and put her hand on top of mine.

"I'm turning sixty, Jake. I want to retire. Gary may want to retire soon too. And Rita's husband is having some health issues. She either needs to hire somebody to stay with him or she needs to retire so she can care for him."

My leg was getting electric shocks, but the pain of Marina's words was a whole lot worse. I felt tired, very tired.

"What would you do if you were me, Marina?"

She sat back. "I knew you'd ask that. You need to change the charter, which you still have the legal right to do. You need to add one more member to the board, so we don't have these three-against-three deadlocks. And you need to let me select the person—somebody experienced so I know I'll have four votes when something important comes up. Perhaps you could set it up for this person to be the board president when I retire, with the kids reporting to him or her for a few years."

Marina's face was tight. "We need to send Cy a signal. Then he can decide whether this is for him. Cy has a sneaky element to his character. He knows that if he gets in control now, he'll be the 'new Jake.' I could be wrong, but from what I've seen, JJ would be the best leader. Lindsey is a sweet kid, but as I said, she isn't ready. The timing is just bad." Her face lightened a bit. "I want to see her and JJ succeed—Cy too, under the right arrangement. And most importantly, I want the company to survive."

I sat in silence for a moment. I couldn't get her comments about Cy's "sneaky element" out of my mind. They hit me personally. If this was an inherited trait, he had me to blame. I could argue with myself and claim it was a learned behavior. But even then, where would he have learned to be that kind of person? It all came back to me.

"You have to do what you have to do," I finally told her. With that, I slowly got up, cringing with the pain. "Well, thanks, Marina. But I just can't take more good news, so I'll move along."

She laughed, then got serious. "You're moving kind of slow. You seem tired. You better take care of yourself, friend, while you're taking care of others."

"Just because you're turning sixty doesn't mean you've become my mother." I smiled. "You are the best, Marina. I can't thank you enough."

She gave me a hug. "I can never thank *you* enough, boss," she said. "You rescued me. I will never forget that, Jake. Never."

A few days later, I needed to return to the North Carolina campus. One assignment was to come up with a short message to God and then write a sermon using that as a title. Marina's heartfelt "You rescued me" hit a chord with me. I came up with a sermon of thanks for God's rescue.

One of my teachers and I shared a beer and conversation after the assignment. We got to talking about God's rescue and his involvement in our daily lives. I said I just didn't think God worried about the minutiae of our day-to-day lives, despite how Gospel reads. I wondered what he thought.

Instead of a direct answer, he told me a modern-day parable: A preacher was running late for an important service. He turned into the huge parking lot and started praying out loud, "God, please provide me with a parking spot close to the entrance. If you do, I promise I will never run late again and put myself in this predicament." Just then, a big car backed out of a space near the front. As he pulled his car in, the pastor updated God, "Don't worry about the parking spot, God. I found one by myself."

Once again, I was away when Susan called with an important update. This time, it was good news, a miracle of sorts. The cancer was gone. She had stabilized. The oncologist and surgeon agreed. She could stop the chemo treatments, but she needed to see her doctor once a month.

Now, simply living a normal life brought great joy. I threw myself into the final stages of my studies with renewed passion. When I was home, sometimes I would quietly sneak back into the bedroom just to watch her sleep as she recovered from the chemo effects. When I looked at Susan, I didn't just love her; I loved God.

The everyday concerns of life soon replaced the anxiety of Susan's cancer. We moved on, almost seamlessly. While Susan, our kids, our family, and our friends all praised God for answering our prayers, I held back some. What about the people I knew who had begged God, prayed harder and longer, and their prayers were apparently shunned? Why would God's plan include such a miracle for us, while others came up dry? In my future life as a minister, how could I pray with people in similar straits and not lead people feeling doubtful or disillusioned?

I finished my studies. The ordination ceremony would take place in a couple of weeks. First, the district council called me about an opening at Saint Peter's in Fullerton, New York, a rural community near the Canadian border. My contact at the district office recommended I interview for the job.

My immediate thought was to decline.

First, Susan remained somewhat weak. We still needed to support her as a family. JJ and Lindsey could not uproot and join us in rural New York—or really anywhere. Second, while my experience growing up on the Range gave me a background for rural living and rural people, I had become a city guy a long, long time ago.

Susan, as always, provided much-needed perspective.

"Jake, I want you to take on this challenge handed to you by God. I will be there on your arm and help in any way you want me to. We've learned firsthand, miracles happen. So Lord, lay another one on us."

34

SUSAN AND I BOTH FELT NERVOUS as we got ready to leave for the airport to fly to Burlington, Vermont. From there, we would rent a car and drive another couple of hours to reach Fullerton.

The phone rang moments before we headed out the door. A voice boomed from the other end, "Is this Pastor Jake?"

"Yes, it is. Who is this?"

"I'm Floyd Mann. I was elected to pick you and your wife up at the Burlington airport. But now I hear from the district that you're renting a car and driving in. Is that right?"

"Yes, correct."

I heard Floyd take a deep breath. "Does that really make sense? I'm planning on picking you up. Are you sure don't want to save the money?"

I didn't like this hayseed telling me what made sense and what didn't.

"Well, thanks, Floyd. Next time. My wife and I wanted to look at the countryside as we drove in. We hear it's really beautiful."

"Okay, then why not just meet at the supermarket on the main highway coming into town? When you get there, tell the girl at the counter you want to talk with Mr. Mann."

That seems odd, I thought as we hung up. For someone basically acting as a chauffeur, he seemed a little too self-important and pushy.

On the flight, I read the reports the church had faxed me. It took me all of five minutes to understand the reality here.

When you added in the surrounding farm areas, Fullerton had over 10,000 people, making it bigger than Mesabi. The capacity of the church building was listed at 200. Just five years earlier, the average attendance was 166 for each of two services, and the worship income was $88,000.

But this congregation had showed a decline every year since then. Now only one service was provided, the average attendance had shrunk to ninety-six, and the total giving was only $67,000.

For those five years, the pastor had been paid the lowest salary in the district-recommended range. Five years ago, this amounted to $30,000 plus free use of the parsonage. I wondered what they would offer me now.

We arrived in Fullerton and followed Floyd's instructions to go to the supermarket. It turned out he owned the place and wanted us to know it.

Floyd was about sixty. He led us out to his later-model black Cadillac to chauffeur us on the tour. Being over six feet, I've had little experience looking up at somebody while conversing. Now, I found myself doing just that with Floyd. He was six-six, sturdily built, mostly bald, but with hair as black as his Cadillac. When we shook hands, my hand felt like a baby's in his grip. I could see his hands were no strangers to hard work.

Susan made some positive comments about how modern the supermarket looked. This statement rang true if you were comparing the store to the rest of Fullerton. We were surprised—dismayed, not to exaggerate—with the number of vacant homes. We noticed litter on nearly every street. More downtown stores were boarded up than open. Mesabi High School, compared to Fullerton High, was the Taj Mahal.

We visited a creamery, quite modern overall, with ten people working. As we walked through, we heard, "Good evening, Mr. Mann." Of course, he owned it too.

He told us he had gone to work for his dad right out of high school and built the creamery two years later. He proudly reported, "I had a monopoly for a few years in the milk business. My dad always said, 'Floyd, I'm beginning to feel like a big teat and you're sucking me dry.'"

After Floyd used the word *teat*, he turned to Susan. "Sorry, ma'am."

I don't think I was imagining it—he looked right at her chest.

Perhaps Susan didn't notice—or perhaps she did—because she laid it on a little thick when she touched his arm and said, "You own half this town, don't you?"

Floyd smiled. "That's an exaggeration, Mrs. Horton. However, we have three restaurants in town, and I'm going to tell you, the one I own is the best. Can I buy you dinner after we visit the church and parsonage?"

The church building was nicer than I had imagined; the parsonage looked its age. The roof showed signs of leaking, and it had been a long time since the interior had gotten attention. I looked for signs of disapproval in Susan but saw none. She remained upbeat.

We drove next to the aptly named Floyd's Restaurant. Floyd joined us in a red leather booth. The supper club atmosphere impressed us, and so did the food. Susan ordered pork ribs.

At the end of the evening, Floyd drove us back to the supermarket. He got a serious look on his face as he walked us to our rental car.

"So, what do you think of our little town and church?"

I took Susan's hand. "We'll pray about it tonight. I'll call Leonard Mattingly in the morning to set up an appointment with the parish council. I suppose you're on the council, right?"

Floyd shook his head. "I'm terrible on committees—time-wasters. Actually, I don't go to church much."

This surprised me. "So how did you become our guide?"

Floyd looked at Susan and back at me. "Well, I told Leonard I wanted to meet you." He made a gesture that was part wave and part shrug. "Maybe I'll see you tomorrow."

With that, Floyd eased his six-six body behind the wheel of his Cadillac and drove off slowly.

Susan turned to me. "Was that strange or what?"

"Strange on which front? Strange because he was more excited to show off his businesses than talk about the church? Strange because he apparently doesn't attend church yet was chosen to greet a possible new pastor and his wife? Or strange because of the creepy way he looked at you every time he thought I wasn't watching? Did you notice how his right hand seemed to shake whenever he talked to you?"

Susan laughed as we got in the car, then she too turned serious. "Tell me— if they offer you the job, will you take it?"

"Would you want me to? We're a team. We won't live somewhere you don't want to live."

Susan winced as we hit one of many potholes. "It certainly would be a change. It wouldn't be forever, of course. But maybe it would be a great place for you to get your feel for the ministry. Maybe you could do great things here. I almost hate to say this, but really, the only way they can go is up."

She put a hand on my shoulder. "Jake, I will support whatever you decide. Where God leads you, I will follow."

I had similar thoughts. "I wish you could join me at the council meeting."

Susan looked deep in thought. "That's okay. Floyd is taking me riding at his horse farm anyway."

Then she smiled.

She had me there for a second.

———

The meeting was in the church basement—which was like every other small church basement I've ever visited: fake wood paneling, acoustic tiles, four-foot fluorescent tubes, and cheap folding tables and chairs.

I got there a few minutes early and found the seven male council members around a large rectangular table. Most were older than me, clearly in their sixties or seventies, with a few around my age. At another table sat Floyd, a teenage girl, and a woman who looked in her early thirties. I thought Floyd would introduce me to everyone, but he just gave me a wave, then resumed talking to the ladies.

A guy about my age stood up and offered a handshake. I could tell my less-than-youthful appearance surprised him.

"You're Pastor Jake Horton? I thought it said on your profile you just finished your schooling."

The room fell quiet.

"That means I either started school really late or it took me a long, long time to finish," I offered with a smile.

This got some laughs.

One of the other men introduced himself. "Let's get started. Pastor, could you lead us with a prayer?"

I took a deep breath. I led a simple prayer asking for guidance.

Then before anyone could say a word, I highjacked the meeting. I asked each member to tell me about himself and how he became connected to the church.

One of the men voiced a cliché I knew I would hear sooner or later in this meeting. "What's important is our youth. If the young people don't stay with the church, there will be no church. That's why I asked Amber over there to be part of the process. She represents the youth." His eyes darted. "Not to be negative, but we were hoping for a young guy the kids could relate to."

I smiled over at Amber, who obviously felt nervous and out of place. I wanted to be careful with her. She had likely never been to a meeting like this before, and I didn't want her to say something she would be sorry for later.

"What do you look for in a pastor?" I asked her.

Just as I was going to let her think about it, she spoke, "I want to be a minister someday, so I want somebody who can teach me to know God better. And somebody who can make more people come to church. It's gotten so I wonder if we'll have a church here much longer."

I was moved by the contrast between the men of the council and this bright light.

"So why do you think people are leaving your church?" I continued.

"I don't think any of us know. I'm youth leader, and we have only seven kids now. Once we had over twenty. Our last pastor was only twenty-three or twenty-four. He did marry a girl from the congregation, but I don't think he liked living around here much. I don't think he liked the people here either."

Leonard wrangled back control.

"Thank you, Amber. We can always count on you to voice your opinion."

With that, the council members continued to ask their questions and voice their concerns. Floyd said nothing. The other woman at the table didn't say a word either. I didn't even know her name.

Arlen, one of the men about my age, said, "Okay, you've heard about our problems. What Bible verses do you think apply here?"

They looked at me in expectation, perhaps for a vision from on high. I thought about making a little fun of Arlen. I mean, what a question. I wanted to reply, "Do you have about a week or so?"

Instead I said, "I can think of two right off the top. I like the twelfth chapter of Hebrews—anyone here familiar with it?"

Heads shook.

"Well, here's what Paul was saying: We all have paths to walk. We all have races to run. He says there are witnesses watching us from the clouds—the saints no longer with us. They are cheering us on. They're saying, 'You can do it. Don't give up!' We all have different abilities, and each of us serves and believes a little different from the next. We need to respect that, even embrace it. And we need to use our own gifts for the glory of God."

Heads now nodded.

"The other reference that popped into my head was Psalm 121. Anybody know it?"

Amber raised her hand. "I lift up my eyes to the hills—from whence cometh my help?"

"Tell me, Amber—from where does your help come?"

Proudly, she said, "My help cometh from the Lord, who made heaven and earth." Everybody became quiet.

Leonard eventually interrupted the silence. "Well, I think we should now get to the official business of deciding if we should accept Pastor Horton."

Awkward.

"Thank you, Vickie and Amber, for joining us," he added.

"Vickie," I said, glad to at least have a name, "what's your connection to the church?"

She stood up. "I'm the administrative assistant. I work for the pastor."

She was attractive, in a "pioneer woman" sort of way. She was dressed in one of those granny skirts, quite the contrast to Amber, in shorts and a tank top.

"How long have you served?"

"It's been five years now," she answered in a neutral tone. "My husband thinks he'll be getting a promotion at work. And when he does, I'll be going back to school."

With that, she and Amber left. Floyd went nowhere, though.

"Leonard," I said, "you made the statement, 'We have to decide whether to accept Pastor Horton.' It's important to note, I've made no offer to serve here yet."

Leonard shook his head as the others looked back and forth at the two of us.

"Make no mistake about it: personally, it's a big decision for me to lead a church that's been on a decade-long slide. More importantly, this is a big decision for your church," I continued. "The momentum here is downward. That's not pessimistic. It's realistic. I respect the importance of this moment in time for Saint Peter's. This building is named after the disciple who denied Jesus yet upon whom God saw fit to build his church. Peter, the Rock.

"But it's not the Saint Peter's building that must commit to the faith. It's the people. Do you care enough to commit to growing this congregation—not just in numbers but in genuine worship?"

I paused to let my words linger.

"Do I have the energy, will, resilience, and creativity to take this on? Do any of us? I don't know. But this I do know: God will be there every step of the way. As that passage from Hebrews is clear, he expects each of us to use whatever talents and abilities we can contribute."

Arlen spoke first. "Pastor Horton, I agree with every single word you've said. I may not be a leader here," he said, nodding toward the older men, "but if you take a call here, I promise to go where you lead me. Or what I mean is, I will go where God leads us."

Two others agreed, each saying softly, "Count me in."

Leonard almost, but not quite, made eye contact with me. "So now let's see if we can work out the terms of compensation with you. Then we'll have all the information to make a decision."

Leonard went on to describe a basic salary and benefit package: a salary of $28,000, a different insurance package than the district offered, and the run-down parsonage.

I let them squirm a little. "Guys, could I live on that salary? Could you live on it? Does that offer show belief in me?"

They were lowballing me, hoping my situation would force me to accept. There was no reason to tell them I didn't actually need to live on my salary.

Floyd shattered the silence. "I will personally add twelve thousand per year to that if you agree in writing to stay a minimum of two years."

I could tell nobody expected this.

"Mr. Mann, that's generous," Leonard said, "but would that be in *addition* to your pledge for the year?"

Now I saw another side of Floyd.

"Leonard, what the hell does that mean? People don't want to come here because of bullshit like that. Offer withdrawn."

Out he walked.

We reached a new level of silence.

"I sure don't want to get involved with any controversies," I began slowly. "So here's another way to look at this: you probably wish you could pay more, but you can't because you don't know if offerings will stay where they are, right?"

They all nodded. Some verbalized agreement.

"I'm not sure if this has been done before, but what if we do a pay-for-performance offer?"

Leonard was puzzled. "You lost me. You lost all of us."

Memories of being a young man negotiating with Leo, Jerrod, and Judy came to mind. Back then, just as now, I was willing to *earn* the compensation

I knew I deserved. One key to growing Sommer's Carpet was to offer bonuses to any employee we could sufficiently challenge and measure. People react to this—why not ministers?

"If I accepted the position here, it would be with two stipulations. One, I need the health insurance offered by the Assemblies of the Lord district. And two, if year-end revenues are over seventy thousand, you would pay me forty percent of the difference."

I could see heads tilting, trying to follow. Arlen, in particular, was tracking.

"So," I reasoned, "let's say offerings go from seventy thousand to one hundred thousand dollars. You would pay me twelve thousand in addition to the twenty-eight thousand dollar base. That would still leave the church eighteen thousand. One thing, though: it would be confidential between us, and it would never be referred to as a bonus."

Leonard squirmed. "Geez, I'm not sure I've ever heard of anything like that before."

Arlen quickly looked at some papers in front of him, then spoke right up. "I move we offer Pastor Jacob Horton a salary of thirty-two thousand dollars, plus the district's health plan, plus additional salary in the form of twenty-eight percent of contributions beyond sixty-one thousand dollars payable in January. I say sixty-one thousand dollars because we'd like you to start March 1, and that was the offering amount March 1 through the end of December this past year."

I understood his thinking—more up front but a lower percentage in the end.

One of the others raised his hand. "I second."

Leonard looked around. "All in favor?"

Nobody opposed.

"Well, Pastor Horton," Leonard said as he let out a long breath, "this has been interesting, to say the least." He paused to draw in another breath. "Do you accept our offer?"

I thought back to the night before—when Susan said she'd support whatever decision I made.

"Yes, with the help of God, I do."

It would be a decision I never would regret.

35

M Y ORDINATION WAS IMPORTANT TO ME. But to Susan, it was simply one of the most important days of our lives. My entire family came out to Fullerton for the event. Mom and Devin, Anna and Judy, Mike and his family, and DeeDee and hers.

Susan insisted on picking up the bill for everybody to stay at the Holiday Inn. She ran into Floyd while making the reservations a few days earlier. He was there talking to a contractor. It turned out Floyd owned 51 percent interest in the hotel.

At first she didn't recognize him, but when she said tentatively, "Floyd, is that you?" his face lit up. He made a big deal about taking his hat off. He even gently admonished the contractor about keeping his baseball cap on his head, saying, "Can't you see there's a lady present?" The guy looked maybe forty, and he all but rolled his eyes as he complied by removing his cap.

Like I told Susan, "Not only is Floyd a giant, but he was protecting the honor of his favorite woman, Susan Horton."

Ordination Sunday, we filled the church. The Horton women sang my choice of hymns: "Crown Him with Many Crowns," "It Is Well with My Soul," "My Hope Is Built on Nothing Less," and "Here I Am, Lord." Their voices blended so beautifully as they sang a cappella.

Judy had volunteered to speak briefly. Her jokes about their new pastor's shortcomings was certainly a highlight. But then she shifted gears, talking earnestly about my strengths and what she's seen in me. It meant a lot.

"Pastor Jake is a doer," she said. "In contrast, I've come across a lot of people who like to tell *other* people what to do. Sometimes this will work in an organization, but mostly it will not. To get a project done, you want a roll-up-the-sleeves person in the forefront. And that's what you got. Pastor Jake will not quit until he's done what he's agreed to do. His track record is well known by people in the business community in Minnesota. He's a righteous man, but he is serious when it comes to his work."

When it was my turn, I stood at the pulpit and gazed out. It moved me to see the church absolutely filled. I could feel the excitement, the Spirit. I thanked everybody for coming and added, "I hope it won't take another ordination for you to come back."

I asked Susan to join me up front. With her at my side, I shared how it was through Susan that God told me this is what he wanted me to do.

"To be completely honest with you, the idea of becoming a pastor came to me out of the blue—God spoke to me. I wanted to follow this path, but I didn't know whether the timing was right. So much was happening in our life at that time."

Putting my arm over my wife's shoulder, I gave her a knowing look.

"But Susan said, 'You must do exactly what God wants you to do. Now, get out there and be the best and most loving Christian who ever came from the carpet business. Bring glory to his name.'"

Then I paused and leaned closer to the crowd.

"Be patient when I make mistakes. But don't be patient when I act too slow or don't appear open to new ideas. Together, with God's guidance, we will get the fire of the Holy Spirit burning here at Saint Peter's Church."

The chair of the district elders knelt in prayer with Susan and me. Then he rose and commanded, "Please stand and celebrate your pastor, Reverend Jacob Horton."

With this, the congregation rose and began applauding. I felt a bit embarrassed and honored at the same time.

After the service, I tried to thank each person there. While I knew I couldn't possibly flag down every person present, at least my little flock knew I tried. These folks reminded me of the Iron Rangers in northern Minnesota. Good people. Sturdy people. Practical people.

Out of the corner of my eye, I saw Fullerton's biggest fish in the small pond, Floyd Mann, trying to sneak out. I recalled the parable about the shepherd and his lost sheep. What happened at the council meeting had likely alienated Floyd further from the church. I knew the others weren't brokenhearted about that, though. Privately, some on the council told me they were tired of his "manipulative ways."

Well, I decided this little lamb wasn't going to sneak out without me thanking him for coming. I maneuvered past several people to chase him down outside. Just as he opened the Cadillac's door, I put my hand on his shoulder.

"Floyd," I said warmly, "it means a lot to Susan and me that you came today, especially considering the unfortunate way your generous offer went at the council meeting. I hope we can do a start-over." I felt I may have laid it on a little thick, so I added, "You know, *many* hands make the work light."

He smiled in a mischievous way. "Yes, but they also say too many cooks in the kitchen spoil the stew."

I looked him in the eye. "Just remember, we're not so different, you and I."

———

After the ordination, I hit the ground running. I had already made some lists of priorities to address. My top priority was to enlist help.

That initial meeting with the council left me with some strong first impressions. Granted, first impressions aren't everything. They don't always predict how someone will work out in the long term. It took me only a few years in business to realize that. Still, I had a good hunch about a few folks.

"I'm going to enlist Arlen and Amber to bring this congregation off its collective dead ass," I declared to Susan.

In one word, she said it all: "Interesting."

That was it.

"Amber is key," I added. "You watch—I'm going to help that girl become a minister someday."

I had a strong hunch about Vickie too. As I got to know her better, I realized she didn't feel her input held value to the council. Several ideas I expressed were similar to ideas she had suggested already.

There was a wrinkle, though: I could see she liked me, which made me think, "Danger, danger, danger." On top of that, her husband frequently traveled on business, leaving her alone quite a bit. When he was at home, he treated her with contempt, based on what I had heard from others.

Monday morning after my ordination, I met with Vickie, Arlen, and Amber in my office at the parsonage. Susan welcomed them in, then turned to leave.

"Would you be willing to join us?" Amber asked her.

This pleased Susan, so she sat down next to Vickie.

The five of us joined hands to pray together. I waited for the right words as I held Amber's hand on one side and Susan's on the other.

"Lord of yesterday, today, and eternity—show us how to support each other. We cannot do this without your guidance. But with your grace, let us strive to bring your message of love and renewal to this, our body of believers."

With the prayer setting the tone, we each brought our ideas to the table. We began by discussing the committee system in place at the church.

Committees were standard format for most churches. For instance, the building committee was responsible for the church property. If you were on this committee, you would likely do some painting, cleaning, and so on.

All three of them told me the committee system only managed to kill new ideas. Some people on the evangelism committee had come up with good ideas over the years, but everyone else mostly just sat around sharing their frustrations of the decline in membership.

Amber chaired the youth committee. She had a plan to bring the kids to visit a nearby Native American reservation, attend worship with them, and then help them update their church. Well, the administrative committee cited possible dangers as well as insurance issues. Ultimately, Amber just gave up.

"Going to committee meetings is a waste of time and effort," Arlen said.

I turned to Vickie. "What do you think?"

"I agree with Arlen about the waste of time," she said, "but I guess I haven't seen much effort. The committees meet once a month, but I haven't seen anything much happen after they meet."

We decided to deep-six the word *committee* altogether. I suggested we abandon the current format and replace the committees with "leadership teams" for evangelism, social ministry, worship and music, youth, and stewardship.

This meeting made Susan a believer. I never verbalized it, but I marveled at how Amber had the intuition right from the beginning to invite Susan to be part of the team. Susan and I later shared our excitement for the core we could build from. In private, we began referring to Arlen, Amber, and Vickie as "bright lights."

I conducted my first change experiment with the council the next week, presenting the idea of the leadership teams. They provided less resistance than I would have guessed.

We immediately implemented the change, with great results. It didn't take long to find the right people for the teams. Within months, those who were committed to the faith and to the growth of the church became more involved.

Another great idea came from another "bright light" member, a mother with a teenage daughter. She suggested that a different person from the congregation speak for five minutes every Sunday on their thoughts about the "Saint Peter's Revival." She volunteered to be first speaker the next Sunday.

She shared her pride and happiness with the congregation and finished by saying, "Thank you, Amber, for making my daughter want to come to church. And thank you, Pastor Jake, for caring about us as you do."

I came to look forward to those five-minute updates. They weren't always positive, but they showed we had life in the people sitting in those pews.

The social ministry team took on the issue of litter and junk in the town. They worked with the town council to implement a plan to both prevent and clean up messy properties.

The evangelism team organized businesspeople to help present a community series on "Finding Meaningful Work." When I heard the plan, I loved it.

"So, Arlen, what would you think about asking Floyd Mann to be on the panel?"

"Brilliant!" Arlen responded with a wink and more enthusiasm than I expected.

"Well, I don't know how brilliant it is, but it's worth trying."

I had fallen into Arlen's trap.

"I've already talked to him, Reverend," he said with a laugh. "He's on board."

We decided to leave the Ladies Aid in place—these were older women who did good work in serving at funerals and other functions. In addition, however, Susan headed a new women's fellowship group. Of course, she drew people right from the start. She immediately looked for somebody in the group to take her place as leader. She knew it was important that the group didn't grow dependent on her.

A men's fellowship soon followed, with Amber's father volunteering to lead. As for Amber, her youth team now had grown to twenty, including some kids from the outside community.

I got into a little argument with Veronica Markingson, one of our long-time members. We finally elected a woman on the church council. We had been looking forward to a new perspective on the council. Unfortunately, her perspective was nothing but negative. I quickly grew tired of it.

"Maybe, it's just me," she said, "but do we really want some of these kids in our youth group activities if they have no tie to our church?"

It was quiet for a moment.

Arlen, now the chairman, finally said, "Yes."

When nobody else said anything, I came on too strong. "Well, this is exactly what we and Amber want. Let's hope you're the only one who feels this way."

Veronica's face turned red, and her hands clenched. Her voice shook from her anger. "I apologize, Pastor, for questioning anything your pet does."

I wanted to light into her. But as I felt the heat go through my chest, I realized maybe my anger was all out of proportion. Susan had once mentioned in passing, "Jake, you are awfully invested in Amber." I had paid no attention to the comment at the time. But now as I sat there, I wondered.

I decided to wait for somebody else to respond. Finally, Leonard—of all people—spoke up quietly.

"I sometimes worry about that too, to be honest. But Amber is doing a lot for the church, and I don't think that statement is fair."

Ultimately, Arlen asked each council member to give an opinion on the matter, and all but two supported my position. We went on and finished the meeting. Veronica gathered her notes and said good night to nobody. She turned to say something more, but instead held it back and left abruptly.

In hindsight, I should have tried to make peace with her. Deep down, I realized she had a point. But in my heart of hearts, I wanted her to resign. I didn't like her. While I had my "bright lights," she was one of the few "wet blankets" who, given the chance, would smother the growing fire we had burning.

I hated to tell Susan about this incident. I assumed she'd seize another chance to tell me I shouldn't hold Amber up in such high esteem compared to the others.

Rather, she mused, "I wonder if you'll be back to all men on the council. I know Veronica from the Bible study group. She's an angry one."

And with that, I let go of any regret for what I had done.

36

I N NINE MONTHS, I WAS TOTALLY IMMERSED in the mission of Saint Peter's Church and, out of necessity, the town of Fullerton. Then one day out of the blue, I got a call from Gary. I almost had to ask him to repeat his name—he seemed like someone from another lifetime. In a way, he was.

"Jake, it's been too long," he said. "Linda needs to go to a conference. I thought it would be a good time to come visit you."

He and I made plans to stay at the casino hotel by Lake Placid. Susan agreed it was a great idea for me to get away for a couple of days and catch up with a good friend.

Driving to the casino, I felt guilty. Very guilty. While I could hardly wait to spend some time with Gary, I had $2,000 in my pocket Susan knew nothing about.

When I sold the business, I had gotten a rather big payoff, which Susan knew. The plan was to roll it into investments. What she didn't know, however, is that I set aside $50,000. I had the investment firm send a separate check to another financial institution, and I used a post office box in Minneapolis as the address for the statements.

It was the kind of dishonesty a man in a questionable marriage might commit, yet I never doubted our marriage. I'm not sure what I even thought I would do with this money, let alone why I needed to be so underhanded about it. The irony was, Susan likely would have said, "It's your money. Do whatever you want with it."

I tried to put it out of my mind. I almost said out loud, *The money is legal. I didn't steal it.* But then another voice in my mind chimed in: *Like the money you "took" from Leo.*

With that, I made a pledge to myself: *Jake, use these funds to somehow pay back what you took from Leo.*

Gary beat me to the designated restaurant at the casino. We hugged and decided to have a burger and a beer before we brought the casino to its knees. Gary was a straight arrow, but if I had to name something even close to a vice, it may have been his gambling. Even then, it was a vice well under control.

"I've been putting money away for this for quite a while," he said. "My maximum loss is five hundred dollars for the two days. How about you, Reverend? What's your max? Or did you take the vow of poverty?"

I sidestepped the question. "It doesn't matter—I don't intend on losing."

We hit the blackjack tables. We started at the ten-dollar-minimum-bet tables. By evening, the casino moved the minimum bet to twenty-five dollars. We were both ahead when we took a break for a couple more beers. I was up $500 and Gary $150.

When we headed back, all the lower-bet tables were filled. The only open spots were at fifty-dollar-minimum-bet tables.

Gary was smart enough to say, "I won't even think about playing for that much."

I normally felt the same. However, I wasn't tired and there was nothing else to do. I felt lucky. Why not try a couple of hands? I told Gary, "I'll play until I lose two hands in a row."

Gary put his beer down. "Whoa—you can lose that five hundred bucks in a hurry."

As often happens, I got into a double-down situation, then the dealer drew to twenty-one. That was tough. After about five hands, it was gone.

It had been a good day, but it was ending on a bitter note. We called it a night.

As I lay on the hardest mattress I had ever tried to sleep on, my mind raced. I decided to go back to the casino downstairs and play a little more. Turns out, I lost another $500. I reasoned, I had the money to lose. Nobody would be hurt—well, other than that the sitting did a number on me. My legs and my right arm ached.

Despite my terrible luck at the table, Lila, the dealer, got to liking me—or at least the five-dollar tips I was giving her. I called it quits when she went on break. We both headed to the bar. I listened as she shared her story about how her husband had gotten sick and died. She found herself broke and alone in Fullerton, of all places.

"Fullerton? I live in Fullerton," I said.

She didn't ask what I did there; I didn't say. When I offered a few names to see if she knew anyone I knew, she brushed past them.

"I didn't know what I would do. Then a local big shot put me up in the hotel in exchange for my services," she said. She still wouldn't give any names.

I was fascinated. "How did you wind up here, then?"

"I fell for a guy I met at a Fullerton bar one night. I invited him to my room at the Holiday Inn. But wouldn't you know—Mr. Big Shot was there that night. It was ugly. He kicked me out. I called a friend who lives near here, and she picked me up. I've been here since."

This had taken a turn I hadn't expected.

"What was the big shot's name?" I asked, already having a hunch but needing to know for sure.

"Forget it," she said. Lila's eyes looked downward, then she looked up and away. She became jumpy. I could feel her anxiety.

I changed my approach. I put two hundred-dollar bills on the table.

"Okay, who is it?"

She shook her head. "Mister, I could use that money. But he said he'd kill me if I ever told anyone about this—and I know he would."

I picked up the bills. "I'll tell you what—I'll give you a hundred dollars for just one initial. No, let me change that. How about a hundred dollars if I give you one letter and you tell me if it's one of his initials?"

She took the bill from my hand. "Okay. What's your letter?"

M is so common, so I said, "*F*, as in *fucked*."

She looked scared. "That's one of them."

I showed her the other hundred-dollar bill. "What's the other letter, Lila?"

"I'm not saying anything more," she said loudly. She up and left, stuffing the bill in her purse.

I cringed and darted my eyes around. A man on the other side of the bar stared back at me, then glanced away. He looked familiar, maybe. Or maybe I was just paranoid. This wasn't exactly the best scene for a pastor: an upset woman leaving a bar in a hurry, flashing a hundred-dollar bill.

I looked back at the man. He had resumed his conversation with his friend. He didn't look this way again. Nor did he look so familiar this time. Still, it was a reminder that life was different now that I was a pastor.

I went back to bed and stayed there this time. It was three in the morning. I felt too crummy to say my bedtime prayers. I needed my rest, but it wouldn't come for a long time.

Big shot. Holiday Inn. The initial *F*. It had to be Floyd. But then again, I wasn't sure.

If it was true, which I guessed it was, it didn't greatly surprise me. I harkened back to my theory that all men are the same, only some have more opportunities and less fear. Perhaps Floyd was a risk-taking thrill seeker, like me.

Like I *was*, that is.

———

Over breakfast, I repeated Lila's story to Gary.

"First of all," he said, "what are the chances of Lila's name actually being Lila? And if she seriously feels at risk with the guy, why hasn't she moved farther away? Fullerton is only fifty miles from here. And why," he added, "were you having a drink with her in the bar anyways, Pastor Horton?"

"Gary, I never stop evangelizing these days," I deadpanned.

He rolled his eyes. "Oh, that's what you call it."

As he looked away, I couldn't help but wonder if he was thinking about the night in Dalton, when he told me to make that fateful call home moments before I headed into Tanya's hotel room.

"By the way, old-timer, what happened to Cyril's brains?"

He was clearly changing the subject, but I had no idea where he was going with it.

"What do you mean? Please start at the beginning," I said.

"Okay, fine—the beginning . . . there once was a horny guy by the name of Jacob, who did the dirty deed with a hot but taken chick, Margie, who conceived, not immaculately, a son named Cyril."

Left unchecked, Gary would gleefully string out his little story for many hours.

"How about we pick up the story where Jacob sells the five-location Sommer's Carpet to a board and encourages everybody to begin grooming two bright and ambitious young men to take leadership positions? Start from there."

Gary signaled a start-over. "Seriously, Jake—I worry a little about Cyril and JJ getting along with the employees and customers and even more so each other. But that's not my main concern about Cy."

I was losing patience. "Gary, would you please get to the point?"

He looked up to the skies, as if asking the Creator to intercede.

"Jake, I think everybody knows you do everything you can for Cy. I don't blame you. But he wasn't thrilled when Marina brought in Marc from Carpet One to take over as board president. He didn't expect it. JJ didn't either, for that matter."

Marc Wentworth was the former president of the huge carpet chain, Carpet One. Marina offered him an aggressive salary and benefit package—actually several thousands of dollars more than she made. He proved to be a no-nonsense leader who moved us up several notches in sales and in service. He had little patience with Cy's infighting.

"Marina tried to convince the kids that Marc's hire was in their interest. JJ seems to be learning a lot. But Cy . . ."

Now I knew where he was heading. "I'm going to ask you a tough question, Gary: Do you think Cy is honest, candid, and transparent?"

Gary weighed his words. "I know Marina explained some of this to you earlier. I don't know why Cy does things he knows he shouldn't. We catch him and slap his fingers, but then he just does it again. I don't get it."

"Do you know the parable of the scorpion and the frog?"

He smirked. "No, Reverend, I do not."

I leaned back. "A scorpion wanted to cross the river. He asked a frog if he could climb on his back so the frog could bring him across the river. The frog, no dummy, said, 'I won't fall for that. You'll sting and kill me.'

"The scorpion looked the frog in the eye and said, 'Why would I do that? If you die, I fall in the river. We both die.' That made sense to the frog, so he allowed the scorpion to climb on his back.

"About halfway across, the scorpion stung the frog. The frog wailed in pain. 'We're both going to die! This makes no sense. Why did you do this?' The scorpion answered, 'I did it because that's who I am.'"

I let the moral sink in.

"Sometimes it's just who people are. I've seen it in others." I was quiet for a long moment before finally speaking a truth Gary already knew. "I sometimes worry Cy has inherited my weaknesses, except they're worse with him. I just hope he can get with the program."

I didn't want to hear this—again—about Cy. But I felt fortunate to hear it from the one person in the world who understood that this was as much about me as it was about my son.

As if someone had just turned up the volume, the sound of casino machines reminded us we wanted to play more blackjack. We hit the tables, agreeing to a $300 maximum loss each. Little did Gary know I still had $900 to invest.

I checked for "Lucky Lila," but she was nowhere to be seen.

37

ANY RURAL OR SMALL-TOWN CONGREGATION holds expectations of their minister. Often, they're unrealistic expectations.

In my case, one unrealistic expectation was that I would always be on call to visit members, their families, and anyone else they designated as needing my services. These requests came in one after another—including on Fridays, which I unsuccessfully tried to declare as my day off.

"Pastor, you need to get out and visit my aunt Helen. I'm afraid she's depressed."

"Pastor, did you hear my dad is having surgery Friday in Syracuse? Can you go see him?"

"Pastor, have you noticed Bill hasn't been in church for a month? I think you should go talk with him."

I realized the congregants would never understand I needed time for my life separate from their needs. But I still did my best to deflect these requests. I tried to educate them, explaining how it was just plain unrealistic to think I had the time to make so many visits.

What I didn't try to explain, however, was the main reason I avoided these calls: I flat-out knew I couldn't be the wise, understanding, patient, interested, caring, and loving pastor they expected me to be during these visits. Fact is, I wasn't blessed with the talent for being interested and compassionate when listening to people's problems, especially their health maladies.

Saint Peter's had a significant number of older people who had plenty of time to think and talk about their health problems. They wanted me to listen to their issues, show compassion, pray with them, and even research what they might do to feel better.

While most everybody felt I was an effective pastor, they eventually came to understand I just wasn't good at this part of my job. So I limited my visits the best I could, going only when I simply couldn't avoid it.

I remember it was a Friday morning when I got a call from Floyd's adult daughter, Ginny.

"Pastor Horton, I know my dad doesn't come to church often, but he hasn't attended in a long time," she said. "I'm sure you've noticed too. Have you talked to him at all?"

Ginny seemed nice enough but came to worship only occasionally. So here was a marginal member calling me on my day off to ask what I was doing to help her father, who rarely attended.

"Well," I began, "I haven't seen Floyd nor talked with him for several weeks. What's up?"

"He's really in bad shape, and he worries a lot about it. But he doesn't talk with me about it. Maybe he would talk to you?"

I was a little frustrated, though she had my interest. "What are we talking about here, Ginny?"

A short silence—I could hear her sniffling. "Dad has Parkinson's disease."

My immediate thoughts migrated to Trent's dad. I could only imagine how difficult it would be to be around the poor, suffering guy.

"I'm really sorry to hear about this," I responded. "I'll go see him. How can I get ahold of him?"

"He's still going into work at the grocery store. But basically, he doesn't want to be around people, so he shuts his office door."

Truth was, I often thought of Floyd. In the first few months after my ordination, I saw him here and there around town. But before long, I found myself running into him less and less. I had indeed noticed his office door shut at the supermarket.

Several times I tried to get in touch with Lila at the casino, without success. The best I could sleuth was that she unexpectedly resigned not long after our visit.

I headed over to the supermarket. His Cadillac was parked near the front, indicating he was in. I knocked on his office door, and he let me in. He was surprised but not unpleasant.

"What brings you out, Pastor Horton?" He motioned me to sit.

I got right to the point. "Your daughter is concerned about you. She asked me to stop by. Is there anything I can do to help?"

Floyd looked grim. "Can you find a cure for Parkinson's?"

Again, images of Trent's dad flew before me.

"I know there's no cure, but lots of people are looking for one, Floyd. Are you on medication?"

Floyd lifted his two hands from under his desk. The left hand trembled noticeably; the right one just a little. He watched his left hand as if it were a stranger to him.

"This damn shaking started a few months ago. The doctor gave me all kinds of pills to try. But nothing works. To be honest, Pastor, I feel like shit most of the time."

I knew Floyd was not one to exaggerate, so I simply said, "I am so sorry. I have a good friend who is a specialist in PD. Maybe you would like to talk to him?"

Floyd kept looking at his left hand. "I wonder what I did to God to piss him off."

I was surprised and moved by the man's honesty. "Floyd, this is a real tough break for you. But this I know—God loves you."

Floyd smiled slightly and looked up. "But this I know, for the Bible tells me so?"

He was referencing the old Sunday school song "Jesus Loves Me." It made my words sound trite. I altered the subject.

"Do you have other symptoms, aside from the tremors?"

"I'm going to level with you—I don't like to complain about it. I don't need people feeling sorry for me. Then again, I know some folks would be glad to hear about it."

I waited in silence. Floyd stood up, then sat down.

"I feel dizzy sometimes," he went on. "And the other thing is, I get these jerky motions with my hands and arms, but only with my right side. My joints hurt more than they did a year ago. But hell—that could just be my age."

I genuinely felt bad for him, which surprised me.

"Floyd, you're a private man. I respect that. Two important actions come to mind, which I would be happy to do: I would be willing to call my friend, the specialist; and of utmost importance, I would pray with you right now."

Floyd looked at me intensely. "You don't know what you're asking God to do."

"Our God says, 'Bring your concerns to me. Knock and the door will be opened.'"

With a bit of wry humor, perhaps, Floyd raised his trembling left hand. "But only if you can knock, huh?"

I took a chance and took his hand. "I'll knock if you can't."

And we prayed.

That was the first of what turned out to be about several visits with Floyd. Despite my concerns about my own "bedside manner," it soon became obvious Floyd looked forward to our time together. He became comfortable sharing his stories, mainly about his business but also about the rest of his life.

After a few visits, I decided to bring up Lila's name and see if he would level with me about her.

"Floyd, do you know a woman by the name of Lila, who lived in Fullerton?"

His eyes showed nothing, looking straight ahead to a point above me. I repeated the question.

Finally, he responded, "Why do you ask, Jake?"

He had revealed nothing, so I decided for now to match him. "I guess it wasn't important."

I felt disappointed, but I also believed he would want to talk more about Lila once he had the chance to think about it.

I called Trent, who was more than willing to call Floyd's general practice doctor. Trent gave helpful advice, and no doubt both Floyd and his doctor appreciated it. But while various drug options were worth attempting, there was no way to get around the inevitability of the disease, no miracle cures.

Floyd's moods got darker. His voice—never loud in the first place—got more and more muffled. The muscles he needed to produce speech were deserting him. I felt profound sympathy for Floyd. Again, this surprised me.

People in the community heard about my "special relationship" with Floyd. Some thought I was trying to bring Floyd's wealth to the church. On this point, let me say, I was not. Others thought it meant I had suddenly developed the talents to comfort sick people. They doubled their efforts to get me to visit various people for various reasons. I still did not have time for this—nor the interest. I often counted the minutes while I half listened to their complaints.

It then occurred to me that I could experience real sympathy only when people had real illnesses. Visiting Floyd couldn't be compared to sitting there listening to someone go on and on about how his sore back made it hard to sit in the pew every Sunday.

I needed to pray for patience and understanding with those other people, yet I just wanted to shake them and ask, "Do you even know what serious problems look like?"

———

Shortly after the New Year, Floyd was on my mind as I headed to the January council meeting. Staff salaries were the main agenda item. It was time to revisit the pay-for-performance arrangement.

Leonard held some papers in hand. "Our revenue for March through December was one hundred eleven thousand three hundred fifty dollars—but then on New Year's Eve, the church received an anonymous money order for fifty thousand dollars. So the total revenue comes to one hundred sixty-one thousand three hundred fifty dollars."

I could hear both nervousness and pride in his voice.

"Last year's revenue for the same period was sixty-one thousand dollars," Leonard continued. "So Pastor's additional compensation will be based on one hundred thousand three hundred fifty dollars. As agreed, he is due twenty-eight percent of the contributions beyond sixty-one thousand dollars. The amount due is twenty-eight thousand ninety-eight dollars." He set his papers down and looked up at me. "Well done, Pastor."

A motion was made, seconded, and passed.

Vickie's salary was also on the agenda. I could sense I wouldn't like what I would hear next. Leonard recommended a cost-of-living increase of 2 percent to her already low salary. This was quickly moved and seconded. When he asked if there was any discussion, I spoke up.

"Let's be frank: for the work she does, we all know she's entitled to about ten thousand more than what you're paying her—even with that two percent increase."

That day I interviewed with the council, Vickie announced she was looking to quit. In rather short order, however, I found out she was as capable as any administrative person I had worked with. She liked to learn and liked to take on additional responsibilities. She and I privately did all we could to groom Amber in her mission to become a pastor. Clearly, Vickie had met and exceeded every expectation. I couldn't help but feel she was being cheated, especially if revenue had increased so much.

Arlen's face was conflicted. "I agree that Vickie does great work. But ten thousand dollars is a sizeable increase. That would be a salary readjustment, and I'm not sure how we'd go about that."

"Yes, don't you think it would raise a lot of questions?" Veronica asked, clearly looking for another fight about a "pet."

As the other council members sat in uncomfortable thought, the dull ache in my right leg had now progressed to cramping. With some distress, I noticed my right foot cramping up as well. It was time to take a stand—literally and figuratively. I rose.

"I'll tell you what—just take ten grand out of my check and pay Vickie what she's due."

I grimaced and limped out, feeling like Floyd in more ways than one.

38

I'M USUALLY NOT GREAT AT REMEMBERING DATES, but I know it was January 8, 1997, when the phone rang. It was just a few days after the council meeting. Susan and I were getting ready for an overnight trip to Syracuse. She had a routine checkup with her oncologist, then we had reservations for dinner and a hotel. We were looking forward to our little getaway. For once, no one could spoil this day off by scheduling a visit or meeting.

I headed to my office to answer the phone. To my surprise, it was the Midwest district senior elder of the Assemblies of the Lord.

"Jake, I'm calling to find out if you think you're ready to pastor at a big new church being built in the Twin Cities. If you're interested, I'll recommend you to the church council." He asked me to think about it and let him know within the next few days. He finished the conversation with, "Pastor Horton, God has worked through you to lift the church in Fullerton. I congratulate you and suggest you pray about a new challenge. Let me know."

As I came back into the bedroom, Susan looked up from her packing. "Who's calling you so early?"

"Just an administrative question about the budget," I answered.

I wasn't being deceitful. I just wasn't ready to say anything yet. More accurately, I didn't know what to say yet.

My mind was flying the entire drive to Syracuse. Thankfully, Susan had brought a book to read, so I had time to sort through my thoughts.

Susan, JJ, Lindsey. But also Amber, Vickie, Arlen, Floyd. Whatever decision I made, it would disappoint someone. If I simply declined the offer without telling anybody else, I could maybe avoid some conflict and hard choices.

But it would be exciting to accept the call, if I got it. I couldn't imagine any pastor not being thrilled to lead a big new church. Moving back to the

Cities would allow Susan to tend to her declining parents. We would be with the kids and my family again. They found it just too hard to get to Fullerton, and I rarely had a day off, let alone enough time for a trip back home. What about my flock here? I was proud of what we were accomplishing at Saint Peter's and in the community. Would the momentum continue if I left?

Once again, my thoughts brought me to the possibilities of being the lead pastor at this new church. I pictured the pride Susan would share. I pictured my mom in the front pew with her atheist husband. Then my mind roared on to Roger and Colleen.

I heard my name called. I nearly jumped. For a moment, I had forgotten I was in the doctor's waiting room while Susan was being examined. My mind traversed quickly back to reality. It was the doctor calling me in to join him and Susan. And the expression on his face told me this wasn't going to be good.

"Jake, I'm sorry to say we've had a setback."

My belief that Susan's cancer had miraculously healed was, sadly, dead wrong. The doctors in the Cities pronounced her cancer-free roughly a year ago. Now this doctor shook his head, mumbled a few guesses, and pronounced Susan's cancer back. It had metastasized, this time to her appendix.

Only when you've heard these words describing someone you love do you know the utter fear it causes in your heart. You hope you heard it wrong. You hope you both heard it wrong. We left in shock.

"We've been through this before," Susan finally said. "Just like last time, let's make a pact to face this tomorrow. Tomorrow, we can decide our strategy and do our best to be optimistic. But tonight, let's avoid talking about it. Instead, let's just try to enjoy our dinner and get a decent night's rest."

Susan needed some personal space to decide her course of action. She would think about me, the kids, her folks, and others as well. I knew all this. "Okay," I said and kissed her.

Memories flooded me of walking into the house a year ago and seeing Susan, JJ, and Lindsey nestled together on the couch.

Neither of us felt like eating, but we went to dinner and had a glass or two of wine. That night in bed, we held each other for the longest time. Finally, Susan broke the silence.

"When I was diagnosed the first time, I prayed to God to let me live long enough to see you preach at your first church. Every day has been a bonus since then. Jake, what a year this has been. The spirit of the people at that church has changed. You have changed. I wouldn't have missed this for anything."

I choked. "No way could I have done any of this without you. I love you. There is so much more for us to do together."

It might have been a perfect segue into telling her about the interview offer for the new church back in the Cities. However, it would have complicated the already overwhelming list of concerns in her mind. And that was about our future—a future I suddenly didn't know whether we'd get to see.

———

When we got back to Fullerton the next afternoon, I headed into my office to check my messages. I was thankful for the diversion. It's surprising how many questions and requests find their way to the voice mail of a pastor. Rarely did I get a call that could be termed an emergency, but now I had one—and the message was already a day old.

It was Ginny, and she was frantic. "Pastor Horton, it's my dad—he tried to kill himself. The ambulance just picked him up. He's asking for you. I'm sorry to bother you, but can you come to the hospital right away?"

I was afraid I was too late.

I immediately called Ginny's number but got no answer. Next, I called the hospital, but they couldn't—or wouldn't—tell me anything. One of my parishioners worked at the hospital, so I called her extension. She had helped before and was eager to help me now.

"Yes, Pastor, Mr. Mann was brought in to emergency yesterday morning. They pumped his stomach. He's going to be okay—this time."

I thanked her, then headed to the hospital.

Floyd looked as though he hadn't slept in a month. I almost joked, "You could go on a trip with those bags under your eyes," but I'm glad I didn't. He grimaced in pain as he sat up, yet there was a trace of a smile when he saw me.

I apologized to him and Ginny, explaining why I hadn't been there.

Floyd's voice was barely audible, but he clearly asked Ginny, "Can I talk to Pastor alone?"

Ginny got up, kissed Floyd's cheek, gave me a hug, and whispered, "Thank you."

Floyd drew me near. "Well, I botched that one. You know I'm a cheap man—but wasting all of those pills . . ."

I said nothing.

"You once asked me if I knew a woman by the name of Lila. I lied when I said I didn't."

Floyd's hands shook, and I could see it was taking everything he had to get the words out.

"I loved her, but I wasn't what she wanted. I tried to keep her in a way that was wrong. Jake, I was a fool." He looked straight at me. "Have you ever cheated on your wife?"

I was taken aback. I wanted to admit and deny it at the same time. But Floyd's gray eyes and unflinching stare demanded an answer.

"Floyd, I've done some very bad things nobody knows about."

"If you know where Lila is or if you can get a message to her, I want you to tell her what I just told you. And tell her I ask for her forgiveness. I've left her some money in my will, but I put it in your name so her name doesn't come up. Understand?"

I leaned so close to him I could smell his breath. "If you die, yes, I will do anything you want me to do. But don't die, Floyd. You need to live."

He lifted his index finger and it shook. "Jacob, you seriously call this living? I did live once—you know that more than anyone else. But now I'm only marching in place and taking up space."

I was thinking this through. Floyd may have opened up about Lila, but he was still leaving a lot unsaid.

"Floyd, Lila claims you threatened to kill her. Did you?" My voice changed a bit. "Tell me the truth this time—you lied to me about your relationship with Lila."

Floyd looked at me with skepticism. I could see he was weighing his words and taking his time.

"You sound out of sorts that I misled you. Was that so important? If you were asking about her, it meant you already knew the truth. And what about Lila? Isn't her privacy more important than your hearing the truth?"

"Floyd," I said, "it's really simple: Did you threaten to kill her or didn't you?"

He turned away from me, his face hardening. "I may have said those words in anger. But you know damn well I wouldn't kill her or anybody else. You're being ridiculous."

"Okay, Floyd—I apologize. I just had to ask so I can tell Lila firsthand. Even if you didn't actually mean those words, she thought you did."

His face melted into sadness. He held his hand out, and I shook it. He whispered his thanks.

"You're my only friend," he said.

"Can we pray?" I asked.

Floyd closed his eyes and turned his head away again.

"God must be mad at me, and I'm not so happy with him either. I think it's best to not talk to each other, at least for now."

———

When I told Susan about the visit and Floyd's concluding words, she reflected, "There's as much faith in that statement as I've ever heard."

I hugged her. "That's what I thought. I feel that way sometimes—like maybe it's best if God and I don't talk. Don't you feel like that too?"

She hugged me back and smiled. "No. I'm a woman. I always want to talk."

With that, I decided to tell her about the possibility of leading a church back in the Twin Cities. Always pragmatic, Susan weighed the pros and cons and came up with her verdict.

"While I love the people at Saint Peter's, I believe the leaders there will continue what you've developed." She paused. "If I have limited time left, I would like to be near family in the Cities. If possible. And while I like my doctor in Syracuse, no facility in this area can compare with those in Minnesota. I would like to be with my old doctors again."

I reminded her, "Don't get your hopes up yet. Remember, I would need to go through the interview process."

Despite my words of caution, I decided right there—I had to launch a plan to get back to the Cities.

39

ECIDING TO RESIGN FROM SAINT PETER'S was one thing. Deciding how to break the news was another. As it turned out, the council members set up a special meeting with me a few days later to revisit the matter of Vickie's salary. It was as good a time as any. I headed to the meeting carrying an envelope with my resignation letter.

I was heartened to learn the council wanted to do the right thing for Vickie after all. At the meeting, Arlen presented a proposal to give her a 10 percent increase plus added compensation in the form of funds to further her education. I thought this was an excellent plan—no doubt spearheaded by Arlen. I thanked the council for their integrity.

After formalizing the motion, Leonard asked if there was any further business to bring forward.

"Actually, yes," I said. "Could I address the council on a development in my personal life affecting Saint Peter's?"

Leonard nodded for me to go ahead.

I wanted to keep it brief, so I got to the point. "I have to start with the news that Susan's cancer is back. We've been told it's extremely serious." I added, "We need to get back to Minnesota."

Silence. The furnace blower kicked on.

As the reality settled into their minds, they realized Susan's condition should be their main focus, but I knew some were also thinking about their church. No doubt, they were thinking, *What will we do from here?* They were getting two bad pieces of news.

Arlen got up and hugged me, tears dripping from his red eyes. He was simply overcome.

As I held him, tears now filled my eyes. In a broken voice, I said, "Arlen, you are the spirit of God here. I can't thank you enough. You can keep this going."

Amber came over and hugged me next. She looked in shock.

All the others now lined up to hug me. Even Veronica hugged me and held me. As we separated, she held my hands.

"Pastor, you have done a miracle here. Please forgive me for what I said. As for Susan, well, like everybody here, I love her and I am so sorry."

I forgave her at that moment, but I wasn't big enough to tell her she had actually been right about my special treatment of Amber.

When the hugs were over, I felt an urge to politely excuse myself and head home. I wanted to be with Susan. Truth be told, the pain in my leg was shooting up and down and screaming for me to leave.

But I couldn't leave yet. I felt as though I was betraying these people by resigning. I thought, in embarrassment, how I had judged them and their small town as unsophisticated, even simple. Now, I realized what a privilege it had been to work side by side with these people, with their big hearts for their church and their faith. The least I could do is sit with them for a few more moments.

"As you can imagine," I began, "Susan will need the best medical attention, and she wants to be near our family in Minnesota. I am so sorry and I hate to leave. I cannot begin to express the thanks, gratitude, and respect I have for all of you," I continued. "You've shown commitment to your church in a way every pastor craves to see. We have served God together. Is our work done? Of course not. As long as we can praise the name of our Risen Lord, we should want to find ways to do it. So it's with deep regret I submit my resignation to you, effective in one month."

Silence filled the room again. There were no words. There was no way to express the sad ending of an unlikely relationship that had been amazingly fruitful. Dare I say, surely, the Lord had his hand in it?

Leonard broke the silence. "Pastor Horton, you and Susan have given us so much. We are all in shock right now, but our prayers are with you both. To that end, please, Pastor—go and be with Susan."

I met with Vickie and Amber together the next morning at the parsonage. While it was irrational, I somehow felt I was abandoning both. Yet I knew they both would go on to do great things.

We sat around the old oak table in our kitchen. Susan joined us for a few minutes before she had to meet a friend for coffee. She too had to break this news to the special people in her life.

The four of us held hands; we prayed together. We chatted until Susan excused herself to meet her friend.

Amber also needed to head out shortly. She was meeting two teenagers who wanted to join our church. I knew an amazing future was ahead of her. Our youth group had become the envy of every church in the area. Amber exhibited an ability to draw not just young people but also their parents into investing in the group.

"Amber," I said, "would you be willing to deliver the sermon at worship in two weeks? I can help you."

She nodded and flushed with pride.

"Amber, let's stay in touch at least until you become a pastor. Yes, that is going to happen," I said as she beamed even more. "I promise."

That left Vickie and me.

In the midst of my own sad news, I couldn't have been happier to tell Vickie the exciting news about her salary and education fund.

She took my hand and kissed it. "I won't say thank you because my feelings are so much deeper than that. Pastor, I will always love you."

With that, she hugged me closely and left sobbing.

It was only about 10:00 a.m., and I felt exhausted.

———

The month went by fast. I had vacation time to use up—and much to arrange for our move—so I was out as much as I was in. Leonard had contacted the district elders minutes after I handed him the resignation letter, so they were hard at work to find my replacement.

The Saturday before my final Sunday, the area absorbed a record-breaking blizzard. It was fitting. That was the day I officiated the funeral of Floyd Mann.

Susan and I arrived at the church before the reception started. For a few minutes, it was just us and Floyd. We stood looking at him, pale in the casket, with a peaceful but satisfied expression on his face. I'm not sure what Susan thought his expression said, but to me, it said, "Nobody knows."

How many secrets can one person have? Would we be better off without them? We wonder about how people feel about us. We wonder who they like best and, perhaps, who they hate most. We think about their money and wonder what they'll do with it. In the end, you can't help but wonder if there really is a God orchestrating this mess. And if you believe there is, you wonder why so much is mystery. Well, that's because God is mystery. And if we're made in his image, that means we too are mystery. We darn well should be able to keep secrets.

Why so much hurt and sadness exist in this world remains unknown. Some feel the need to try to explain why. Your opinion has as much credence as mine. I will listen to you.

But nobody knows.

Susan took my hand and held it. "Jake, what a friend you were to Floyd. You have to be glad for that."

I couldn't tell Susan how much I had in common with the guy. As he unburdened himself with me, I was somehow able to unburden myself.

During one of my visits, I told Floyd how I had noticed him lusting after Susan and how it had angered me. He had reached that point in life where there was no value in pretensions. So he just gave me a sad smile.

"Jake, I'm quite sure you looked at plenty of good-looking women and thought . . . what you thought."

The first funeral-goers began trickling in, breaking me out of my thoughts. My sermon emphasized that Floyd was a private person but one hell of a businessman. I sanitized the story about him and his dad and the creamery. He treated his employees well.

During the luncheon afterward, I wanted to mingle about the room, but I had to sit down. I got tired much more easily of late. As I looked about the church basement, with its fluorescent lights and folding tables, I recalled how Floyd had stormed out of it nearly a year earlier.

A couple of well-meaning people asked me, "Are you okay? You look a little pale."

Was I okay? Well, my wife had cancer—bad cancer. I was at the funeral of a good man and friend. I was resigning from my position, moving back to Minnesota, and perhaps taking on another parish. And truth be told, my right leg and my right arm ached more and more, I couldn't sleep much, and my balance occasionally felt a little off. Susan told me to make an appointment with my doctor back in Minneapolis; I added it to the to-do list.

Back at the parsonage that evening, I looked out the window in a funk, watching the snow continue to fall. For my final Sunday, the council had decided to offer just one service, so the community could unite for my farewell. Now I doubted anyone would attend.

I called Leonard. "With this weather, should we just cancel worship?" I didn't say it out loud, but I preferred that.

"Pastor," Leonard responded, "I talked to Arlen about this an hour ago. I know the weather is bad. But none of us would miss the chance to say thank you and say good-bye. I think people will walk through the snow if they have to."

———

He was right. Susan and I arrived a half hour early, and the church was already two-thirds full. When the parishioners saw us, many came over to shake our hands and hug us. I marveled at the love I witnessed for Susan, especially.

Amber had written a song of thanks for the occasion. Her youth group sang it. At the end of a beautiful tribute, she presented me with a wonderful painting of the church, signed by twenty-six youth members.

She fought her tears and said simply, "Pastor, I will never forget the first time I met you. Never. I felt hope. You leave us more faithful. You leave us realizing we can, with God's help, change our course. You've made us proud of our church and how we serve God. You and Susan have truly been a gift from God. We just wish you could have been with us forever. We don't want to share you!"

Her face shining like the bright light I knew she truly was, she added, "The Lord will preserve you from all evil."

It was Psalm 121, our connection from that first meeting.

I responded with the next verse: "He will preserve your soul, Amber."

With that, I delivered a sermon of thanks and celebration.

Much to my surprise, my mother, DeeDee, and Trevor had been squirreled away at the Holiday Inn and now came in. Trevor, always the preacher,

introduced himself and asked Mom, DeeDee, and Susan to join him in leading the congregation in song. They sang beautifully.

Trevor thanked the congregation for loving Susan and me. He finished
with an interesting statement: "God sent Jake and Susan to a land far away,
and they labored hard to show that God is everywhere."

The people gave us a standing ovation. I had been holding my tears back,
but now I couldn't help it—their affirmation moved me to sob like an eight-
year-old who had just found out his dog died.

We all joined hands for the last time.

40

TWO DAYS LATER, WE WERE BACK IN MINNEAPOLIS. I met with the district elders to "exchange information" on the position of lead pastor at Celebration of Christ Christian Church.

My experience with churches in general was that the governing organizations sought to avoid mistakes rather than try new paths. Celebration Church, on the contrary, was hardwired to be independent and aggressive in pursuit of their mission. They had tried many different initiatives—failing at some but succeeding at more.

As the suburbs surrounding Minneapolis exploded with new houses, this congregation grew to the point that their existing church building needed to be expanded. It was all thanks to ardent evangelizing. In a forward-thinking move, they purchased expensive but strategically located acreage in the heart of the expansion. For almost a year, the congregation had been meeting in a high school auditorium while the new building was under construction.

The previous pastor had led the congregation ably for eight years, but he was fulfilling his call to be a missionary in Tanzania. The interim pastor knew he could not be considered for the permanent position, and he was anxious about finding his own church to lead. With the pulpit essentially vacant, the congregation was pushing the district elders to get a pastor in place before the new church was ready for occupancy.

After vetting candidates, three strong potentials remained. Surprisingly, I was one of them. I assumed the elders' first choice was a former businessman in his early forties who was serving his third year in a church in Ohio. They were also impressed with a pastor currently serving a Lutheran church. He had a strong resume but was disillusioned with the Lutheran organization.

There were only three final candidates because the congregation had added an additional qualification for the lead pastor: they wanted a man who, beyond the standard qualifications, had "experienced life." Meaning, in a roundabout way, they wanted somebody at least forty years old.

They further wanted this individual to have experience with budgets and management. Apparently, the previous pastor frustrated the membership with his lack of business acumen.

On my end, I was savvy enough to stick to the truth with the elder. The truth as I knew it. When the elder got to the tried-and-true question about strengths, I certainly had to share the story of Sommer's Carpet and Tile and how we grew by taking innovative steps and by building on the advice of others. And when we got to matter of weaknesses, I boldly admitted my short-comings—I mean, the shortcomings I was willing to express. I freely admitted I struggled in visiting hypochondriacs or those just seeking attention. I knew the elder liked what he heard.

Two weeks to the day, I received a call from Lars Olson, who identified himself as the "facilitator of the Celebration of Christ Christian Church call committee."

I couldn't help but laugh out loud on the phone. "Mr. Olson, I'm sorry. I couldn't help but think you should be the chairman—then it would be a lot of Cs."

His laugh grew louder when it dawned on him. Once he gained his composure, he said, "Can I say 'congratulations' as another C word? We would like to interview you."

I thought of responding "Cool" or "Copy that," but I got serious.

"It would be my pleasure and honor to interview. Do you have a date, time, and place in mind?"

"How about Tuesday at two p.m. at Lincoln School, where we hold our services right now?"

"Sure. I know where it is," I answered. "I worshipped last Sunday with you."

Olson seemed pleased. "We'll want to know what you thought of us. See you Tuesday."

———

As I drove up to the school the day of the interview, Susan was on my mind. She had told me her only prayer was to hear me preach again. Her cancer was looking more and more incurable. I shouldn't have been interviewing at all. Yet I found myself picturing being in the pulpit, delivering a sermon dedicated to my wife.

I showed up at the school about fifteen minutes early. Memories of meeting with the council at Saint Peter's came rolling into my brain. I let the receptionist know who I was and took a seat.

Moments later, a young man—perhaps about twenty-six or twenty-seven—came and greeted me.

"I'm Lars Olson, we talked on the phone. Jake Horton, I presume. Come in."

As he led me into the school's conference room, I quickly counted the heads. There were twelve. I suppose like the disciples. No women—also like the disciples. That surprised me a little.

For forty-five minutes, they bombed me with questions. There was nothing difficult or controversial until the oldest-looking man, Luke, piped up.

"We assume you read, know, and live by your Bible. Do you recognize homosexuality as a sin? And what, if any, role do you see for them in the church?

Internally, I admonished myself for not preparing for this question. Homosexuality was currently a hot topic for the church. I knew what Luke wanted to hear, but I couldn't say it. I thought of Judy and Anna.

Before I opened my mouth, Jeff, another council member, stepped in.

"Luke, we all know where you stand on this one issue, but do we really have the time to go over every possible sin and get his opinion on it? Why didn't we ask the other candidates this question? And I need to remind you, and let Pastor know, we are far from consensus on this question within the congregation."

I still felt I needed to say something. "Could I just make a short response to Luke's question? When it comes to the church, we can and will have differences of opinion. We should talk about those differences with the idea of listening to each other and considering and respecting beliefs different from our own. One of my core principles, though, when it comes to our church is, 'All are welcome.'"

Luke eyed me with some suspicions, but the rest of the men seemed satisfied with my comment. If there was one aspect about Assemblies of the Lord that I wasn't fond of, it was that it tended to attract judgmental types such as Luke. And what did Jeff mean when he said the other candidates hadn't been asked this question? Did the council do a background check on me and uncover information about Anna and Judy?

The church treasurer, Milt Meyer, took his turn. He asked a variety of questions, from the use of computers to income and expenses. It became obvious to all in the room I had more experience than any of them when it came to business matters. I wondered why these issues were taking interview time, but I was comfortable with my answers.

Each council member was given the opportunity to ask one more question. Sure enough, someone asked, "I'm sorry to hear of your wife's cancer, Pastor. But I'm concerned about your ability to give this church the energy it needs. Do you understand my concern?"

I hesitated. "Yes, I understand. And it's a valid question. My wife, Susan, and I have prayed and agonized over this. She earned a theological degree and has loved the church her entire life. Before I left this afternoon to meet with you, Susan told me she is praying for the chance to see me preach again. One way or the other, I'm committed to this."

Lars, as council chair, asked the final question: "What do you know about our church, and why do you think you're a good fit to lead?"

This question, while expected, was of utmost importance. I was ready to reply. It was almost a sermon itself.

"The biggest problem with organizations in general and with the church, specifically, is too much talk and not enough action. Celebration of Christ Christian Church has a reputation for not being afraid of trying new ways to help people know the Lord better. You can't get to know somebody without learning more about them. That's why we need to study the Bible—to get to know Christ. How can you love somebody if you don't know anything about them?

"Christ cares about our relationship with him. If we make this relationship the most important thing in our lives, we will want to serve others and we will want others to know the Good News. As it's written in James 1:22, we are to be not just hearers of the word, but doers. When we have our relationship right in Christ, we will want to use our talents to glorify him.

"I love the story about a minister leading his congregation in an appeal to raise money to expand their church. He told his congregation, 'In regard to the financial goals for our appeal, I have some good news and some bad news.

The good news: we have the money to meet and exceed our goals.' The congregation clapped loudly. 'However,' he added, 'the bad news is, the money is still in your wallets and purses.'"

I paused and smiled as they laughed loudly.

"Whether we're talking about the talent to make money or the talent to lead a prayer fellowship or the talent to care for church property, we need to dig deep. Not because we feel guilty, but because we want to share the light of Christ.

"I never could have built a business from one to five stores by just talking about it. You get consensus, make sure you've got a plan to get to where you need to go. And then you act with the end goal in mind."

I smiled.

"You are my kind of church. I think I'm your kind of pastor."

I shook everybody's hand, thanked each one, and headed out. Back at home, I told Susan I thought the interview had gone well.

A few days later, I received a letter with their employment offer and a start date in less than a month.

It didn't take long to settle back into our house in Apple Valley. We enjoyed being close to the kids again, especially considering the circumstances with Susan's health.

But there was still unfinished business. Susan and Colleen had never truly mended the rift from that argument when we first told them about her cancer and my decision to become a pastor. And now here we were, with news of her cancer's return and my new position. Susan, still upset, held out as long as she could.

Finally, I told her, "Enough is enough. Invite them over."

It was awkward at first, but a couple of glasses of wine softened the somewhat stiff conversation. I held my breath for a moment when Susan bragged about my work in Fullerton.

She then leveled about her appendix cancer. There were tears, and there was more wine.

I never knew whether Colleen couldn't hold her liquor or whether she just drank more. But either way, I wondered where she was going when she raised her glass to toast and began with, "Susan, I am just plain jealous as hell of you."

Not exactly what you expect to hear when you tell someone you have incurable cancer. I thought, *Roger, tell her to shut up.* I looked at him, and his expression must be how somebody looks just before a car crashes.

"Look at this place where you live," Colleen continued. "Look at this guy you're married to. Look at what you did in that godforsaken place up by the Canadian border or whatever. Forgive me for making those comments about the Assemblies back then. Because now—well, Roger, you tell them."

Roger took a sip of his wine. We all did.

"Yes, here's to the Assemblies of the Lord—I'm a finalist to become pastor at the new Celebration of Christ Christian Church. Lutherans everywhere, forgive me."

Susan and I didn't dare look at each other. Roger noticed the quietness.

"Seriously, this is a once-in-a-lifetime chance. And you know how Colleen would like to come back here to the Cities. Pray this would be good for all."

I sipped my wine. Actually, I took a fairly healthy swig.

"Roger, Colleen," I began, "this is difficult, but I must tell you. I was offered the job at Celebration Church. I accepted two days ago."

Colleen broke the silence. "Son of a bitch!"

With that, she left the room crying.

41

R IGHT FROM THE START, THE LEADERS OF Celebration Christian
Church amazed me with their commitment and creativity. This
body would have grown without a church building. The membership had grown to over a thousand active members.

About two months after my ministry began, the contractors were ready
to put the finishing touches on the new building. The church elders decided
that the first service would be a joint celebration for the new church and the
new pastor.

In the days leading up to the first service, I wondered if Susan would still
be here with us for the commissioning of this beautiful new building. Once
so vibrant, she now felt exhausted to the point that she often stayed in bed
until noon. Her once beautiful skin now looked almost ashen. The hair once
so beguiling to me now lived only in my memory. Lindsey spent a lot of time
with Susan and me. We both found her presence something to look forward to
every single day. In particular, I looked forward to her arrival so I could go to
work. I had a job to do, and I did it. Truth be told, I wanted to be home with
Susan. But bravely continuing with the truth, I found it very hard.

———

Just as my new life kicked off at Celebration, a little piece of my old life in
Fullerton came calling. I heard from the Syracuse law firm handling Floyd's
estate.

Floyd had awarded Ginny, one of his three children, the grocery store and
the restaurant. She already managed the restaurant. With her love of people
and her innate honesty and friendliness, she had the tools to do well.

Floyd already had a buyer for his creamery. For his partnership in the Holiday Inn, he had an agreement with the other partner: Ginny could either make an offer to buy his partner's shares, or she could sell Floyd's shares for the same amount. Any proceeds were to be divided between the school and the five churches in town.

Lest any misunderstandings occur, he made it plain that his two other children were to receive nothing. They had ignored him these past years, so he would return the favor now.

A sum of $600,000 was left for me to distribute. One half of this was designated to right a personal wrong, which remained confidential as far as the estate was concerned. Of course, I remembered Floyd's instructions.

With the other half, I was to advance Amber's education—and I was to use the remainder in any way I saw fit. As the will read, this could include paying any unanticipated medical expenses to "care for his beautiful wife."

As I read the document to Susan, she could only shake her head.

"Floyd, Floyd, Floyd," she repeated.

I knew I could trust Gary to help me locate Lucky Lila and keep the matter confidential. Gary found her family through public records. When he offered $100 to whomever got the address to him first, he had her new location within a few minutes.

Gary called to share the irony with me. "Jake, you'll never believe this— she's dealing blackjack at the Mystic Lake Casino about ten miles from you."

I wanted to act quickly, so a couple of nights later, I surprised Lila by bellying up to her table. Her eyes grew big and her lips quivered. Two half-drunk women were the only other people at her table. I gave each one a fifty-dollar chip to move.

"What do you want?" she asked as she nervously dealt me a hand.

"I want you to relax and promise you'll talk to me when you have a break. Trust me—you'll be surprised, and you'll be happy."

Lila became quiet as we finished up the hand. As it turned out, I drew to twenty-one. For the first time, I noticed Lila had beautiful blue eyes. And while a little thin, she had delicate features that contrasted with her shrewd dealer personality. I could see how Floyd fell in love with her.

I picked up my money and told her I would wait in the bar. About twenty minutes later, she came over and sat down.

"Okay. What do I have to do, and what are you going to give me if I do it?"

I shouldn't have been surprised, remembering the arrangement she had made with Floyd.

"Well, I have three hundred thousand dollars for you. What do you have to do? You just have to listen to what a man named Floyd Mann wanted to tell you before he died."

She stared at me. "Floyd's dead? What happened?"

"Parkinson's disease. He had a tough year before it finally got him."

Even with all that money possibly in the balance, she blurted, "I'm not going to lie—I'm glad I won't have to run from him anymore."

"Why did you think you had to run?"

She shuddered. "I told you—the night he kicked me out into the street, he said he would kill me if I said a word about us."

I found myself wondering about her intelligence. As Floyd told me, he didn't mean those words. They were unfortunate, yes, but nothing but hot air. Most people would have understood that. I did now.

"I got to know him very well, Lila. Floyd wasn't about to kill you or anybody. He wanted you to know he loved you, but he just didn't know how to show it. He was in a marriage without any love and couldn't leave his wife. He told me to tell you that after you left, he never lived a day that he didn't think of you."

Her face softened a bit.

"Lila, he asked me to find you and give you this money as well as his sincerest apology. He knew this money might not make a difference in how you feel about him, but he hoped it could help you improve your life."

I took the check from my pocket along with a receipt for her to sign, acknowledging she received the money free and clear. I handed her the check and asked her to sign the receipt.

She smiled for the first time. "I'm definitely going to celebrate tonight. Want to join me?"

Believe it or not, my sleazy side had me looking around to be sure I didn't know anybody. She had already progressed from not bad-looking to attractive in her own way.

But I just shook her hand. "You can change your life with this money. Spend it well."

———

One of my favorite aspects of Celebration was that every member belonged to a "friendship group." Each friendship group included eight members who agreed to get together at least once per month to eat, play, study, and pray.

Susan and I joined a group with three other couples. We loved the members in the group right from the start. Dr. Feldman was in our group. For our first get-together, we enjoyed dinner at his and his wife's home.

After a delightful evening, Dr. Feldman asked if Susan and I could stay a little longer as the others headed for their cars.

"There's something I've been wanting to ask you," he said.

Susan and I exchanged glances. Honestly, we were both exhausted. Susan, especially. Even a dinner with good friends was a major undertaking for her these days. But we nodded and followed him as he invited us back into the living room to sit. His wife, Liz, made a deliberate beeline for the kitchen.

"I'm sorry for all the mystery," Dr. Feldman began, "but I wanted to speak to you confidentially. Pastor Horton, I hope I'm wrong, but I believe you may have Parkinson's disease."

My immediate thought was, *Susan doesn't need to hear this.* My second thought was, *I need to call Trent.* The very word *Parkinson's* terrified me. I had seen the disease up close more than once. Parkinson's had taken down a giant, Floyd Mann, with little ceremony—efficient and cruel.

I looked at Dr. Feldman, not wanting to say anything, waiting for him to finish. I wanted to get the hell out of there. Susan squeezed my hand.

"I'm sorry," he continued, "but tonight at dinner I heard you mention issues on your right side. And I've noticed you move rather slowly and don't blink your eyes."

While he clearly wasn't saying I had Parkinson's for certain, I knew him well enough to know he wouldn't have said anything unless he was reasonably sure. Still, he was only a general practitioner, not a specialist.

"I suggest you see a neurologist—and sooner rather than later," he added, as if reading my thoughts. "I could recommend one if you would like. They can help people with PD these days."

"Thank you," I said calmly. "Actually, a good friend of mine is a leader in Parkinson's treatments. I'll be sure to contact him."

On the way home, I was still calm, yet I found myself hoping I had imagined the whole conversation. Susan and I didn't speak until we got into the house.

She took my hand. Her hand seemed so weak and fragile. She already had the weight of the world on her; now she knew she couldn't count on me to be there for her.

"Jake, let's take this one step at a time. Tell me—what are you thinking right now?"

"I guess it would be good to know what's wrong," I said. It was a lie.

Two people now occupied my thoughts: Floyd and Trent's dad. Had I ever thought I might have Parkinson's? Only very briefly. But many other conditions also came to mind aside from the dreaded disease. I wondered if it were a brain tumor.

My work as pastor at Celebration had been my refuge from the tragedy of Susan's cancer. Now, I'd likely need to spend my time addressing my own health as well as Susan's. As much as it broke my heart, I knew Susan's issue would resolve itself sooner than we wanted it to. But me, I was now on a long-term track. It wasn't like I could ask for a few weeks of medical leave, then pop back all better. Parkinson's is debilitating. There's no cure. You don't get better.

———

The next day, I called Trent and set up an appointment, explaining my symptoms and Dr. Feldman's hunch. I wondered if Trent fell for my phony brave tone at all.

After making the call, I climbed behind the wheel of my car and just drove. I needed to be by myself. I wanted to be away from the house. Away from the church. Away from my life. I wanted to pray, but I wasn't ready. It was as if I needed to practice and find the right words for God.

I went through the rest of my day in a fog. With Susan's cancer, I was already bankrupt of any positive thoughts. Now I began to imagine how this whole new scenario with my health would play out for JJ and Lindsey.

For the first time in a long time, I decided I owed myself a drink. The Thunderbird Hotel lounge had been a comfortable place for me in the past, so I went a little out of my way to end up there. Their Old Fashioned was legendary, so I didn't waste time thinking about what to order.

I suddenly didn't want to be alone. I figured maybe this was a good time to call Cy. Twenty minutes later, he joined me at the lounge. He ordered me another round and a draft beer for himself.

As Cy flirted back and forth with the waitress, I couldn't help but notice what a good-looking young man he had become. He possessed his mother's dark eyes and wavy, thick, shiny black hair. For a very brief moment, I missed those days when attractive women looked at me with the interest this waitress now showed Cy.

Cy turned to me. "How's Aunt Susan?"

"To be honest, she's not getting better. She's a brave one, though. We're just thankful for every day. Thanks for asking." I paused a beat. "Tell me, Cy—I know we don't typically talk about this, but how are Roger and Colleen doing?"

Cy took a sip of his beer. "Well, if you're asking if they're still pissed off at you about your new church, I would say, my dad is happy for you, and my mom sometimes makes life a bitch for my dad. He often suggests she should go spend time with Aunt Susan. Jake, my mom is an unhappy woman."

I was shocked by this candor, so I went on. "What about Margie? How often do you see her?"

Cy took a deeper drink. "When we get together, it's good, but I try to think about Roger and Colleen, my mother and father, in all of this. Really, I don't see her very often." He eyed me. "I've often wondered if you ever think of her. You know something happened between her and Vince, right?"

I looked at him in surprise. "What do you mean?"

Cy shook his head. "One weekend she called me and said, 'Well, Cy, we have something new in common—we're both single.' I don't know what happened. Aside from that, though, I think she's doing okay."

Old habits, I guess, made me mentally make note of this. I wanted to ask more about Margie, but I moved on. "How about you? I hear you're getting serious with that girl, Amber, you've been seeing."

In comparison, JJ was engaged and Lindsey likely soon to be, once she and her longtime boyfriend graduated from college. I wondered if Cy, at twenty-eight, would ever settle down.

Apparently Cy didn't appreciate the line of questioning.

"Uncle Jake, I don't think that's your concern. Actually, I find it pretty fucking ironic to have you sitting here asking me about my love life. Did you forget how I came into this world?"

With that, he got up, threw down two twenties, and left before I could stop him.

I sat there reeling for a few minutes. Finally, I downed my drink and headed home.

Susan kissed my cheek as I came into the living room. "Have you been drinking—a little happy hour, perhaps?" she asked with a surprised smile.

I gave her a hug. "Guilty. I had a drink with Gary for old time's sake."

She looked confused. "But Gary just called a bit ago. He didn't say anything about having a drink with you."

Shit.

With all the tragedy in our household, I hated that I had lied to her. But I also hated having to address the difficult truth. "Okay, I had a drink with Cy. I just said it was Gary instead because I know how you get when Cy's name comes up."

She was pissed. She turned, went to the spare bedroom, and shut the door.

I slumped in the chair. I felt too exhausted to even think about following after her. I could go in to apologize, but it wouldn't be sincere. We just didn't see eye to eye when it came to my "nephew."

Peeking in on Susan a while later, I wasn't surprised to find her sleeping soundly. I decided to let her rest and make some food before waking her. She needed to take her meds after she ate. Though I didn't feel like it, I made her favorite casserole and placed it in the oven.

About seven in the evening, Susan walked shakily out of the bedroom with a single comment: "Smells good."

It occurred to me I couldn't smell anything.

Susan and I sat at the kitchen table. She took my hand.

"Jake, I don't know if I was angry because you found it necessary to lie about meeting Cy or because you want to treat Cy like your son. As you've said many times, I get upset by this for all the wrong reasons. Maybe you can invite him over sometime."

I kissed her hands. I think both of us knew it was unlikely that Susan's cancer would allow this to take place.

After dinner, I felt somewhat energized. I cleaned the kitchen and began working on my pastoral tasks at hand. Susan sat near me reading a novel for a while,
then headed to bed while I watched the news.

I was just getting ready for bed myself when I heard her calling for me
weakly.

I rushed in to find her holding her side in obvious pain.

"Take me in. Take me in!"

42

We arrived at the emergency room twenty minutes later. Susan's physician was called. The ER doctor asked me questions and shared his opinions, but I was in a trance.

Susan, it seemed, had slipped into a coma. I was ushered to a semi-private waiting area while they treated her. The doctor suggested I call the kids and anyone else I felt should be there. I knew Lindsey was at home, so I called her. She said she would pick up JJ and bring him with her to the hospital.

I looked up at the clock and noticed it was five past midnight. One of the worst days of my life was over. But I had every reason to believe this day would reach a new low.

I tried praying. I tried reading the Bible. I felt thoroughly exhausted, as if I were walking in my sleep, robotically.

Just as I got up to drop a quarter in the vending machine for some coffee, the lead doctor came over and shook my hand.

"Pastor, your wife is awake—for now. She wants to see you."

I stared. "What do you mean, for now?"

He looked down, then back at me. "We'll do all we can, but her heart is so weak. I just think I need to prepare you. Come this way."

As I followed him to her room, I wanted to scream, "God, don't do this! God, don't do this!" I tried to put on a brave face. But I choked.

She looked so tiny, so vulnerable, so pale.

I put my hand on the side of her face. Out of habit, I touched her ear. She lifted her hand and locked her fingers in mine.

"Jake, come close," she whispered. "Remember the first time we saw each other and I sat on your lap? I knew then, you know."

She closed her eyes for a few seconds.

"Please forgive me for being jealous of Margie and Cy. I've loved you every single day . . . you know that. I believe in heaven, and I know you'll be with me someday. Still, I don't want to go . . . yet. The kids . . . all so good." Her words were breaking up. "Jake, can I sit on your lap once more?" she managed to ask.

I was afraid of hurting her somehow, and I was afraid of pulling the tubes from her frail body. But she wanted this one thing, and I couldn't deny her.

JJ and Lindsey arrived just then. Slowly, they opened the door to see me kissing Susan as she sat on my lap on the bed. They stood transfixed for a few moments. It had not been unusual for them to see us being affectionate, but they knew we were saying good-bye for the last time.

They waited, then came in and put their arms around us. Their mother looked at them and mouthed, "I will always love you."

Then her spirit left.

43

AS THE DAYS PASSED AFTER SUSAN'S DEATH, the extreme hurt dulled. I settled into the reality that my world had simply lost its joy.

The kids and I sort of circled the wagons. I planned on delivering the eulogy, but JJ and Lindsey begged me to let somebody else do it. So I wrote it and asked DeeDee's husband, Pastor Trevor, to deliver it for the family. Actually, my first thought was to invite Amber to read the eulogy, but I opted to not risk hurting Trevor and DeeDee's feelings.

We held the visitation the night before the funeral. So many good and caring people had been attracted to Susan's essence. Some of the stories and the people sharing them were strangers to me.

A woman in her seventies came with her daughter. I was confused when they thanked me profusely for my support. It turned out Susan had helped them purchase a used but reliable car so they could get jobs, but she had told them it was my idea. That was so Susan—she lived humbly and gave credit to others.

Seeing Trent filled me with as much discomfort as comfort. He expressed his condolences, then began asking me about my suspected Parkinson's. Funny—we once cruised around Mesabi looking for parties. Now, here he was, an authority on Parkinson's. And here I was, at my wife's visitation, doing my best to deny the disease had me in its clamps.

Trent practiced at the Cleveland Clinic, but he maintained a professional relationship with the Mayo Clinic in Rochester, Minnesota. He mentioned he would be there on Wednesday. If I made an appointment, we could discuss further options. I knew this was generous of him, so I took him up on it. As he shook my hand, we both noticed it trembling.

Cy stopped in. He and Lindsey were talking. As I approached, he raised his voice a little too much so I would be sure to hear him.

"Aunt Susan was a wonderful woman. I came here to tell you that. I hope you and JJ are doing okay."

Then he came over to shake my hand. "Seen Margie yet?" he asked.

DeeDee had told me Margie was in town for the funeral, but she decided not to attend the visitation.

"Not yet. But thanks, Cy, for coming by."

When Roger and Colleen came in, I immediately went over and welcomed them. Colleen put her head on my shoulder and just sobbed.

I said nothing except, "There were far more good than bad times with the two of you. Think of the good times. She loved you so much."

My entire family made it, though I wasn't surprised. They loved Susan and they loved JJ and Lindsey.

I wondered what was going through Mike's mind, knowing Margie would be at the funeral. Mike and I had an unwritten rule to not go there. I wondered if Sharri knew the story and if she knew Mike would love Margie right to the grave. Yet he loved Sharri too and no doubt would be loyal to the end. More loyal than I had been to Susan.

Over the years, I came to see that Mike resembled our dad in all his good ways. But unlike Dad, Mike was no fake. Sometimes I wished I hadn't insisted that Anna tell me the story about why she left Mesabi. But if Anna could forgive Dad, I certainly should. Anna was more concerned about loving Judy and being her true self than dwelling on the past.

As if reading my mind, Judy walked over. She and I tended to gravitate toward each other in larger gatherings such as this. For her, perhaps she sought me for comfort. She knew how much I liked and respected her. For me, it just made me feel good that somebody so smart would converse with me. Judy may have been the smartest person I've ever known, at least in business matters. She taught me to be a better businessperson and a better person in general. I thought about the old saying, "We may not remember what somebody said, but we remember how they made us feel." So true.

Judy and I talked about Sommer's Carpet, Marina, and Rita. Then almost in passing, she commented, "My dad died a month ago Friday."

I was shocked. "Oh, no. I am so sorry, Judy. Had he been sick?"

Judy proceeded to tell me how the stress her mother had thrust on her dad eventually led to a severe heart attack.

"Judy, we're family. Why didn't you let me and Susan know?"

She touched my hand and said softly, "Jake, we knew you were dealing with so much. Anna and I decided you didn't need more."

"So what about your mother?"

Judy hesitated then looked me in the eyes. "When it comes to my mother, the less I see or talk to her, the better. When we held a small service for Dad at the local funeral home, she dropped by with her current love interest. She said nothing to anyone and left abruptly. Truly, I don't care if I ever see her again. Aside from Anna, my dad was my best friend, and my mother made life hell for him." She shook her head. "I'm sorry for the diatribe. I know I shouldn't feel this way. But I literally hate her."

My heart ached for this great human being who had been saddled with the worst mother ever.

"I'm sorry, Judy. You and your dad deserved better. You're one of the best people I've ever known, and you did it without having a nurturing or even decent mother. I hope you know how much I respect you. This only makes me respect you more."

Judy had tears in her eyes. "I don't think I believe in God, but sometimes I wish I did just so I could ask him what he was thinking when it came to my mother. Why was she so evil?"

As a pastor, this type of question can be frustrating. You want to help. You want to say some magic words. But then again, you ask the same question about people in your own life—people like Frank Nazar, who almost methodically ruin people's lives.

"Judy, I would like to know that too. We've both experienced the miraculous as well as the deep sadness. We need to choose to dwell and live with the miraculous. Is it too much of a pass to give credit to God for the miraculous but not the sad stuff? I don't know. I believe it's not only good but prudent to give thanks in all circumstances."

I looked around, suddenly aware of where I was standing: at my own wife's funeral. It gave new perspective to my words.

"Sometimes my feeling of thankfulness is just too strong to share with only people—I need to thank something or someone beyond. So even as I contemplate life without Susan, I feel so enormously thankful for all the moments we spent together and, of course, the family she left me. I choose to thank God. I believe I will meet him face to face someday. I hope he's a forgiving guy. There's much he could take me to task for. But if he allows me to ask him questions, yours will be near the top of the list."

Judy hugged me. "Jake, you should have been a minister—oh, that's right. You are one! No wonder you're so good at it."

I thought, *If you only knew . . .*

———

Life was a blur. Before I knew it, I was standing in the back of the church a few minutes before the funeral service began. I looked up, and there was Margie.

My first reaction was to go give her a hug, but I had thought about this earlier and decided I wanted to concentrate on Susan and the kids. I still didn't trust myself around her. I couldn't help but wonder how she thought of me now.

But enough of that. It was time. Margie and Cy joined Roger and Colleen. The four of them trailed behind the kids and me as we followed the casket into the church. It reminded me of Dad's funeral, when Margie joined our family. Each time, it was simultaneously awkward yet comforting.

The procession was the longest walk of my life. Emotionally, of course, it was hell. Physically as well. The two aspects fed each other. When I felt a little nervous, I got a slight tremor in my right hand. When I felt serious tension, pain radiated from my arm and my hands grew stiff and hurt. As I proceeded with the casket, my right leg, my right arm, and my right foot checked in with various levels of hurt. My balance challenged me as I leaned to the right. But I made it.

The funeral service would have pleased Susan. I was told it was the largest gathering ever at Celebration Christian Church.

It's an honor when the district elder attends a funeral. He did more than attend; he delivered the message. I had thought about asking Roger to do this but decided to use him for a less stressful part of the service. Roger lived with regrets for that fateful dinner when a wedge was driven between our wives. He would have had trouble feeling honest up there.

After the service, we buried her in the church's new cemetery, then headed back for lunch in the new community room.

A group of eight came in from Saint Peter's in Fullerton. Amber was enrolled in her first year of seminary and seemed so much older.

Arlen and Leonard told me the new pastor was doing well. Arlen winked at me and added, "But between us, he didn't get the pay-for-performance plan."

At first, I didn't even recognize Vickie. She had gotten rid of ten to fifteen pounds of fat—and at least 200 pounds of a lazy husband. She was now divorced and eager to let the world know it. I wondered who had helped her select her clothes. No pioneer-woman dresses for Vickie anymore.

Vickie took me aside and mentioned she was thinking of moving to the Cities. Apparently, she wanted to start over and she had heard me say good things about life here. I assumed there was more to it, but I just let it go. She asked if I knew of anybody looking to hire somebody with her background. Well, I did, as a matter of fact. Pastor Roger Lund.

I brought her over to meet Roger. Even under the unusual circumstances, introductions went well.

"I would love to learn more about you and your experience, Vickie," Roger said. "Could we set up an interview?"

"I'd like that," Vickie replied. "But I'll just need to finagle a way to get to you . . ."

"Actually," I chimed in, "would Wednesday work? I have an appointment in Rochester, so I'm heading that direction. Vickie, you could ride with me. I'll wait for you during the interview if you don't mind waiting for me during my appointment."

Both Vickie and Roger were happy with the arrangement.

When someone beckoned Roger over, Vickie leaned in to me and whispered, "Thank you—but are you sure this isn't too much of a hassle for you?"

"I would love the company, Vickie."

She beamed. And touched my arm.

I made my way around the room during the luncheon but never crossed paths with Margie. She always remained in my periphery. I wasn't sure if that was by my design, hers, or a combination. I did hear her name mentioned once, though. One of my mother's friends said in a rather loud voice, "That Margie sure doesn't look like she's forty-eight, does she?"

Chatting with each person was exhausting yet uplifting. These conversations of everyday matters helped me see how life continues for those left behind. These chats were inane, insane, or just plain, but each was a reminder that, like it or not, my life would continue.

Before long, people began trickling out. JJ and Lindsey wanted to join Judy, Anna, and Mike's crew at a local hotel. Again, memories flooded me. This time of my fortieth birthday party—though I quickly shook that particular memory away before I had to relive my dance with Colleen. I encouraged the kids to go, though I politely declined to join them.

I was beyond tired. If I had been just another funeralgoer, I would have left the luncheon an hour earlier. As both pastor and husband of the deceased, though, I had to wait until the last guest left to show my appreciation. Eventually, all I had left to thank were the hard-working members of the funeral lunch bunch. Then it was just me, Mom, and DeeDee.

Mom put her arms around me and held me in a hug, rocking back and forth. She leaned back to see my face, though without releasing the hug.

"Jake, Susan was the perfect wife for you. And, son, and you were a perfect husband for her. When we first met her, I thought she was a little quiet for you, but I soon saw she was a deeply principled, loving person. This is such a loss for our whole family. I'm so sorry to see you go through this tough time, Jake. You had a special marriage. This is so tough on JJ and Lindsey too."

DeeDee got up and asked, "Can I join the hug fest?"

My leg was aching, but I extended my arm out to her.

We held each other for a long moment, then Mom kissed my cheek. "I should get going. Devin is waiting for me. We're heading to the hotel too. Please join us if you want, Jake. But we understand if you just want to go home."

As Mom headed out, DeeDee smiled shyly. "I know this is an odd thing to say right at this moment, but Margie is staying with Trevor and me for a few days. I've kept in touch over the years. If you feel up to it, I know she'd like to see you. Were you able to say hello to her today?"

"No. I didn't get a chance to talk to her. I barely saw her. I just wasn't sure if she was uncomfortable and wanted to avoid me," I admitted.

"Well, think about it." She reached out for one last hug, tears coming to her eyes. "You arranged a beautiful service, Jake. Thanks for including my hubby. I know he was honored. I miss Susan already. You have a tough road to travel. I'm happy to help in any way."

Now, I was alone. I walked back upstairs and sat in the front pew looking up at the huge wooden cross. It loomed above me. I thought of DeeDee's comment about a rough road in front of me. I thought of the challenge Parkinson's presented—if indeed I did have it, which I most likely did. I thought of the huge hole in my life left by Susan.

I looked up at the cross and prayed, "You know I am lost right now. Please show me the way."

44

O DOUBT, MY APPOINTMENT WITH TRENT weighed heavily on my mind. Yet the time had come to do something about these symptoms before they interfered with my work and, well, my life. Susan had piled on the guilt by saying, "I can't be here to hold our family together. Jake, it's up to you to take care of yourself."

I picked Vickie up on Wednesday morning. My first thought was that she dressed a little too sexy for an interview—let alone one with a pastor. She wasn't fully over the top, but just a little.

During the drive, I found it fun to catch up with so many names from Fullerton. By the time we reached Roger's office at his house, she had begun talking about her husband—ex-husband now.

The two of them had attended high school together in Fullerton. He left for college; she stayed true to him. When he flunked out of college two years later, he returned to Fullerton feeling like a failure. They got married and stayed with her parents for another two years while he tried to find a decent house. Her mother did not like the new son-in-law. He didn't like his mother-in-law either.

Vickie shook her head. "When he got a job selling some kind of lubricants for farm equipment, we all knew he would need to travel. We all were glad for that."

They hobbled along like this until he got into an argument with his boss and was fired. Again, he came back a failure. The mother-in-law said he could stay at the house for one month and that's it.

Vickie smiled. "I was glad when the thirty days were up. I asked him, 'Do you want a divorce?' He answered, 'Where would I live?'"

Thankfully, we arrived at Roger's right on time. I didn't need to hear more about her ex.

I escorted her in, then said I'd be back once they were done. I looked for Colleen in the house but didn't see her, which was odd. Roger no doubt told her I'd be here to drop off Vickie. I was planning on chatting with her while I waited for Vickie and Roger.

I decided to walk around outside. The church was nearby. Finding the doors open and the church empty, I walked in and sat near the back in the silence.

The building itself impressed me. The brick and oak exterior showed it to be well kept. The interior showed a congregation with traditional worship values. The centerpiece, an oak cross about ten feet tall, reminded me of the one in our church.

I bowed my head and shared my concerns of the day with God: *I pray it's not your will for me to live with Parkinson's. But if it is, I need courage.*

My prayer was interrupted by the sounds of somebody moving about the front of the church. Startled, I looked up to see Colleen cleaning the brass cross on the altar.

It made sense now—no wonder I couldn't find her in the house. She was deliberately trying to avoid me. In turn, I almost slunk low in the pew to avoid her seeing me. Instead, I decided to get up and head to the front.

Once she saw movement out of the corner of her eye, she jumped back and drew her right hand to her heart. Her face registered a different type of surprise once she recognized the figure approaching her was me.

"Jake, what are you doing here?"

I sat in the front pew. "I'm pretty sure Roger told you I was bringing Vickie to interview today," I said.

She knew she was caught, so I went on.

"Do I make you so uncomfortable that you don't even want to see me? Maybe you should tell me what you think I've done."

She stood there in her jeans and University of Minnesota sweatshirt, holding a dust rag in one hand and the brass cross in the other, not knowing what to do or say.

I coaxed her. "Why don't you first put the cross down so you don't try to bury it in my head?"

Her old humor came back. "I wouldn't do that, Jake. I just cleaned it."

I patted the spot next to me in the pew. "Come sit by me."

She sat down. We just looked at each other for a few moments. It sounds uncomfortable, but it wasn't. I saw an intelligent and attractive woman who had supported her husband through thick and thin, who raised another woman's child, and who likely felt deep disappointment in the outcome. I wondered what she thought of me.

I broke the silence. "Why don't we get it all out on the table right here? Roger is tied up with Vickie. It's just you, me, and the cross."

She had been tearing up, but now she straightened. "Well, the problem isn't you. I know that. It's me and its choices."

I leaned back. "Tell me about them, and tell me why you tried avoiding me today."

"I guess it's no secret to you," she breathed. "You remember the night I humiliated myself at my own sister's house. I've felt like a whore since then."

"We didn't have sex."

She half smiled and looked down. "No, but I've played that whole scene over too many times—I wanted to have sex with you. And I'll never forget what you said as I threw myself at you: 'Not here, not now.' What did that mean, Jake?"

She had turned the table on me. "It just meant, not here, not now."

She looked directly into my eyes. "I think it meant you would have taken me right there, but you knew Susan or Roger might show up any minute. Is that true or not?"

I decided to be real. "I hate to admit it, but yes. I've been fascinated by you since I was a kid in youth group in Mesabi."

Colleen glanced away now. "I really had the feeling then that you would cheat on Susan if you had the chance."

I held my breath. If she pressed me further, if she came right out and asked me the hard question, it would be nearly impossible to escape the truth.

Thankfully, she didn't. Instead, she said, "I thought about warning Susan, but how could I? She wouldn't have believed it anyway. She would have dismissed it as just jealousy, my jealousy. Susan lived in Apple Valley. That's what I wanted. You had a successful business and built that beautiful house. I lived in a church parsonage in a hick town. You guys did fun things, you had two kids. We had little money, and I was barren. Then you became a minister, and the two of you succeeded in that godforsaken place in New York. And after years of me trying to convince Roger he needed to take control of our future, you got the job we prayed about every day for a month. And then there's Cy. We don't have to go down that road—you know where that one takes us."

She took a deep breath.

"I know most of this is not your doing, but these are the things that make me ashamed and make me act like a bitch to the people I care about. So much, that I didn't help my beautiful, wonderful sister as she walked the path of suffering and death. Do you think I'm being overly dramatic? I feel as low as I can feel."

I felt ashamed myself. When I first encouraged her to talk to me, I thought I would end up saying, "I forgive you." How simpleminded.

"Colleen, I'm sorry for my part in all this. As I told you at the funeral, Susan loved you. She could have reached out to you as well." I took her hand. "Is there anything I can do today to make things better?"

She gave my hand a squeeze. "Not really. Just try to understand."

———

As I made my way back to the house, I thought about Colleen and her disappointments in life. My mood was dark, but my timing was good. Vickie and Roger were done with the interview.

Vickie did most of the talking as we drove to Rochester. She felt the interview had gone well, but she wondered if she wanted to live in another small town. I suddenly wished I hadn't encouraged the interview. I realized now the new Vickie wouldn't be happy for long in Roger's small community. Oh, boy.

I let Vickie take the car after she dropped me off at the main entrance of Mayo Clinic. The place had scads of volunteers with blue outfits to point people in the right direction. Someone guided me to Trent's office area, where I told the receptionist I had a two o'clock appointment.

It surprised me in a good way when she responded, "Dr. Podominik told me to bring you right in."

She brought me back to a bigger office. Trent greeted me and motioned for me to sit down at a table with him and his assistant.

"Well, Jake, after visiting with you at the visitation, there's no question you have Parkinson's. You've had it for at least a couple of years."

That was it.

It was just a matter of time before I looked like Trent's dad or Floyd. I lost my wife, and now I lost my life.

"Tell me about your symptoms," he pressed.

"Symptoms," I said, still trying to process it all. "Well, what's probably been bothering me most is my right leg. At first, I would get this shooting pain in my upper right leg every so often. Starting a year ago or so, I noticed it had worsened. It hurt more often, and I also felt it in my right foot. Then a month ago, I noticed I had pain in my right hand, like it was stiff. Now, I notice pain in my other leg as well. I also don't feel quite 'with it.' My balance is a little off. I lean toward the right. I think I do this because my arm feels limp and heavy."

Trent's assistant took notes as quickly as he could.

"Have you noticed any other problems with your health," Trent asked, "whether you think they have anything to do with Parkinson's or not?"

I thought for a moment. "I need to have my eyes checked. It's gotten hard to read. It may be because my eyes are so dry."

"What about tremors?"

"Maybe my right hand a little, when I feel stressed."

Trent then asked me to perform several exercises designed to see how the disease had progressed. It made me acutely aware my right hand had become my weak hand.

"Jake," he said, "there's a saying I've found to be true: 'show me one case of Parkinson's, and I'll show you one case.' It's like snowflakes; no two are the same. There's no cure, but through meds, we can slow it down. With your permission, I'd like to contact a top Parkinson's guy I know at the U. I'll get you two together, but I'll be partnering with him all the way." He put his hand on my shoulder. "Jake, you can still lead a productive life for many years."

Despite his optimism, I felt the walls closing in on me.

Trent went on to explain the pills I'd need to take, but I couldn't follow him well. Thankfully, his assistant wrote down the regimen: pills at 6:00 a.m., pills at 10:00 a.m., pills at 2:00 p.m., pills at 6:00 p.m., and pills before bedtime. The grand total of this daily schedule would be thirty-two pills per day. I dreaded it, but Trent said this would be the price for living a more normal life for longer.

Thankfully, I had incredible insurance from the church—no deductible. I shuddered at the cost of this medicine and wondered how many people were not able to get it because they didn't have insurance like mine.

I had told Vickie to start looking for me at the front entrance after three thirty. I thanked Trent and reaffirmed how lucky I was to have him for a friend. I was still in a daze as I made my way out.

Vickie pulled up, then started to get out of the driver's seat. I waved her back in to drive.

"Where to?" she asked.

I felt parched. "How about a bar?"

We drove for a while, heading to the outer reaches of Rochester, where the hotels were located. I motioned out the window.

"How about that bar over there, next to the Holiday? What's its name?"

Vickie looked. "Clever. It's called the Library."

We took a booth near the back. I wondered if she noticed the male patrons eyeing her up and down. I wanted a Manhattan, and I wanted it now. She settled on a screwdriver. Here I got a lucky break—it was two-for-one happy hour.

One and a half screwdrivers made Vickie braver. "So," she said brightly, "what did the good doctor have to say?"

Both the question and the casualness surprised me.

"The good doctor says I have Parkinson's disease."

I could tell she regretted the question. She put her hands in mine.

"I thought when people had Parkinson's their hands shook. Yours don't."

I met her gaze, and she continued to hold my hands. Suddenly we realized the waitress was standing at our table. Vickie let go of my hands. We ordered the house special, prime rib, and another round. I didn't want the two-for-ones again, but there they were.

My plan had been to stop for a drink or two, with Vickie driving us back to the Cities. Thanks to happy hour, that turned into two or four drinks. While I may have been a little drunk, she was a lot drunk. My dad's death loomed in my mind.

"How about getting a couple of rooms next door so we don't get in a car accident trying to drive back?"

"I don't have anyone to account to," she slurred.

The Holiday Inn waited all of three or four blocks away, and thankfully the streets were empty. I was sober enough to handle the short distance, but I still found myself driving as slow as I possibly could.

My Parkinson's seemed like old news. Instead, I had a new inner conflict. It seemed clear where Vickie and I were headed, and that troubled me. This wasn't a dilemma of right and wrong, however. It was about not wanting to make a fool out of myself.

From the moment we left that morning to the drinks at the Library, she seemed eager to show her affections for me. On the other hand, what if I read her wrong? How would that play? I'd be a fifty-one-year-old guy—who lost his wife the week before and just found out he has Parkinson's—manipulating his thirty-seven-year-old former assistant to sleep with him. Sounded sleazy. I decided she'd have to make the move.

I pulled into a parking space near a side door and shut off the engine. I felt her stare.

"Jake, you're the reason I've begun a new life. Do you find me pretty at all?"

I couldn't wait to reply. "Do I find you pretty? Yes, all of you."

She surprised me a little next. "My ex, he could be a supreme asshole. But he did tell me he was a tit man. He loved my tits."

With that, she took my right hand and slipped it into her blouse and into her bra. She put her head back, closed her eyes, and partially reclined her seat.

Not that I wanted to complain, but it seemed odd she would just lay there while I played with her breasts. To be fair, I had to agree with her ex.

Finally, she pulled me over and brought my mouth to hers. I hated to break the spell, but I couldn't see having sex in this well-lit parking lot. Not to mention the frequent cramps I now got.

"Hold this thought," I whispered. "Let me go and check us in."

Sure, I felt sleazy, but I got the registration taken care of in record time. I asked for a room near my car so we could use the side door and not go through the lobby. Asked and granted.

As I hurried back to the car, I envisioned Vicki passed out and half naked. I wasn't too far off. She had resumed the same goofy pose from earlier—eyes closed and reclined.

"Vickie, you want me to carry you in?"

"Yes, carry me over the threshold," she mumbled.

Why I suggested this, I have no idea. Ever the gentleman, I got out and opened the passenger door. She worked her way toward me and extended her arms toward my neck. I could imagine my vertebrae screaming at me, "Don't do it, Jake."

With one big effort, I picked her up, but we both could feel her slipping out of my grasp. I was about to experience my first benefit from Parkinson's: it's a built-in excuse when you really need an out.

"Vickie, I'm sorry, but the Parkinson's has made my right arm worthless."

She was sorry. I know because she said it twenty times. I opened the door, and she stumbled in after me.

I purposely left the lights off inside the room. I peeled back the covers and slipped her into the bed.

"Jake, love me. Love me."

She tried to unbutton my shirt. Parkinson's or not, I had more dexterity than my partner. She next tried her hand at taking my pants off, but the zipper proved way too challenging. This frustrated her, and she took out her frustration by grabbing my manhood in a way that put me in that "no-no land" in between rough sex and finishing my game in the third quarter. It crept in my mind to return the favor, but I didn't want to hear again about what her former husband liked to do with or to her.

The kindest way to say it was that I *managed* to have sex. She fell asleep almost immediately afterward.

I got up to use the bathroom and stood looking out the window for a few minutes. I put my briefs back on, crawled into the bed, and put my arm around her. She awoke and forgot we had already made love. She asked me to love her. It didn't take much to get me in the mood.

The second time was similar to the first. This time, though, I barely survived a panicky moment. While Vickie and I were at our passionate high, I felt my right leg tighten up at the thigh. I got cramps frequently, but never had I experienced one during sex. I barely made it through, then jumped out of bed.

"Hey, is everything all right?" she asked. The words barely left her mouth before she fell asleep again.

We were both glad about that.

I endured a relatively sleepless night, which was becoming the norm. I showered, dressed, and decided to get coffee around six thirty. I left her a note letting her know I would be back by nine to check on her.

When I got back, she was ready to go. Of course, she had the same clothes on from the night before, sans the makeup, but her looks stood up to the morning sun. I asked if she wanted breakfast, but she wasn't hungry. Funny— when I was hungover, I usually felt famished.

As I drove north, we talked a little. She told me she hoped I would call her when we got back. I assured her I would. It sounded weak even to me. She moved next to me, put her head on my shoulder, and went to sleep.

Why all this seemed wrong, I wasn't sure. I reflected on Susan and hoped she hadn't witnessed last night's events. I thought about Parkinson's and how it would change my life. That led me to think about my church, Celebration of Christ Christian Church. Could I do justice to this active congregation as my symptoms increased with this "degenerative and incurable" disease?

I thought about major league ballplayers who hang on too long. Their young teammates watch these pathetic guys take up space. They can't help the team much, and they repeat stories over and over from the past. Finally, these old guys have no choice—somebody fires them for the good of all concerned. I didn't want to hang on to my job until somebody said, "This guy is over the hill. We need to let him go."

I should have stopped and stretched a couple of times during the drive. My right leg hurt in several spots, and I was risking another cramp. But I was so focused on getting back to the Cities. I just wanted to drop Vickie off and get her out of my car.

Vickie kissed me as I pulled up to her hotel. She had nice, soft lips. Interesting what she said as she left the car: "Jake, I can never repay you for what you've done for me. I love you for that. Bye."

I don't think she was talking about the sex.

45

THE NEXT EVENING, DEEDEE CALLED TO INVITE me for dinner. As she put it, "Margie leaves tomorrow. This is your last chance if you want to see her."

To tell the truth, I wasn't sure I wanted to see her. On top of that, I wasn't sure how a reunion would feel with my sister and Trevor there. But I accepted.

When I got to DeeDee's house, I recognized Roger's and Cy's cars in the driveway. I just about turned my car around. What the hell?

I rang the doorbell. DeeDee came to the door and gave me a hug. I motioned her outside with a frown.

"You didn't tell me the Lund family would be here."

She seemed surprised by my reaction. "Geez, Jake. She's leaving tomorrow, and I thought they would want to see her too. Is it a problem for you?"

I sighed. "It's not your fault. Let's just see how it goes. If I leave early, forgive me."

A bottle of wine was already pretty much history as I entered the room. I felt a little relieved the usual gender division was in effect. DeeDee dropped me off with Roger, Cy, and Trevor in the living room while the ladies were in the kitchen.

Roger shook my hand, placed his left hand over the two of ours, and held it there. The "minister's shake." I hated it.

"You said you would call Wednesday night. How did your appointment with Trent go?"

I truly felt sorry I hadn't called him back. I tried not to think about why I didn't.

"Well, bottom line: I have Parkinson's."

Of course, everyone knew this was a distinct possibility. Roger and Trevor expressed their sympathies.

I thought it was damn-near priceless when Cy blurted, "Is it hereditary?"

I smiled. "No, and it's not contagious either!"

We joined the girls when dinner was ready. Colleen seemed warmer to me than she had been of late.

And then there was Margie.

I had rehearsed our reunion in my mind—meeting this old friend. However, I hadn't expected it would happen under a microscope, with our son by birth and his adoptive parents.

When we saw each other, we both wanted to hug. I could feel it. We embraced. When I released her from our hug, I looked at those eyes and freckles.

"You look amazing!" I proclaimed.

She seemed pleased. She did a half curtsy. "Thank you, Pastor Horton."

As we all sat at the table, the last thing I wanted to talk about was my Parkinson's. But it became apparent that's where we were headed.

Thank you, Roger.

We talked about the symptoms and the prognosis. Someone had to say it, so it was DeeDee who declared, "They're finding cures for so many diseases. I'm sure they'll find a cure for Parkinson's too!"

I'm glad she's sure, I thought.

"So, Jake, how does this change your plans, if at all?" Roger asked.

I explained the parallels to an aging ballplayer.

Roger then surprised me with a thought-provoking story. "I'm not the greatest pastor around—nor even in this room," he began. "I learned more from Pastor Lutz than I did in the seminary—"

"Well, that's not saying much," Trevor butted in.

Roger smiled and went on. "Anyway, Lutz was dying of cancer. Everyone knew it. He talked about it in his sermons but didn't dwell on it. He often described his cancer as his challenge. He said everyone has their own cancer, their own challenge. He often warned us it would be wise to consider that and to be kind." He paused. "Seriously, Jake—I know you could make it work."

I had been thinking only about the negatives of Parkinson's. But here was Roger giving me thought-provoking and helpful encouragement.

———

We all chatted for a few hours after dinner, then Roger, Colleen, and Cy left. DeeDee grabbed Trevor's arm and said they would clean up in the kitchen. Margie glanced toward the living room.

"Do you have time to visit, Jake, or do you need to go?" she asked.

"Well, I do need to go—to the bathroom, that is."

She laughed.

"But yes," I added, "I would love to visit some more."

When I got back to the living room, Margie was sitting on the far side of the couch. I had a choice here: I could sit right next to her, or I could sit in the chair adjacent the couch. I thought it may be too forward to sit next to her, so I chose the chair.

"Margie, I have to say it again—you really don't look much different than you did twenty years ago."

She giggled. "I guess your eyesight isn't what it used to be."

"Nor is the rest of the machinery," I said with a laugh.

She took my hand and locked her fingers into mine. "Tell me how you feel about this Parkinson's disease you have. I'm really sorry, but I don't know much about it."

I gathered my words. "It's like an unwanted visitor knocking on my door in the middle of the night. Sometimes the knock is louder than other times. I like it best when I can forget there's somebody out there waiting for me."

She was processing this. "Are the 'other' times when you don't feel any symptoms? That is, you don't feel like you have Parkinson's when the symptoms aren't bad?"

I was surprised how well she understood the comparison. "Exactly. When I don't hear the knocking, life is good—but I still know that damn visitor is out there."

I wanted to know about her life. She told me the whole story of how she met Vince at his father's funeral and how the two of them helped each other through the pain—at first.

She sat looking at her hands in her lap. "The Nazar cruelty eventually started to show itself," she said quietly. "It reached the point where I became afraid for my life. He became jealous if I talked to any man. Then he became jealous if I got close to other women. He accused me of being a 'closet lesbian.' Cy sent me some money so I could move an hour away and hire a lawyer."

The thought of Margie fearing for her life yet again filled my brain—but so did the realization that Cy had lied to me at the Thunderbird. He not only knew the details of Margie's separation but had even assisted her with it. I was proud of him, yet royally pissed. Here was another Lund coming to the rescue and keeping me in the dark. Some things never change.

"The first thing my lawyer did was to issue a restraining order," Margie continued. "Vince ignored it. Like his little brother, he was put in jail. He got out. Ignored it again and went to jail longer the second time. With the divorce settlement, he's not allowed to be within fifty miles of me without my written permission. In the settlement terms, he agreed to a full year in prison if he violates the agreement."

"Speaking of his little brother, do you know where Frank is?"

She nodded. "Yes, I do. Believe it or not, he lives with Vince up in Washington, near Olympia. He works at Vince's mill. I hope the two of them can stay out of trouble, but I doubt it."

"Margie," I said carefully, "does Mike know all this about you and Vince?"

Her eyebrow arched a little. "I would say no, and I would rather you didn't say anything about it. It was good to see Mike. I'm very happy for him—his wife and kids seem wonderful."

She grew quiet again. Then she smiled and said something I didn't expect.

"Back when Mike and I became friends, he once asked me if I could ever forget you, Jake. I told him, 'Sure.' He looked at me for a moment, then said, 'I'll be right back. I have to get something.' He walked away, then came back a few seconds later pretending he was carrying something very heavy. He told me it was the Bullshit Meter. He pretended to plug it in, then made me repeat my 'sure.' He said the needle went far to the right! God, we laughed."

Just thinking about it made me laugh, but then the real meaning sunk in. We were both quiet then.

"Sometimes," she said slowly and just above a whisper, "I wish we hadn't met until later. We were so young. And my thinking was already warped from Frank. I treated you like my personal ticket to get away from him. Going through all that with Frank and then getting pregnant"—she shook her head—"what chance did we have? Fact is, Jake, a lot of good people in your life got hurt because of me. Think about Mike and your dad."

"Okay, I will think of my dad. If he were here, he would say, 'I'm glad Margie got that miserable bastard out of her life.' I can tell you with no reservations, my dad had no regrets in helping you. No regrets at all. He cared deeply about you."

Margie gave me a small smile. She let out a cleansing breath and steered the conversation in a new direction. "Cy seems to be doing well. I think he turned out to be a wonderful young man, don't you think?"

"Yes," I said—and left it at that. Now I wanted to steer the conversation elsewhere.

"DeeDee says you may leave tomorrow. Where are you going? Not Washington, I hope."

"It's a sad fact: here I'm approaching fifty with no real home. I'm certainly not going back to Washington. But Mesabi isn't home. My parents passed away. They were both depressed. I hope I don't have that gene." She shrugged. "I like Minneapolis. I may find a place to rent while I'm regrouping."

"Good decision," I said spontaneously. "Minneapolis can use more beauty."

That sounded like a conversation closure. We both got up at the same time. Our faces were inches apart.

Margie put her arms up and around my neck, as she used to. My hands seemed to have minds of their own as they found themselves on Margie's butt, as they used to. I pulled her close and we kissed. My hands moved gently over her body. Still locked together, we eased down on the sofa.

Then Margie pulled away and shook her head. "We can't do this."

I got the feeling she wanted to be convinced otherwise, but it was hard to say.

We agreed to stay in touch.

As I drove south to Apple Valley, I couldn't help but feel excited about the events of the evening. Margie was still a knockout.

What power did she have over men? I thought about the jealousy she provoked in both Nazars. Then I thought of her hold on me. I didn't express it through jealousy, necessarily. But here I was over fifty—I lost my wife a week earlier, and I made love with my former administrative assistant the night before—yet Margie still excited me.

As far as I knew, Margie had only been with three men: Frank, Vince, and me. And none of us seemed able to move on from her. I shuddered a bit at lumping myself in with those two SOBs.

I turned it around in my mind until I settled on a reasonable rationalization: I was different than the Nazars. Their unhealthy attraction to her was more a symptom of their mental illness than Margie's "powers," specifically.

I grinned to myself. *Jake, are you a psychologist now . . . or are you just horny?*

46

FTER TAKING A WEEK OFF, I MET WITH THE PARISH ELDERS before I returned to the pulpit on Sunday. They assumed we'd discuss how having lost my wife might affect my ministry. They were shocked, then, when I shared the additional complication of my Parkinson's. I encouraged an open discussion about how we should go forward.

"Given this development with my health," I asked, "does anyone want to ask for my resignation so you can replace me?" Being realistic, I wanted this option up front so we could parse it.

Lars looked around the table. "If anyone feels this should be considered, please speak now."

Heads shook. I saw nothing but support from the group.

"You don't know how much I appreciate your commitment and confidence in me," I began. "That said, gentlemen, I'm not asking for any free passes because of Parkinson's or the loss of my wife. We are blessed with a vibrant church here. Our congregation needs a strong leader, period. So you need to let me know if and when you have concerns about my ability to perform my responsibilities."

"How will you address your health with the congregation?" Lars asked.

"I plan to be open with them. So little is known about Parkinson's—I hope people can learn more if I share my experience. I also hope my sharing will allow us to share with each other our hopes, our fears, our ups, our downs."

One of the younger elders spoke up. "Pastor, do you think it would be prudent that we begin a search for an associate pastor, who might ease some of the load for you?"

These guys amazed me. The idea of a new hire would scare off most church leadership, even if the hire was needed. But here at Celebration, they thought about service first, not budgets. Still, I wasn't prepared to hear what Lars said next.

"How about Pastor Roger Lund, the Lutheran refugee who was our second choice when we hired Pastor Horton?" He turned to the other elders. "How do the rest of you feel about me approaching Pastor Lund to see if he would be interested in this position?"

I sat there in shock as Lars made the motion and it was seconded.

"Any further discussion?" Lars asked.

I raised my hand slightly. "Under the heading of 'It's a small world after all,' I should disclose that I know Roger Lund. I know him very well. Not only did he confirm me when he served Saint James Lutheran up on the Iron Range, but he's also my brother-in-law. Roger's wife, Colleen, is Susan's older sister."

It grew quiet as they took this information. Then the elder closest to me asked, "Is there any information you could share in confidence about Pastor Lund that could help us make the right decision?"

"Roger is a fine man," I replied without hesitation. "A solid man of faith. I know of no information that would say he isn't the right man. However, would it be uncomfortable for you that we know each other so well and are related by marriage?" I rose to my feet. "I think I should excuse myself from further discussion so you can discuss this in private."

I decided to leave them that thought to chew on. Plus, my right arm ached and the inside of my legs were telling me to get up.

Lars called the next morning. They decided to make an offer to Roger on Monday. I told Lars I would keep the news quiet until they had approached Roger directly.

Lars ended the conversation, "Jake, we're thrilled you'll be preaching Sunday."

———

To my surprise, the congregation had planned a "Welcome Back, Pastor" celebration for me on Sunday. Lars had personally called everyone in my family as well as most of my friends.

When I stepped up to the pulpit, seeing the church filled with people touched me deeply. But then a quick surge of loss made me grip the pulpit.

Every Sunday, I had always started my sermons with a quick smile at Susan, and she had always returned the smile.

I looked out to the first row and found Lindsey. I felt Susan's encouragement. I looked further and saw JJ and Mom next to Lindsey. In the next row sat Mike and his family, Anna and Judy, and DeeDee and Trevor. Gary, Trent, Marina, Rita made up another row. The Lunds were there too. Roger gave me a discreet thumbs-up. Cy and Colleen met my gaze.

And next to Cy sat Margie. She smiled and wore that same look of pride I had seen on her face at my dad's funeral so many years ago.

With that, I could begin my sermon with a reading from First Corinthians, chapter 12. It compares the church to a body: there are many parts, but all are important; when one part suffers, all suffer.

I moved away from the pulpit and confided, "I need your prayers and support more than ever. Days after losing Susan, I found out I have Parkinson's disease."

I could hear gasps and see hands fly to cover hearts and mouths. Near the front, I found Dr. Feldman. He gave a simple nod of encouragement.

"It's left me broken," I continued. "It will be some time before I feel whole."

I shared the analogy of a rope. A rope consists of individual filaments that once joined together are strong and cannot be pulled apart.

"It's in the joining of these fragile strings—every man, woman, and child here—that makes our church strong," I said. "We can't be pulled apart. Every filament is important. Every one of us."

I moved on to the second lesson from Second Corinthians, chapter 12.

"Brothers and sisters in Christ, if there were an all-star team of people who have advanced the Christian faith, no doubt the Apostle Paul would be a unanimous choice. Before he became a disciple of God, he was named Saul. You know, 'Saul, why have you forsaken me?' You know, Saul, whom God chose to bring the Good News to Europe. Saul became Paul, but it wasn't just a name change or a coat of fresh paint. He threw his old ways aside and became One in Christ. Oh, did he ever!

"But wait—in chapter twelve he says he has a 'thorn in his flesh,' which challenges his ability to share the Good News. Theologians of our day have speculated his 'thorn' may have been stammering of his words, arthritis, bad eyesight, or a host of other physical or mental problems. I'm not trying to be controversial when I say that, for all we know, the thorn could have been a terrible past sin or even homosexuality. I find it brilliant that we are not told. That means each of us can substitute our own thorn, whatever it may be.

"What's keeping you from serving God with all your heart and all your soul? Will Parkinson's be my thorn? Rather, I pray God will use this disease to help me grow in faith and in my devotion to God and to you.

"Is my thorn the grief I feel in losing the wife he blessed me with? Susan would not want that. Let us pray for honesty in dealing with the thorns keeping us from serving God with all our hearts, all our minds."

From time to time, a pastor knows when his sermon, his message, is the just the right one at the right time at the right place. It's just right on. You feel affirmed in your trade and in your calling. It's hard to describe, but trust me, it feels good.

And boy, did I feel good as I finished my sermon that Sunday.

Roger called me, surprised and happy, immediately after the elders offered him the position of associate pastor. He and I shared hours of conversation, but Colleen excused herself from the discussions. She told me, "This is a huge decision for Roger, and I want *him* to make it."

Even though Colleen refrained from the decision-making process, I believe her lifelong wish to return to the Cities was the number one reason he ultimately accepted the position.

I was so pleased Roger would be joining the Celebration family. As I told him during our discussions, I saw it as a great honor to work alongside him. What I didn't tell him is that if, for whatever reason, he and I didn't work well together, I would simply resign.

Resignation was always in the back of my mind, Roger or no Roger. I wanted to be a pastor forever. But since I had reluctantly accepted that I had Parkinson's, I had begun to hear the unwanted visitor knocking louder and louder at my door.

I needn't have worried about working with Roger. He proved to be the perfect person for the position. He used his strengths to dovetail, not compete, with mine. He shared Lutz's "Eleven Commandments," recommending that these guiding principles become our operating standard. I agreed.

In addition to hiring Roger, the elders also created a third position. Allen Larsien became our "visiting pastor." This young man wasn't an ordained minister, but within Allen beat the heart of a person who loved people.

He also loved beer. And it showed. Like Roger, Allen didn't worry too much about his wardrobe. People would sometimes tease Al about his gut hanging over his belt. He would just pat it with great pride and say, "Paid in full!"

I was grateful that Allen took on the responsibility of visiting shut-ins, people in hospitals and nursing homes, and anyone else who requested his time. Now more than ever, I struggled with that duty.

Allen fit his role exceptionally well. A confirmed extrovert, he shared his faith with only a modest amount of encouragement. He loved people, and people loved him. However, he did feel a little uncomfortable with the title "pastor."

During visits, a common question would be, "Where did you go to school?"

He would answer, "Red River High School in Grand Forks, North Dakota."

Of course, the next question would be, "So where did you go to college, then?"

He would acknowledge he hadn't attended any theology school. Rather, he had attended the University of North Dakota off and on. It was during an off period when he received an offer he couldn't refuse. He had been involved in professional boxing for years, and he found himself managing one of the top heavyweights in the country.

It was through training boxers, he would tell his visiting companion, that he learned about discipline, pain, sickness, health, redemption, hopelessness, and hope.

Then he would listen.

After a Sunday sermon, an older woman told me her sister had suddenly suffered a stroke and had been sent to hospice. I jotted down the information but told her Allen was using some PTO time this week. I said I'd leave him a message so he could visit her as soon as he returned to work. But she and I both knew there was a good chance her sister might not last that long.

After dinner at home, I couldn't get the woman and her sister off my mind. I was exhausted, but I decided to go to the hospice. The whole way there, I prayed for guidance. It was extra tough for me to visit people who had only days to live. And it was especially tough when I didn't even know them or their beliefs.

The door to the woman's room was slightly open. I peered in and saw, to my surprise, Pastor Allen and the woman holding hands and praying together. He had heard my message and felt called to respond.

He could have been her son, with the connection they had. Maybe, in that moment, he was the Son of God to her.

47

A T FIRST, IT ANNOYED ME WHEN WELL-INTENTIONED congregants, friends, and nearly everyone else, it seemed, shared stories of the unfortunate people they knew with Parkinson's. Often, they wanted me to visit these PD folks.

I'm more than Parkinson's, I'd silently retort. *What do I have in common with these people besides the damn disease?*

As time went on, though, I came to welcome these visits. Much to my surprise, I was fascinated by hearing how others coped and didn't cope. Sometimes I didn't even tell them I had the disease, though I knew their pain all too well. Sometimes, Pastor Allen would visit with me. If laughter really was the best medicine, we were quite a dispensary.

My personal gospel was good old First Thessalonians 5:18: "Be thankful in all circumstances." I witnessed people dealing with far worse PD situations than mine who lived by the same gospel, though perhaps they expressed it a different way. One common statement I would hear is, "There are people a lot worse off than me." Or, "What if one of my children had cancer?"

I had never been good with sick people before. Now I could see God was making a change in me. I found meaning in supporting these hurting people. The faces of Parkinson's were being revealed to me.

Statistics reveal that roughly 55 percent of people with Parkinson's are men. I did meet some women who suffered with the disease, but they certainly didn't make up 45 percent. I don't know whether the statistics are wrong or whether women don't want others to know they have the disease.

There was the guy in his early seventies who loved his wife of 44 years. He told me, "What I really hate about this disease is that it makes me mean to my wife."

There was the guy in his sixties, a former high school teacher, who told me, "I mumble so much now—why even try to talk with people? They pretend they understand what I'm saying, but I know they don't."

There was a guy in his fifties, a successful attorney, who had been fun-loving most of his life, but now he told me, "Why leave the house? My muscles freeze up, and I get these sudden twitches. People look at me like I'm a freak."

I had one guy I knew from the carpet store tell me, "You notice first my Parkinson's face—no expression. I tell my daughter I love her, but it doesn't show on my face."

I talked to another guy, a positive, energetic person, who told me, "I've always felt sorry for those unfortunate people who are depressed—now I'm one of them."

It's all too easy to get depressed when you find out you have a disease that will only get worse and for which there's no cure.

Now I had a sixth sense for recognizing people who had the disease, sometimes before they knew. Well, I guess it would be a "fifth sense," because I can't smell anything.

One of the bright lights on our church council, a fitness nut, tripped my PD radar. He said while he was out biking, enjoying a nice summer day, he almost ran over a freshly dead raccoon. He almost crashed.

Somebody asked him, "Wasn't that smell overpowering?"

"No," he replied. "It's funny, but I didn't smell anything. I don't have much of a sense of smell."

I thought, *I sure hope you don't have Parkinson's.*

But he did.

Trent had told me, "When you've seen one case of Parkinson's, you've seen one case of Parkinson's." Each is unique. This gave me hope. Could I be a lucky one who wouldn't be affected as severely? I had what some called "painful Parkinson's." The upside was that I had no visible tremors or other obvious motor-control signs of the disease. The downside was that I hurt like hell.

As I became more open about my PD, one of my favorite lines was, "A benefit of Parkinson's is that you get better looking." It must be true. When people hear I have Parkinson's, they often tell me, "But Jake, you look great!"

I hadn't been told that for years.

At first, I tended to be somewhat sloppy about taking my meds. But I soon realized that if I stuck to the regimen, I could live most days feeling almost normal. Sometimes my arm and hand pain wouldn't even be present. These moments gave me reason to send arrow prayers thanking God. Sometimes I asked forgiveness for the thousands of days when I hadn't given thanks for simply feeling good before Parkinson's came knocking at my door.

———

Then there were the days when I remembered there were two visitors knocking at my door—Parkinson's and the grief of losing my wife. I felt an ache in my gut when I thought about Susan, which I did many times a day.

In the midst of this sincere grief, I still harbored my old desires when it came to women. I had become close friends with Lars, and we could confide in each other. I took the risk of sharing with him my desirous feelings about women.

"Hey, Pastor," he said, "you know as well as I do, that's the way the Creator made us. It's called propagation of the species. There's nothing wrong with looking at women. It's like going to an art museum. You admire the paintings, but just don't take them home." With some humor, he added, "Even Elder Luke would approve of your dirty mind—as long as it's women and not men you crave."

Lars's perspective was reassuring. I was thankful to share these feelings with him. I could never share them with Roger, who by all appearances did not experience the same "normal guy" feelings that Lars, I, and possibly the rest of the male human race had in common. Then again, maybe Roger didn't need to think about other women. He was married to Colleen . . .

Still, women were on my mind. One in particular. I got excited when I thought of Margie and kissing her.

It had been a few weeks since our reunion at DeeDee's. Margie was staying with a cousin in Fridley while she "regrouped," as she had called it. I knew she needed some space and time, but I was eager to see her again. Eager to see what the future might hold for us.

What held me back, though, was respect for Susan's memory and con- cern about what others might think if I rushed into a relationship with my old flame. I also couldn't easily dismiss another thought: a relationship with Margie would be quite different at this point in our lives. We wouldn't be two teenagers in heat climbing in the backseat of a car anymore. We wouldn't even be like Vickie and me having an impromptu, drunken romp in a hotel.

Yet whenever I thought of Margie, I wondered if we were meant to be together all along. It seemed we had never lost that special connection—from the very first time I saw her at the armory dance to the night we kissed at DeeDee's. When Margie looked at me, I still felt loving feelings. And they felt good, even right.

That was it. I picked up my phone and called her.

"Hi, Margie," I began. "How have you been? Have you made any decisions about staying here in the Cities? Would you maybe like to get together and talk sometime?"

I could immediately sense hesitation. "Jake, I guess I would rather just say this on the phone. I know you'll think I'm an idiot, but I'm going back to Vince. He really needs me. He says he's getting help."

I tried to persuade her to meet so we could talk about this. I nearly begged her to not go, but to no avail. It was a short conversation.

Even though it was still morning, I felt very tired, and it felt like a giant toothache was invading my arm. I sat down and actually said out loud, "Well, that's that."

I felt bad for myself, yes, but I felt worse for Margie. She had to realize she was about to become a cliché—the woman who says of her abusive husband, "I know he loves me. He just doesn't know how to show me sometimes."

As a pastor, I worked with people in dysfunctional relationships. I would often recommend M. Scott Peck's book *The Road Less Traveled*. One simple statement often helped: "Love is as love does." The message being, don't let somebody tell you they love you if they don't treat you like they love you.

———

I got together with Roger and discussed this development about Margie, including how I'd hoped we'd get another shot at a relationship.

"I'm really sorry to hear this, Jake," he said. "I admit it: I too was hoping you might get together. I thought, given your whole history, why not close the circle with the two of you together? Quite frankly, I'm shocked she went back to Vince. He must have been convincing."

"Roger, was that pun intentional?"

He looked confused.

"You said Vince must have been convincing. Like con-*Vincing*?"

He finally got it and smiled broadly. "Nobody ever said I was clever. I guess they were all wrong. But seriously, it perplexes me. She's smarter than that now. Maybe you should talk to Cy—maybe Margie has confided in him more."

The thought had occurred to me, but after my conversation with Cy at the Thunderbird, I doubted another would be productive.

Instead, I asked, "Will you be seeing Cy soon? Do you think you could probe a little? He might open up more to you."

"As a matter of fact, "Roger said, "I'm seeing him tonight."

———

A couple of days later, Roger stopped in my office, and I could tell he had information.

"Jake, I've been waiting for the chance to talk with you privately about Margie. Turns out, she's not going back to Vince at all. Cy told me she has a girlfriend on the East Coast. She's staying with her and looking for a job out there." He paused. "Cy said she lied about Vince as a way to close the door, so to say, for you."

"Close the door?" I repeated.

Roger touched my arm. "I wish I didn't have to tell you this—in fact, I've spent the last few days debating whether I should just keep my mouth shut."

He took a deep breath. It was clear he hated having to say whatever he had to say. He cleared his throat, twice.

"Margie told Cy she doesn't want to get involved with you because you have Parkinson's. She told him, 'I took care of my mom and dad in the end, but I didn't have a choice. I have a choice now, and I choose not to sign up for helping Jake eat and pushing him around in a wheelchair.'"

"Thank you," I said graciously, almost as if I were the one consoling him. "I appreciate the honesty. It's okay. I'm just glad to hear she's not back with Vince."

I then changed the topic, which put the sun back into Roger's day, if not mine.

But it wasn't okay. In the days that followed, I vacillated between wondering if Margie had lied to Cy about Vince, if Cy had lied to Roger because he knew it would get back to me, or if it was the truth.

I couldn't let it go. I needed help. I usually went to Gary for such confidential matters, but I had a hunch this mission needed a woman's touch. I asked Marina if she would do me a favor.

With a twinkle in her eye, she said, "I knew sooner or later you would ask to sleep with me!"

After I stopped laughing, I told her I wanted to find out if Margie was with Vince. She had an idea. She said she'd call Vince and ask to talk to Margie. She'd find out one way or the other if Margie were there.

The first time Marina called, Vince just hung up. The second time, she came up with a story—something about Margie winning some prize money in a drawing. She said she needed to know where to send the check.

Vince was interested in the money. He gave his correct address. Marina pressed on, saying it was necessary to speak to Margie so she could verify the address. At that point, Vince got angry.

"She's not here, and she's not coming back!" he barked.

With mixed emotions, I accepted this as the final proof I needed. I was relieved she wasn't with Vince after all. But I was crushed that this meant Cy was telling the truth. My mind still couldn't believe Margie cared so little for me.

I came to see a sort of justice in this. I made the decision to leave her— twice. First, when I found out she was pregnant and still having sex with Frank. And the second time was after Cy was born, almost thirty years ago. From Margie's perspective, I went on to enjoy a satisfying and happy life married to a beautiful woman who shared my best years. Was it fair to expect Margie to come back after all that rejection and be my wife in my declining Parkinson years?

Rationally, I agreed with her decision. Emotionally, I still winced when I thought of her expressing such cold words about me.

48

A FEW DAYS LATER, MARINA CALLED ME to return the favor. She asked if I would attend a special board meeting with the leadership team at Sommer's. Part of me was happy to oblige. I appreciated that they valued my opinion. Another part of me wished I could bow out somehow. I knew I owed it to Marina to be there, but I didn't feel quite up to par.

After realizing my original regimen of meds was losing the battle, if not the war, to Parkinson's, Trent and my doctor, Will Sharp, had recently upped the dosage. My leg, my arm, and my hands hurt less. This was welcomed. On the other side of the ledger, I noticed sometimes, especially later in the day, my balance seemed a little off as I leaned to the right.

My steps were also growing smaller. This observation troubled me. I feared my smaller steps would become the "Parkinson's Shuffle," which might in turn lead to dyskinesia, or uncontrollable movements. I also wondered if I'd be like the guy who told me about the time he absolutely froze in place at a grocery store. There he stood as his feet refused to take orders from his brain. He asked a helpful shopper if she would bring him a grocery cart, which she did. Using the cart as a walker, he was able to get to a phone and have somebody pick him up.

All this had me feeling less than top-notch, to say the least. But that wasn't the biggest reason I wanted out of the meeting. Marina didn't say, but I knew what was on the agenda. Her retirement was looming; it was time to make her recommendations for the future of the company.

The writing was on the wall. One of my sons would leave the meeting elated, and the other would leave crushed. As difficult as it would be, I needed to represent the company's past as it moved into the future.

———

The meeting was scheduled for 8:30 a.m. in the main store's conference room. The oversized clock on the wall read 8:25. Five minutes later, we were still waiting for Cy. Marc and I indulged in small talk. I looked around the table and could see JJ pretending to study a report in his hand. Gary played with his hands when he was nervous, and I noticed he was folding and unfolding them like crazy. Rita stuck to her natural way of handling awkward moments—she doodled. Lindsey gazed out the window, clearly wondering where Cy might be.

To everyone's relief, we saw his Mustang arrive. He parked next to the front door, in a "Customers Only" space. Moments later, he sat in the empty chair across from me, between Marina and JJ.

"Sorry," he said nonchalantly. "That construction traffic on 494 held me up."

I felt a surge of admiration as Marina began the meeting. What a gamble I took in hiring her, but she succeeded in spades because she had all the right tools along with a relentless desire to prove herself. Shades of Judy.

She began by thanking everyone and reminding them the store would be opening in an hour and so we needed to attend to business. After going through some agenda items, she moved to new business.

"First, I am handing you my resignation, effective in two weeks. I truly believe Sommer's Carpet and Tile can continue to prosper and be a great place to work if you vote for the leadership changes I will now recommend."

Around the table, breaths were held.

"It is my recommendation," she continued, "that JJ becomes the CEO, taking my place. My reasons are many. We can discuss in more detail later if it's important. But in sum, I feel he has the ability and commitment to continue our mission. He also has earned the support of the employees."

I would have felt totally proud and happy under different circumstances.

Marina turned to Cy with resolve. She knew she was right, but she also knew this could be trouble.

"So, Cy, where does that leave you? You've said and done things to hurt JJ's position with other employees and vendors. I have specifics I will withhold for now, but again, I can go into more detail later if you wish. The conclusion is, you have not demonstrated the integrity and people skills needed to lead this company. Further, I am convinced you would be a divisive factor going forward under JJ's leadership."

She paused for effect.

"I recommend you hand in your resignation and that the board pay you fifty thousand dollars severance and buy out your contract. If you choose not to agree to the conditions, your position will be terminated and you will receive zero severance, except for what's due in regular compensation now. Either way, Cy, this will be effective immediately."

With that, she handed Cy the documents. As he grabbed the papers, he looked at me with hate in those black eyes, then he scanned the room. He looked at JJ last.

"Good luck," he said. And out he walked.

The room was silent for a moment, then Marina reached over to JJ to shake his hand.

"Congratulations, JJ," she said with a smile. "You'll make my decision look brilliant."

The others joined her in congratulating him.

"Got to hand it to you," Gary told him. "You're the right man for the job."

When JJ turned to me, I walked over and we hugged.

"Dad," he said in front of the others, "I hope I can be as faithful to the business and our employees as you have been."

As Lindsey stood up next to hug JJ, Marina took the opportunity to put her arms around both of them.

"Jake, you should be proud of both of your kids. I don't see an ounce of jealousy between them. Lindsey, you could be extremely valuable to both JJ and the company if you choose to work here full-time."

Marina next turned to me.

"Jake, I think all of us would like to know how you feel about *your* company today. This was an important moment, especially for JJ, but everyone around this table has contributed."

I hesitated, then began. I suddenly realized I had so much to say and so much to be thankful for.

"I wish Judy could join us today. I'll never forget how she had the confidence in me to make this whole company possible. When we were partners, she was brilliant. She understood the importance of thinking big and thinking little. She burned with the desire to be the best and to treat people that way. I love her and learned so much from her.

"It's appropriate to mention Susan. She was my partner too. Time I spent here was time not spent with her and the kids. She understood sacrifice, and she expressed pride in what I was doing. She knew I considered this my mission."

JJ and Lindsey nodded and smiled.

"Marina and Rita," I said next, "we blazed a new trail with you. Right from the start, you sold circles around *almost* all the men—and I'll come back to this later. Your fingerprints are on this company today. Marina, your prints on our administration. Rita, your prints on our training. I've loved working with you from the start.

"But there was one man who was not intimidated by our two trailblazing ladies. Gary, you've been a constant here, even when you decided to teach. You treat everyone right. You're honest. You're loyal. You have a lot to do with the person I am today. Susan loved you. Sometimes I wonder whether because you are low-key, you didn't get the credit you deserved. I'm sorry for that."

Gary stood up. I could tell he was near tears.

"Jake, my best friend, I loved working with you, and I loved being part of your family in many ways. Your life hasn't been as easy as some people think. The success of this company makes me nothing but proud." Gary looked at JJ and Lindsey and smiled. "One more comment: I love your two kids. They're their own personalities, but they also have your and Susan's traits."

Gary sat down, and I gave him a quick smile. It was time to address my kids.

"JJ, you understand the responsibility that comes with being a leader. Love what you do, always! Lindsey, you have outstanding potential. Everyone sees it. Thank you for the good work you have done. Time will tell if God has this path in mind for you. Whatever you do, you'll do well. Give yourself all the time you need."

I sat down.

"Well," Marina said, "with that, I declare this meeting over."

———

Just as I was ready to leave, I saw Vickie, of all people, sitting at a desk. I ducked out of her sightline, then headed over to Gary.

"Do you know that gal over there with the plaid skirt?" I asked quietly.

He nodded. "I meant to ask you about her. That's Vickie, your old—I mean, former—administrative person at that church in the boonies, right? She interviewed with Marina and started last week. She'll be JJ's assistant."

I wasn't sure how I felt about all of this. But before I could even formulate one thought, she glanced up and spotted me. I knew it would be decidedly odd to walk out without saying anything to her.

I strolled to her desk. "Hello, Vickie."

"I suppose you're here to take me to lunch," she said with a wink. "How about a salad or sandwich next door? I'm starving. But please—this one is on me."

I still found her newfound confidence, along with her new look, an amazing turnaround. A real Pygmalion. I wondered who had carved her out of that ivory.

I had known other women who left their husbands or whose husbands had left them. Many threw out the "old" as they adopted new lifestyles, found new friends. For some, it all boiled down to showing up looking good at some singles' bar. More and more, I sensed Vickie had that singles' bar personality.

I wondered how this would bode for JJ.

Vickie's break started in fifteen minutes, so I headed to the local diner to grab a booth. When she made her way through the door, I realized that what I found alluring about her was the same thing I found distracting about her.

Yes, she did indeed possess a classic, sexy build with her curvy features that were once hidden behind granny skirts. But now she came across a bit too anxious to show those features. As she sat across from me, she sat erect and even lifted her hands up around her neck to extend her chest. What man wouldn't be drawn to that? I remembered too that for her interview with Roger, she wore a skirt with a slit on one side. That night at the bar in Rochester, she had crossed her legs for maximum impact.

I liked subtler. But even today—without a drink—I nevertheless contemplated another visit to the not-so-subtle.

I almost surprised myself when I asked point-blank, "What are you doing tonight?"

In the worst acting performance of the year, she looked upward, as if referring to some mental calendar. "Hoping I'd be with you."

I needed that.

Her new apartment was located near Lamp Lighter's Bar, one of my favorite bars. I toyed with the idea of meeting Gary and Linda, but then it occurred to me how awkward it might be.

Over the years as a pastor, I had told so many people, "We all grieve different." While true, I wasn't so sure my showing up with the less-than-subtle Vickie would qualify as an approved grieving process to them.

As it turned out, it was "Tango Tuesday" at the bar, with free drinks for participating couples out on the dance floor. Even after a third drink, no way would I consider trying to tango. My date, on the other hand, had attracted some single men. Without much persuading, she was out on the floor looking ridiculous.

I've seen couples tango and found it incredibly sexy. But what I viewed that night had little resemblance to the art of tango. Each of her partners had to grab anything he could to keep her from hitting the floor.

I wanted out of there.

Ultimately, these guys gave up. She wound up asking me to bring her home so we could do some "real dancing." It turned out to be our first encounter all over again. Though drunk, she was a beautiful woman, and she proved again to be incredibly responsive to me.

What wasn't responsive, much to my frustration, was everything below my waist.

The last time I'd seen Dr. Sharp, we discussed several PD symptoms. "Difficulty in achieving an erection" was one of them. He went on to say this was not at all unusual with Parkinson's patients. I assured him I didn't have that problem.

Never, ever, had I even pictured this happening to me. Vickie did everything she could to please me. Really, she was over the top. But to no avail.

When she got up to use the bathroom, I moved as fast as I could to find the clothes I had once been so eager to shed. I dressed quickly, but my guilty conscience couldn't bring myself to leave without at least saying good-bye.

I knocked lightly on the bathroom door. When there was no response, I opened it slowly. There sat the Lamp Lighter's "Tango Rookie of the Night"— asleep on her toilet. She looked content and safe, so I left quickly and quietly.

The drive home gave me time to punish myself with a variety of random thoughts.

What the hell am I doing? Am I preying on Vickie just for my sexual satisfaction? Why would I do that?

And "sexual satisfaction"? Who am I kidding? Is sex only in my past now? What if Vickie tells people about my flaccid performance?

Maybe Margie was wisest of all.

As I plunged into dark thinking, I remembered Dr. Sharp warning me, "Over fifty percent of Parkinson's patients become clinically depressed. If you start to feel down, call me. Don't wait until it's too late."

Why would I be depressed? Susan was gone. I missed her. I really missed her. I hurt. I was getting worse. I took thirty-two pills a day. And now I had a limp dick and couldn't have sex anymore.

And guess what, Jake—it's going to get a lot worse.

Out of habit, I repeated the admonishment from Paul in First Thessalonians: "Be thankful in all circumstances."

49

OVER TIME, I CAME TO THE REALIZATION there's some bad in all good and some good in all bad. My mind moved to people with more advanced stages of PD, then my thoughts jumped to the Gomez family.

Celebration had begun to attract people of Mexican descent. As far as earthly possessions go, many were poor. However, those who came to our church were hard-working people who loved God and loved their families.

Our outreach team accepted an invitation to attend several community gatherings in a neighborhood mainly populated with Hispanics. At first, some in the congregation questioned these outreach efforts with the Hispanic community. People assumed they were all Roman Catholics. We knew this wasn't true because several families were already attending Celebration.

In our outreach conversations, we discovered these folks wanted an opportunity to worship together. So, we offered the use of our building for their own worship services as a ninety-day experiment. It wasn't long before they asked if one of our pastors could participate in their service. To our surprise and delight, the entire group decided to simply join our fellowship.

We celebrated with a "Mega New-Member Sunday." Our church added an additional service to accommodate the increase in numbers, and our social ministry team became involved with advocating for their community.

Joseph Gomez and his fourteen-year-old son, Joey Junior, attended most Sundays. Joseph joined a friendship group. His wife, though, never came to worship.

Joseph approached me after service one Sunday when my sermon mentioned my Parkinson's. As it turned out, his wife, Ricci, had advanced

Parkinson's. She couldn't even turn over in bed without assistance. I offered to come by their home to visit her. He took me up on it.

What I saw brought tears to my eyes. She was only forty-five but had been suffering with the disease for ten tough years. Joey knew her only as a near-invalid. As she reached out for my hand, it shook out of control. Her eyes told me it hurt simply reaching out.

I was moved to help this woman. I had an idea.

That year, in 1997, the FDA approved a treatment called deep brain stimulation (DBS). During this amazing procedure, a patient is under the influence of medication but still conscious. Holes are drilled into the scull, and a metal crown is installed to make the head immobile. The surgeon next enters the brain and carefully inserts probes, called leads, at strategic points. The leads are connected to a neurotransmitter, which sends pulses to the brain. These pulses help control Parkinson's symptoms and side effects.

The success rate for DBS is quite high. Unfortunately, the operation was only available to certain patients, and they tended to be people of means.

Trent had told me about the early success of this operation. He said that, down the road, this may help me. However, he said my symptoms at this point did not warrant the operation.

I immediately thought of Ricci. The Celebration council agreed to engage a physician to see if Ricci would be a candidate. Of course, I called Trent, and he collaborated with a specialist at the University of Minnesota. The two of them felt Ricci was indeed an excellent candidate for the procedure.

From there, Celebration embarked on a fundraising mission. In just a couple of weeks, through a combination of fundraising groups, the church was at the halfway point of its $40,000 goal. The target was met when the church received $20,130.58 from an anonymous donor.

Nobody knew. That is, nobody knew it was me. I had been watching for the right opportunity to purge myself of the money I had embezzled from Leo so many years ago. Nobody knew, for that matter, my shame, of which I couldn't so easily purge myself. I had never once told the story to another human being.

Side satisfaction: I so preferred Ricci to have the money rather than have Leo's son-in-law inherit it.

Ironically enough, I came close to sharing the story just a few days after donating the money. That was when Roger got a call from an old acquaintance from Mesabi.

"Do you remember Roberta Chesnia?" he asked me. "I kind of recall she may have been in Luther League with you."

I thought of that night before Dad's funeral, when she waited on me, Judy, and Anna at the Holiday Inn bar. I could have slept with her. I wonder how I resisted.

Not that I could tell Roger any of that. Instead, I managed, "Yes, I remember her. Vaguely."

"Well, she called me out of the blue today. Her soon-to-be-ex-husband is incarcerated at Stillwater. She says she's afraid he'll kill himself. She wonders if I can go see him."

"What's he in for?"

"Sad story. Roberta's dad owned a bar, and her husband embezzled over ten thousand dollars from him."

I said nothing. *But*, I thought, *by the grace of God.*

"Roberta never wants to talk to him again, but she wants me to visit him," Roger continued. "I'll do it—but I don't get it, really. Am I just standing in for her and absolving her from guilt? As is, she feels no love or responsibility herself, yet she wants me to help him."

"That's a good question," I said. "You probably are. Cheap grace. You'll be Christ to him. And it likely won't be the last time you'll do something like this. There's so much hurt out there within our own congregation we simply don't know about. Yet."

"So, would you do it?"

I looked at him. "You know I would. That guy is lower than low, no doubt. His wife is gone. His reputation is gone. His future is gone. Guess what? That leaves God. And guess what else? You have the honor of being God's hand. So, be like the Good Samaritan, and don't delay."

"What could make a man steal from his family?" Roger wondered aloud.

It was rhetorical, but I answered it. And perhaps a little too quickly.

"You never know what people have done. And just think—before this happened, you might have thought he was the nicest guy you'd ever met. Each person we encounter has something they wish they hadn't done. This poor soul just got caught."

A few moments of silence.

Finally, Roger ventured, "Jake, you almost sound as if you have something you want to tell me."

I took a deep breath. I could tell him about the money. I could tell him about my infidelities. Hey, I could tell him about his wife. I could tell him half-truths that didn't address the whole truth. Or I could just dismiss him.

"Roger, you have enough on your shoulders. But if I ever need to confess my sins to somebody here on earth, I'll think of you first."

I am glad I didn't tell him. Experience tells me bringing garbage to light doesn't make it any prettier or make it smell any better.

———

The day of Ricci's surgery, Roger and I went to the hospital to pray with her, Joseph, Joey, and a waiting room nearly full of family and friends.

Trent reported the operation seemed to go well. Two days later, amazingly, Ricci walked for the first time in almost three years. Trent emphasized to all that this was no cure—there was none for Parkinson's. The medical team didn't know how long the positive results would hold. Even with no guarantees for tomorrow, the family simply exuded joy today.

News swirled about this "miracle." Celebration received another large group of new members from the Hispanic community. Ricci's brother, a new member, owned a landscaping company. He showed Roger and me a magnificent plan to landscape around our church.

"I have people who want to volunteer for this," he said. "It will be free, just to share, just to show our thanks."

A week later, it moved me to see at least thirty of our new Hispanic members working on this project. Several long-time members were helping out as well. The finished product became a source of delight and a symbol of our unity. More than one person told me they literally gasped when they drove up to the church. So much joy filled the air.

Ricci Gomez got a miracle. The members of Celebration of Christ were part of that miracle too.

———

But miracles are unpredictable, as is Parkinson's.

Bill Henderson, a long-time member, had suffered from Parkinson's for fourteen years. He requested DBS through his health insurance plan and was approved. Bill had met with me several times to commiserate about PD as well as discuss his unhappy marriage.

He shared the pain of being married to a woman he loved but who did not seem to love him. He asked her to join him for a meeting with me. She refused, saying, "Bill, you have the problem. Not me."

"I tell her I love her," he told me, "and I ask her to say the same back to me. But she says we don't need to do that—we don't need to say the words."

"Have you ever just asked her point blank, 'Do you love me?'" I offered.

He shook his head. "I'm afraid."

In time, though, he decided he needed to know. So one night as he sat across from her at their dinner table, he asked her the question.

"You know what, Bill?" she responded. "I am so tired of your nagging. No, I don't love you. I want a divorce."

Within a week, she was living with another man, a friend of Bill's.

Now he lived with the advanced symptoms of Parkinson's and the mystery and hurt of his wife's leaving him. To get by, he needed significant amounts of medication every day.

Once the DBS was scheduled, his doctor instructed him to stop taking his meds two days prior to the operation. When his son picked him up to bring him to the hospital, he was alarmed to see his poor father shaking with tremors as never before. After two days without his needed meds, Bill grimaced in pain. He couldn't walk unaided, and his arms were flailing. He mumbled rather than spoke.

It proved difficult keeping Bill's flailing arms and legs in the car so the door could be closed. They arrived somewhat late for the operation. His son sat him down in the lobby while he brought the pre-operation forms to the front desk.

Suddenly it occurred to Bill he had left his meds on the front seat of the car. In a panic, he left the lobby without his son noticing.

Bill stopped a young man, gave him his spare set of keys, and asked him to get his meds from the car. The kid took the keys—and the car was never to be seen again.

The son was furious at Bill's stupidity. The two of them got into an argument, with Bill shaking and flailing. The operation was called off.

Two days later, a burglar visited Bill in the night, no doubt via the extra set of keys. Bill got to his phone and kept dialing 811—never realizing his error.

Meanwhile, the burglar went through his medicine cabinet and stole all kinds of pain meds. Before he left the house, he also took Bill's TV and some cash. Bill hid under his bed and stayed there the rest of the night.

I went to see Bill the next day. He was traumatized and depressed.

"My son told me I need to move to a nursing home," he said flatly.

Roger took Bill under his wing, encouraging him to hire a helper to check on him so he could remain in his home. I played my Dr. Trent Podominik card one more time. The DBS was rescheduled.

Bill turned out to be less than a model patient. To be fair, it's daunting having a metal halo screwed into your skull prior to the operation. And yes, it's daunting to have surgeons working on your brain for twelve hours while you're conscious.

When the operation was over, Bill first words were—and I quote: "I will give you ten thousand dollars if you'll get this fucking thing off my head."

The halo came off, but I don't think anybody got $10,000.

Bill's results were not as impressive as Ricci's. But three years later, Bill was still able to live alone.

"I'm sure glad I did it," he told me. "Most days."

Be thankful in all circumstances, I reminded myself.

———

And indeed, I needed to be thankful in my current circumstances. Both Susan and Margie were gone. Even Vickie was gone, deciding to move to New York City. (I was relieved for both JJ and myself.) With so many people exiting my life, I became thankful for the people who entered it. So many people came out of the woodwork to seek my counsel about Parkinson's disease. As I listened to their symptoms, it amazed me that nobody matched my exact symptoms.

I met Robert, an attorney who had battled Parkinson's for fifteen years. He spoke in a soft, monotone manner but with a twinkle in his eyes. As he shared his story with me, I think he counseled me more than I him.

"I used to present arguments in court," he said wistfully, "but now I would need a microphone for people to hear me. As my voice got more and more muffled, I needed to retire early. My wife and I talk more now, actually. That is, I'm always repeating myself, and she's always saying, 'Speak up, Robert—I can't hear a single word you're saying.'" He added with a wink, "Jake, I don't have the heart to tell her it's her hearing that's gone bad, not my voice."

I smiled.

"True story," he began. "My wife was having her hair done at the beauty shop in the mall. I needed to pick something up at the other entrance of the mall, so I told her I would pick her up in an hour. I dropped her off and parked the car on the other side of the mall.

"I found the store I needed, then still had almost twenty minutes before I needed to pick up my wife. I get tired in the afternoons, so I sat down for a couple of minutes on a bench outside. The wind felt brisk. As I stood up from the bench to head back to the car, though, the wind now was at my face."

He shook his head emphatically. "Jake, no kidding—I could not walk against the wind. My leg would go up, but then my foot would come straight down. I retreated to the mall and sat down again, breathing as if I'd just run a marathon. What was I going to do? My wife was going to be pissed as well as deaf.

"I came up with a plan. I used to sail, so it occurred to me, I should walk at an angle through the wind instead of directly into it. It worked—not easily, but it worked. I was huffing and puffing, but I got to the car. I could still make it on time. But then I couldn't get my damn key in the ignition.

"I thought it was because my hand was shaking so badly. Well, there was another reason: I was sitting in somebody else's car. I got out and staggered to mine. By the end of the ordeal, I was only ten minutes late to pick her up. My wife failed to see the victory in all this. To top it off, the wind had blown her hair into a style I had never seen and for which she shouldn't have had to pay."

As I played this remarkable story back in my mind, all I could think was, *You can't change the wind, but you can adjust your sails.*

50

As a pastor, I felt I worked in the comfort business. Yet I seldom looked for comfort from others. But if I did need to talk to somebody, it typically meant a call to my mother.

Now seventy-six years old, Eva had recently buried her second husband. She had a small, private memorial for him in Colorado.

She and Professor Whiteman had made a very special pair. He sometimes spoke in an intellectual way, with an added dose of jargon, which made him difficult to understand. When he spoke that way in Mom's presence, she would say, "Honey, if you don't want us to know what you're saying, that's fine. But if you do want us to understand you, please talk normal." Other times, Mom would interpret his words for the rest of us, as if he were talking Swahili or something. Without him, Mom never would have become a teacher, which allowed her to fulfill much of her post-child-raising purpose.

Devin and I got along well. We wanted to like each other, so we avoided discussions of politics and faith. Our commonality was Mom. We both loved her, and we both were happy she enjoyed us in her world.

Mom answered the phone at its first ring.

"I knew it was you," she said. "You're the only one who calls in the middle of the day. Mike calls me early, and the girls call me in the evening. Anyway, it's always good to hear from you, son. How's it going?"

I lied a little. "I'm hanging in there, Mom. How about you?"

Sometimes when I called Mom, she was in a mood to philosophize. I loved it—if I had the time. On busy days, I had to keep her from going down that path. Today I could tell she was in that mood. I decided I could spare the time.

In retrospect, I'm glad I did. Little did I know that two days later, she would never be quite the same.

"I've been thinking: your father and Devin were polar opposites as far as men go," she began. "I feel fortunate to have experienced both, so I know what to look for in my next man."

We both laughed. But then I added, "So, if you did get together with another man, what could he offer that Dad or Devin didn't?"

She liked the question. "I have an answer for that. But first, I'm going to look at the big picture. Most women know they had a loving relationship with their kids and grandkids. At my age, I can't tell you what that has meant to me and what it still means to me today. I know some other old women who have everything except this. They would trade anything for the relationship they're missing with their children. It's the second most important relationship anyone can have."

"But Mom," I interjected, "your relationship with us isn't accidental or just lucky. You are the best mom we could have had."

"Well, Jake, do you know what they say is the secret to being a good parent?" She paused. "Having good kids."

"You mean like Mike?" I challenged.

"I'll give your dad credit for that one, for the way Mike turned out," she said candidly. "The four of you are so different, but you're all the same in at least two important ways: you believe in God and you all know the value of honest work. Aside from that, I know we made mistakes with all of you. In your case, Jake, I should have supported you—I should have taken that first-grade teacher to task for her overreaction to your love of purple, right?"

We laughed again.

"But seriously, Jake, there was a time when I should have supported you more and trusted your decision. It was a bad mistake on my part. Thanks to your good judgment, you didn't let it lead you to a mistake as well, which would have had life-changing results. Do you know what I'm talking about?"

"The fact that I refused to play hockey?" I kidded.

"No, but you were right about that one too. You would have been horrible at hockey. I would've needed to defend you with the other hockey moms."

Mom seemed to take a deep breath.

"I'm talking about Margie. I am so embarrassed when I think about my selfishness, pushing you to reconcile with her. I wanted that grandchild so bad, I didn't even think about your future. I thought the two of you were drawn to each other. But just think—you wouldn't have found Susan. There would be no JJ and no Lindsey. And you wouldn't be a pastor."

She let out her breath. "I suppose Margie's life needed to go down a different path too, as difficult as it may have been. I hope she's doing well. DeeDee hasn't heard from her since she left the Cities. All any of us knows is what she told you, that she was going back to Vince."

I hated to go there, but I decided to lay it on the line. "Well, Mom, you're right—I'm still drawn to her. While she was in town, we talked about maybe getting to know each other again. The next time I reached out to her, though, she made it very plain she was going back to Vince. Since then, I've found out she actually didn't go back to Vince. In truth, she just didn't want to get back together with me because of my Parkinson's. She said she didn't want to push a crippled husband around in a wheelchair."

Mom literally gasped. In the long silence that followed, I actually thought the phone connection may have been lost.

"Jake," she finally said, "I'm so sorry. I never would have thought Margie could say anything like that. It's so hard to believe. Are you *sure* she said this?"

"Yes," I said simply.

"Well, then, she's not who I thought she was. And she's certainly not good enough for you."

I responded with the obvious: "You're my mother—of course you feel that way. Honestly, I've come to accept Margie's decision. I don't like it. It still hurts. But I think I understand it." I was quiet for a moment, then I switched gears. "But Mom, you never answered the original question: What would you have wanted in a spouse that neither Roy nor Devin was able to give you?"

"I told you the number two gift in life is your loving relationship with your kids. The number one gift is your personal relationship with God."

I knew to be patient with this latest nonanswer; she would eventually bring this all together.

"Nobody is perfect," she said. "Roy was basically a good man. He took earning a living and supporting his family seriously. He could have been nicer to me, but I have no real complaints. The good outweighed the bad. He went to church with us, and I think he believed in God, though he kept his thoughts to himself. His family meant a lot to him, and all of you know that.

"Devin and I, on the other hand, began our relationship with no kids to be concerned about and no financial worries. So, some things can be easier with age. He was sweet and fun, yet he challenged me to grow. But as you know, he did not believe in God. Period. And I was never comfortable with his professor friends. They liked to sound smart, but often at the core, they were passionate only about sounding smart."

I could tell she was getting to the heart of it now.

"I hate to say this, Jake, but I think I grew tired of your dad and his ways. Devin and I laughed together more in a day than Roy and I did in a month. Again, no real complaints here. But to me, a man who truly believed in God and sought to grow in his personal relationship with him . . . as well as with me . . . would have been perfect."

"But Mom, nobody knows. How could you know what's *really* in a man's heart?"

"When faith lives within a person, you know it," she said. "Those who truly believe in God live life differently. We know that whatever happens in this life can be managed when we turn to God. You remember Psalm 121: 'I will lift up my eyes to the hills—from whence come my help? My help comes from the Lord.'"

"I know it well," I said, smiling to myself.

"I've known people who live happy lives until something serious happens. Then it's, 'Why me?' But those with faith believe we can face anything because God does not break promises. Faith gives us something that won't fade like everything else. I am thankful for the two men I loved, but God didn't give me a husband who felt that way. He did, however, give me a son like that."

We talked a little longer and exchanged our "I love yous." As I hung up, I pondered why a man in his fifties still cared so much about his mother's approval. I wiped the tears from my eyes.

She was right. God does not break promises, especially not in the difficult times. I could face Parkinson's knowing God didn't expect me to battle it alone. My help cometh from the Lord.

———

Two days later, life once again proved not to be a long highway, where you can see miles and miles, but instead a curving mountain pass, where you have no idea what's coming up.

As Mom left worship at her church in Colorado, she suffered a stroke. I got the call from Anna. I bought tickets for DeeDee, Mike and me, and we flew out the next day.

Judy found a highly regarded specialist for Mom. After three days in the hospital, Mom was released to recover in a nursing home.

"Your mother is remarkable for her age," the doctor told us. "She has a long road of physical rehabilitation in front of her. But if she keeps a positive attitude, she may walk again."

We gathered as a family to discuss our next steps with Mom. Anna and Judy used the opportunity to share the news that Judy's cancer had returned—and the fight would be extremely difficult this time. Memories of Susan's battle flooded me. With she and Judy facing their own challenges, Anna reluctantly agreed Mom would be better off in Minnesota, where the three of us could help her.

DeeDee invited Mom to move in, but Mom stayed true to her lifelong sentiment that she never wanted to live with any of her kids. The next week, we moved her to a nursing home about halfway between where DeeDee and I lived.

While Mom worked hard to recover from her stroke, she wasn't able to walk again. In most other ways, though, she recovered.

While it pained me to see Mom adjusting to her challenges, I knew she wasn't facing them alone. Her help too came from God.

51

I T WAS ABOUT SIX MONTHS AFTER MARGIE LEFT when a letter arrived. Holding it in my hands, I just kept looking at the envelope in disbelief: Margie Kolar, 3015 East Central, Chicago, Illinois. The tremor in my right hand caused the envelope to almost seem alive.

These days, I found myself becoming more reflective. I tried to guess what she had to say. I figured she had heard about Mom's stroke from DeeDee and was writing to say she was sorry. She did love my mom.

I was half right. She did want to see Mom and wondered if she would be welcome. But the main thrust of her letter was to apologize.

I read in disbelief her words: "Jake, I'm sorry I lied about returning to Vince. I guess after all these years, I still feel you are much more intelligent and well-read than I am. You make new friends easily. I'm still afraid of holding you back. I'm also sorry I lied to Cy about not wanting to help you with your Parkinson's disease. Again, it was just fear talking. Those aren't my true feelings about Parkinson's disease. Jake, just as it meant a lot to me to help your brother, Mike, I would find meaning in helping you—the only man I truly love—through the rough spots when you need help."

She ended the letter with, "I don't blame you if you say stay away. But over the last six months, I now know for sure I love you and always will. Here's my phone number if you want to call me."

I'd heard about people needing to read and reread written words in apparent disbelief. Now I was one of them.

I rarely drank liquor anymore because of the unpredictable results of combining it with all the pills I popped. It took me a while to even find the bottle of scotch I knew I had. Once in hand, I poured some on ice and sat down again with the letter.

While I debated what to do, I couldn't help but notice how I just wanted to hold this letter and not put it down. It began to dawn on me: I felt the same way about Margie. I wanted to hold her and not let her go.

I finished my scotch and dialed her number.

"Hello," she answered.

"Margie," I said. "I got your letter a few minutes ago. I have only one question: When are you coming?"

I could hear her smile as her voiced perked. "Jake, I'll get there today if possible, tomorrow at the latest. I'll call you when I get to the Cities. I love you."

"I love you too."

I hung up the phone and picked up the letter to read it again.

In the midst of this, I needed to get to the church for a funeral service for Trisha, a fifteen-year-old girl who had been killed in a car accident. The parents, Brett and Sandra, were in terrible pain.

What had made the tragedy even worse is that Trisha had just told her parents she was pregnant. Brett had screamed at her to get out of his sight. Three hours later, she was dead. No chance to take back what he had said.

I pictured Lindsey at that age, and I just closed my eyes.

I knew Brett and Sandra. Good people and loving parents. I remembered seeing Brett and Trisha together. They were tight. But now all those good times were blocked by the harsh and hurtful words he had unleashed on her.

In her pain, Sandra screamed at Brett. She screamed that he killed Trisha and the baby she was carrying. And he agreed.

Pastors are expected to comfort people in such circumstances. As I drove in, I reminded myself how important my words would be. I decided my funeral message would simply be focused on Brett and Sandra. I would talk as if it were just the three of us in their living room.

I was honest. I shared my thoughts about my own daughter, that I couldn't know their pain, and that it was only natural to ask or even yell, "Why?"

I repeated myself, much louder: "*Why?*"

The loudness and hollow tone of my voice seemed to bounce off the church walls. It surprised even me. The church was void of sound.

"When the ancients suffered tragedies, they shook their fists and demanded to know 'why,' but to no avail," I continued. "Over the centuries, as human beings, we have drawn from an ever-increasing body of knowledge, but the answer to this heart-wrenching question is still not forthcoming. My dear sister and brother, don't be misled—nobody knows 'why.'

"My own father was killed in a highway accident he caused. I prayed for answers. As a pastor, I've seen good couples like Brett and Sandra suffer tragic blows far too many times. I'm going to be very direct: what I've found is that their marriages either grew stronger as they survived together, or they didn't make it. One sad tragedy added unto another."

I gazed out at Brett and Sandra. "I beg you to get through this together. I love you. These people around you love you. Let us help you through your sadness. I promise you, it may seem to take a long time, but the sun will shine again."

As the service closed, I made my way to them. I was surprised and pleased to see them holding hands. Taking their clasped hands in mine, I implored, "Never let go. Never let go."

Roger caught up with me as people began heading downstairs to the luncheon. "Jake, that was so perfect, really amazing. God's Spirit could be felt and heard." He put his arm around my shoulder. "You look beat. I can take it from here."

I didn't protest. "Walk me to my car, would you?" As we left the church, I told him, "You won't believe who's coming over to my house tonight. Margie."

Roger looked surprised. "Oh, I didn't know she was around. I don't think Cy knows either. Did she say what she wants?"

Suddenly I wondered if I had picked the wrong guy to share with. But I decided to put the truth out there anyway.

"She wants to get back together. So do I. What do you think of that?"

Roger stopped walking and put his hand back on my shoulder. "I think, Jake, it doesn't matter what I or anybody else thinks. I think you're a good man, and I think she realizes truly good men are in short supply. And I also think she's a very special woman. Go for it. Let your relationship bring joy and surprise every day!" He hesitated, then added, "Susan wants that for you."

———

Back home, I looked out the window, watching for her. A taxi drove slowly into my driveway. The driver got out and retrieved one suitcase from the trunk. She paid him, and he backed out and disappeared.

I got up slowly, as I usually did these days, and went outside to greet her. I took her hands, looked into her lovely dark eyes, and kissed her.

I thought about the first time she had captivated me at that armory dance. I remember thinking it was too good to be true. Now, decades later, I felt that way again. Actually, I wanted her even more now, but in a different way.

"I am sorry, Jake," Margie whispered in my ear. "I hope in time you can forgive me."

"And I beg for the same blessing from you," I whispered back. "Let's go inside."

I picked up her single suitcase in one hand and held her hand with the other. We entered my house—our house, if she wanted. I didn't know how long this phase of my life would last. But I intended to love every moment I was given.

EPILOGUE

"**C**'MON, JAKE—HELP ME A LITTLE BIT HERE. You can lift your arm a little so I can slip this nice shirt on. You're having company today, and we want you to look nice."

This is Bethany—maybe in her late twenties and grossly underpaid at Golden Valley Nursing Home. Unlike some of the other staff, she at least seems to remember that just because I can barely speak, it doesn't mean I can't still think.

Then again, the jury is out on whether you're better off here if you can or can't think.

I am no longer Pastor Jacob Horton. I am not a father or husband depended upon to bring home the bread or anything else. I am now a "resident" with advanced Parkinson's.

The workers here come and go. Incompetence doesn't surprise anybody. Nursing assistants start out at about a buck above the minimum wage. I could tell the administrator how the latest hires spend most of their time talking about the want ads, looking for a way out. That doesn't quite jibe with the high-minded mission statement: "Serving God by serving our residents in a way that delights and surprises both our residents and their families."

At first, I was disappointed that the staff talked in front of me as if I couldn't understand or couldn't hear them. As if I were a fence post rather than a human being.

Now I'm used to it. When I listen to their insane comments, I'm mostly glad they don't talk to me. I wonder what kind of intelligence tests some of these people could have passed to get a job here. In half-exasperation, half-prayer, I think, *Judy could you have straightened these people out?*

Bethany introduced me to a newbie "care-worker" yesterday—Akeem Mohammad. Or was it Mohammad Akeem? He's from Malaysia. I can't speak any foreign languages, so I give him credit for working on his English. I could understand most of what he said.

Akeem and I witnessed something yesterday that upset us both. Backstrom is one attendant I try to avoid. It's plain that taking care of people is not his calling. Yesterday, he was trying to get Mrs. Blakely to move out of the dining room. She has poor hearing, but apparently he thought she was rebelling. He leaned up close and held her wrists as if he were being affectionate. But he was hurting her, and he meant to. The tears in her eyes said so. Akeem saw this too. He looked at me, knowing I knew, he knew.

I promised Mrs. Blakely I would report this. And dammit, I will.

I'm one of the lucky ones, at least. I have family watching what happens, and they're not afraid to stick up for me.

Speaking of family, Bethany reminds me today is a "big" day—there will be a birthday party and I will get to eat cake, she gushes.

Wow. Spare me this excitement.

Okay, I admit it: I am eager to see my family.

The party will be at ten this morning, so I need to eat breakfast and get ready. Bethany has Michael assist in getting me into a wheelchair, then he pushes me to the dining room and locks the wheels at my spot at the table by the window. He turns to Margaret, my least favorite person around here, with the exception of Backstrom.

"Be sure to keep him clean. The family is coming over around ten."

Margaret shovels eggs into my mouth as I try to swallow them. The picture in my mind is an old photo I once saw of a train engineer shoveling coal into a boiler.

Margaret's supposed to keep me clean, which worries me. Her mother must not have impressed upon her that "cleanliness is next to godliness." Her apron looks as though it hasn't been laundered in the past couple of years. Maybe she washed it the last time she washed her hair? She wears a black shirt under the apron, and it's littered with dandruff. Meanwhile, she's engaged with another young woman in a conversation about their boyfriends.

Lucky guys.

I would love to have a drink of my water, but I need her to hold the glass up so I can suck on the straw. I raise my hand and try to point at the straw, but she doesn't see me as a person, much less see my finger move.

But this apathy toward my needs will come to an end now. The sheriff just arrived in Dodge City.

"Can't you see he wants to drink that water?" the sheriff snaps.

"Oh. I guess you may be right, Miss Evangeline," Margaret says with a little attitude.

Margaret brings the glass to my mouth, nearly getting the end of the straw in my nostril. I go a little overboard in my act to suggest I may need to be brought to the emergency room for extreme dehydration.

I mouth an insincere thanks to Margaret, then attempt my best smile for the law.

"Good morning, Mom," I mouth.

Mom wheels her chair next to mine. She turned one hundred a couple of days ago and still has a purpose in life—me. Yet I'm the son. I should be taking care of her now.

Bethany brings my mother's plate with a smile. On it is a pancake decorated with strawberries and some Ready Whip that reads, "Happy Birthday, Miss Evangeline."

I can see Mom is pleased as she lifts her arms up to hug Bethany. She takes a bite out of a strawberry.

"This may be the best strawberry I've ever eaten," she says grandly. She puts the balance of the berry in my mouth.

Margaret has left me high and dry for her cell phone. Mom moves her plate next to mine. She cuts a small piece of her pancake, dips it in her syrup, and moves it toward me. I open my mouth. It tastes pretty damn good. I don't mind admitting it: I feel loved as she does this.

"Jake, do you still like pancakes?"

She expects me to nod, but instead I signal for the letter board Lindsey made for me. I point to the P, O, and then T. Before I keep going for the next letters, she gets it and laughs.

"No, I won't make you potato pancakes!"

We smile at each other.

Mom names about a dozen family members coming over for her birthday party. She says, "I wish they wouldn't fuss over me like this." But she doesn't mean it.

We get wheeled to the party room. Fortunately, Bethany drives my chair and knows where to park me.

"Here you go, Jake. I know you like the way the morning sun feels on your face. Is it okay if I leave you here alone for a little bit while we help your mother get ready?"

She looks at me as if I have a choice. I appreciate that. I nod and whisper, "Sure."

Looking out the window, I see a young family outside enjoying each other. It has me thinking of the people of my life—those who have come and gone.

I married Margie one year after that night the taxi dropped her off. I love her to this day.

JJ was not happy about our marriage, though. Lindsey thinks it's because he wants to honor their mother's memory. I suspect my finances may have had something to do with it. That and because Cyril and JJ are no longer friends. Far from it, in fact.

Cyril took his $50,000 from the buyout and wasted little time breaking his noncompete agreement. He opened a carpet and tile store across the street from one of the Sommer's locations. JJ chose to fight him tooth and nail. Who could blame him? Well, JJ ultimately won, but as the saying goes, "Whoever wins, it will be the lawyers."

Cy found that out too. He married a woman who ended up taking him to the cleaners not long ago. Cy can blame the lawyers for that as well. Though if I had to guess, the real blame would fall on infidelities. I know I'm hardly one to talk, but if Cy treated his marriage the same way he treated his business dealings, he lacks integrity. The good news is, if he's sick of living this way, he could change. I heard he's broke. I expect JJ will be hearing from Cy one way or the other.

Both Roger and Colleen have passed away now. Cy should feel fortunate to have his birth parents still around. I know his relationship with me is con-voluted. But he hasn't even treated Margie as a son should. She knows she can't count on him for anything.

Yet he is indeed her son, which means Margie has issues with JJ. She knows Cy created his own mess at Sommer's, and she knows he's selfish. But she still sees JJ seemingly happy with a wife, kids, and a successful business career. She compares him to Cy. Maternal instinct.

More importantly, she thinks of my love for Susan every time she sees JJ. It's no different than how Susan felt about Cy. To her, he was a reminder of my love for Margie.

Judy died of cancer five years after Mom's stroke. But the damned cancer knew it had battled with the best. She fought it with courage, resourcefulness, heart, and all she had.

I loved her and she knew it.

As a bucket list checkoff, she wrote a novel about a bitter and dangerous woman from a daughter's perspective. It's one hell of a book.

Anna moved back to Minnesota. Judy had willed her a significant amount of money. Anna and I became financial partners in a hospice, a respite for the dying. Anna and I made certain every one of our "pilgrims" were treated with dignity and love.

After my retirement from the ministry at Celebration, I stopped by the hospice nearly every day, comforting people who accepted their impending deaths. I loved the work.

Truly, this was Anna's ministry too. When we drew up the plans for a new building, she refused the comforts of a large office. When I saw the cramped space that became her office, the first words out of my mouth were, "Judy would be pleased." We laughed.

Anna too is gone now, but she lived a life worth living. My kids and grandchildren loved her. We all did.

DeeDee took Anna's passing very hard. Anna left DeeDee and Trevor some inheritance money. Though happy, they were struggling financially. The money from Anna has helped them enjoy their retirement years more.

Mike, Sharri, the boys, and their grandchildren are all doing well. So much seemed especially unfair in Mike's early years. I thanked God for how his life evolved.

When I think about Mike's life, I remember to be thankful for my father.

Who I'm truly thankful for is Lindsey. She reminds me how much I loved her mother. She walks like her mom. She sounds like her mom. She has those same green eyes and sandy hair and wears it as her mother did. I see the way her husband, Jason, looks at her. I hope he treasures his time with her and their kids. I think he does—or at least as much as anyone does when they think they have all the time in the world.

Lindsey stops by often. One time she said, "I know you love Margie, and so do I, Dad. But do you still miss Mom?"

I used the letter board to point out, "*EVERY SECOND EVERY DAY.*"

She held my hand and we cried like a couple of two-year-olds.

Then I spelled, "JUST LIKE I LOVE YOU."

She knows she is my Susan.

The story of my life didn't start with Susan, nor did it end with Susan. But she will always be the heart of my life.

I became a minister because Susan encouraged me. She believed in me. She pushed me. I felt that if she was so convinced about this path for me, she had to be right—God was answering *her* prayer.

And deep down, I wanted to help her beat cancer. I knew I couldn't do that, but becoming a pastor brought happiness and fulfillment for her. I never regretted serving God in this way.

As I reflect on my ministry, I realize some people put pastors on a special pedestal, as if they have superhuman gifts. I was no more special than the woman who uses her singing to praise God or the wealthy man who feels good about sharing his wealth for God's glory.

If I did have a special gift, it may have been my shadow side. I need God's forgiveness more than most. I understand what it's like to have sinned maliciously and know you cannot make it right. But God still expects me to try.

Sitting here at the Golden Valley Nursing Home, at age seventy-five, I have too much time on my hands. My mind goes back to what I regret, to what I might have done better. I think of that fortieth birthday party. All those friends. The independence and choices I had. To think I took most of it for granted, never imagining it would change. I was a young fool.

And yes, I think of what happened that night with Colleen. Sex. Did it all come down to sex?

Frank Sinatra sang a song called "It Was a Very Good Year." God, I wish I could get somebody here to play that song for me. I remember some of the words. Sinatra sang about remembering when he was seventeen, twenty-one, thirty-five—how these were good years. Then he got to "the autumn of his years" and began appreciating women in his life.

I look back now on making love with Susan after nearly doing the same with her sister. I look back on all those other women. I am so damned ashamed of my stupidity and blindness toward what I possessed. I had it all.

Maybe I would have been better off had I not been so clever at keeping my indiscretions secret. I do know this. It comes back to my old theory that nearly all men fantasize about being with other women, while only some of us have the means to act upon it. I'm quite sure this is the way we're built.

However, I knew many men who could have cheated on their wives but didn't. I knew godly men such as Roger who wouldn't allow themselves to be put in a situation where they would be tempted. Not surprisingly, liquor greased the slide in my case.

I don't believe God seeks people out to punish them. I hope not. But if he does, I can understand the justice of why I'm here today.

Somehow, I thought I would have all the answers by this time in my life. Not so. I find myself still feeling like David felt in Psalm 121. I still need to lift up my eyes to the hills. My help still needs to come from the Lord.

Party time. I can hear the Hortons in the corridor. The birthday cake has been set up on a table near me.

As Mike wheels Mom into the room, he jokes, "We wanted to light one hundred candles, but the fire marshal said code wouldn't allow it."

Margie is here now. She smiles, kisses me lightly on my lips, and says she loves me. I know she does. And I love her.

Mom interrupts. "Jake, could you lead us in prayer?"

I mouth "Yes" and "Thanks." Lindsey hands me my letter board.

They know the prayer will be simple but slow. I'm pleased I can do this. "BE THANKFUL IN ALL CIRCUMSTANCES."

Amen.

ACKNOWLEDGEMENTS

THIS BOOK IS *ALMOST* ENTIRELY FICTION.

I doubt I would have found the time to write *Nobody Knows* except for Parkinson's disease kicking me out of bed at 4:00 a.m. every day. My first pill feeding is at 6:00 a.m., so those two hours from 4:00 to 6:00 became my writing time. Some mornings, my arm and my hands would be really hurting, yet I wouldn't want to stop writing if the words were flowing easily. Quite often, I would write for over four hours, missing my 6:00 pills. Then I'd need to adjust the rest of the dosages scheduled for 9:00 a.m., 1:00 p.m., 4:00 p.m., 7:00 p.m., and 10:00 p.m. You might think, "What a pain." Well, it does get tiresome, and the pills cause some problems. But all things considered, it's a small price to be living a relatively normal life.

So, suffice it to say, while this story is fiction, it's the dead truth where Parkinson's is involved. All references to PD are factual, a composite of what I've experienced, but *mostly* what others have revealed to me.

Nobody Knows is dedicated to those who fight Parkinson's tooth and nail. I especially want to thank Gary Mortenson. Parkinson's checked into his body almost twenty years ago, but the man never gives up. I try to do two spinning classes per week along with a boxing lesson. Gary struggles to get on the bike, but he wants no help. At boxing, he often falls, but don't try helping him up. I asked Gary what he and his wife, Maryanne, did on their anniversary. He said, "We went canoeing." Yikes. Though I shouldn't be surprised.

So, thanks to my early-morning writing sessions, I finished my first hundred pages quickly. With some trepidation, I e-mailed them to Hanna Kjeldbjerg, managing editor at Beaver's Pond Press. Nobody can encourage a writer more than Hanna. I would send her copy nearly every day, and her responses made me feel I could do this. And this went on for maybe a year until the book was ready for the next step.

Angie Wiechmann, editor, you are a treat. For your belief in the book; for never tiring of reminding me, "Larry—show, don't tell"; for your enthusiasm for a storyline or even a meaningful turn of a phrase; for your thinking as a daughter, wife, and mom: I can't thank you enough for your contribution to *Nobody Knows*. No contest, Angie—*Nobody Knows* is a much better book because of your suggestions.

The cover was created by Athena Currier. A lot of thought goes into the design, content, and message. I've gotten much positive feedback on your work, Athena. Thank you.

Several friends provided helpful input:

Jeff Larson, thanks for your enthusiasm and the great laughs we shared going over chapter after chapter.

For a long time, I've admired Susan Strong's ability to proof the Schneiderman's Furniture advertising. I asked her if she would be willing to take a final look at the manuscript and she responded enthusiastically and, as always, with great competence. Thank you, Susan!

Wayne and Patt Grazzini, thanks for your candor and your suggestions.

Pastor Don Ludemann, what a generous guy you have been with your help. Our experiences with Mother Church have much in common.

Bill Derrick—what can I say? Your critiques have been so valuable to me. You really dug in. You're an amazing guy. While fighting cancer, you were willing to give me detailed feedback. Just for the record, Bill said he would recommend the book to his friends but would warn them about the "adult language." Let it be said, I think the language is accurate for the people in the story, but it's not the way I talk either.

Rick Garlick is another friend who has fought PD for much longer than I have. Rick, thank you for your encouragement and your stories.

Many of my friends asked about the book frequently. I shared the plot with Cheryl Abramson, and she said, "How about this for a title . . . *Nobody Knows*?" I guess I like it!

Parin and Jeff Winter, thanks for your thoughts and interest.

And thank you, friends from the book club and their brilliant partners in the magazine club. And thank you to Shelly Boldon, Jay O'Shea, Jim Larson, Jim Pohle, Marcus Cary, Rosie Lebewitz, Al Erickson, Mark O'Brian, Ryan Welle, Amanda Daubert, Jerry McGraw, Mike Abramson, Jon Vomachka, Kevin Ringhofer, Jerry Vitek, and Robert Liukkonen for your interest often accompanied with good humor.

Thank you, friends from Schneiderman's Furniture and also in our Performance Group. Really, so many of you have asked frequently, "How's it going? When will it be done?" At times, the process seemed slow, but the story was simmering nonetheless. (Not that we have a Crock-Pot going.)

Do you have a friend whose laugh rings out through an entire restaurant? I do, and I love it. Chuck Waletzko, you own a matching big heart.

Jody Mabry, thanks for always being willing to share your ideas.

Al Larsien, you're one of a kind. I am so sorry we didn't get the book published before your wonderful mother passed away.

Finally, I say thank you to my family for reminding me every single day how fortunate I am. Sheila, Jason, Natalie, Jodi, Chris, Jenna, Collin, and Quinn—I love you all!

You make me thankful in all circumstances.

ABOUT THE AUTHOR

Larry Schneiderman lives in Lakeville, Minnesota, with his wife, Sheila. They have three grown children they're thankful for and proud of: Jason, Jodi, and Jenna.

Larry has loved being in the retail furniture business all his adult life and even before then. When he wrote *Call of the Couch* in 2014, he had no interest in retirement. Parkinson's disease changed that in January 2017. He retired after serving as CEO for forty years. But he is proud to see the company continue to prosper since his son, Jason, became the owner.

Larry won a Midwest Book Award in the Business/Memoir Category as well as an Axiom Award for Business for *Call of the Couch*.

Nobody Knows is his first novel. Outside of the details about Parkinson's, it's fiction. Yes, both Larry and Jake grew up on the Iron Range. Yes, both work in retail. Yes, there are other similarities between Jake and Larry, just as there will be similarities between Jake and the readers. But to his friends and acquaintances, Larry wants to confirm, "This is fiction." And louder, "THIS IS FICTION!"

Visit his website at www.larryschneiderman.com.